Just My Luck

Rebecca Rennick

ISBN: 979-8-218-33362-1

Cover & Interior Art by Speckled Plum
Formatting by Rebecca Rennick

For the unlucky in love.
Remember everything happens for a reason.

Part of

The Gummy Bear Orgy Series

Sweet but naughty Rom-Com's

Irish sentence translations

Leamhan Beag: *Little Moth*

Mura turasóir thú thabharfainn abhaile thú, stóicfinn thú agus líonfadh mo choileach thú go dtí go screadfá m'ainm: *If you weren't a tourist, I would take you home, strip you and fill you with my cock till you screamed my name.*

Sílim go bhfuil do ghuth agus asal shapely tarraingteach: *I think your voice and shapely ass are attractive.*

Tá tú chun mé a mharú Leahman Beag: *You're going to kill me, Little Moth.*

Ba mhaith liom na liopaí foirfe seo a phógadh. Ba mhaith liom a fhios ag gach orlach de do chorp. An ligfidh tú dom? Mo Leamhan Beag: *I want to kiss these perfect lips. I want to know every inch of your body. Will you let me? My Little Moth.*

Ar mhaith leat dom fuck tú, Leamhan Beag?: *Do you want me to fuck you, Little Moth?*

An maith leat é nuair a labhraím Gaeilge leat?: *Do you like it when I speak Irish to you?*

Tá tú liom anois, Leamhan Beag. Agus níl mé ag ligean duit dul riamh: *You are mine now Little Moth. And I'm never letting you go.*

Is tusa an grá a cheap mé nach bhfaighfinn choíche agus an grá nach scaoilfidh mé as: *You are the love I thought I would never find and the love I will never let go of.*

Irish Terms you may want to know

Arse: ass/butt
Bollocks: (curse slang) damn it
Carpark: parking lot
Eejit: dumbass/idiot
Feck/Fecker: (curse slang) fuck/fucker
Flat: apartment
Gobshite: (curse slang) asshole
Going for a ride: having sex
Holiday: vacation
Jumper: sweater/sweatshirt
Joggers: sweatpants/lounge pants
Lad: a male, guy, boy, man
Lift: elevator
Loch: lake
Love: a term of endearment usually to a female
Mate: friend
Mobile: cell phone
Mum: mom/mother
Nan: grandma
Petrol: auto fuel/gas
Ring/ringing: call/calling
Shite: shit
Trousers: pants
Twat: (curse slang) an obnoxious person
Washroom: bathroom

1 – Emma

Patience, meet end of rope

I'm sorry, can you repeat that? I think I blacked out." I ask in the nicest tone I can manage given my understandable confusion.

It's only two hours into my workday, when my research into the last ten years' statistics on avalanches in the Alps is rudely interrupted by my boss calling me into his office. I have no idea what this could be about. The last time I even spoke with Mr. Hinkle was to discuss labeling my food containers in the break room fridge. He isn't a super cool boss who hangs out with the employees after work on a Friday at the local neighborhood bar. We're lucky if we get a passing nod of acknowledgment. To be called into his office is never a good sign.

Sitting across from the middle-aged man who uses too much aftershave, I'm pretty sure I misheard what my boss of nearly two years said. There's no way he said those nightmarish words.

"You're fired."

Nope. I heard him correctly.

This job was supposed to last me at least five years before the statistical likelihood of a termination. It is a well-established company with loyal customers and plenty of market demand. I did my due diligence, researching each company in the city and the position I qualified for. Listing out all their past years' numbers, hiring and firing rates, benefits and pay. Risk assessment is always needed, and I'm a top earner in the private sector.

How could I have miscalculated this? What did I miss in my own evaluation? This should have been the one thing in my life I could depend on.

"What? Why? Did my numbers not meet satisfactory goals?"

My words are rushed and pleading.

This must be a mistake. Surely, they read the name wrong, and they meant to bring in Ella Jones from the third floor, not Emma Johnson from the seventh.

Every month, they do an evaluation of each agent and their productivity rates. My numbers are always high above average. I'm a thorough researcher. Statistics are my life. Literally. They've saved me on more than one occasion, and it's because of that that I went into risk assessment.

"No, Miss Johnson, your numbers were exemplary. The company is simply moving in a different direction with the new advancement of AI." Mr. Hinkle states flatly, as if no further explanation is required.

Further explanation is most definitely required. For a risk assessment agent, I need a lot more data to satisfy my statistical brain.

"AI? What AI?"

"The AI that's cutting the company's costs in half and multiplying productivity by ten. It calculates faster and more efficiently than any person. Collecting data in minutes or hours instead of days and weeks. You've simply been replaced, Miss Johnson. I'm sorry."

He doesn't look sorry. He looks like he's trying to hide his smug smile behind those tortoise-shell glasses he always wears. Mr. Hinkle isn't a mean man, but he's also not a friendly man. A "company lapdog" as my best friend Jules calls him. Always working in the favor of the company and never supporting the employees. If forcing mandatory overtime and denying vacation days helps the company, he'll do it. I considered this when applying for the job, and still, my numbers showed my continued employment for longer than twenty-two months.

"But . . . I . . ."

What response is there? I can't argue with him. If the company is firing me, and I can't change their minds.

"You will clean out your desk by noon today. You are required to turn in your badge at reception when you leave," he explains while typing out something on his phone, paying me little attention. As if he has better things to do. "Do not forget, according to the contract you signed when you were hired, you are not permitted to work at a competing company for the next year—"

"What?!"

I don't remember that in the contract. Where the hell am I supposed to work then? They're all competing firms.

"You are also to refrain from disclosing any proprietary knowledge of the company or speaking out negatively against the company publicly, as per your NDA. If we discover you ranting online about your mistreatment while employed here, the company will take legal action."

My fingers dig into the crisp cold leather of the armrest. Despite my planning, research, and dedication to this job, he assumes I'll spill everything on reddit. It's like he hasn't paid attention during the entire time I've been here. Not surprising if he's happy I'm being replaced by a computer algorithm.

Something deep in my chest ignites and whirls. I can feel it churning and accelerating. Gnawing at the pit of my gut, seeping into my blood stream. I would really like to slap this man right now. I've never gotten mad about my bad luck before, but this time it's testing my limits.

Mr. Hinkle slides his cell phone into his inside breast pocket, seemingly unperturbed by my growing scowl and vice grip on his chair. Straightening his back in his fancy ergonomic chair behind his streak-free glass desk. His navy-blue suit pressed within an inch of its life. His ungodly amount of aftershave sticking to the back of my throat like tar.

"As you have not been with the company for a full two years, you will not be receiving a payout for your unused vacation and sick days."

"What?!" I shriek, standing so abruptly my chair screeches and slides back a few inches on the laminate flooring. "That is totally unfair. You can't do that."

I'm now towering over the cocky man still calmly sitting in his chair protected by his desk, as I lose my battle with patience.

My bad luck has done me dirty in the past, but this is ridiculous.

"You legally have to pay that out to me. Those are *my* hours that I accumulated working here, and I deserve that pay."

My voice goes shrill and squeaky the angrier I get.

Mr. Hinkle sighs, annoyed. "Miss Johnson you will lower your voice and sit down, or I will have you removed by security."

I ignore him, and his threats. What do I have to lose at this point?

Leaning in and placing both hands flat on his desk, hoping

they'll leave an imprint on the clean surface, I glower down at him. A strand of red hair falls into my face. I ignore it too. Determined to be menacing.

He doesn't flinch.

"That pay is rightfully mine, and I will get it. I know the law."

"Do you know how to read? Because it clearly states in your contract *that you signed*, that you will only be paid out vacation and sick days after being with the company for twenty-four months. That's two years." He holds up two fingers at me like a kindergartener. "And you've only been with the company for . . ." He clicks on his computer a few times, pulling up my employee file. "Twenty-*two* months and five days. Therefore, as you agreed to, you will *not* receive a cash payout for those hours."

Patience, meet end of rope.

"This is so unfair!" Slamming my hands on his desk, I rattle the obnoxious crystal statue for service excellence he likes to show off.

My now *ex*-boss calmly reaches over and presses a button on his phone intercom. "Security."

I growl in frustration. More angry at myself than anything. I should have read that damn contract closer, or at least considered the fact I might not work here for the five years I anticipated. I was just so eager for a stable job I let my hope get in the way.

Damn me, and my stupid hope that my bad luck curse wouldn't be this harsh. So much for that. I should have known better.

We have a silent stare off for a few long moments before I can't stand looking at his smug face any longer. Security will be here any second. As I look at the undeserved phallic crystal award for service excellence, my anger multiplies. I remember when he received it last year. Being rewarded for the outstanding service and record numbers in his department. That award was for the work of the entire department, and he's the only one with something to show for work we all did. None of this is fair, and that award belongs to me more than him.

Grabbing it, I stand tall on my low sensible heels, swaying only slightly.

"You don't deserve this."

Without thinking, I spin to leave, intent on taking the award with me. A little trophy to remind myself of today. What I hadn't realized was just how sweaty my palms had become in my fever pitch. As I spin on my heel to leave my arm helicopters and the award goes flying. Just my luck. It hits his glass shelf that matches his stupid glass desk and holds fragile awards, picture frames, and pompous knick-knacks.

Glass shatters and everything falls to the floor.

Loudly.

Oops.

Out of the corner of my eye, I can see everyone frozen outside the glass wall of his office staring. *Why is there so much glass in this office?* Correction, almost everyone is frozen. Two large men in suits are making their way into his office now. No doubt my security escorts.

The four of us stand staring at the pile of glass and metal rubble that used to be a shelf. Mr. Hinkle no longer sitting smug and calm behind his desk but standing furious and pointing a rigid finger at me.

"Escort Miss Johnson off the premises and make sure she is

never allowed entry again."

Fuck a duck.

This will not look well on my resume when I apply for another job. People in this industry talk as they do in most. By next week every risk assessment agency in the state will know about my "fit." I suppose it's a good thing that I won't be able to apply for a job at any of those companies for a whole freaking year. Maybe by then they'll all have forgotten about this little hiccup in professional decorum.

The security men allow me to retrieve my belongings before forcefully removing me from his office, then make sure I return my badge. I'm out the door on the street before they release their hold on me.

It isn't even ten o'clock on a Tuesday, and I'm already back at the bus stop waiting to head home. Jobless. Without a letter of referral or recommendation. The bus driver, Jimmy, eyes me curiously when I step on to the bus I ride to and from my apartment every Monday through Friday.

"You not feeling well today, sweetheart? Heading home early?" he asks, concern etching his wrinkled face. Jimmy is a sixty-five-year-old retired veteran and the nicest man you'll ever meet. Always asking about people's days, remembering your name and commute schedule. Being genuinely nice and thoughtful. He even knows my birthday and gave me a red frosted cupcake when I got on the bus that day. Saying the red reminded him of my hair.

Why couldn't Mr. Hinkle be more like Jimmy?

"Yeah, something like that." I don't tell him the whole sorted story. It would take too long to explain why I got so upset.

It wasn't purely because my ex-boss was a jerk and

withholding my payout. It was also because Unlucky Emma strikes again. My ability to have continuous bad luck should go in some sort of record book. I've lost jobs before, sure. But none like this. None that cut me and poured lemon juice on the wound simultaneously. It will be hard to get over this one. Especially since I have no idea what I will do for work during my forced year absence from the competitive world of risk assessment.

Do I even have any other skills? My customer service is pretty good. Maybe I'll get a job at a call center and work from home. That would be ideal. It would cut down on possible accidents that could occur while commuting.

After swiping my metro card, I take my usual seat on the bus. Not too close to the door to get bumped into with a backpack and not too far back to be trapped when I want to exit. Slumping down in the scuffed blue plastic seat, I feel the hem of my skirt catches on a wayward screw pulling out the stitching and tearing it. It's the least of my concerns today. I should be happy I even caught a bus so soon.

I don't have to take the bus. I know how to drive and have a license. I was tired of paying parking tickets and getting trapped in traffic, causing me to be late to almost everything. Driving possesses its own list of possible negative outcomes. Riding the bus has fewer risks as the luck and planning of others outweighs my bad luck, ensuring I make it to work and doctors' appointments on time. When others are in control of the schedule, it's harder for my curse to sway the events.

When I get off at my stop, I wave meagerly at Jimmy and make my way to my third-floor walk-up apartment. You'd think that would be a turn-off, but really, it's for the best. Even if there was an elevator, I've gotten stuck in four in my life. I only use them when absolutely necessary.

My apartment building is average, nothing special about it. Just a standard multi-story apartment building with a gray exterior. Closer to downtown, there are no balconies, and all the halls are interior, making the building self-contained. It has the normal amenities, but no pool or gym. I'm paying over the average for rent, but it was this or the fourplex that looked like a crack house.

After the morning I've had, vegging out on the couch, eating mint chocolate-chip ice cream, and ranting to Jules about that jerk Mr. Hinkle sounds nice.

It isn't until I make it to my floor that I realize something is off. The carpet in the hall is soggy. As I approach my front door, it only gets worse.

Shit.

Reluctant and expecting the worst, I unlock and open my apartment door to find just what I expected.

Water.

Everywhere.

It sprays in a light sprinkle from cracks in the ceiling, covering everything. The couch, the TV, the dining table and chairs. *Everything* is soaked. I don't know if it was a slow soaking for the past two hours since I left for work or if there was one large down pour, and this is the aftermath. Either way, there will be no vegging on the couch for me anytime soon.

2 - Emma

It does smell very similar to wet dog in here

My apartment is now a child's splash pad. The blue carpet squishes under my borrowed rubber boots from the building manager as I pick up items and wring them out.

Thank goodness I believe in a sizable renter's insurance.

A lot of things are ruined. I'm mainly trying to save the important items. Such as the Afghan my grandmother knitted for me, some of my special edition books and family photo albums. Thankfully, I only own a laptop, and I took it to work with me. Most of the furniture is done for, though.

"Look at this mess, Jules." I flip the camera view on my phone to show my best friend what used to be my couch and is now a wet gray blob.

I called her as soon as I informed my building manager of the flooding. I needed someone to commiserate with me and help make me feel better. Jules knows everything about my life, and all the unfortunate "accidents." There isn't even time for me to process being fired, and now, I have to deal with a flooded apartment. Best friend encouragement is desperately needed right now.

"Damn, Emma. What happened?"

Her caramel-colored eyes widen as her brows shoot up her forehead.

"Some sort of busted pipe or some such bull. It leaked straight through the ceiling in a network of cracks, just to make sure it got almost every part of my apartment wet."

The carpet makes a gross shlurping sound as I step on a saturated area, sloshing a small wave across the floor. Paper from books and mail float around like tiny little lifeboats. I better not get a bill for all this water. This was so not my fault and there's no way in hell I'm paying for it.

"What is the landlord going to do about it? They better pay you for all the damages. If they don't, you let me know, and I'll sic my lawyer on them."

Her face turns serious, enraged on my behalf.

Julia, or Jules and I became fast friends when she hired my old firm to do some statistical analysis work for her five years ago. She's independently wealthy and basically a daredevil who does anything and everything she can think of. The crazier the better. But she's also not stupid and likes all the numbers in front of her before she base jumps off a cliff. Just to make sure her probability of surviving or dying is acceptable. The most recent numbers I ran for her were for cage diving in South Africa with great white sharks. It's remarkably safe these days but still something I wouldn't risk.

We've only met in person a few times over the years, since she lives in New York, and I live in Texas. But ever since we worked together, we've been best friends. We talk nearly every other day if not every day. She fantasizes about what daredevil stunt is next, and I tell her about how I tripped on flat ground and scuffed my elbow and tore my pants.

Jules is who I dream of being, and I live vicariously through her since I could never do anything she does.

Instead, I work a nine-to-five office job in a cubicle, making educated decisions to ensure I'm never in a position for a freak accident that will cut off a finger. Thus far my preparedness and smart choices have allowed me to keep all my fingers.

To many, my story of bad luck is "all in my head." To others like Jules, they believe me and don't call me crazy. In fact, she actually helps me, giving me tips and ideas to avoid the small inconveniences it causes me.

It's never caused anything life threatening or done permanent damage. It's more like it wants to make my life just unpleasant enough to cause distress. Today is the biggest stress it's caused to date. It may just push me over the edge. A person can only take so much before they snap.

Picking up my limited edition *Bridgerton* series, I deflate even further, almost breaking down into tears. The book is destroyed, tattered and torn, the pages dissolving at my touch. I love my books. They allow me to escape my boring life and experience the things I'm too afraid to do. Go out with friends to bars, try exotic foods, learn how to snowboard, go on dates, take vacations and have adventures. Things I'll never have the courage to attempt, fearing what my bad luck would affect.

I drop the book on to the bowing dining room table, not even trying to save it. There's no point.

"Whatever their insurance doesn't cover, mine will. I made sure I had the best renter's insurance before signing the lease."

Giving up on trying to salvage anything more from the

living room, I make my way to my bedroom, where, thankfully, the water only damaged the floor, flowing in from the living room flooding. The ceiling in here remains intact, so my bed and clothing were safe.

"Are you going to stay there tonight? It must smell awful."

She's right. It smells very similar to wet dog in here.

"Maybe. I'm going to call my brother and see if I can crash there for a few nights to figure things out." Pulling out a small black suitcase and duffle, I set them on my moss-green comforter to pack the necessities.

I live minimally, only buying things I need or make me happy, like my books. Packing is easy if I'm not having to include those.

"Which brother? The married one, the annoying one or the cute one?"

"You know their names. Don't act like you don't."

"Yeah, but it's more fun this way." She grins widely at me through the phone screen.

I crack a small smile. "The annoying one. He has the extra space and isn't home much."

My brother Danny is a firefighter and works multiple day long shifts where he stays in the firehouse, leaving his two-bedroom apartment empty. He's not really annoying—okay, that's not true. He can be annoying. He just likes to mess with Jules and tease her. I think he might have a thing for her. I bet if they lived in the same state there would be a lot more to it than teasing.

"Oh, well, if you must. I guess," she huffs and flips her blonde hair over one shoulder. Acting uninterested in Danny, even though I can tell she is.

So she can watch me pack, I prop my phone against a

picture frame of me and my three older brothers on a camping trip.

Opening the dresser drawer, I pull out shirts, underwear, and socks. Stacking them in the suitcase with very little organization or care. Pulling open more drawers and packing clothes without paying attention to what I'm packing.

"I haven't even told you the best part of my day."

"There's a good part?" She looks hopeful I might tell her something positive. One look at my face, and she realizes I'm being sarcastic. "Oh. Unlucky Emma strikes again?"

"Yup."

"How bad?"

"Got fired."

"No," she gasps.

"Yup, *and* I'm not getting paid out for my unused vacation and sick time." I add in a sweetly sarcastic tone.

"That's not right. They have to pay that out."

"Apparently not when you sign a contract that says they don't have to if you haven't been with the company for more than two years."

I throw a pair of jeans into my suitcase with a little more force than I intend on making a muted thump as they land haphazardly in the half-packed case. Letting out a frustrated groan, I drop on to the bed amidst my scattered clothing. Dropping my head into my hands and resting my elbows on my knees.

I'm still wearing my pencil skirt from work and the too big, borrowed rubber boots. I should really change. Instead, I stare down at my knees and the freckles scattered there. My freckles are everywhere, and not in the adorable, cute way where they're delicately scattered across the bridge of my nose.

Nope, my Irish heritage made sure I have a wealth of freckles all over my body.

"What am I going to do? My life is a freaking mess, and all because of my stupid bad luck."

"You can come visit me!" Jules suggests brightly.

I would love to visit her, and it would definitely make me feel better. But would it solve any of my problems? Probably not. I need to get rid of this bad luck following me around my whole life like a cursed shadow. Lurking right behind me, waiting to pounce.

"You know I would love to, Jules, but I can't. With the streak I'm on, who knows what'll happen, and I don't want to put you through that."

"I don't mind."

"I would be a horrible friend to be so selfish."

"Maybe you need to be more selfish."

I pause, lifting my head to stare at her face on the tiny screen across from me. "What do you mean?"

"You're always being so careful and precise and saying no instead of yes. Hiding in your apartment and never doing anything fun. I know you want to, and I know why you don't."

"Yeah, for good reason." Standing I pace the room, my boots quietly squishing with every frantic step. She's going to try to convince me to do something again, swearing it won't be affected by my curse. "You know what happened last time."

"Yes. But," she continues before I can argue, "this time I think you might like my idea."

"Doubt it." I grumble, continuing to pace pack and forth in front of my phone, Jules eyes following me on each pass.

"What if you could turn your bad luck into good luck?" She smirks at me as I stop and stare at her disbelieving, giving her my best *are you serious* face.

"Hear me out."

Turning to face the phone fully, I cross my arms over my chest and wait. Her ideas are always good for a laugh. I suppose I could use a little humor right now to make myself feel better.

Jules clears her throat and focuses on me. "You go to Ireland."

"Ha! Me, travel internationally? Are you insane? There are so many things that can go wrong don't even get me started."

"Maybe but . . . you could go to Ireland, the homeland of your people, and soak up all that Irish luck. Aren't they like known for it or something?"

I'm not laughing. *Why am I not laughing? Am I seriously considering her suggestion?* She's not wrong. The luck of the Irish is well known. I could find a four-leaf clover, maybe be blessed by a leprechaun or something. Perhaps being in the country will nullify my bad luck.

No. What am I thinking? That's nonsense.

Isn't it?

"Sooooo?" Jules prompts in the silence of my nonresponse. "Good idea, right?"

"It's not completely horrible."

"Woo-hoo! I knew you would like it. Okay, I'm going to look up flights right now."

On the screen, she moves to another room, sits at a desk, and starts typing.

"Jules, I can't just up and go to Ireland."

"Sure you can," she argues. "You have no job, your apartment just flooded, so who knows how long that'll take to fix, no children and an empty passport. You have no reason not to go."

I can think of a dozen reasons not to go. The plane could crash, I could catch some strange disease, the airline will definitely lose my luggage, I'll be kidnapped and sold into human trafficking. The list in endless.

Jules doesn't think of these things, though. To her it's just another normal day of adventuring and laughter. I'll have to convince her with more logical, believable reasons.

"I can't afford it. And I have to deal with the insurance and replacing my stuff. Not to mention I need to search for a new job." And maybe a new apartment. Something on the first floor, perhaps.

None of this deters her one bit. She just keeps on typing and clicking. Not even looking at me as I plead logic with her.

"Don't worry. It's my gift to you. You need a vacation anyway to clear your head and de-stress, and, yes, maybe even have a little fun. And you don't need to be in the country to deal with the insurance. Just take a bunch of photos and video and document everything, make a comprehensive list, and I'll make sure it all gets taken care of. What else is a rich best friend for?"

"Emotional support and love?" I suggest flatly.

"Always. *But also* all expenses paid vacations," she sing songs, happy as a clam to be doing this for me.

I've never let her use her wealth to pay for anything for me. It just doesn't feel right. I don't want her as a friend because she can buy me things. I want her as a friend because she's a good person. One who always listens and makes me laugh and forget about my shitty day. Kind of like she is right now.

I open my mouth to argue, but she catches me and stops typing. Picking up her phone, she brings it inches away from her face.

"Emma Marie Johnson. You listen to me, and you listen good. Pick up your phone and pay attention."

Picking up my phone, I hold it close to my face, so I'm theoretically nose to nose with her. Sighing, I prepare myself.

"You are a beautiful human inside and out, and if I say I want to buy you something to make you feel better, you are going to let me buy it for you. Because it will make me feel good putting my money toward someone worthy. I will not hear any arguing, and you will go to Ireland and have your very own adventure and maybe even find some Irish luck to bring home with you. Do you hear me?"

How can I say no to that?

"Fine." I concede to her demands, albeit somewhat reluctantly.

"Besides, I have, like, five hundred thousand frequent flyer miles I need to use before they expire, so this is happening. And hey, maybe you'll even find some hot Irish beef to taste while you're there." Jules wiggles her eyebrows suggestively.

"That's disgusting."

"Okay, fine. Then just find some sexy ass man with a huge dick and get railed six ways from Sunday while he whispers dirty things to you in his panty melting accent."

With my luck? Not likely. But it makes for a nice daydream.

"I'd go with you, but as you know, I have a date with a great white. So, you'll have to go on your own this time. But next time we're making it a girl's trip."

There's a part of me that's giddy at the idea. I've always wanted to go to Ireland. Explore the homeland of my family. Discover my heritage and roots and all that. My family came to American four generations ago. We still have ties to Ireland, although remotely. I know none of the supposed relatives, but they're there, somewhere.

When the realization hits me that my bad luck curse might finally end, my giddiness becomes pure elation. To think me, Unlucky Emma could be Lucky Emma. My brothers will never believe me.

3 - Conor

That has to do with my pretty face

A slick sheen of sweat covers my bare chest and face as I circle my sparing partner, searching for an opening. I spot it and take advantage, swinging a right hook at his jaw. My biceps flex as my fist makes contact, spittle flying. Not giving him anytime to recover, I crouch and bend forward, shoving my shoulder into his stomach. Grabbing behind his knee, I pull his leg between my thighs and clench. Walking forward to throw him off balance, he stumbles on his one remaining leg, falling back to the ground. We grapple, and I get him locked under me. When he knows he's lost, he taps my arm, and I release him.

Spitting out his mouth guard, he rubs his jaw. "For fuck's sake. How do you get me every time?"

"It's called talent mate. Try finding some if you wanna win."

Shoving at his shoulder playfully, I know he knows I'm fucking with him. Niall has been my sparing mate for years now. He's been trying to go pro and getting close. He's just not as good as I am.

"There's no way that's all talent. You're just lucky."

"Oh, just luck, is it? Well, then, call me Lucky the Leprechaun, lads, because I'm burstin' with it." I do a little jig and dance around him, smacking him on the back of the head as I pass.

Niall spins and tries to catch me off guard, which, of course, he doesn't, and he ends up in another headlock. The kind I put my sisters in, his head tucked under my arm at my side with him bent over.

"Just luck, eh? What do you call this, then?" I give my bicep a little flex.

"All right, alright ya eejit. Let me go." His protest is muffled by my armpit.

I ruffle his hair like a kid before releasing him with a laugh. We both exit the ring and deglove. Rory, my manager and cousin, hands me a towel to wipe off the copious amount of sweat I've worked up. When I went pro and started getting into the bigger fights, I realized I needed someone to manage everything. Rory was attending university at the time and was always organized. When I offered him the job of keeping me on schedule and booking everything, so I didn't have to worry about the tedious crap, he agreed. He worries about scheduling fights, flights, and hotels, and I focus on training and winning.

I love fighting. The sweat and blood, the skill, and talent it takes to do what I do. MMA (Mixed Martial Arts) isn't for the faint of heart, and I am no softy. Not one part of me is, I'm made of hard muscle and even harder resolve. If there's something I want to do, there's nothing anyone can do to talk me out of it. And I want to fight.

When I was younger, I'd always grapple with my cousins, learning the most effective way to take them down. That translated into team sports in secondary school and university. Joining the MMA and becoming a main card fighter was a dream, and I snatched it. No one knows better than me that when an opportunity presents itself, you take it. With my natural inclination toward the sport, I moved through the amateur fights quicker than most, and when I was offered a main card fight, I didn't hesitate.

"He's right, you know. You are one lucky bastard. No one has a record even close to you when it comes to takedowns." Rory offers a towel to Niall and tosses me a water bottle. I catch it and take a long pull of the crisp cool liquid.

"I'd like to think all my time spent training has something to do with it," I argue.

I may have the luck of the Irish on my side, but I also spend six days a week training. Working my arse off to perfect my moves and sharpen my reflexes. Muscles and moves like mine don't just appear overnight. It's taken years to get to this point, and I've made the commitment.

"Aye. That it does. But if you're gonna tell me that being able to take down every one of your opponents with every try doesn't involve some sort of luck, you're crazy."

"Not to mention his luck with the ladies," Niall adds.

"That has to do with my pretty face, unlike your ugly mug."

Niall flips me off before turning to head toward the locker room, wiping sweat off his face and short brown hair with the towel. After three hours spent sparing with me, he's spent and ready to head home. I walk in the other direction, picking up a skipping rope and dropping my towel and water bottle on a bench nearby. I'm not nearly done for the day yet. It's still early afternoon, plenty of time left in the day to get in a whole workout.

Running my fingers through my thick auburn hair, I try to push the strands out of my face. I'm only partially successful. I should probably get a haircut before my next fight. Can't risk it falling over my eyes and obstructing my view just as my opponent strikes. Or it getting tangled "accidentally" in their fingers and ripped out. There's plenty of time to get a trim. My next match isn't for another couple weeks.

Finding my footing, I begin to spin the rope and jump in fast succession. Keeping my heart rate up, and my body loose on my toes. Bouncing and shifting, picking up my pace.

Rory sits on the bench and watches. "So, what's your plan?" he asks.

"My plan for what?"

"Your next fight with Becker in a few weeks."

"Win."

"That's all well and good, but how? You need to have a plan of attack, know his weaknesses and strengths. Learn his patterns and where he leaves himself open to attacks."

He rattles on about all the research I should do on my German opponent to prepare for the fight. He should know better by now that I don't do that, I don't need to. I'm good at what I do and that's all I need. The lads are right though, I am naturally lucky. I'm always able to read my opponent and just know what to do and when. Making the right move to attack or defend at the right moment. And I always take them down when I want to. Why should I change my ways now? My way has always worked for me in the past, and it will.

"Yeah, you know I'm not going to do that, mate. If you want to learn all about Mr. Becker, you're more than welcome to, but I'm going to spend my time right here keeping in peak physical condition and doing what I always do."

"Fine. Leave it all up to fate, then." Rory eyes me as I continue to jump, spinning the rope faster. "Don't you ever take a break? You've been here all day. Go home, relax, go out to the pub, and take a night off."

We've had this conversation many times. He thinks I work too much and need to take a break; he's out of his mind because I want to work more. I love being in the gym and ring, it's where I feel at home. Where the world aligns, and everything is right.

Pausing my jumping, I watch Rory. He's younger than me by half a decade, but he's already engaged and buying a home. Planning for a family with his fiancé, Erin. I still live in the same flat I have since I was twenty. I've had girlfriends, but I wasn't in love with any of them. If I'm going to tether my life to another, she better be the love of my life. Since I haven't found that, I remain one of Dublin's most eligible bachelors.

With my rise in the MMA world has come popularity and my face on a few magazines and websites. Which has also resulted in quite a few of those girlfriends being nothing more than gold diggers and fame seekers. I do all right for myself, but I'm no millionaire—yet—and my fame is strictly limited to fans of the fight. When they realized I wasn't the limelight seeking celebrity, they thought I was the relationship ended pretty quickly.

"Just come out with us tonight. Clear your mind before the practice match tomorrow."

Rory scheduled an off-the-books fight with a local amateur fighter tomorrow. Something I do every so often. I know he will not be able to win or fight at my level. I do it to teach. It's good for them to learn what a fight with a real pro is like before they can advance to the professional level.

Normally, I do the exact opposite before a fight. I work out and train nonstop to make sure my reflexes are sharp, and my muscles are warm and loose. It may only be a practice match with an amateur, but I still treat it like a paid professional fight. It's only respectful to the other fighter to do so. Taking a night off to "relax" doesn't fit with my routine, and he knows it.

My hands grip tighter to the jump rope hanging at my sides. "That's not how I prepare for a fight."

"I know, but maybe just this once you could try something different. Like Niall said, you're a lucky lad and one night off isn't going to undo all your years of training."

I suppose he has a point. And it is only a practice fight. There are no real stakes. It doesn't affect my record, and I'm not getting paid for it.

Standing here after spending almost six hours working out and training, I realize he may have a point. I could switch it up just this once. Plus, I'm thirty-two, and I'm not gettin' any younger. If I want any future or family after I retire, I'm not going to find it in here. I'll find it out there, where there are people not just sparing mates.

"Fine."

"Wait what? You're agreeing with me?"

"Yeah. I'll take a break, go out to the pub, have a pint. Be a 'normal' lad for the night."

Rory jumps from his seat and crosses to me, gripping me at the shoulder. Removing his hand just as quickly, he cringes and wipes his sweat covered palm on his trousers. "All right then. How about we meet at Temple Bar at eight?"

"Seriously? A tourist bar?"

"How else are you going to meet new people?"

"I want to meet a nice local Irish girl, not a tourist looking for a story to tell her friends when she gets home."

He shrugs, chuckling. "Locals go there too."

I groan. I said I would go out, and now, I will have to deal with the consequences. Hopefully, there aren't a lot of MMA fans out tonight or drunk American girls. They're the worst.

"Fine, but if I end up on some girl's Instagram feed, drunk and half naked, I'm blaming you."

"As long as it gets you out of your flat. And if that happens you should be thanking me."

"Oh, I'll thank you alright, with my boot up your arse. Because being hung over during a fight is definitely *not* professional." I shove him in the shoulder as we walk toward the locker room.

"Yeah, but getting a ride always helps ease the anxiety and clear your mind."

"I am not spending the night with anyone but myself tonight. Going for a ride will just have to wait for another day."

"Ouch. Well, I sure as hell am letting Erin ride me all she wants tonight. That's what having a partner means. Sex any day, every day, without dealing with the walk of shame," Rory gloats and rubs his amazing relationship in my nose . . . again.

Not all of us are lucky enough to find their perfect match first day at University. My luck in fighting and getting laid doesn't seem to include finding an all-encompassing love to rival all relationships before. Lust? Sure, there's plenty of lust and sex, but love? Haven't felt anything near it.

People may look at me and see a big lad covered in muscles and tattoos who could kill a man with my fist. But I want the same thing most others do. To find a partner that I love to the point of pain who loves me just as fiercely. The heart is a muscle too and mine is as big as the rest of me. Sometimes I wish people could see that better. I suppose the savage beatings I give my opponents in the cage doesn't help.

Stepping out of my flat hours later, showered and dressed casually wearing a shirt my sister gave me for my birthday last year, I flag down a taxi and make my way to the pub to spend an evening with my friends. Something I haven't done in far too long. Perhaps Rory is right. I won't tell him that, though.

When I arrive at the pub, it's practically empty, which is strange for a Thursday night. None of my party are here yet. The hostess seats me at a table, and I order a pint. My mobile vibrates in my pocket. When I pull it out and open the text, it's from Rory, saying they're running late and to order while I wait.

Fucking of course.

Now, I get to sit here at a table for four, drinking by myself. I will either look desperate or pathetic. Hopefully, no one takes it as an invitation to keep me company.

I ignore everyone, including the redheaded woman sitting alone at the table behind me, and sip my beer, deciding what I want to eat.

4 – Emma

My collection of stolen cutlery

Traveling overseas was as horrible as I thought it would be. Although I flew first class thanks to Jules and her generosity, I was seated next to a man who smelled like fish and snored. The flight was delayed due to the plane needing a replacement part. A spare part that the plane can technically fly without but isn't allowed to. Because of it, my arrival was six hours delayed, and when I landed, I went straight to the hotel to sleep it off.

After getting a semblance of sleep, enough to function, I get out and explore. I made it all the way here, so I'm going to at least try to enjoy it. My all-inclusive tour package doesn't start until tomorrow. With the time difference and probable delays, I figured arriving a day or two early would be best. This also gives me time to wander the city before heading out on my seven-day bus tour.

The tour is scheduled to circle the island, hitting all the major stops. The Blarney Stone, Cliffs of Moher, and the

Giants Causeway. Figuring I can soak up the luck of the Irish in one or more locations. We chose one that started with kissing the Blarney Stone. Better to begin with the best luck possible. For now, I have no real destination, choosing the way based purely on what I can see. If the street looks interesting, lined with shops and restaurants, I take it.

This city is nothing like Dallas. The buildings are old in a way that seems timeless. Built with stone and brick. Shops line the street level while apartments fill the standard two to three floors above. Colorful awnings stretch out covering windows filled with locally sourced and made goods. A few touristy stores are scattered among them, but most look like independently owned specialty shops. No big-name brands or stores.

Stepping in to one such store, I look around their wares. Touching all the wool knitted items and shaking a snow globe with a leprechaun and a pot of gold inside. If I weren't positive the glass would break in my suitcase on the way home, I would buy it. Instead, I purchase a book of Irish folktales and a keychain in the shape of a sheep made with real sheep's wool. It's cute and fuzzy, and I attach it to a ring to my purse.

Well, I call it a purse, but it's more of a small messenger bag. Made of soft charcoal gray leather, I've kept it in relatively good condition for how long I've had it. The strap hasn't broken; the color hasn't faded, and I picked out a color that goes with everything. It has a zipper closure and a flap with a magnet for added security. Which is why I feel safe carrying it. Knowing it's difficult to pickpocket.

The white of the mini wool sheep stands out against the leather, and I know it will get dirty, but I don't care. I'm here to change my luck and stop worrying about everything going wrong.

I leave the shop, stepping out onto the sidewalk and bump right into a woman's shoulder. Knocking her into the man next to her who spills some of the contents of his standard disposable to go coffee cup. I guess my luck hasn't changed much yet.

My stomach rumbles as I apologize again to the couple and make my way farther down the street. I find the nearest restaurant, a place called The Temple Bar Pub, to grab some dinner at. Googling it on my phone it's supposed to be a popular place to visit when in town. Stepping through the bright red exterior, I nearly trip on the threshold, catching myself before I face-plant and make a fool of myself again.

Wrapping my arms around my middle, I pull my oversized pewter knit sweater closer to stave off the chill the Irish spring temperature brings. Gray clouds roll in overhead, no doubt carrying the rain that is always present in this country. I don't mind it. After the rising heat of spring in Texas, I'm more than glad for the reprieve.

A friendly, bright-eyed hostess seats me at a small table with two chairs after I inform her I'm alone. Sitting in the seat that faces the front, I enjoy the ambiance of the classic Irish pub.

It isn't huge, but it's not quite a hole in the wall either. With paned windows on two sides of the corner building, it creates a feeling of openness within the dark wood interior. The ceiling is a cherry red, painted to match the color of its eye-catching exterior. A large and well-stocked bar lines one wall and there's a small stage in one corner for live music performances. None are there presently, the music being piped in through wall-mounted speakers. A few other patrons drink their beers and chat quietly.

It's better that it's slow and not packed. Makes it easier for me to relax and enjoy myself without worrying.

Perusing the menu, I decide on the hot pastrami sandwich and "chips" which I learn are their version of French fries. Here's hoping I actually get what I order because it sounds delicious.

Going against my better judgement, I order a light beer or "pint." I stay away from the Guinness that looks far too dark for my taste. Before it arrives, I pour a nickel-sized helping of salt into my hand to throw over my shoulder. I know superstition says to do it after spilling salt, but I can use all the help I can get to rid myself of bad luck.

I toss it over my left shoulder and immediately regret the action.

"For fuck's sake. What the hell?" a deep and agitated male voice cries out behind me.

Bollocks.

I should have checked no one was behind me. That's on me for not looking. I should know better. Turning abruptly, my hand swipes the table, and my butter knife goes flying. Crashing to the ground and clattering loud as a gong.

I curse, probably loudly enough for everyone to hear, though I don't intend to and pick up the dirty knife. I set it on the table far out of elbow reach. Turning back to the man, I apologize profusely.

"I'm so sorry. I didn't look, and I should have. Did I get it in your eye? That happens sometimes, and I know how much it stings."

I'm rambling, trying to see around the man's broad shoulders to check his eyes and make sure I didn't blind him.

"No, not in my eyes, just my pint." His voice is smooth and deep, with an alluring Irish accent that stands out from all the others I've spoken with since arriving. It's . . . luscious.

The man glances and me and does a double take before turning to face me, and of course, he's gorgeous. I just had to throw salt on a handsome Irishman.

Good job, Emma. Men love it when you throw spices on them. That's not what they mean by spicing up a relationship.

The man has thick lush dark auburn hair that falls in untidy waves brushing the tips of his ears and soft jade eyes that watch me intently. A slight stubble covers his strong jaw, and he is far bigger than I first realized. As he turns to face me in his seat, I see now the full scope of his muscled body beneath his well-fitted black shirt.

"I-I'm sorry."

"It's not a problem, Love. A little salt won't hurt me. Although I am curious, how often you get salt in your eyes." He smirks and his eyes light up, brilliant and clear and focused on me.

He rests one large arm on the back of his chair, sitting almost sideways. My heart does a little flip in my chest.

"Oh, well, it happens more often than you think. I'm glad I didn't blind you with it. That would sort of defeat the purpose of throwing it over my shoulder."

"Yes, I believe it would."

I fiddle with the cuff of my sweater as he continues to stare at me. *Do I have something on my face?* I haven't eaten yet, so it's not likely. That doesn't mean there isn't something smudged across my cheek all the same. Discreetly, I reach up and rub at my cheek with my sleeve covered hand. I pull it away clean. Good.

"You're American."

It's a statement, not a question, but I still feel as if I should answer.

"Mhm." I nod.

"Are you here on holiday?"

"Yup."

He peers around me to my empty table. "Alone?"

All the travel blogs say let no one know you're traveling alone. You never know who might be a human trafficker searching for their next pay day.

"No," I answer after a beat.

The big man squints at me. "You don't sound so sure, Love."

"Oh, I am. My friend is with me. He's just . . . running late."

"Okay then," the man stands, towering over me. *Wow, he is really tall.* Grabbing his drink, he steps around to the empty seat across from me. "Would you mind keeping me company until my friends—and yours—arrive? It's awfully boring drinking alone."

"Oh, um . . ." I take another look around the bar. There's plenty of people here that if he tried anything I could easily scream, and they would help. There's nothing he can do here in a public place. "Sure. I guess that's fine."

He sits and stretches out a hand. "Brilliant. I'm Conor. And you are?" I automatically accept it. The warmth it produces is welcome against my cool palm.

"I'm Emma."

"Emma," he repeats in a soft whisper, his accent curling the vowels in a way no American man can. My toes curl in my sneakers under the table. "It's a pleasure to meet you."

With him sitting directly across from me I can now see his entire left arm is covered in black lines of an intricate tattoo.

Thick lines break it into sections, the one on his forearm forming a swirling tree. The rest I can't decipher as they are hidden under the rolled-up sleeves of his shirt.

Here I am getting a chill while wearing a thick sweater, and he's rolling up his sleeves and still radiating heat.

I pull my hand back from his and place it in my lap, not quite sure what to do now. I wasn't expecting any company figuring the locals would see another American tourist and ignore me.

"So, what brings you to Ireland?" Conor sips his dark beer and watches me over the rim of his glass, leaning one arm on the table.

"Just taking a break from everything. My family is originally from Ireland on my dad's side, and I thought it high time I see where it is we come from."

The server appears with my pint in hand and sets it down in front of me. Not looking at me, she watches Conor with a flirtatious grin on her face. Guess his good looks affect everyone.

"Are you not waiting for your mates anymore?" she asks sweetly.

"I am. I just thought I'd keep my new mate Emma here company while I did."

The server is pretty, far prettier than me. With silky chestnut hair that falls in waves around her shoulders and ample cleavage under her low-cut shirt and athletic build. Apparently, the cold doesn't bother her either. I'm a little softer around the middle, and my breasts aren't as large as hers, though you can't tell any of that through the sweater. I'm what I call an everyday Emma, the girl you see every day, average and ordinary.

A man like Conor is far more interested in a woman like our server over me. So, why is he sitting with me, making idle conversation? He could have chatted up the server at his table. Yet here he sits at my table asking her to deliver his meal to him here if it should arrive before his friends do. There must be something wrong with him. There always is when an attractive man shows interest in me. The men I have the pleasure of attracting are basement dwellers and mama's boys. Gaining the confidence to talk to me only through vast alcohol consumption or peer pressure. Conor most certainly does not fall into those categories.

Conor thanks the pretty server and returns his attention to me, and my pint sitting in front of me, untouched. "Aren't you going to drink that?"

"Right." I raise the glass to my lips and take a small sip. It's good, far better than any beer back home. I'm still going to baby it. Too much alcohol makes for a bad night for me.

"Good?" Conor asks, leaning back in his chair, his hand loosely gripped around his half empty glass.

"Yes. Much better than anything I've had back home."

"And where's that?"

"Home?"

He nods.

"Dallas, Texas."

"And your *friend*. He from Texas too?"

Ah, right. I'm not supposed to be here alone. "Yeah. He's a cop, actually." Hopefully, thinking I'm waiting on an officer of the law will deter any nefarious thoughts he has.

"Oh, really? He a good friend? Perhaps a boyfriend?" He's being cheeky now. He knows I'm lying, but I'm not willing to give up the farse yet.

"No, just a friend." I take another sip of my beer. Trying to hide my smile behind the rim of the glass. My cheeks warm under his attentions.

"And does your friend have a name?"

"Uh-huh."

"Which is?"

"Steve."

"Steve?"

"That's right. Steve."

His laugh is a low rumbling in his chest. He's enjoying messing with me.

"So, you and *Steve*, are you staying in Dublin or are you venturing out to the country?"

"I have a bus tour booked. It's going to take me all around the island to all the sites."

Wiggling in my seat, I pull one leg up under me and shift closer to the table, trying to get comfortable. Where I was once cold, I'm now growing warm under my sweater.

"Just you?"

"What do mean?"

"You said I instead of we. Is Steve not going with you?"

Well, there goes that lie. I was never a good liar. I don't respond to his question, covering up my reluctance with another sip of beer.

"There is no Steve is there?" A gotcha smirk spreads across his handsome face. Thankfully I don't have to answer because the cute server is back with our meals.

She sets a large meaty delicious looking burger in front of Conor and . . . a plate of oysters in front of me. Dammit. I really wanted that pastrami sandwich. I frown so hard I can feel it pull at my entire face. The smell reminds me of the man on the plane, and my stomach roils. Couldn't they at least bring me something not fishy?

Conor picks up his burger, mouth wide open and about to bite in when he looks up and spots me scowling at the offending shellfish.

"There something wrong with your oysters?"

"Other than the fact I order a pastrami sandwich? Not a thing."

On impulse I slide the tiny oyster fork off the tray and casually slip it into my purse hanging on the side of my chair. One more to add to the collection. That's one thing that wasn't ruined by the water in my apartment. My collection of stolen cutlery. Every time a restaurant has gotten my order wrong, I take a utensil as a reminder. My collection is extensive. Ariel would be jealous.

"You didn't order that?" Conor sets down his burger and joins me in frowning at the oysters.

"Nope." I prod a shell with a finger, contemplating if I can suck them down. There's no point in trying to send it back and get what I really ordered. They'll never get it right.

"Then let's send it back." He waves a hand for the server, gesturing for her assistance.

"Oh, no, don't bother. It's okay." I try to wave him and the server off, but I'm too late. She appears in seconds, as if she were staring and waiting for him to call her from across the bar.

"She didn't order this," he tells her flatly.

Oh no. This will not turn out well for me. I'll end up with so much spit in my food. To my surprise, instead of giving him attitude the server is apologetic and polite.

"Oh. I'm sorry. Let me get that out of your way. What can I get you instead?" she asks Conor, not me.

"She would like the pastrami sandwich, please."

"Chips?"

Both Conor and the server, surprisingly, turn to look at me.

"Yes, that's fine. Thank you."

"Of course. And, naturally, it'll be on the house for the inconvenience."

The server vanishes in a flash, taking the smelly shellfish with her. Nodding, Conor returns his attention to me but doesn't pick up his burger. Instead, taking a long pull from his pint, ignoring the food in front of him. He's waiting for me to get my food I realize.

"You don't have to wait for me. Go ahead and eat. It'll probably come out wrong again anyway."

His brow furrows as he cocks his head slightly. A lock of his dark hair shifts and falls across his brow. The light hits it just right and a sheen of red flashes as he moves. I've never met a man with red hair quite like his. It's dark, almost brown, but the color shifts in the light glowing deep red. I wish my red hair were as luxurious as his. Instead, it practically glows in the dark with how bright red it is.

"Why do you say that?"

I return my attention to his face, and his question rather than his beautiful hair that I want to run my fingers through.

"Because it always comes out wrong. Such is my curse."

"You're cursed?" He leans back a little as if my curse were a tangible thing that could reach out and bite him. It might.

"Not really. More like I don't have the best of luck with . . . well, anything. My meals are *always* wrong when I order out. Sometimes not so much as that." I cock my head in the direction the server went with the oysters. "But something is always wrong. The wrong dressing, the wrong toppings, they forgot a side dish."

Conor's lips pinch together and twist as he listens to my

tales of restaurant ordering woe. "And you never send it back to get it fixed?"

"In my experience that only makes it worse."

Just to prove me wrong the server walks up with a plate in hand and places a fresh steamy hot pastrami and chips before me. Conor orders another pint, and I stare in fascination at the food. It's exactly what I ordered.

"How did you do that?"

"Just lucky, I guess."

With my food delivered Conor digs into his burger, and I do the same. Enjoying every freaking bite.

5 - Conor

Personally, I like freckles

The woman sitting across from me is cute in a way that catches my full attention. When the salt scattered over my shoulder and into my pint, I had no intention of conversing with the person responsible. Not only is there no live music tonight to entertain me while waiting, but the normal plethora of noise created by a packed pub is missing. I was hoping to fade into the crowd until Rory showed up. But it seems the luck the lads seem to think I possess is missing tonight. Which left me open to such interactions.

I knew there was a woman sitting behind me, and when she began apologizing in her American accent, I had even less intention of speaking with her beyond brushing her off. Then I turned around and something about her contrite expression caught my attention. Not to mention those sultry hazel eyes.

Rory, Erin, his fiancé, and our mate Murphy are the ones running late. It's their fault I'm sitting at this table with Emma. Which I would have considered the lowest part of my day on any other night.

Tourist girls are good for a temporary distraction if I'm looking for one. They swoon over my accent, touch my muscles, compliment my tattoos and hair color then generally want to take me for a ride. Especially if they know who I am. Emma does none of those things, and she most definitely has no clue who I am. I find it a refreshing change of pace.

Maybe that's why I sat with her. She didn't swoon or flutter her lashes or thrust her tits at me. In fact, she seemed more opposed to me joining her than interested.

It's obvious she's lying about this guy, Steve. She's here alone. Smart of her to lie, though. You never know who someone might be. Especially being a woman traveling alone in a foreign country. Doesn't mean I won't tease her about it and get her to admit it to me. She was about to when the server showed up with our food.

How in the hell could they mistake oysters for pastrami? She claims to have bad luck, which she calls a curse. When she told me she was cursed, I thought I would have to run out on my tab and mark Temple Bar off my list of acceptable pubs. I don't mess with curses. No Irish person takes those lightly. No way in hell was I sticking around if she said some dark priestess cursed her for stealing her boyfriend or some such shite. Good old fashioned bad luck however can be easily remedied. Especially in Ireland.

Across from me, Emma bites into her pastrami sandwich and lets out an oddly arousing moan of delight. Her mouth overflows with bread and meat as she devours the sandwich as if it's been years since she last ate.

"That good, eh?"

With her mouth stuffed, she nods absentmindedly, keeping

her eyes glued to the sandwich in her hands. I don't think I've ever met a girl who was more interested in her food than me, other than my sisters.

I huff a laugh and pick up my burger, taking a hearty bite as well. If she's not being dainty about eating, neither am I. With my size, I could never be dainty at anything.

Emma is halfway through her food before she takes a break, gulping down some of her beer.

"Oh my god, this is so good."

"Hungry, are ya?"

"You have no idea how fulfilling it is to get exactly what I ordered. There have been times I've craved something only to have it denied. For my first Irish meal to be so drastically wrong was a huge disappointment. I guess I should be thanking you for getting it corrected for me."

"No need. I still don't understand why you wouldn't tell them it was wrong in the first place." I set down my half-eaten burger and watch her. Far more curious about this girl than I should be. She's a tourist, here today gone tomorrow. Why do I care so much about her story?

Because I was stranded here and left to wait by people who forced me to come out tonight. I'm just filling the time until they arrive, or she leaves. It's better than sitting alone.

At least that's what I tell myself to avoid admitting I find her enticing and amusing.

She snorts a laugh. I didn't realize something I said was so funny.

"If I had pointed out the error, the server would have just argued with me saying that was exactly what I ordered, and if I wanted something else, I would have to pay for both. Then the second item that came out, if correct, would be either cold, burnt, contain someone else's DNA, or completely wrong again. It's just best to eat what's put in front of me and be happy I have food at all." She huffs an exasperated breath, her brows pinching cutely in her agitation. It quickly vanishes when she returns to her pastrami. The edges of her lips curl in a small smile of contentment when she takes another mouthful.

She sure can fit a lot of meat in her mouth. Makes me wonder how much of other things she can fit in her mouth.

Stop thinkin' about her mouth, you eejit. This is not the girl to start that with.

My inner self is right. There's no reason for me to think of anything beyond this meal and conversation because it will never happen.

Clearing my throat, I refocus my attention, and my dirty thoughts, keeping the conversation on more appropriate topics for a pub.

"Is your luck really that shite that your food never comes out, right? Seems a bit overexaggerated to me."

Not even bothering to finish chewing she speaks with food shoved in the pocket of her cheek. She looks like a chipmunk. It's cute.

"Oh, yeah. It's that bad. Would you like to hear about everything that went wrong on my journey here from Texas?"

Her grin is mischievous and livid at the same time. The hazel of her eyes sparkling with determination to prove me wrong.

"By all means. Do tell." I gesture with my hand for her to continue.

She finishes chewing, swallows, wipes her mouth with her napkin and begins.

"Well, to start, my flight was delayed six hours due to

needing a replacement spare part for something that's a redundancy. Why they didn't just get us a new plane, I have no idea. I had to sit in the airport and wait while they *drove* the part to the airport. After that I was sat next to a gentleman who smelled of fish. And not the light white kind but like the dead rotten kind. Because of my flight delay I arrived at my hotel dead on my feet, and my garden view was actually an alley view. Then while I'm dead asleep trying to recover from massive jet lag, get this," she laughs, but it lacks any humor, "the fire alarm in the hotel goes off. Now I don't know if you've heard fire alarms in America, but they sound nothing like the ones here. So, naturally, I had no idea what was going on and tried to turn off the offending sound by using the TV remote, flicking light switches and pushing any button in the room I could find. It wasn't until I called down to the front desk, and they informed me I would have to evacuate the building that I knew what the hell was going on."

"Feck." I curse at the luck of it all. Or rather bad luck of it all. She wasn't kidding. Maybe I should leave in case it's contagious.

"Fuck indeed. But that's not all."

"You're shitting me."

"No sir I am not." She takes a sip of her pint before finishing. "To top it all off, when I returned to my room, it had been gone through."

"You were robbed?" For some reason I'm enraged anyone would dare do such a thing to her. A wave of odd protectiveness washes through me, and I want to put my strength and right hook to good use.

"Attempted. There was nothing there of value for them to steal. I learned a long time ago to keep all my valuables on me at all times, no matter what."

Emma leans back in her chair, seaming exhausted from telling her tale. It wore me out listening to it. My hands relax in my lap, unaware I was even clenching them. I don't think I've had even a fraction of that kind of bad luck. Someone had to have cursed her to be that unlucky. Why someone would do that is beyond me. Emma seems to be a funny, polite, friendly, attractive woman. Not the kind that would be on the receiving end of a curse.

"Getting the oysters instead of this delicious pastrami was just my bad luck kicking me when I'm down. I don't think I could have swallowed down any of those after the fish man on my flight."

I grunt my agreement. It's understandable. I wouldn't have been able to either. I'm surprised she's even upright and as put together as she is right now. She's hiding under an oversized jumper, but I can tell she's got a body underneath it I wouldn't mind seeing more of.

She acts as if every man in this bar didn't give her a once over when she walked in, which I'm sure they did. I did, even if it were cursory. Even in a country where redheads are abundant, she stands out. She may not know it, but she does. The red of her hair is vibrant and bold with golden highlights woven throughout, nothing like the darker auburn shades that are so prominent everywhere. It's stick straight, long and thick, tucked behind her ears which are adorned with simple gold stud earrings.

Her beauty is subtle, understated. Instead of reaching out and slapping you across the face, forcing you to pay attention, it lures you in bit by bit. Only once you've paid enough attention can you see it for all that it is.

Subtle freckles dance across her cheeks and around her eyes haphazardly. I can see a few trailing down her neck below the collar of her shirt and jumper. There's probably more beneath, scattered across her chest, arms, and thighs.

My thoughts wander to all the places she may have freckles. Picturing her stripped to her panties, discovering those freckles has my dick twitching in response.

I've heard there are girls who don't like their freckles, hiding them under makeup and using products to diminish them. That's not as popular a practice in Ireland. Personally, I like freckles. They create a road map on a woman's body to follow. I like that Emma doesn't hide them. As I watch her more and more, it doesn't appear she's wearing much makeup. If she is, it's unrecognizable, at least to me.

Amidst my ogling something she says filters through the perusing and X-rated thoughts, and I smile, knowing I get to tease her again. I wait until she's distracted, dipping a chip in ketchup to strike.

"And where was Steve when all this happened?"

"Who?"

"Ha!" I cry triumphantly, pointing a finger across the table at her. I've caught her in the lie now. "I knew there wasn't a Steve."

"Shit. Fine. I lied okay. Happy now?" she grumbles and gives me a playful glower. She's a feisty one.

"Yes. Immensely. But why lie about being here with a lad?"

"It's safer if people don't know I'm traveling alone. Human trafficking and all."

Before I can commend her on her smart traveling habits, my mobile vibrates in my pocket. Pulling it out, I swipe the screen and read a text from Rory.

Rory: *Change of plans. Meet us at O'Donoghues. Murphy met some girl there and doesn't want to leave.*

Of course he did. Typical. I finally agree to go out with them, and they leave me waiting for—checking the time I realize I've been chatting with Emma for nearly forty-five minutes. Wow. Didn't seem like that long. She's easy to talk to. Funny, too, even if it's accidental.

"Everything okay?" Emma asks. Clearly concerned.

"What?"

"You're frowning. Is everything okay?"

I didn't realize I was making a face at my mobile. Trying to relax my face and give her a small smile, I respond to Emma at the same time I type out a response to Rory.

"Yeah, everything's fine. My mates are just changing plans on me."

To Rory, I send an annoyed and curt text.

Me: *I'll be there when I get there.*

My mobile buzzes with his response, but I ignore it. I'll finish my meal and the surprisingly engaging conversation with Emma first. Then I might consider joining them. Maybe.

Ten minutes later I'm paying my bill and apologizing to Emma for taking off. Which is strange since I didn't come here with her. It's not like I'm bailing on her. Yet I feel the need to.

She smiles with her whole face when I thank her for a lovely evening. I don't get her number or try to give her mine. She's not the tourist hook up kind of girl, and she'll be here only for a short time then gone again back home to the states. There's no point in getting any further involved.

I leave her and the bar and decide against meeting the others. Turning instead to head home. My night has already been better than expected. No need to ruin it.

6 - Emma

It's like googling John Smith

Last night was oddly fun. I haven't gone out to a bar nor had a regular conversation with a man I just met in a long time. They rarely end well. This one did. Conor finished eating, paid his tab, said goodnight, and left. Thanking me for a lovely evening. He didn't ask for my number or ask to take me home. He wasn't skeevy or creepy. I can't believe guys like that still exist.

For a while after he left, I regretted not getting his contact info. He was attractive and easy to talk to. You can never have too many friends, right? We could be international friends. You know the kind that shows the other around when they're in town and texts every so often.

Who am I kidding? I want to jump this man's bones so hard they break. I want his number, so I can convince him to let me take that body for a spin. Conor is a big man, with big hands, and we all know what that means . . .

Big dick. I'm talking about his dick.

With my luck, he probably would have a huge cock but have no idea how to use it—or, even worse, be a two-pump chump. My imagination is probably better than reality. As that's just my luck, isn't it?

I waited till this morning to call Jules and tell her all about him. I had to call her anyway to make sure I was going to the right travel agency for the bus tour. I regale my evening with Conor to Jules while I walk to the address on the booking confirmation.

"And he didn't ask to take you back to his mom's basement and photograph your feet?"

To be fair, that's a legitimate question, although it only happened once.

"Nope. Just thanked me for a lovely evening and left."

"Did he actually say *lovely*?" Jules eager voice filters in through the bud in my ear, her face on the screen still disheveled from sleep. It's still early back in the states. Jules still curled in her bed, hair unbrushed.

"Did it sound lovely in his accent?" she asks dreamily mimicking an Irish accent that doesn't even compete with Conor's.

It did sound lovely in his smooth Irish accent. I wish I could have recorded it just, so I could listen to it on repeat. Late at night—in bed.

Shaking my head to clear it of the dirty thoughts, I answer Jules. Trying to keep the lust out of my voice. "Yeah. His accent was really nice. I could listen to it all day and never tire of it."

"I would think not. What was his name again?"

"Conor."

"You didn't get a last name?"

I laugh and sidestep a crack in the cobblestone sidewalk.

"Didn't seem pertinent."

"How am I supposed to google him and stalk him online if I don't know his last name?" she pouts. She totally would, too. Me meeting a hot Irishman was literally on her list of things I need to do while in Ireland. "Fine. I'll just have to use what I have. Conor, male, late twenties, early thirties, Ireland," she dictates as she types into the search bar.

I can hear the weird fake keyboard click of her smart phone as her FaceTime video pauses while she searches.

The address on my paper reads 104, and I check the address on the building. I pass reading 98. Almost there.

Excitement bubbles in my stomach. Most people get excited about their trips when they leave their house or board the plane. I don't until I get to my destination. Now that I'm here, the bubbles are nonstop. Over the next eight days, I'll be traveling around the country seeing living history and having the adventure I was always too afraid to take.

When I told my brothers I was going on a trip alone to Europe, they rightfully laughed. They know me and the way I've structured my life to ensure the safest and most desired outcome. Which usually means the least fun. Their words, not mine. I have plenty of fun. It's just mitigated fun to safeguard myself. Things like renting a new movie on a streaming service and making dinner at home. Or spending an afternoon at my brother's house with my sister-in-law and nephew. Things I suppose people like Jules would consider boring or lackluster but to me are considered an eventful day.

Jules's groan of disapproval pulls my attention back to my phone, once again seeing her half-asleep face.

"Do you know how many Conors there are in Ireland?"

"A lot?"

"A LOT. Like astronomical. It's like googling John Smith in the United States. Without a last name I'm never going to find him." She buries her face back in her pillow, letting the phone slump in her hand.

"Sorry. If I happen to run into him again, I'll make sure to ask his last name, so you can google him."

"You better," she scolds. "He sounds like a hottie, and I wanna see."

I sort of wish I had taken a photo of him. You know for those lonely rainy days at home when I want to daydream about being swept off my feet in a whirlwind romance while on Holiday in an exotic foreign country. Partaking in primal, sweaty, passionate sex. The kind that could turn Jules's cheeks red.

It would be just my luck to meet the perfect man only for him to live in a different country. It's probably for the best I didn't get his last name or phone number. And definitely a good thing I didn't get a photo or recording of his sinful Irish accented voice. In my imagination he is the perfect man, and my curse doesn't interfere. In reality, everything would fall short. I have to accept that it will never happen for me.

Stopping in front of a boarded-up storefront, I reconsider the black metal number nailed to the crossbeam over the locked door and then back to my booking confirmation and back to the door. This can't be right. The paper says 104, the numbers above the obviously out of business store front says 104.

Fuck a duck.

I sigh loudly, Jules's head pops up from her pillow to stare at me through strands of unkempt hair.

"What is it?"

"You're not going to believe this."

"What?" she asks warily.

Turning the camera on the phone to front facing, I show her the boarded windows and doors. "See this?"

"Yeah . . ."

"This is the travel agency where we booked the bus tour I'm supposed to be taking this afternoon."

"Ah, fuck."

Ah, fuck indeed. Looks like my optimism about my luck changing was unfounded. Meeting Conor last night was a fluke, a momentary lapse allowing me a tiny respite before bitch slapping me harder than an angry pimp.

Jules may have used her frequent flyer miles to get my plane tickets, but the tour had been paid for. It was all inclusive. Transportation, hotel, and tickets into any site that required them. Now . . . nothing. All my plans shot to hell.

How did this happen? How does an out of business travel agency continue booking tours and taking payment? If they weren't already out of business—and most likely broke—Jules would ensure they would be by the end of the day.

"I don't understand. We paid and got confirmation. We took precautions to make sure this was taken care of. All the online reviews were outstanding, and nothing even hinted that they were closed."

She stands from the bed and makes her way to another room, sitting down on the couch with her laptop. No matter what she finds or who she yells at the issue remains. I am in Ireland with nowhere to stay, and no way to get to the places I want to go.

Groaning I pinch the bridge of my nose. A soft breeze blows down the charming cobblestone street brushing stray strands of hair across from my face, I tuck them behind my ear and stare back up at the storefront. I brought a scarf with me, but it's not as warm as it looks, letting the chill of the air filter between the fibers. Ireland is famous for its wool. I'll have to buy a new one while I'm here. Except I'll most likely not have the spending money I had anticipated with this new turn of events.

"There's nothing online about it closing or being closed. Everything looks copasetic. Wait there's a phone number I can try. Maybe it's just that location that's closed, or they're doing some remodeling. Let me call you back, okay?"

Without waiting for me to answer she hangs up to call the travel agency and possibly tear them a new one. Leaving me standing in the street, staring like a fool at bare plywood and an empty shop.

Deciding I need to do something more than stand here I search the area map on my phone looking for something I can walk to close by. I find a church called St. Patrick's Cathedral. It looks amazing. I might as well get some site seeing in while we figure out what's going on with the travel agency. There's no need to panic yet, and I stuff down the desire to do just that.

I'm not even a block away from the boarded-up shop when my phone rings with Jules's name on the screen. I answer and bring it to my ear.

"Hey. What did you find out?"

"According to a lovely recording that I only got to after choosing a dozen items through their automated menu, they are closed for business. Permanently."

"Seriously?"

"Seriously. They really didn't want people to know they were shutting down business because that information was buried deep in the bowels of the automated system. I'm reporting them now so that no one else gets robbed like we just did."

I feel like hot garbage on a summer's day in Florida. I knew something like this would happen, which is why I never allowed her to pay for anything in the past. This always happens. I finally get a glimmer of joy and pleasure in life, and my curse strikes it down.

I should never have left the US. I should have never left Texas. Things are safe there. I know where all the risks are, have calculated them down to the hundredth decimal. Nothing can surprise me there that I don't already know will go wrong and have compensated for.

At least I can be thankful I'm alone and this hitch can't affect anyone else. Except for Jules bank account, which only makes me wince more.

How am I going to pay for everything now? I hadn't budgeted for it since Jules was paying for the tour package. If all hotels cost what the one I'm in costs, I won't be able to afford much of anything. Not to mention food. How am I going to eat? I'm going to starve.

There goes all the cute Irish souvenirs I had planned on buying. A teacup and tin of tea, a music box that plays an Irish melody, a new sweater and scarf made from locally sourced wool, and maybe one of those twisty Celtic knot necklaces. I had little time to make a full list of items. Those are just the ones I thought of on the flight over.

And now I won't be getting any of them.

For the first time in a long time, I'm not only angry about the situation my bad luck has created but dismayed. I'm in a foreign country, *alone*, with limited funds and nowhere to go and nowhere to stay. My flight home is secure, but it's not for another eight days. No matter how much it hurts I am not going home early. I made it all the way here, and I'm not going home with my tail between my legs.

"I'm so sorry Jules. I knew this would happen. I shouldn't have let you pay for it." I say quietly into the phone. Stopping at a street corner, I sit on a low stone wall rounding it.

"No, Emma, don't be sorry. This was not your fault. We'll figure it out. We'll find another agency or book another bus and hotel for you at all the stops. It'll be okay, all is not lost." She coos in soothing tones.

People pass on the street, going about their business. Their days not completely ruined by an invisible force set on ruining their lives. My elbows drop to my knees, and I hang my head. Closing my eyes, I try to take a steadying breath. It helps . . . a little. I still feel like I want to cry, but don't let myself. Too many tears have been shed in my life over things I had no control over. I won't give the curse anymore.

"You still there, Emma?"

"Yeah, I'm here," I mutter.

"Look, I'm going to figure it all out for you. Okay? We'll get hotels booked, find a new bus and—"

"No. I can't let you do that, Jules. This is my problem, and I'm going to fix it. I'll deal with it."

Sitting up straight on the stone wall I force down the despair and resolve settles in my chest. I've dealt with the repercussions of my curse before, and I'll deal with them now. I'm a grown twenty-seven-year-old woman. If I can't handle this, I'll never believe in myself enough to handle anything that may come.

"Are you sure? I don't mind. It's easy enough for me to do."

"Yes, I'm sure. I'm a big girl. I tie my own sandals and everything." I quip weakly. Using my Disney quote knowledge to try and lighten the mood.

"What?"

"Never mind. Don't worry about it. I can book my own hotels as I go and find my own way around. It can't be that hard."

Even though I don't have my computer to research statistics and create a spread sheet to make me feel better, I'm determined to make this trip a success. I stand and cross the street when the light turns green, heading toward the cathedral, which is now my first official stop on my new journey.

One with no plan and no schedule. One I haven't researched and vetted. One I have no statistics for other than the ones that are always present when traveling as a single woman in a foreign country.

When life gives you lemons, make lemonade, right?

"Well, if you insist. But *I* insist you let me send you some extra money. I don't want you staying in questionable hotels that don't lock and have bed bugs just because you're on a budget. And I won't take no for an answer. This is unnegotiable."

I shut my mouth that I had opened to do just that. I suppose accepting a little help wouldn't hurt in this situation. "Fine. But not too much."

"You got it."

I hang up with Jules as I enter the park area surrounding the cathedral. It's green and lush, with sprawling spaces filled with a scattering of people on blankets and walking through the winding pathways. The cathedral itself is breath taking. A tall tower with a pointed spire juts toward the sky at one end of the long building. It's not massive, and it's no Notre Dame, but it's beautiful all the same.

Wandering around a sputtering fountain and flower bed filled with small purple buds, I stroll through the park and surrounding gardens. Letting the peacefulness of it all sink into my bones. Letting it realign my fluttering heart into a calm, steady beat.

I will not let this curse control me. It won't ruin my one and only adventure I've ever had. The only vacation I've ever taken that wasn't just to the beach for a weekend. I may not meet the man of my dreams or have a perfectly scheduled tour, but dammit, I will enjoy myself if it's the last thing I do. And I will nullify this horrid bad luck curse while I'm here.

Ireland is known for its luck, and as much of it as I can while I'm here. Because I am not going home without it.

Spotting a patch of leafy green clovers, I take my first step toward that good luck. Finding a four-leaf clover. Statistically, there is one four-leaf clover for every five thousand three-leafed. Finding one is just a matter of time. I can search through five thousand clovers easily. Many people have found four-leaf clovers in the past and even with the curse I know that statistically I *will* find one. Bad luck can't stop that from happening.

7 - Conor

You know you can buy them at a gift shop

I woke up this morning refreshed and renewed. Damn Rory for being right. I hadn't wanted to go out last night, but it seems it did some good. Rory was pissed I didn't meet them at O'Donoghues. I didn't explain why or tell him about Emma. He would have gloated with his "I told you so's," and I didn't feel like admitting defeat to him.

It's Rory I'm on my way to meet at the practice fight, at a gym in central Dublin nearer to Temple Bar where I was last night. Whereas my flat and gym are outside of the busy central hub.

Some like to live in the heart of the city, but I like being just outside it. Near but not in the middle of it all. After spending my youth living in the country on a farm, there's only so much city living I can take. Still needing my own space and fresh air away from the hordes of people and tourists.

At least once a month, I head out to my parent's place to do just that. Rory says I never take a break, but I do—just in my own way. A couple days a month, I leave the city and stay at my parent's place basking in the peace and quiet. Except for the sheep. There's always a constant hum of sheep bleating since they run a sheep farm where they produce wool. The sounds are familiar and comforting, like the ticking of a metronome. It's a small farm, nothing large enough to sell to huge companies. They only sell their wool to local weavers and shops throughout Ireland.

Last year, my oldest sister Bridget helped get their wool and yarn into a few shops in Dublin, Belfast, Galway, and Cork. Expanding their business but not growing it beyond their capability. Moving their products into a more profitable market.

Bridget has plans for a website to start selling directly to customers, but they haven't quite made it there yet. Having to inventory and sell and ship requires infrastructure and employees they don't yet possess.

The farm has been in the family since my grandparents started in nearly five decades ago. It's because of my nan and her love for all things yarn that I know how to crochet. She tried to teach me how to knit, but I couldn't manage the two giant needles.

I have more jumpers, scarves, hats, gloves, vests, and socks than any man will ever need. When living in Ireland, they're all needed but not to the extent of filling a wardrobe with them all. Especially since I don't get cold easily. Yet I still get at least one hand made wool item for my birthday and Christmas. I don't mind the socks; I like to wear them around my flat like slippers to keep my feet nice and warm on rainy days.

Although today is shaping up to have some rain this afternoon, I left the wool socks at home, dawning one of my many jumpers. This one is black made by my nan a few years ago for my birthday. It's one of my preferred that I wear frequently. Worn in and stretched to the perfect fit.

Thanks to the extra pep in my step, I'm running early for the fight. Making my way through the gardens around St. Patrick's Cathedral, killing a little time. For some reason, I felt the need to take a walk in my good mood. It's something I rarely spend my time on unless I'm out at my parents' walking through their acreage.

The slight clouding overhead blocks out any direct sunlight as it slowly drifts across the sky. There aren't too many people out on the grounds, just a handful here and there. One in particular catches my attention. There's no way it could be who I think it is. That would be far too lucky.

Circling around her to keep from getting too close just in case she isn't who I think, I see her profile and straight red hair and those chaotic freckles. It is her. Emma, from last night.

Looks like my luck is that good. I take it as a sign that I was meant to see her again. Even if she is American and only here temporarily. Doesn't mean we can't be friendly.

Emma is lying flat on her stomach in a patch of shamrocks, combing through the leafy greens, seemingly searching for something. Her legs are bent at the knee, kicking her feet in the air focused solely on what her hands are doing.

She's not hiding beneath a giant gray jumper today. Instead, she's wearing a fitted hunter green shirt under a denim jacket that shows off her backside. Her jeans hug her arse in a way I cannot ignore. It's round and ripe and made for grabbing. The position she's in ignites dirty thoughts, which, in turn, stirs my cock to attention.

Shaking my head free of the naked images or her and I, I

watch her for a moment entranced. She doesn't seem to notice me, or anyone else for that matter.

She shifts to a kneeling position still hunched over, searching through the clovers. What is she looking for? Don't tell me she's hunting for a four-leaf clover.

I approach her slowly from behind not wanting to frighten her and lean down to place a hand gently on her shoulder.

"Hey there, Love—agh."

My words are abruptly cut off as I go flying over her shoulder. Somehow, she twisted, grabbed my arm, and flung me over her, landing me flat on my back in the patch of clovers she was just looking through.

How the fuck did she just do that? I have to have at least six and a half stone on her. Most of it muscle. Yet she is strong enough to flip me on my back. From a seated position no less. That wasn't your average I-was-shocked-and-reacted flip. That was practiced with precision.

I stare up at the sky and her freckled face staring down at me, the wind momentarily knocked out of me. Her cheeks are rosy, and her brows are furrowed in concern.

"Oh my goodness. I'm so sorry, Conor. I didn't realize it was you. I just reacted."

"What the hell kind of reaction is that? Most people just jerk away or shout. Not body slam a lad."

I grunt through gritted teeth. Sitting up, I rub the back of my head where I knocked it on the ground. It's only slightly sore, no headache or bump, so I think I'll be okay.

"Most people don't have three older brothers and a father who insist on training you in self-defense beyond what is reasonable or necessary."

Emma smiles shyly at me, reaching around to brush her

fingers across the back of my head and through my hair, checking the spot I was rubbing. Her touch is soft and warm, making me want to lean into it and nuzzle her palm. There's just something about this girl. I can't stop staring at her.

"Doesn't seem like there's any permanent damage. You look like a tough guy. I think you'll be okay."

She withdrawals her hand and its absence is palpable. I want her to touch me again. To run her fingers through my hair and across my skin, marring me with her heat.

"What are you doing here?"

It wasn't the line I had planned on opening with, but it's what comes out of my mouth.

"Oh, um . . ." she turns away, hiding her face under the curtain of her hair. "I was looking for a four-leaf clover. Remember how I told you about my bad luck?"

I nod. "Yeah."

She sits back on her heels and fidgets with the fluffy white keychain dangling from her bag. I remain seated but shift into a more comfortable position with my knees bent. Big guys like me can't sit crossed legged on the ground, our thighs won't allow it.

"Well, the curse struck again today. The travel agency I booked my tour through is apparently closed for business. Permanently. So now I'm on my own. Figured maybe if I find a four-leaf clover it'll help with the rest of the trip."

Turning her head, she looks up at me through long lashes. Those bright hazel eyes inquisitive.

"Had any luck finding one yet?"

"No," she grumbles. Frowning adorably. Pursing her lips and scrunching her brow.

"You know you can buy them at a gift shop for like three

euro."

"Yes, I know." Her voice is soft but stern. She seems dead set on finding one the old-fashioned way.

She says she has bad luck, but I consider running into her twice in twenty-four hours good luck.

Maybe she's looking at it all wrong.

Checking my watch, I still have a little time before Rory will have a fit. I wouldn't mind spending more time with her. Maybe this time I'll remember to get her number.

"Would you like some help?" I offer, shifting my position to better see the clovers under and around us.

I've never gone clover picking, but how hard can it be? You count the leaves, and when you find one with four, you pick it.

Emma pinches her mouth to one side. "I don't know. I thought you had to be the one to find it in order for the luck to work."

"I think you just have to be the one in possession of the clover to reap the rewards. It's like having a winning lottery ticket. You don't have to be the person who buys it you just have to be the person who cashes it in."

She looks down at the clover field and the thousands of green leaves she'll have to look through.

"I suppose it would make it go faster with help. Then I'll have time to figure out how I'm going to get to the Blarney Stone tomorrow."

"Still want to kiss the stone for luck, even after finding a four-leaf clover, eh?" I quirk my lips up in a smile at her as she resumes looking through the clovers.

"Can't be too careful. With my bad luck I can use all the good luck I can get. I plan on soaking up every bit of it while I'm here."

Emma picks a clover and lifts it to her face before throwing it over her shoulder. Apparently, not a four-leaf. I ignore the clovers and watch her instead. There's a colorful jade green and azure enamel pin on the front of her jacket that looks like some sort of butterfly.

"What's this?" I point to the pin but don't touch it.

We're less than a meter apart, and I could easily reach out and touch any part of her, but I resist. If she could put me on my back without seeing my coming, I can only imagine what she could do with a little warning. Kind of makes me want to get her in the ring and grapple with her. See what she's capable of. I'm a large lad, and it's not easy to take me down. She didn't even break a sweat.

She stops picking clovers and looks down. "Oh, it's a lunar moth. I find them fascinating."

"Those are the ones that are the size of your face, right?"

I vaguely remember seeing one on the telly once, in some movie or show. It was large, with soft wings and thin long tendrils dangling from either side. They were beautiful.

"Yeah, they can grow rather large and are usually shades of soft mossy green and bright ultramarine blue. There are different species that can be pink and yellow too. I would love to see one in person someday," she adds absentmindedly.

"Why haven't you?"

"They aren't exactly native to Dallas, Texas." She rolls her eyes and looks up at me as if I should have known this.

"You could have gone to see them somewhere else."

She barks out a laugh that startles me. "Haven't you been listening? Traveling isn't exactly easy for me."

"And you don't consider the reward worth the risk? You flew all the way here. Why not travel to see the lunar moths?"

She pauses and lowers her lashes, contemplating. I don't think it ever occurred to her that the slight setbacks and delays might be worth it if she gets to see something she's always admired.

"Yeah, I guess you're right. I could manage a flight delay and fire alarm if I got to see them. Maybe I will someday."

"You will."

We sit in silence, examining each other. Emma licks her lips and rolls them together, moistening them to a glistening pink. I stare at them without blinking. The clouds overhead shift and a soft ray of sunlight breaks through, lighting up her hair and face. She's a golden glowing goddess. The dickhead American who snags her as his own will be one lucky fecker.

She could be mine. There are plenty of people who date others from a different country. My fights are all over the world. I've gone to many EU countries *and* America for them. I could live anywhere and still do the same thing I do now. I wonder if her job is mobile. I hadn't even thought to ask what she does for a living. We've been too focused on her luck.

Before I have the opportunity to ask her about her job or anything else, she breaks the silence between us.

"Okay. How about that clover? It's not going to find itself." She turns away from me and starts looking again.

Turning my attention to the ground, I brush the hand across the tiny stems, shifting the leaves, so I can count them. I'm only looking for about a minute when I spot what look like four leaves on one stem.

Plucking it, I hold it up and count. One, two, three, and four. That wasn't that hard.

"Found one."

"What? Impossible."

Emma turns her bright eyes to me and scoots to my side, pressing her thigh against mine. This close, I can smell her scent. It's a clean, crisp scent. Like freshly washed linen drying on the line. A soft breeze through the rolling hills around my family's home. It's not a bottled scent, either, like a perfume or body spray. It's too soft for that. It must come from her soap or shampoo. I take a long inhale, soaking it in.

She snatches the clover from my hand momentarily brushing her fingers across mine. I can see her mouthing the numbers as she counts to four.

"How did you find one so fast? I've been here for over half an hour and not found one."

I shrug but don't move away from her, enjoying the closeness. "Just lucky I guess."

"Well, I hope you don't mind if some of that luck rubs off on me. Because I could really use it."

"Not at all."

Her smile is wide and easy, as if I just handed her a stack of gold bars. It makes me smile. As does her ensuing giggle of joy and little bounce on her bum.

Lifting a long gold chain around her neck, she holds up what looks like a glass ball about the size of a two-euro coin. She twists the little nob on top and the orb breaks in half and falls open on a hinge.

"What is that?"

She places the clover inside and closes the two halves, flattening the clover between. The glass magnifies it.

"It's a glass locket. This way I can keep the good luck with me always."

She finishes locking it closed and lets the pendant hang down between her breasts against the textured green fabric of her shirt. It's harder to see the clover against the green, but I know it's there.

I notice another shorter gold chain around her neck, this one with an upright horseshoe dangling from it.

Every bit of luck indeed.

"Do you think that'll be enough?" I ask, trying and failing to remove my eyes from her chest.

"Not in the least. Which is why I'm kissing that dirty old stone tomorrow." Laughing, she looks up to me and throws her arms around my neck, pulling me close to her. Forcing me to place one hand on the ground behind me to keep from toppling over.

The long silky red strands of her hair tickle my nose and that windy linen scent is stronger, invading my senses. The hug is unexpected but welcome. I wrap my free arm around her back, returning the embrace, letting my face sink a little deeper into her neck without obviously nuzzling her.

"Thank you. I probably never would have found one without you," she whispers into my ear, and her breath across my skin sends a shiver down my spine.

This woman.

She does things to me I've never experienced before. I love it and hate it. She's a foreigner on vacation. What could come of this? Even knowing that I still want to find out.

When she leans back, I'm about to ask for her number when I'm rudely interrupted by my mobile ringing loudly in my pocket. I can't remove it while sitting, so I apologize to Emma and stand to retrieve it.

It's Rory. Feck, I'm late.

"Hi, Rory, I know I'm late. I'm on my way now."

"Damn right you're late, you gobshite. Get your arse over

her now. This may not be a sanctioned fight, but it still deserves the respect of being on time," Rory practically yells in my ear.

"Okay, okay. I got it."

Rory continues to yell at me through the speaker as I turn back to Emma.

"I'm sorry. I really have to go. I'm late. Maybe I'll see you around again. We could—"

"Who are you talking to?" Rory demands through the mobile in my hand. "Never mind, I don't care. They're not important. Stop what you're doing, move your arse and get here NOW!"

"Right. Sorry again." I tell Emma before turning on my heel and jogging across the grass toward the gym.

8 - Conor

Am I going to need to ice my balls tonight?

When I arrive at the gym, Rory is standing outside the entrance, arms crossed over his chest and a frown on his face. I will never hear the end of this.

"Where the hell have you been? You should have been here long ago. What, you forget how to drive?"

"No, you eejit. I just got distracted and lost track of time okay."

I push past him into the gym and search for the locker room sign. Finding it in the back right corner, I make my way toward it. Rory hot on my heels.

"How exactly did you get 'distracted'? You are never late for a fight. What's going on?" He sounds both pissed and concerned.

It is unusual for me to be late, but being late once in my entire career isn't much of a concern. And it's only training. Not like it's the headlining main card fight being televised I'm late for.

Pushing through the swinging doors to the locker room I pull off my jumper and shirt and pluck my shorts from the bag Rory brought and has open and ready for me on a bench.

"Relax. It was one time. I got caught up with someone and didn't realize what time it was. Won't happen again, so chill."

Stripping down naked I pull out my black shorts and quickly slip them on. My cousin has seen me naked more times than I care to count. It's nothing he hasn't seen before and won't see again. Besides, I have nothing to be ashamed of. My package is substantial. He should feel honored seeing me in all my glory. I've had plenty of offers from magazines and reporters to bear all to them. None succeeded in convincing me. Nothing is worth that kind of publicity. I may be well endowed, but photos of my junk don't need to be on the internet for all eternity. And the PR lady who calls occasionally from my sponsors might have a seizure while yelling at me and Rory for it. So, to save her the hospital bills, I refrain.

Rory steps up to my side and holds out my glove for me to slip my hand into, doing the same with the other. His hands tighten around my wrists and hold me in place when he's done. Forcing me to look him in the eye.

"Who?"

"Who, what?"

"Who distracted you?"

"Just some girl." I shrug, pulling my wrists out of his grip. He could try to fight it, but I am far stronger than him. Making my way to the door, I give him my back, so he can't see the lie on my face. I have a decent poker face, but Emma's scent lingers in my nose, and I'm not sure how convincing I can be at the moment.

Keeping her scent in the back of my mind, I clear the rest

for the fight ahead. It's never a good idea to go into a fight, professional or practice, with a clutter mind.

Stepping back out into the gym, Rory follows as I begin a quick warm up to loosen my muscles. Bouncing on the balls of my feet and swinging my arms, shaking out my neck.

"Just some random girl, eh? If that were the case, you wouldn't be so evasive. What's her name?"

"Weren't you the one who told me who I was talking to was unimportant and to stop and get here now?" I quote his words from the phone before when he interrupted me and Emma.

Shite.

I stop mid bounce. I fucking forgot to ask for her number again. Damn Rory and his poor timing. Now I'll never see her again for sure.

"Yeah, I might have said that. Doesn't mean I'm not curious about you getting caught up talking with a girl. So . . . who was she?" he inquires again.

I return to stretching and prepping. Now fully trying to push Emma from my mind. It's pointless to think of her. The odds of running into her again are practically nonexistent now.

"Doesn't matter. She was a tourist, and I didn't get her number," I bite out. A little irritated at that last bit.

"Oh well. You don't want a tourist anyway, right? No, you want a nice Irish girl because women from other countries aren't good enough for you," he mocks.

Normally I'd agree, but not about Emma. She was too good for me. I could tell in her smile. She'd have me on my knees with one word. Or on my back with one swift movement. Fuck, a girl like that is a turn on. Strong and sweet, obviously sincere and kind. That's the kind of girl I want to take home to meet my parents. Whether she's Irish or not. Which technically

Emma is. She even said so. She has distant relations here on her father's side. So, technically, she does fit my limited criteria.

I'm going to add more to the criteria. For one, I never realized I wanted a woman who could put me on my arse. It was hot. She should also find joy in the little things, like clover hunting. As well as have sultry hazel eyes and be a little quirky.

Apparently, my attempts to clear my head of Emma have failed. Shaking my limbs out a little more aggressively, as if I could shake her right out of my system, I ready myself for the fight.

We walk toward the ring where my opponent is already waiting. A lad in his mid-twenties, a little shorter than I but with almost just as much muscle and bulk. This should be a decent fight.

"Now remember, he's just an amateur. Only been fightin' for a few years so go easy on him, aye?"

I laugh darkly. "Not likely. You know I never go easy on anyone."

He laughs in response. Shaking his head good naturedly. "All right then, just don't hurt him too bad."

"No promises," I say as I step into the ring and greet my

* * *

"I told you to go easy on him *not* let him win. What the fuck was that shite I just witnessed?" Rory berates me as I stumble back to the locker room with his help.

He has every right to be upset. I fucking lost. I *don't* lose.

Especially. to newbie amateurs. That kid better mark this day in his diary because it will never happen again.

"I don't fucking know. He got the jump on me somehow. I didn't see it coming."

"You didn't see it coming? Since when do you miss an obvious hit like that? I saw it from three meters away. And what was that shite you tried to pull at the end? It was the weakest attempt at a takedown I've ever seen. And not just from you, from anyone. That wouldn't take down my baby niece. He's supposed to be the amateur, *not* you." Rory sucks in a frustrated breath and blows it out harshly. "You're lucky this was a practice fight. If you perform like this at your fight with Becker, you're going to lose your sponsorships. Do you want that?"

"No, of course I don't. I also don't want to lose," I growl back at him, dropping to sit on the bench in the locker room. My ribs ache, my ankle feels twisted, my fists burn, and every part of my face is throbbing from the hits he landed. I haven't had this many injuries— even minor ones—since I started in MMA over a decade ago. This fight would have been embarrassing were I an amateur. As a professional, it's fucking disgraceful.

"Well, you're gonna if you fight like that again. What the hell happened out there?"

I wish I had an answer for him. Honestly, I have no fucking idea what happened. It was like fighting through sludge. I felt slow and delayed. Like I wasn't seeing his movements until they were already making contact. I poke my tongue at the split on my lip that's still bloody. One of many hits I should have seen coming. I always see them coming, can predict and react without thought always slipping free of their attempts to take me down, and can catch them in my own holds. I couldn't lock in a hold once in that fight.

It's as if that special ability I always possessed that made me so good at the sport is gone.

This better not be fucking permanent. MMA is my life. If I can't do that, then what the fuck am I doing?

"I just had an off day okay. I'll be fine for the Becker fight," I say more to reassure myself than him.

"You sure about that? Because that shite is unacceptable. You're better than that Conor. You, and I both know it."

"I know." I sigh, dropping my shoulders in defeated acceptance. This was a fight I should have won with my eyes closed.

He grips my shoulder and ignores the dripping sweat and splattering of blood that fell from my nose when I was caught off guard by an impressive kick. "Good. Now get cleaned up. I think we need to get back to the gym for some training."

I clean up after Rory's not so grand pep talk. Wiping clean the blood smears and quickly showering off, redressing in my jeans and shirt I wore in. Pulling on my boots, I tug at the laces, tightening them when one snaps right off as I do so.

"Bollocks," I curse at the broken bit in my hand.

First, I don't get Emma's number, then I'm late for a fight I lose, now a broken shoelace. This is not my day.

Chucking the lace in the bin, I tie the long end to the short in a messy knot. It'll hold till I get home. Shoving my gear back in the bag I zip it up and make my way out of the locker room and then the gym without speaking to anyone. A few lads try to get my attention, but I stride past. I'm in no mood to make friendly small talk or give advice to wannabe professionals.

Outside, I trip over a lip in the cobble stone walkway nearly falling face first into a light post. Cursing even more colorful expletives at the ground and offending light post.

Fisting my hand tight, I can feel the stretch of tender skin across my knuckles. Even with the gloves, they're red and irritated more than usual. Just one more pain to add on the growing list I've received this afternoon.

I make it to my car without another tripping incident but knock myself in the shin with my driver's door when I yank it open a little too aggressively.

What the actual fuck is happening?

Not only do I get stuck in a traffic jam leaving the city, but almost get into an accident when some twat cuts me off in a round-about trying to exit and nearly killing me in the process instead of rounding once more and exiting properly.

It takes me twice as long to get back to the gym, having to circle before finding a spot to park. Rory is already there waiting for me, with Niall at his side.

"What took you so long?"

"Don't ask," I growl as I stomp past them to get changed.

I pay no attention to the other half dozen lads in the locker room as I strip naked and put my shorts back on. Grabbing my gloves without putting them on, I stomp back out to the main room of the gym.

I've been training in this gym for years. The ring, the bags, weight machines, and various other training tools are embedded in my brain like DNA. I know where every single piece lies and could navigate it in my sleep. Yet as I make the short journey from locker room to ring, I stub my goddamn toe on a bench press and nearly punch the lad nearest me.

"FUCK!" I let out a scream, gaining the attention of everyone in the gym. All sounds and movement cease as all eyes turn to me. Some curious, others irritated I interrupted their workout or training. I ignore them all and the throb growing in my foot and join Rory and Niall with a scowl so deep it'll be etched into my features for days.

"You okay, pal?" Niall asks hesitantly, eyes wide and cautious. He's already shirtless and changed into his yellow shorts, gloves tucked into his waistband.

"Oh, I'm just fucking peachy. Why do you ask? Could it be the split lip, swollen nose, or possibly broken toe? None of those? Maybe it's the obvious stench of failure wafting behind me."

My anger spills out, and I lash out at Niall, I need someone to expel my ire on, and he is the lucky bastard to receive it. My fists are clenched and every muscle in my body is pulled tight as a violin string. One false pluck, and I'll snap.

"Woah, easy pal." He holds his hands up in surrender. "Just wonderin' why Rory called me in for a last-minute training when I knew you had yer fight with the amateur earlier. Didn't think you would need me today and would be out celebrating another win."

Rory winces, and Niall catches it, immediately aware he said something wrong but clueless as to what.

"What did I say? Am I going to need to ice my balls tonight?" He cringes and reflexively reaches down to cover his groin with one hand.

One session I may have been in a bad mood and took a shot below the belt on purpose, knocking him square in the sack. The mood I'm in I'll probably do permanent damage if I do that again. I should attempt to restrain my hits to recoverable damage.

Growling, I sneer at him. My anger more at myself than

anyone else. They shouldn't suffer for my shortcomings. Unfortunately, I need to expel this frustration and Niall will end up icing something tonight.

"He had a bad fight," Rory supplies.

"How bad?" Niall asks, clearly worried.

"He lost," Rory states flatly. "And he's being a big baby about it." He turns a glower to me, and I grunt at him.

Apparently, I've turned into a caveman.

"Shite. Like lost on a technicality because the ref was an arse, lost?"

Oh, Niall, I wish it were that kind of loss. Your day wouldn't be about to take a turn for the worse if it were.

"No." Rory doesn't elaborate, thankfully. He doesn't need to.

Niall groans and grips his groin even more protectively now with both hands. "Do I really need to be here? Maybe he should go home and decompress before returning to the ring."

"No."

They both turn to face me when the rejection rumbles from my chest.

"Come on, mate. I just started seeing this fuck hot girl, and I would really like to be able to use my dick," Niall wines in protest.

"Don't worry. I'll steer clear of your precious dick. It would need more than one night of icing to recover from what I might do to it right now."

Oddly my reassurance doesn't reassure him. He steps back, horror written all over his face. The color drains from his cheeks, leaving his skin a ghostly white.

"That doesn't sound any better mate. I think I'd like to call in sick today."

"Probably a good idea," I agree. I may actually break something if we fight right now.

Needing to disperse this twitchy funk I've found myself in, I move to one of the open bags. Dropping my gloves on the floor, I don't bother with them and begin pounding into it. The bag sways and shifts with each hit. The chain jangling overhead.

The leather gives under my fists but still rubs the skin there raw. Causing more chaffing and redness. The pain feels good. I deserve it after the performance I put on earlier. Every new thought is punctuated by a forceful hit of the bag.

I knew I shouldn't have gone out last night.

Right hook.

Breaking my routine caused this.

Left hook.

Ignoring my instincts caused this.

Upper cut.

Listening to Rory caused this.

Jab.

Emma . . .

My rhythmic punching falters when I think of Emma but resumes a moment later.

She didn't cause this. Thinking of her eases some of the tension in my body though, slowing my frantic pounding into a smoother rhythm.

I can't blame her. She has nothing to do with this. It may have been because of her I was a few minutes late, but that didn't cause my epic failure. No one could blame anything on such a lovely woman. Just the thought of her has my blood heating for reasons other than anger. I wouldn't mind seeing her again, no matter how unlikely it may be.

Behind me I can hear Rory detailing the fight to Niall. I listen to his description of my movements as seen from the outside. They were just as bad from the spectator's point of view as they were from my own.

A little of the steam burns out of me by the time they finish going over the fight, and I stop hitting the bag. There's a light smearing of blood on it from my knuckles. If I don't stop now, I'll regret it later.

"Sounds like he lost all that luck he's known for."

"It's not luck—" I begin to protest, but my words are cut short as that train of thought leads me somewhere unexpected.

The thought strikes me like the foot did earlier to my face. The only thing that has changed recently was that I met Emma. A woman who says she's cursed with bad luck. I thought it was good luck running into her twice in twenty-four hours, but perhaps that wasn't luck at all.

What if she really is cursed? And now, so am I.

Can someone pass a curse onto another person by just being near them? That seems rather ridiculous, otherwise everyone she came into contact with would have her bad luck. But I did something for her that has me questioning my own sanity.

I found her a four-leaf clover and told her she could have some of my good luck. What if Niall is right, and I was lucky all along? And now I've handed over all my good luck to Emma? I can't fight Becker in two weeks if that's the case. It would ruin my entire career. But I also can't back out.

But if I were to get my luck back . . .

The idea has merit.

I could simply find Emma and make her give me back the clover, and I'll get my luck back and win the fight against

Becker.

I sound like a crazy person. Thinking I handed off all my good luck to a woman I just met in the form of a leafy green weed. Yet I can't bring myself to disagree with myself. What do I have to lose at this point? Besides another fight, and my entire career.

Seeing Emma again has me more excited than the idea of getting back my luck. It has my dick excited too. There's only one thing. I didn't get her number . . . again. How the bloody hell am I supposed to find her? It's not like she lives in the area, and I'll just bump into her on the street. That can only happen so many times. She could be anywhere on the entire island.

However, I know where she will be tomorrow. She told me at the cathedral. She wants to kiss the Blarney stone. Luckily, I happen to know someone who works there.

"I think you're right Niall."

He jerks to face me and stares, a pinch between his brow. "About what?"

"I should decompress. Take some time to work through the . . . *loss*." The word comes out through clenched teeth, unable to fully annunciate it. "Maybe even take your advice, too, Rory."

Rory looks at me one eyebrow twitching up. "What advice would that be?"

"Take some time off. Clear my head."

Rory looks like he's about to lose his mind. Contorting his face in shock and confusion. He should be happy I'm taking his advice. He's been telling me to take a holiday for years. I'm just doing as he suggested.

"No, no, no, no. That was when you were winning and not having a mental breakdown. Right now, you need to be here, training. This is not the time to take a holiday, mate."

"I think it's the perfect time to take one. I've been meaning to visit my little sister. Then I'll head up to my parent's place for a few days, get away from all the noise and commotion. It'll be grand, you'll see. I'll come back a changed man."

Changed as in I'll have all my good luck back and won't have to worry about losing epically to Becker, and I'll be hunting down a rather enticing redhead. But I keep that bit to myself. The lads would have me committed if they knew what I plan on doing.

9 - Emma

It's thicker but still delightful

Booking my hotel near the Blarney Castle and finding a new way to get there goes smoother than I ever thought imaginable. Maybe my new lucky charm is actually working. I found the cutest little hotel, with old world country charm and one of those old school elevators—sorry *lifts*—with the accordion gate door. I might feel lucky enough to try it when I arrive. Which will be in a luxury coach.

That's right I found a luxury coach that makes daily trips between the two cities and many others. I may use it for the rest of my trip.

I'm sitting in the luxury coach in my oversized seat with full armrests and complimentary water and snack, when I see a sign outside my window. Cork. *I made it.* Without the bus breaking down, without having diarrhea in a bus bathroom, and without losing my luggage.

When I travel, I only use a carry-on suitcase. I've had my luggage lost or misplaced too many times to ever check a bag ever again. I learned to create a capsule style wardrobe, so I could pack small but smart. Allowing for the greatest number of outfits without an excessive number of clothing. The skill has come in very handy. Though, sometimes, I wish I could purchase more interesting pieces, with patterns and interesting cuts. But every time I buy anything not solid colored or simplistic in style something always goes wrong. I buy a striped shirt and look like a referee or old school prison inmate. I buy a funny cat shirt, and all my other shirts end up dirty, forcing me to wear it to school. I buy colorful, humorous underwear, and my pants rip flashing suggestive illustrations of eggplants and peaches to my boss. Don't even get me started on wide flowy skirts and dresses. Me and flowing skirts don't mix.

Therefore, I've curated a wardrobe consisting of neutral colors, like black, white and gray, with only a few accent complimentary colors. Mainly forest green, royal blue and burgundy in simple minimalist styles that fit in any situation.

On a bus, however, all bags, even carry on suitcases, go in the undercarriage. Leaving me with only my messenger bag, which sits on the empty seat next to me. That's right *empty* seat. There's only two seats to each side and the one beside me was empty the entire trip.

This may be my most relaxing and comfortable traveling yet. No smelly row mate, no cramped legs. I feel like I won the lottery.

Do normal luck people feel like this all the time? Booking hotels and luxury coach transportation without issue? If so, my life will be drastically different now.

Even with all the apparent good luck, I'm still not holding my breath. Not until I kiss that smooth ancient stone will I breathe easy and accept my new existence. Until then, I'm not letting my guard down. But that doesn't mean I can't enjoy it all.

Sipping my cold water, I watch the scenery slide by as we enter the city. I spend the last half hour admiring the culture and history of it all.

Once we arrive at the bus terminal in Cork, I have to transfer busses to get to Blarney, where the castle and stone are located. I've reserved a room at the Blarney Castle Hotel. Just to make it easy on myself.

The short drive out of the city is just as pleasant and easy as the one from Dublin, and I arrive with no fuss. This experience is the most enjoyable one I've had since . . . well since ever, I suppose.

The bus stop is only a few blocks away from my hotel, so I decide to walk. Walking is always best if able. It has the least probability of difficulty and setbacks. As long as I triple check before crossing the street, I'll be fine. Having chose the first bus out of Dublin it's barely ten in the morning. Giving me plenty of time to check in and make my way to the stone.

It's another chilly day, and I pull my scarf tighter around my neck and chin. It doesn't do much. This is what I get for buying cheap. Trying to balance quality and cost when clothes shopping is a delicate skill. Not wanting to buy something expensive for fear that it'll be ruined, lost, or stolen is a real challenge. But not wanting to buy something cheap that'll be see-through or rip the first time I wear it is also an issue. Finding a balance has been a well-honed and researched skill.

First thing on my shopping list is to find and buy a new scarf, and maybe a hat to match. Can't not have a matching pair. It gets cold in the winter in Texas. It's not like I won't use them.

Obviously, my last-minute scarf purchase of this gray woven flimsy thing was a bad choice. I didn't have the opportunity to do my regular research and comparison in the short time I had before leaving. Not to mention having to pack up almost all my possessions so they could remove the water-damaged items and strip and replace the flooring.

Which reminds me, I should check in with Jules and Danny to make sure everything is going well on that end. My brother promised to help out in person at my apartment while Jules coordinated everything from her place in New York. I hope they haven't ripped each other's heads off yet.

Deciding it best to get over with as soon as possible, I check the app on my phone that calculates the difference in time zones. If it's ten a.m. in Ireland, that means it's . . . four a.m. in Texas. Hmm. Is that too early to call? If he's on shift at the station, it might not be. Should I risk it? Probably best not to. I'll just wait a few hours, then call him.

Turning left at the next intersection I find the hotel halfway up the block. Three stories tall with dormer windows on the topmost floor. The front is painted a soft robin's egg blue, separating it from the shops and businesses around it. They're connected with shared walls in a row down the street. It's quant and cute and everything I hoped it would be.

Stepping through the front door, I enter a small foyer decorated with sapphire and gold jacquard wallpaper and gold framed drawings of horses. A small white porcelain chandelier hangs over head illuminating the space in a warm golden glow. To my right is a check-in counter and lobby. To my left stretches out a pub and bar with small tables filled with a handful of people eating. Good to know they have a restaurant, so I have one less thing to worry about.

"Welcome to the Blarney Castle Hotel. How can I help you today, Miss?"

Turning toward the voice, I see a man in a tan polo shirt with a logo embroidered on the chest standing behind the check-in counter, already smiling broadly at me. He appears to be in his forties with expertly slicked back copper colored hair and soft brown eyes. A name tag on his shirt reads Finn.

I'm still surprised by how many gingers I've seen here. Even though I know that ten percent of all Irish people are gingers. That may seem like a small percentage but considering only two percent of the entire world population has red hair that's a lot for one small island. It just means I blend in more here than I do back home where blonde is the preferred hair color among Texan women. Whether natural or bottled.

Finn's accent differs from Conor's. Conor's is lighter, smoother, silkier. It slithers under your skin and seeps into your bones in a way that lingers. Finn's doesn't do that, it's thicker but still delightful.

"Hi. I have a reservation. The name is Emma Johnson."

Finn types on his computer, smile still in place. It twitches when he reads the screen but readjusts itself.

"I see your reservation here Miss Johnson. Unfortunately, there was an issue with your single room . . ."

Fuck a duck.

I knew this newfound good luck wouldn't last. Maybe four-leaf clovers have a limit and negating my massive bad luck sucked all the good luck out of it faster. I clutch the pendant, holding my clover around my neck, hoping I'm wrong.

Please don't crap-out on me now.

"But not to worry miss," Finn continues, shocking me back to skeptical. Maybe my clover is still working. "We've upgraded your reservation to one of our king rooms for the inconvenience. There won't be any additional charge, since the error was ours."

"Oh, well, thank you."

"Of course, Miss Johnson."

Finn takes my info and hands me my room key. And not an electronic card key or even a standard house key but a golden brass antique style key. One that looks like those old school skeleton keys. It hangs from a blue tasseled keychain. He directs me to the lift to take to the third floor where my room is located.

Carefully I enter the elevator, lined in wood and gold accents with a tasteful indigo carpet, and no mirrors. I always found it uncomfortable when an elevator is lined with mirrors. I know it's to create the feeling of open space, but it's just awkward because no matter where you look you're staring at someone.

Closing the accordion gate, I push the button numbered two. Which was confusing at first until I realized they consider the ground floor level zero instead of one.

The elevator dings and ascends smoothly. Passing the first two floors without issue and stopping on my floor with another pleasant ding.

I exit and roll my suitcase through the simply decorated hallway, stopping in front of the door numbered 312. The same number engraved on the golden key in my hand. I slide the key in the hole; it turns and opens without struggle.

The room inside is heaven. As in I've literally died and gone to heaven. That's how cute and cozy this room is. Although the furnishings are simple, everything looks clean and comfortable. With golden-yellow-and-ivory striped wallpaper on one wall, matching the butter yellow suede chaise and fluffiest most comfy looking comforter I've ever seen. Making me wish for heavy rain so I can stay inside, wrapped in a blanket, and enjoy tea while reading a book from the downstairs borrow shelf.

There's even a wooden trolly with a ceramic tea set on top, ready and waiting.

I take a quick inventory of the room and make my way to the bathroom. Where proof of my death and subsequent ascension to heaven sits on the white ceramic tiles. A legitimate iron claw-foot tub.

Heaven.

My trip to the Blarney stone may be delayed an hour or two.

Stepping out of the hotel after the most relaxing two hours of my life, I begin my walk to the Blarney Castle to kiss the Blarney stone. It's now noon, and I figure late enough to call Danny and check on things.

Pulling my phone from my bag, I tap his name on my list of favorites and hold the phone to my ear. He answers after the third ring.

"Hey, li'l sis. How's the emerald isle?"

"Pretty great, actually. Started off rough, but I think things are taking a turn for the better. I may return home the luckiest person you've ever met."

Danny laughs. His voice is loud and good humored,

obviously wide awake. At least I didn't wake him up.

"That'll be the day. Considering you're the unluckiest person I've ever met, that will be quite a feat." His tone is disbelieving—which I completely understand—but also optimistic.

My entire family would love for me to reverse my luck. Not only for my sake but for theirs as well. It tends to bleed over sometimes, and I hate when it does. I feel like it's my fault, even though I know it's not.

"Just you wait and see."

"So, your plan to soak up the luck of the Irish is working, then?" Again, he's disbelieving but curious.

I cross the street when the little illuminated sign shows the figure of a walking man, checking both ways first. There's a large green space with bright green grass and spread-out lush trees on the other side. Not a forest but more like a large well-manicured park. According to the pamphlet I took from the lobby, a lot of green space surrounds the castle. The peacefulness of birds, wind, and the occasional distant car is fine by me. Nothing like the noise of a busy city.

I relax even more. The mix of the hot bath, tea and soothing sounds is magic. Jules was right. I needed this trip. With or without finding good luck I needed it.

"Seems so. I don't know why I didn't do this sooner. Could have saved myself a lot of grief."

"Mhm," he hums in agreement. Knowing very well all the trials and tribulations I've been through for everyday living.

"How's everything going with my apartment? You haven't sent assassins after Jules yet, have you?"

He huffs an annoyed laugh. "No, not yet. But I have considered prank ordering her twenty pizzas. But then I realized she'd probably like that. The apartment is moving along. They've removed all the damaged furniture and are set to remove the carpet tomorrow. It'll have to dry out for a few days before they can do anything else. I think the ceiling repair people will be patching up the cracks in that time, too."

Danny pauses as I make my way deeper into the green space. Finding the main path that will lead me directly to the castle. It's made of gray stone, well-worn from decades of feet and shoes traversing its path to seek the luck of the Blarney Stone. The pathway makes wide, leisurely curves and turns through the greenery, and I stick to it like Dorothy on the yellow brick road.

"You sure you want to stay in that apartment after this? Might be a good time to look for something new." Danny asks in my ear.

I have thought about it, but with the curse it wasn't a logical course of action. With the curse nullified, I might find something worthy of moving.

"Maybe. Perhaps when I get back, I'll look into a new place. I am on a month to month and the landlord isn't charging me for the weeks it's going to take to repair all the water damage."

"I think that would be a good idea. I don't like the idea of you living in that unsafe building any longer. If the damage had been any worse, or you had been home, the entire ceiling could have collapsed on top of you." Danny's voice goes airy and quiet. Softening as he considers the possible outcomes that could have ended with me severely injured. "I don't want to show up at a call and find you trapped under a mountain of debris, Em."

"I know."

It's been a long-standing concern of his, and my parents.

One day he'll suit up and arrive to a scene to find me injured or worse, dead. That was the leading force when I was younger that pushed me toward risk assessment. If I could know and understand the statistical likelihood of any event, I would know how to avoid it. Or at least increase my chances of surviving it. I just never thought that would be my career. There was always something else I wanted to do but could never risk exploring for fear of the damage I could inflict unwillingly on others.

"You're being safe there though, right Em?" Danny continues, avoiding any more direct talk on the matter.

"Of course, I am big bro. Everything is great here. I'm just about to kiss the Blarney stone."

"Be careful. You know that stone hangs over at least a five story drop through a hole in the floor."

I am well aware of the precarious placement of the stone, which is why having the four-leaf clover first comforts me enough to risk it. Reaching down, I clasp the glass locket, holding it in my palm. Reassuring myself it's still there.

"I will. They have people here to help me to ensure I don't fall. I'll be fine. Say hi to everyone for me, okay. Talk soon."

"Fine, but I want you to text me after so I know you're safe."

"Can do," I agree. It's nothing I haven't had to do before.

"Good. Love you sis."

"Love you, too."

We hang up, and I pick up my pace to reach the castle. If I'm going to manifest the future I imagined with Danny, I first have to make sure I'm rid of the curse for good. Which means finishing this trip as planned.

10 - Emma

Perhaps the Irish Friendly is the American Flirting

The Blarney castle is magnificent. I round upon it and see it standing tall and strong, consisting of multiple structures. Smaller towers surround the massive foreboding castle, looming tall overhead. Squared off with uneven squares lining the top, right where the stone resides. At the tallest point of the castle.

That looks a lot higher than five stories, closer to six or seven. My nerves begin to vibrate and rattle thinking about hanging upside down and backward over a sheer drop with nothing to stop me should I fall. With only two metal bars to hold on to and no security harness.

Maybe this was a bad idea.

Do I really need to kiss the stone? Is it that important? I have my four-leaf clover now, and it seems to do the job just fine.

I ponder this, standing here, gazing at the castle, building up the nerve to go inside the ticket booth and buy a ticket.

If I went home without kissing the stone, I would regret it, and Jules would never let me forget it. I wish she were here with me. That would make it a lot easier to go through with it. Knowing there was someone standing next to me to watch over me, supporting me. It would make all the difference.

"Well, look who it is."

I turn abruptly at the deep voice behind me and find the last person I expect to see standing about six feet away, Conor. Wearing a similar sweater to when I ran into him at the cathedral in Dublin, only this one is a cream color with light brown flecks. He looks like a model ready for a cover shoot of "Hottest men in Ireland" or something. His dark hair is brushed back and tamer than before, as if he took time styling it before leaving the house.

He looks sexy as sin, and he knows it.

His muscles fill out his sweater and jeans perfectly, and I have the fleeting desire to be wrapped up in him. Held close, safe and secure within the circle of his embrace. What an odd feeling to have for a man I barely know.

"Conor." His name comes out on a winded exhale as my eyebrows touch my hairline in surprise.

"Hello, Love." His accent fondles the word, causing gooseflesh to run across my back making my nipples tighten beneath my sweatshirt and shirt.

Wow.

"What are you doing here?" I ask, distractedly.

Part of my brain still functioning enough to question his presence here, in a city, hours away from where I met him.

Conor's smile is wicked and beautiful and mischievous. As if he has a secret he's not telling me.

Realizing this is the third time I've seen him in three days and the second time he's appeared out of nowhere, I'm concerned it might not be accidental. Sure, our first meeting was, I threw salt on the man, but the others, a little too coincidental.

"Are you stalking me?" Raising an eyebrow at him, I eye him with wary curiosity.

The sexy mischief drops from his expression, but his smile remains. "What? No, not at all. I just . . . it's just a lucky coincidence."

"Mm, I don't know that I believe you." I cross my arms over my chest, holding onto the strap of my bag just in case his apparent friendliness and disarming appearance are false, and I need to run to escape.

I have pepper spray in my purse, curtesy of my oldest brother Sean. It's police grade and can cause some serious damage. It wouldn't take much to reach into my bag and spray him. My brothers made sure I practiced the action enough for it to be second nature so I would never fumble when I needed to use it. I've already used it once, and I have no qualms about using it again. Even on the gorgeously handsome Conor. He'd recover.

"My sister works at the visitor center; I came to visit her. Bumping into you was just accidental. I swear."

Conor pulls his hands out of his pockets and holds them up in surrender, showing his empty palms.

His smile is softer now, pleading for me to believe him. I watch him but don't move closer or relax my hold on my purse strap.

"Look, I'll even introduce you to her if that makes you feel better. Her name is Aisling O'Shea, and she's annoying on the best of days, but I still love her."

Conor chuckles and lowers his hands, keeping them outside

his pockets this time only slipping his thumbs inside. I don't know how he fit them in his pockets in the first place. They're huge. Like mitts. I almost forgot how large they are. Then my mind makes the not so far jump to his dick, and my eyes flick down to his groin.

I can't quite tell what he's packing behind that denim. Nothing is bulging out. Maybe the two sizes aren't comparable. That would be unfortunate. I suppose if he uses steroids that could explain a teeny weeny. If he's on roids, though, he could also have roid rage. And I'm back to contemplating using my pepper spray on him.

"Eyes up here, Love. Although I do love it when a woman checks out my package, you're makin' me a little self-conscious here."

My eyes shoot up from his groin to his face, where he's smirking at me. Playfulness dancing in his mossy green eyes.

"Sorry. My mind was wandering, and I zoned out a bit."

"Wandering, eh? I'd like to know about what." His voice goes low and syrupy, and I almost want to tell him. Then his eyes rove up and down *my* body.

After my relaxing bath I put on my black leggings, gray T-shirt and a black crew neck sweatshirt that fits loose and long and is made of the softest terry cotton. It was one of my pricier purchases but worth it for the extra bit of style and fit I got. I love the feel of sweatshirts and hoodies but dislike the sporty look of them. When dressing, I was going for casual comfort, with my hair braided in a long plait and draped over one shoulder. I ditched the scarf. It wasn't helping anyway, and I didn't want to lose it from the top of the castle.

My attire doesn't inspire arousal or scream sex appeal, but Conor's eyes on me make me feel naked under his attentions.

As if they aren't layers of fabric between his gaze, and my skin. It's as if he can see my body for what it is underneath and appears to appreciate what he sees.

The thought makes my entire body shiver and heat up at the same time. The warmth stinging my chilly cheeks. The things I would do with this man if I were able.

Conor finishes his appraisal of me and returns his gaze to mine, not an ounce of shame or embarrassment for his long perusing. I doubt a man like him would ever have a reason to feel embarrassed.

"Have you kissed it yet?"

"What?" My brow shoots up, breaking my daydream of a naked Conor.

"The stone. Have you kissed the stone yet?" he clarifies.

"Oh, not yet. I was just working up the courage to. It's a lot higher than I thought."

I turn sideways to face the castle but also keep Conor in my line of sight. It's still as imposing and tall. A small black and white bird flies across the sky, landing in one of the nearby trees. From the corner of my eye, I see Conor raise and lower his arm. But when I turn to see what he's doing his hand in back at his side, and he's looking up at the castle.

"What did you just do?" My curiosity gets the better of me before I can stop it.

"Do when?"

"Just now. You raised your arm or something."

"Oh." He chuckles. "Habit. I saluted the magpie that just flew by." Raising a hand, he gestures to where the bird remains perched on a branch a few yards away.

"Why would you salute a bird?" I pinch my brows in confusion. Is there something special about the bird I don't know?

"It's an old Irish tradition." His eyes shift, watching me from the corner of his eye. "For luck. A solo magpie is said to bring sorrow and saluting it is supposed to cancel it out."

"Oh. Should I have saluted it too? Am I going to have bad luck now? Is it too late to try?" I'm rambling but if there's any possibility this will cause bad luck or "sorrow" I'm desperate to remedy the situation immediately.

"You could give it a try. I've never heard there being a time limit. The bird is still in view so give it a go." Conor waves at the bird, who is watching us and waiting.

"So, I just . . . ?"

Lifting my arm, I position my hand near my temple, questioning my pose with a look at Conor. He nods and grins, shifting his eyes to the bird again.

It feels a little stupid saluting a bird but, when in Rome, or I suppose when in Ireland would be more accurate.

I do my best impersonation of a soldier, straightening my spine and holding the salute for a few seconds. Just in case. As if it were waiting for me to salute it the bird shakes and puffs out its feathers before lifting off of the branch and flying away.

"Did I do it right?" I ask, turning back to Conor, giving him a sheepish smile.

"Perfect."

The heat in my cheeks intensifies, and I press my palm against it to cool the deepening blush.

I turn my attention back to the castle, letting my heart calm as I motivate myself to go inside. A warm large body appears beside me. Conor. I have to look up to make eye contact. I haven't stood side by side with him yet, and although I could tell he was tall, I hadn't registered just how tall.

He must be well over six feet. At five foot eight I am neither short nor tall, and he's at least half a foot taller than me. Some guys can be on the shorter side, coming eye level with me or just above. They don't like it when I wear heels and look down at them. I like a man who's larger than me. Able to look over me and not have his masculinity endangered just because of height.

"Shall we go in?"

"You want to come in with me?" This man just keeps surprising me. He came here to visit his sister and now he wants to come with me to kiss the Blarney Stone? "I thought you came to visit your sister?"

"I did, but I see her quite frequently. We can stop in after to say hello."

I was just thinking how nice it would be to have a friend at my side while I risked death to kiss a rock hundreds of feet in the air, and here he is. My big muscular friendly Irishman offering to keep me company.

"You're not murderer, are you?"

A barking laugh bursts from Conor as he turns an amused look at me. "Why on earth would you think that?"

"Because this is the second time in two days you've appeared out of thin air to try and seduce me."

"Seduce you? Here I was thinking I was just being friendly."

"Perhaps the Irish friendly is the American flirting." My cheeks redden as I say the words.

I wasn't trying to flirt, but here I am, flirting away. I can't help it. Who wouldn't flirt with a guy like Conor? Even knowing we live in different countries, he's just too much to ignore.

"Oh well flirting I was *absolutely* doing."

One corner of Conor's mouth quirks as he softly bumps

me with his elbow.

"Flirting aside," I chide, "I still only just met you. How do I know you won't kidnap me and use my hair to weave into a doll and bury me in a patch of clovers somewhere."

"That seems a little extreme. Are you one of those girls who watches crime documentaries for fun?"

"I like to be informed," I shrug.

Bantering with Conor is fun. I don't really think he's a murderer, but it's best to be sure.

"Well, if you're really concerned, then google me."

"My friend already tried that." The admission slips from my lips unbidden, and I slap a hand over my mouth as soon as I realize what I've said.

"So, not only have you told a friend about me, you also tried to cyber stalk me? Who's the creep now?"

"I did not cyber stalk you. *She* tried to google you and was unsuccessful because Conor is a very common name in Ireland."

Crossing my arms over my chest once again, I take a defensive stance. I'm interrogating him, *not* the other way around.

"I promise if you use my last name you'll come up with different results."

I side eye him. "What does that mean?"

"Just type in Conor O'Shea, and you'll see."

"M'kay."

I don't know what he's getting at, but I placate him and pull out my phone, opening google and typing in his name. Immediately the search results appear, his face, name, age, height, and profession. Irish mixed martial artist.

Scrolling, I see more photos of him practically naked and

fighting other muscularly built men in a ring. Sweat sparkling on his rippling abs and the black swirling intricate tattoos that cover his entire left arm and shoulder, even stretching over his pec. In some of the photos, there's blood splattered across his beautiful body and face. More than not, his opponent is the worse of the two. He looks gorgeous and dangerous. It only makes me want more of him.

No wonder he's so built with hands like bricks. He's a professional fighter.

I steal a quick glance at him. This close, I can spot small evidence of it on his face. A slightly swollen bottom lip with a tiny cut on one side, a slight angle to his nose as if it's been broken more than once and a shadow of a bruise across his cheek bone.

This man beats people up for a living. He's good at it by the looks of it and seems to enjoy it too. Not sure that's any more trustworthy than a murderer. People who fight for a living can have anger issues, be abusive and aggressive.

He nods his head at the phone in my hand. "See. Not a murderer. Although I fight for a living, I'm not going to hurt you, Leamhan Beag."

His voice rumbles low and churns in my belly. His Irish words doing something to my insides that has them melting. My fears of his unknown anger and aggression drifting away. Eased by the soft smoothness of his voice and his easy, open smile.

I believe him. He's not going to hurt me. At least not physically. He's already breaking something inside me, though, that has me leaning toward him.

"Come on, Emma. Let's go kiss that stone. Eh?"

I can only nod. If I were to speak, it would come out in a

pathetic, mousey squeak.

11 – Conor

Oh, how I would love to be wrong right now

When I saw Emma standing there staring up at the castle, I nearly backed out. Sneaking up on her again would seem suspicious to anyone. To some like Emma, so astute and keen, I was sure she would see right through me. Knowing I came here seeking *her,* and run away screaming. Thankfully she didn't. She actually seems a little sweet on me.

Initially I kept my distance. Not only to make her feel safe, but to save myself the embarrassment of another take down. I'm still in shock over that one.

When I was sure she would not freak out or retaliate, I made my way closer to her. Even dressed in casual leggings and jumper, she's appealing. Clutching her bag strap as if to use it as a weapon against me. I don't blame her. The situation is rather odd on a normal day.

I'm here to get back my luck as a clover—still feel like an eejit believing that nonsense—but that doesn't mean I can't enjoy my day.

It's been years since I've ventured up the castle to the stone. Pretty sure the last time I was up there was when we were kids, and my parents brought me, and my siblings here on holiday. Living in a country filled with so much history, I'm ashamed to say I barely notice it anymore. We pass by it, and it's a part of everyday life, yet we never interact with it.

Perhaps kissing the stone won't be beneficial only to Emma but myself as well.

I guide Emma toward the ticket booth in one of the smaller buildings by the small of her back. She doesn't tense or pull away from my touch, and I take that as a good sign. The more comfortable she is with me the more likely she'll be to willingly hand over the clover.

If she were local, I'd ask her out, get to know her even more. Work my luck out of her in a more personal and physical way. As she *is* a tourist, I don't have such luck. Strange how I thought meeting her was lucky and now I'm cursing my luck that she won't be around longer. Or that I met her in the first place. Had I never met her, my life would be what it was before. I would have won that sparring match, and I would be back in the gym training for my fight with Becker.

Instead, I'm here, about to kiss the silly Blarney Stone, hoping to convince this sexy stranger I accidentally gave her my good luck in a clover and now need her to give it back.

Out of everyone it could have been I suppose Emma would believe me, considering her "curse."

My agitation dwindles as I purchase my entry ticket and follow Emma inside the castle grounds. It's not a bad view from behind. I thought she looked enticing in jeans. I was not prepared for her in leggings.

Her legs are shapely and strong as she easily climbs up the stone steps and through the uneven ground. She must be a runner or at least on her feet a lot.

We follow signs through the castle, passing other rooms and spaces without exploring, heading upward to the stone on the roof.

"Now that you know what I do for a living, what is it you do, Emma?" I ask her as we continue up stone steps somewhere around the third floor.

"I'm a risk assessment manager."

"I don't know if there's something lost in translation, but what exactly is that?"

She chuckles the sound amused as she stops and looks over her shoulder at me from a few steps up. She's at eye level with me, and I want to pull her close and hold her tight, feel her hidden figure beneath her loose clothing.

The look she gives me says, *are you serious*? It's not my fault I have no idea what the fuck a risk assessment manager is. It's one of those random jobs no one knows exists.

"Lost in translation? We both speak English," she scoffs.

"I speak Irish, and you speak American, *not* English. There's a difference."

She doesn't seem to believe my weak argument of a language barrier as she turns to face me, her scowl becoming comical. Her mouth twists and pinches while her eyes squint at me under lowered brows. Her freckles shift on her cheeks as she does so making them stand out against her pale skin.

Stepping close enough to wrap an arm around her waist, I lean in close so she can feel my words on her skin.

"Mura turasóir thú thabharfainn abhaile thú, stóicfinn thú agus líonfadh mo choileach thú go dtí go screadfá m'ainm." *If you weren't a tourist, I would take you home, strip you, and fill you with my cock till you screamed my name.*

Emma's face immediately softens and her eyes dip to my lips as I speak naughty things to her in Irish. Women, especially Americans, love a man with an accent. And speaking anything in Irish is no doubt an instant aphrodisiac. I could recite my shopping list, and it would make her swoon.

I'm most definitely not reciting a shopping list. I was blatantly telling her what I would do to her if I had the opportunity, and she has no idea.

But it's obvious she likes what she hears. Would she still like it if she understood it? The rosy pink in her cheeks says yes.

Her body sways toward me almost brushing her tits against my chest, and I so badly want to lean in and close the remaining distance between us.

"Is that your way of saying Irish is a sexy language? Because you would be correct. Irish is one of the top three accents people find most attractive, and eighty percent of people find that accents make a person more attractive. Considering you're already so physically attractive I would imagine that percentage to be higher."

Her voice is low and quiet, and the words tumble out as if she's not even paying attention to them. Just random facts and numbers that sit inside her brain waiting to be spoken at any moment.

My own eyes dip to her lips, which are a soft natural pink. Not a hint of lip-gloss or lipstick. Bare and waiting for someone to taste them.

"Sílim go bhfuil do ghuth agus asal shapely tarraingteach." *I think your voice and shapely ass are attractive.*

I breathe the compliment in Irish against her skin, slanting my mouth to trail over her cheek without touching her. Inhaling her fresh scent of morning rain and grassy fields.

When I lift my head, facing her once again, she continues to watch my mouth with hooded eyes. Does she want to hear more? There is plenty more I would love to say to her. The growing situation in my jeans however has me holding in the Irish that wants to slip free of my lips.

She's a tourist. She's not staying. You can't have her. I remind myself. It sucks that my inner voice is such a gentleman. Because the rest of me wants to be the opposite of gentlemanly with Emma.

I step down, backing away from her, removing the temptation to kiss her.

"So, what is a risk assessment manager?"

"Hmm? Oh, um I assemble and analyze data to identify risks in a variety of areas," she answers off handedly. Her eyes still searching my face and waiting for more Irish to spill from my lips.

I keep a tight seal on the words bubbling in my brain and climbing up my throat. I want nothing more than to seduce her with my voice, my words, my mouth, but I can't. It wouldn't be right. But, oh how I would love to be wrong right now.

"Identify risks? Like what?"

I gesture for her to continue up the stairs as there have been a couple of people walking around us. She obliges and turns back around, continuing up the stairs. Keeping her eyes ahead of her and going slow enough to not lose her footing, giving me a wonderful view of her arse once again.

"Well, for example, if you applied for health insurance and the company wanted to know the risk of covering you, they would hire someone like me, to figure out how often you're likely to need coverage and how much. What kind of injuries you would sustain and how much they cost to treat. It helps insurance companies decide how much you should pay and how much coverage they should give you. But other companies and people use it to figure out other risks. Car accidents, shark attacks, investments, et cetera."

"Shark attacks? People really need to know the risk of a shark attack?"

She has to be messing with me. How many people need to know that?

"That one's not as frequent. It just popped into my head because my friend Jules was planning a trip to South Africa to cage dive with great whites, and I had to make sure the likelihood of her being eaten by one was minimal."

"Your friend sounds like a real daredevil."

"That's an understatement. If there's something outrageous and possibly life threatening, Jules wants to do it."

I can hear the smile in her voice. This Jules must be a close friend. I wonder if it's the same friend who tried to google me. Before I can ask about her daredevil friend, we reach the top floor and the short line of people waiting to kiss the stone.

The roof top is wide open with a waist-high stone wall around the edge. Emma eyes it cautiously and keeps well away from it, unlike most people who approach and easily lean over to look down to the grounds below.

"You don't want to take a look over the edge? It's a nice view of the grounds."

"No, thank you. I'm fine right here. I think hanging over the edge to kiss the stone is risk enough for me today."

Emma crosses her arms over her chest protectively, focusing her attention on the person laying backward and holding on to the iron bars kissing the stone.

A man sits on the edge of the square hole, holding on to the lad who puckers up and plants a full-mouthed kiss on the stone below the surface.

Gross. Besides the risk of falling, I hadn't considered that other people's dirty mouths would be on the stone. From the looks of it they don't wipe it off between each person either.

"Hey, Emma?"

"Yeah?"

"What's the risk of contracting mono from kissing a stone others have kissed?"

Emma cocks her head and scrunches her nose adorably, doing some mental calculation in that pretty little head of hers.

"Well, they would have to have Mono in order to spread it. So as long as no one has it the risk is zero. If someone has it and kisses the stone, the risk is greater. Especially if it were recently. If it were more than a day ago the risk is also minimal. The likelihood of contracting it is statistically low. In all the calculations I did about kissing the stone contracting Mono hasn't occurred to me."

She looks at me with a thoughtful expression, impressed with my extreme concern for contracting a disease from a rock.

"What had you considered?"

Since the first thing I thought of was sharing spit with a stranger, I'm surprised it isn't something she thought of.

"Falling through the hole to my death on the ground below. Falling through and getting my scarf caught around my neck and hanging myself, catching my face on the iron bars and ripping my lips off, the attendant being in a bad mood and pushing me out of the hole. Basically, anything that ends in my death. Illnesses I could recover from weren't a top priority."

A surge of laughter escapes my chest and the fear I saw

growing on Emma's freckled face eases at the sound of it. She relaxes enough to smile back at me, chuckling lightly at herself as well.

"You really thought you were going to catch your mouth on the bars and rip off your lips? How high of a risk is that?" I ask through my continued laughter.

"It is extremely low but still a possibility." She points a finger in the air at me and raises her eyebrows defiantly.

"Has that actually happened to anyone in the history of people kissing the Blarney Stone?"

"No, but there's a first time for everything."

She's serious. She actually believes that could happen. Even though I'm sure she's the first person in history to consider it.

My laughter deepens, and I have to hold my stomach and take deep inhales to calm. Emma's own giggling laughter rings out around me as her tension releases.

"I promise I will not let you rip your lips off while kissing the stone. It would be a shame to lose something so lovely."

Without thinking I run the pad of my thumb over Emma's bottom lip. Her lips part in a soft sharp inhale at my touch, and I desperately want to slide my thumb between them and into her hot mouth. My dick twitches in agreement. I should pull my hand away immediately, but I can't. It lingers. Feeling the soft skin of her neck on the back of my rough knuckles and the slight wetness of her lip on my thumb.

A low growl rumbles in my chest. Thankfully low enough, it's not obvious I'm aroused by the sight of my finger on her mouth.

Smoothing my thumb down her chin, I remove my hand and discretely adjust myself while her eyes are fixed on mine.

"It's almost your turn."

I nod behind her, and she whirls around to see the short line has shrunk even more to only two people between us and the stone. We close the distance, getting a much closer look at the square opening in the floor where the stone resides.

A middle-aged woman is being pulled up after kissing it, and I take a peek through the opening. The drop is sheer and straight to the ground far below. No net, no harness. Just the young lad holding your waist and the two bars to hold on to.

Why the hell does anyone do this?

"I'm not sure I want to do this anymore."

Emma backs away from the opening. Backing into my chest and pressing close. Wanting me to what? Hold her? Comfort her? She trusts me to do such a thing after only meeting me three days ago?

Reaching up, I wrap my hands around her biceps squeezing, letting her know I'm here for her. I'm here to support her. Even though my motives aren't altruistic. My being here was not to support her but take something back from her and right now I feel like utter shite for it. I wish I had run into her accidentally and decided to spend the day with her without having an ulterior motive behind my actions.

I take in a steadying breath to fortify my own nerves and shove the thoughts away. Instilling all the assuredness in my tone, I can to show her, or perhaps myself, that I am here for her. No matter the reason for my presence at the castle.

"I'm right here for you, Emma. I'll be with you the entire time. Thousands of people do this every year, and how many have fallen to their deaths?"

"None."

"Exactly. And you won't be the first. The attendant will be holding you the entire time."

Her body shudders under my touch, leaning into me but not settling. Her nerves getting the best of her as I make us take another step closer as one more person takes their turn.

"What if he loses his grip? What if I'm so sweaty I slip right through his fingers? What if—"

"None of that will happen."

Leaning over her shoulder, I try to grab her attention away from the nearby hole in the floor.

Her body is soft and warm, fitting perfectly against me. If she were to tilt her head back, it would slide into place on my shoulder against my neck. Her temple would rest perfectly at my lips, making it easy to kiss her whenever I pleased.

That thought only multiplies when she turns her head up to glance at me. Her head almost resting exactly where I imagined it would.

"How do you know?"

"Because I will also hold on to you if that makes you feel better."

Her nod is immediate, quick sharp movements eager for my assistance. It warms my chest in a way that has me questioning my motives.

The last few people take their turns and then it's ours. Emma worries her lip between her teeth, and I want to kiss her to stop it. I don't, and I can't.

Gently I push her forward. She slips the strap of her bag off over her head and places it well away from the opening.

"Hello, miss. Sit down here facing away from the opening."

The lad sitting with his feet dangling over the edge looks to be in his mid-twenties. Working here while at university no doubt. He looks strong enough but not as strong as me, and for some reason, I feel the need to push him out of the way and hold Emma all on my own.

What if Emma was right and his hand slips? Would he be strong enough to catch her, hold her? Lift her up to keep her from falling?

The lad looks at me, confused, when I crouch down at Emma's side. I don't sling my legs over the side, but I kneel at its edge. I give the boy a look that has him zipping his lips but scowling at me.

Emma scoots into position, her back to the stone her hands fitfully wringing at the hem of her jumper. I place my hand on her thigh right above her knee, drawing her attention.

"You'll be fine, Love. I'll be right here with you."

She nods but doesn't speak. Her nerves making her fidget and worry that pink bottom lip of hers between her teeth again.

Scooting back the attendant grips Emma's hips and helps position her.

"All right now, just slowly lean down and lay on your back then scoot your bum toward the edge, and I'll steady you. Reach out over your head and grab the two bars with both hands. Once in position, you can pull yourself close to the stone and kiss it."

Emma again nods and does as he says. Gingerly shifting to reach the bars before pulling herself over the opening. I keep a firm grip on her thigh, letting her know I'm here. As soon as her lips make contact with the stone, she immediately pushes off, wiggling her way back to sitting.

"I did it!"

Her smile is pure joy, even though it's laced with her residual anxiety.

"See nothing to it. You did great, Love."

A giddy laugh bubbles from her smiling lips. "I have never done anything like that before," she admits.

"You were brilliant."

We remain locked there watching each other, her sitting and me kneeling. My hand still firmly in place on her leg, her hands reaching toward me gripping my arm and bicep.

"Now, it's your turn, mate." The attendant looks at me, and I look at him then the stone. I suppose I came all the way here.

Nodding I help Emma to stand and retrieve her bag before taking her spot on the floor and getting into the same position. I have far less distance to cover reaching out for the bars, as I am much taller than Emma.

I pull myself forward and gingerly place a kiss on the stone, right in the very spot Emma kissed. It's still warm from her lips, slowly cooling from the chilly breeze that blows up and through the chasm I'm currently dangling through.

When I stand, Emma's there to greet me with the same wide smile on her lips. Wind brushes the loose strands of her golden red hair across her rosy, pink stained cheeks. She looks cold even under her jumper.

"You look cold. Don't you have a scarf or something? Springtime in Ireland can get chilly."

"So I'm learning. And yes, I do have a scarf, but it doesn't do shit against the breeze."

We make our way back down through the castle, stopping only when I slip on a step and fall on my arse, which gets a hearty belly laugh out of Emma. I like Emma's laugh. It's contagious.

A gift shop and information center sits inside a small outlying building, where we'll find my sister, and I guide us in that direction. Knowing my sister, this should be interesting.

12 - Emma

Get on your knees and start looking

Conor directs us to a gift shop in what appears to at one time have been a barn or stable that has since been repurposed. People mull about through the store, looking at bits and bobs. Trinkets and souvenirs to take home with them. There's even pressed shamrocks in clear cards by the register, just like Conor had said. Seems like a short cut to me. Good thing I already have mine.

Behind the counter stands a young girl with long curly red hair the reaches her butt and bright emerald eyes that practically sparkle as we approach. She, like me, has freckles dotting her face, but hers appear to be deliberately placed in a pleasing pattern. Unlike mine, which are scattered like shattered debris across my face.

"Conor! I was expecting you earlier."

The girl bounces around the counter and jumps into Conor's arms. This must be his sister. Conor lifts her in a tight hug before placing her on her feet once again.

"Sorry about that. I got distracted."

Conor eyes me over his sister's head angling in my direction. She's much shorter than him, shorter than me, even. She spins around her eyes wide and alight with curiosity, landing on me.

"And who might this be?" Stopping directly in front of me in less than three steps she extends her hand. "Hi. I'm Aisling, Conor's little sister."

She grips my hand without waiting for me to extend my own shaking it adamantly. My arm jostles in its socket.

"Oh, hi. I'm Emma. Conor's . . . friend?" I don't know if we would be considered friends or not at this point, but how else am I supposed to introduce myself?

"An American. Conor's never brought a girl with him before. Let alone a foreigner."

Aisling drops my hand and grins at me and then her brother who's come to stand at her side. Stepping closer, she elbows him, and he elbows her back. A friendly sibling interaction of teasing. You can tell a lot about a person by how they treat their family and how close they are. This shows me Conor and his family are close and loving. Teasing one another in good humor. There's probably a lot of laughter when they're all together. It warms the part of my heart where my family lives. We're the same.

When I was younger, I would always follow my brothers around, wanting to do everything they did. Considering my bad luck always made things more interesting than they should have been they didn't always want me to tag along, but they never told me no. They were and are protective of me even when we annoy each other.

Which reminds me, I should text Danny before he freaks

out, thinking I fell from the roof of a castle in Ireland. Taking my phone out of my purse, I pull up my messages and type out a quick one to Danny.

Emma: *Kissed the stone, didn't die.*

Danny: *Good. No more stunts while you're there.*

Emma: *No promises.*

I'm pretty sure Danny will type out an entire essay on safety, but I'll just have to read that later. It's nothing I don't already know or haven't already heard a dozen times before. Big brothers are wonderful people, but sometimes, they can get a little overprotective.

Turning my attention back to the siblings in front of me, who are currently having a brother-sister moment of their own, I catch Conor responding to Aislings wiggling brow.

"I didn't bring her, Aisling. She was already here. We only just met back in Dublin two days ago," Conor explains.

"Oh, well, I can see why you were distracted. She's quite pretty, Conor. You should ask her out."

Conor chuckles and ducks his head but doesn't dispute his sister. I think I would like it if he asked me out. A vacation fling might be fun. He's attractive, friendly, has that sexy accent, and he seems to like me well enough. Whatever he said before in Irish didn't sound innocent either.

"We didn't come here to get dating advice from you Skittle." Reaching out Conor ruffles his sister's hair in a manner very similar to my own brothers.

"Hey! Don't mess with the hair mate."

Aisling smooths a hand down the hair her brother has tousled, scowling at him in mock anger. This is behavior I'm more than familiar with having three brothers of my own and a smile pulls at my lips.

"Did you already kiss the stone, then?" Aisling asks me. Ignoring her brothers teasing in favor of getting to know the new and interesting American.

"Yes, we did."

"We? Did this big twat actually kiss the stone, too?"

"Language, Aisling." Conor chides his sister, who although younger is plenty old to be cursing. At least I think it was a curse. I'm not completely versed in Irish slang.

"I am not a kid. I can say whatever I damn well please."

"That may be, but you are also at work."

Aisling startles as if she has forgotten where she was, looking around to make sure no one was in earshot of her bad language.

"Right, then. So, you both kissed the stone?"

"Yes."

"Do you feel any luckier?"

Conor stares down at his sister, his face neutral yet something behind his eyes says more than he's showing. Aisling stares, waiting for an answer he will not give. She turns her attention back to me.

"What about you, Emma? Do you feel luckier?"

"Sort of. I feel lucky I didn't fall when kissing it, and I don't normally feel lucky at all."

"No one has ever fallen while kissing the stone. It's perfectly safe."

Conor gives me an *I told you so* look, to which I respond with an *I already knew this* look.

We chat with his sister a while longer about nothing in particular. Conor inquiring about her classes at University, Aisling excitedly telling us about her plan for a tourism company she wants to start after graduating with emphasis on smaller, more intimate tours. Most focusing on incorporating Irish lore, history, and mythology into its excursions. It all sounds very fascinating and her enthusiasm and ambition are palpable in her animated explanation.

After Conor agrees to dinner with Aisling, we say our goodbyes, and she returns to assist a customer as we make our way outside.

Walking side-by-side, Conor keeps his hands shoved in his jean pockets, watching me from the corner of his eye. Unsure what to say we walk for a minute in companionable but charged silence. Which is only broken by Conor clearing his throat and rubbing a hand against the back of his neck. He looks a little nervous.

"I have a rather unusual request, that I hope you don't judge me for."

I stop walking to face him. Curious what he could have to ask of me when I've only just met him. Is this when he asks to come back to my hotel for a night of wild, sweaty sex? Do I want that? Should I say yes? Squeezing my thighs together, I know the telltale ache there tells me I would most certainly agree to let him ravage me. My previous sexual encounters with other men have been less than satisfying. With my newfound luck this time could be different. The idea stirs low in my stomach, making me clench my thighs together tighter.

"Okay." Is all I can say to encourage him to keep going. Far too interested now in what he has to say.

"It seems I may have inadvertently given you my good luck when I gave you that four-leaf clover."

Conor points to the pendant hanging around my neck. My unexpected arousal instantly fades, and I frown down at my glass locket. It sits unassuming against my chest. I look back up at him completely at a loss. What does the clover have to do with anything?

"I would like you to give me back the clover."

My brow furrows, and I shake my head once. "I don't understand."

He sighs and cringes, fidgeting and rubbing his jaw. Searching for the words to explain what the hell he's talking about.

"You see, I didn't realize that by finding the clover and giving it to you I would also be giving you all *my* good luck. Since I gave it to you, I've had the worst luck. I lost a match, almost got in a car accident, have stubbed my toe more than once, lost my favorite pair of socks and was kept up all night by noisy neighbors I've never heard before."

My frown is so severe it hurts. I ease my eyebrows out of my eye sockets, relieving some of the growing tension. At least the physical tension. My brain is still trying to compute what he's said.

"Are you trying to say it's my fault you had a run of bad luck?"

"No, not at all." Conor waves his hands in front of him in a placating manner, trying to ease my growing frustration. "It's completely my fault for giving it to you. I would just like it back now. You see, I've never lost a match, and I have a big fight coming up, and I can't risk losing it. So, if you could just give me back the clover, I would be eternally grateful."

"So, you're saying when you gave me the clover you gave me your good luck and took my bad luck, and now you want me to give it back to you?"

"Yes."

His shoulders drop with a deep exhale. Relieved to have

gotten it off his chest? Was this all he wanted from me? Is that why he's here today? Was this all just a weird ploy to get my clover? This makes absolutely no sense.

My stomach drops and a strange sadness flitters through me. He wasn't actually flirting with me or interested in me, and he sure as hell doesn't want to have some sexual tryst with me. Stupid me for thinking a man like him would ever be interested in me. Plain, boring, unemployed, dirty freckled face Emma. I probably look like a frumpy slob to him in my boxy sweatshirt and leggings.

He must be used to leggy gorgeous super models with perfect makeup and skintight sequin dresses fawning over him. Hell, he probably has one on speed dial. Shit, I hadn't even thought of that. What if he has a girlfriend and was just being nice to get back the clover? But then why would he have talked to me at the bar and the cathedral. No, I don't think he has a girlfriend. That doesn't mean his interest in me was real.

The curse strikes again. Even with my new good luck, apparently thanks to him handing his off to me unintentionally, I still get the short end of the stick. The man I'm interested in isn't interested in me. And that thought makes me mad. Mad that I still haven't escaped the bad luck curse, and it's brought this on me now. Mad that just when I'm finally enjoying myself and moving on past it, it's still here.

Why should I relinquish my clover to him? It's mine now. And according to him it's who possesses it that reaps the rewards, and for once, I will be the lucky one. I'm not giving it up now that I've found it. That was my whole purpose in coming here.

"Why should I?" I demand, crossing my arms over my chest and protecting the clover inside my glass locket. Conor seems taken aback by my refusal to instantly hand it over.

His face falls and the growing relief there dissipates, replaced with the confusion I just felt.

Doesn't feel good to get taken off guard now does it?

"Well, because it's my luck, and I didn't mean to give it to you, and I want it back."

"Now it's my luck. And I'm pretty sure I need it more. If all you want to do is win a fight, then just train, and you will. I highly doubt I've taken your ability to do your job."

My tone grows in strength, becoming stern and unmoving. I've drawn my line in the shamrocks, and I'm sticking to it. If he wants better luck, he can go find it like I did.

"I am perfectly capable of performing my *job*," he growls through clenched teeth, "but I never lose a match. And if that's because of my good luck then I'm going to ensure I have it before I enter the cage. I won't risk my career and standing within the MMA because I gave a girl a clover."

Conor is getting irritated now, too, his voice going deep and terse. The sweet-talking Irishman from earlier gone in the wake of my refusal.

"That's why you're here today isn't it? This wasn't an accident. You being here when I am."

He opens his mouth to say something, to argue perhaps, but we both know I'm right. It was all too "coincidental" running into him here. All those sweet words and gentle touches were nothing more than buttering me up to give into his request. It makes me want to cry, to scream and rant and beat on his chest for the unfairness of it all.

"You're not getting the clover. It's mine now. If you want to find some luck get on your knees and start looking. I came to this country for the express reason of finding good luck to cancel out my bad. I lost my job my apartment was flooded, and I was sick and tired of nothing going my way. If I've finally found that good luck, I am not giving it up.

"I have suffered through twenty-seven years of bad luck and structuring my life around it, and I'm done with it. It's my turn to have a little peace and maybe even enjoy life."

Heaving in a large breath, I ease back and try to calm my racing heart. He doesn't deserve all my wrath. It's not just him I'm angry with, it's everything.

"I think I should go now." My face falls at the realization, and even though I was just mad a second ago, I feel miserable having to leave Conor again.

My hopes for anything with him wiped away in one clean sweep. My heart hurts at the loss of even the blooming friendship I thought we had. I know we live on different continents and any relationship between us would have been fleeting, but I still feel its loss. The shadow of what could have been drifting away on the cold breeze that once again slips under my clothing and sends goose bumps across my skin.

I can see that same sadness reflected in Conor's eyes. Whether it's solely at losing his luck or of me as well I don't know. But it only intensifies the tightness in my chest. Unthinkingly I grip at my chest and fist the material covering my traitorous heart.

Without another word I turn to leave. I only get a few feet away when I'm stopped by a large hand on my arm, forcing me to turn around to face Conor again.

"Wait. I'll give you whatever you want for it. I never believed in this luck business until I lost it. I don't think I'd be where I am without it. Ask of me whatever you will, and I'll give it to you."

I stare at him dumbfound. He's trying to bribe me, buy me, or rather my clover. There's no price he could pay for something so valuable to me.

"I don't need anything."

"Wait! What about your trip? You said the tour company was closed and your tour canceled. What if I . . . I could drive you." He offers, unsure. Still thinking through his proposition as the words are coming out of his mouth. "Aye. I'll drive you wherever you want to go. How long are you here for again? A week or two? I can take you anywhere you want to go. My fight isn't for another week and a half. I can be your personal chauffer and butler until then. I'll help you find all the Irish luck you want. And when we're done, you give me the clover, and we both get what we want."

He's scrambling now. Offering me something he knows I need. But do I want it? Do I want to spend all that time in a car with him, knowing he's only there to get something from me?

"No. I think I can manage just fine without you."

I pull my arm from his loose grip and resume my journey back to my hotel. My brain and heart arguing with one another. One adamantly agreeing with my refusal of his help, knowing his motives, the other disagreeing and desperately wanting to spend more time with Conor.

In the past, I've always agreed with my head. It's kept me out of trouble and saved me on more than one occasion. Logic always being my safe default. Saying no to anything that could be potentially disastrous. With my knowledge of disasters and statistics, that's basically everything.

This is just another one of those times. I could say yes and let him drive me around, possibly have a decent time, maybe more. However, it might all go horribly wrong. In this case, there are too many variables and outcomes that all end with me worse off than when I started. It would be better for everyone if I say no, and we part ways now.

Conor jogs to round in front of me, stopping me in my tracks.

"I disagree. I think it would be better if you let me drive you. Buses can be historically unreliable. Not to mention a pretty girl like you traveling alone screams *take advantage of me*. You would be safer with me, and I would feel better knowing you have protection from creeps."

Those beautiful green eyes of his soften as he looks down at me. His warm hands once again loosely gripping at my biceps, holding me still, so I can't run away again. I can tell he's not going to give up that easily.

"If I recall correctly, I managed to take you down quite easily the second time we met." Squinting up at him in indignation, I challenge him and his masculinity.

I am perfectly capable of defending myself from anyone who might desire to mess with me.

"Yes, you did. But I wasn't trying to kidnap you. Someone who is, will be more vigilant and attack you when you can't fight back. Possibly even subdue you before you even know they're there."

His thumbs brush up and down my arms, searing me through my sweater. Sincere concern laces his words and causes his determined scowl to fall into something close to unease.

Before I left, I may not have had time to research everything but something I did investigate was human trafficking. People like to think it doesn't exist, at least not in their country. Not in the first world countries. But in reality, it's everywhere. It's back home in America, it's in the third world countries of Africa and it's even here in Ireland. The threat is real and so is his concern. I know I can hold my own, but if there's a human trafficking faction that wants someone bad enough, they will get them. Especially if they're traveling alone.

Fighting off a handsy drunk guy in a pub differs from fighting off half a dozen armed attackers with sedation drugs.

He may have a point.

"And if I were to agree to this?" I hedge. Offering him the tiniest of hope, his easy smile returns. He hasn't won yet.

"You're the boss. You tell me where to drive, and I drive. We stop where you want to stop, go to whatever sites you want."

"And I don't pay for gas?"

He shakes his head adamantly. "Not a drop. I'll pay for all petrol, and my own hotel. Just consider me your personal bodyguard and tour guide."

This will probably turn out to be a bad idea, I know it. Again, I war within myself. Should I agree and have a big strong, trained fighter as my escort to ensure my safety and drive me wherever I please, but in the end give up my four-leaf clover and possibly my good luck? Or be greedy for once and keep my new good luck charm and take the bus like I had planned to all the sites I want to see but also possibly risking kidnapping and human trafficking . . . ?

Fuck a duck.

"If I agree to this"—I begin, and instantly, the light in his eyes sparks—"you will do all that you say and help me to make or find good luck. You won't make fun of me or question me, and you won't attempt to take the clover from me while we travel."

"Fine. Whatever you like. You give me the clover when we're done, and I will be yours to command until then."

Skeptical, I eye him. Waiting to see if he flinches or wavers in his resolve. To see something in his face that betrays his words. There is nothing. He's not lying, and he means what he says. He may not be my friend, and I may not completely trust him, but I can trust he's telling me the truth now. I want to ensure that continues.

"No more lying."

He looks offended I would even need to clarify such a thing, but I do. He's been lying all day, making me feel . . . special. I'm not special. He just wanted something from me.

Tightening his grip on my arms, he sets his mouth in a firm line and nods. "No more lies. I swear."

Taking in a steadying breath, I let it out slowly. I am so going to regret this.

"Fine."

"Yes?"

"Yes," I grumble in agreement. My reluctance about as great as his delight. This trip just got a lot more complicated.

13 - Conor

You can sleep on the couch

I'm sorry, sir, but we're completely booked for the night."

Of course they fucking are. This bad luck shite is really starting to piss me off. I barely made it to Cork in one piece in the first place, and I circled that damn castle for an hour before Emma finally showed up. I thought the curse would keep me from finding her. Thankfully it didn't. But it seems it was waiting to strike until now.

"Maybe you can call your sister? Sleep on her couch for the night?" Emma suggests.

She's not exactly trying to be nice, but she's also not trying to be mean. She's just offering a solution. Little does she know my sister has three female flat mates, and they all tried to ride me last time I visited. *At the same time.* There's no way in hell I'm sleeping at her flat. I'd wake up with my dick in one of their mouths for sure, and not in a good way. The only mouth I want on my dick is Emma's. With the way she's been looking at me after my little confession earlier that's not looking like a possibility any time soon.

"I can't stay at Aisling's."

Emma turns suspicious eyes on me, raising one of her eyebrows in question.

"Don't ask. She has flat mates, it's a whole issue. But I can't stay there."

Cautiously I prepare myself before asking her something I'm sure she'll refuse, but at this point, it's that or sleep in my car. I'm a pretty big guy, and the back seat, although comfortable to sit in, isn't the best for sleeping in.

"What about your room?"

Emma's head snaps in my direction, her eyes narrowing on me dangerously. If I were a weaker man, my balls may have shriveled up at that look. But I'm not. I'm big, strong, and very determined.

"You must have a couch or something I can sleep on in your room," I hedge.

"Not a chance." She turns abruptly heading for the lift, and I follow. I'm not taking no for an answer.

"Come on, just one night. I don't even snore. You won't even know I'm there."

"Yes, I will, and the answer is still no."

The lift arrives, and she shoves open the gate. I pull it the rest of the way open for her, but she ignores my chivalry and steps in, trying to close the gate on me before I can enter. She is unsuccessful. I block it with my body and slip in next to her.

The lift is small and even standing as far away from me as possible she's still only about a dozen centimeters away. I could easily press up against her and blame it on the tight space, but I don't. Instead, I try to give her the space she desires. Pushing her now won't garner me the answer I need.

She growls in frustration as the lift door closes, and she pushes the floor button so hard I'm surprised she doesn't sprain her finger.

"You are not sleeping in my room Conor. I just met you, and I don't completely trust you yet, and . . . and . . . I just don't think it's a good idea." Emma crosses her arms over her chest, and her cheeks turn a bright red in frustration.

Is she blushing? My Leamhan Beag has a dirty mind and is thinking about me and her in dirty ways. I think I like it.

"I promise I'll keep my eyes closed the whole night. I won't peak, not even once." My voice is low and husky and reveals just how much I would like to peek at her. As I promised her before, though, she is the boss, and I will do whatever she wants.

The lift signals our arrival on the top floor with a soft ding and Emma opens the gate as soon as it's accessible, bolting straight out into the hallway. I follow, of course, never letting her more than half a meter away from me.

She stops in front of the door numbered 312 and inserts her key. Opening the door only wide enough to slip inside, she tries to evade me by slamming it in my face, but I'm faster. Reaching a hand out I stop it before it latches, pushing it open wider but not forcing myself inside.

"Please, Emma. Just for tonight. I'll make sure to get my own room in the future. But there aren't many hotels around, and I really don't want to have to sleep in my car."

Emma tries to fight the door closed, but I hold it firm, looking down at her with an expression I hope conveys my sincerity and desperation. The temperatures at night aren't the most comfortable to be sleeping outside in, and I really don't want to cramp my legs and freeze my balls off.

We stand there for a long minute staring at one another. Her deliberating on whether she can trust me to be in the same room while she sleeps, searching for a reason to say no. While I am hypnotized by the chaotic freckles on her face. They have no discernable pattern like Aisling's. I always found her symmetrical freckles a little odd and unnerving. Nothing should be that perfect. I prefer the scattering of unkempt toffee-colored spots on Emma's cheeks, nose, and even on her temples.

"Ugh. Fine. You can sleep on the couch."

She opens the door wider and gestures for me to enter in a very unwelcoming manner. She's reluctant, but at least I have a warm, comfortable place to sleep tonight. That is until I see the "couch" which is not a couch. It's a chaise lounge, and a rather short one.

"That's not a couch."

"For all intents and purposes, it's a freaking luxury king size bed to you. If not, you're more than welcome to leave."

I kind of like snarky Emma. That's going to make this trip a lot more fun.

Emma made me change and go to "bed" first and turn to face the wall, so I couldn't see her in her pajamas. Shame really. If she didn't want me to see them that badly they must be delectable. Or she's just shy about her body. She does like to keep it covered.

I managed to get a list of all the places she wants to go however, which is useful. The next stop on her list is the Cliffs of Moher, the city of Galway, then a coastal drive to the Giants Causeway and back to Dublin and basically anything interesting in between. Easy enough. Nothing too outrageous. Although considering who Emma is, that's no surprise. Tomorrow, we'll leave for the cliffs, which are only a few hours' drive away and spend the night there. The long drive will be from there to the Giants Causeway all the way in the north.

Not sure if Emma wants to spend a whole day in Galway or make it a stopover on the way. I guess we'll find out.

When I wake up, there's a kink in my neck, and my left foot has fallen asleep. Rolling over, I almost fall off the edge of the chaise but manage to make it into a sitting position. Planting my bare feet on the plush carpeting, I feel pins and needles up my leg. The sun is barely shining through the thin curtains, and when I check the bedside clock, it reads seven.

Emma's still fast asleep, burrowed under a mass of blankets like a mole rat. Just a lump on the bed across from me.

There's no way I'm getting back to sleep, so I decide to get in a shower before she wakes. Maybe the hot water will warm my muscles and relax the tightness that's built up over night.

Gingerly I extricate myself from the spare blanket I used, untangling it from my jogger clad legs. I rarely sleep this clothed, but I doubt Emma would approve of me sleeping in my customary birthday suit. It gets too hot at night to sleep in so much clothing, but I'll do it if it makes her comfortable.

Standing I stretch out the kinks and quietly make my way toward the washroom door. Stepping as lightly as I can so as not to wake Emma. She doesn't move, and I silently turn the doorknob and press the door open, slipping inside.

Inside there is a large dormer window that lets in a lot of natural light. Even in the dusk of morning, it's more than enough to see clearly, so I leave the overhead light off.

I shut the door behind me just as quietly as I opened it. Stripping my shirt off, I set it on the porcelain sink and place both hands on the edges. Leaning with my head down, I take in a long deep breath and let the morning air filter through my lungs and center my mind. I turn on the hot water, waiting for it to warm before cupping it in my hands and splashing my face. I turn it off and dry my face with the hand towel before looking up at the mirror above the sink.

My jaw is covered with the beginnings of dark stubble. If I leave it for too long, it'll be a beard within the week. For now, it's acceptable. I don't need to shave just yet.

Rubbing my hand across my stubbled jaw my eye catches on the clawfoot tub directly behind me and under the dormer window, and I freeze.

Emma was not the lump in the bed because she's currently laid back in the tub, covered in foamy white bubbles with her hair tied in a knot on top of her head and ear buds in her ears. Her eyes are closed, and she sits perfectly still, with her head resting back against a folded towel on the edge of the tub.

Fuck, she looks gorgeous like this. Being bathed in the dull morning light, the quiet stillness surrounding us. For a moment I can imagine her like this on other mornings, asking me to join her in the soapy, warm water.

If she catches me now staring at her like this, she will have a fit. I should leave before that happens, no matter how much I don't want to.

Turning around, I keep my eyes trained on Emma no longer a reflection but real, tangible, touchable and within reach. Focusing on her peaceful face and relaxed body. Her arms rest along the sides of the tub her hands draped over its edge.

Instead of stepping away, I take one step closer before I catch myself. At this angle I can see a small glimpse of the swell of her breasts under the bubbles. Those freckles I spotted before trail down her neck and across her collar bone and shoulders. Light red-brown flecks in a widespread dusting across her pale skin. Everything else is concealed by those blasted bubbles. The sight is enough to wash away the last dregs of sleep clinging to my consciousness.

It's a good thing she's covered. If she weren't, it would be far more difficult to turn away and leave. *Which is what you should be doing, right now.*

I listen to what can only be my conscience and start to back away toward the door. My hand connects with the golden nob just as Emma opens her eyes and lazily sweeps her gaze across the room and lands on me.

She shrieks and jerks wildly, sitting forward to shield her already hidden naked body even more, pulling an earbud out of one ear and scowling darkly at me.

"What the hell are you doing in here?"

Letting my hand drop from the nob, I decide to go with it now that she's caught me. Might as well have a little fun. I cross my arms over my bare chest and lean my big arse against the sink, getting comfortable. I don't miss the way her gaze lingers on my naked torso. Wanting her to see more of me, I uncross my arms and place my hands on the sink at my sides. Flexing just a little.

"Well, I was going to take a nice hot morning shower to work out the stiffness sleeping on that "couch" caused, but the tub appears to be occupied already. That is unless you're willing to share."

I give her a smirk and a wink.

Emma flings one arm wildly toward the door, pointing with a bubble coated finger. "No, get out! You shouldn't be in here. Why didn't you knock or something?"

"It's not my fault the blankets on the bed looked like you were still in them. And the light wasn't on, and it was quiet. How was I to know you were in here so early in the morning?"

"Uh I don't know, maybe because the door was closed," she scoffs and glowers. Clearly trying to appear menacing but only succeeding at making me want her more.

My dick swells in my joggers becoming obvious even in the low light. Then again, my cock is obvious even when it's not hard, so this is nothing new. I don't shift or move to hide or adjust it. Leaving it for her to see or not. That's up to her. I'm not ashamed of my body's reaction to her.

"Lots of people keep their washroom doors closed when not in use," I argue.

"Well, not me. Now get out."

I stay right where I am. I like seeing her skin flush pink from the heat of the water and her ire. "So that's a no on sharing your bath?"

"Yes."

"Yes? That's lovely then." Pushing off the sink, I reach for the waistband of my joggers and begin to pull them down, revealing the top half of my bare pelvis, almost about to free my cock, when she yells at me from the tub.

"No! No, you cannot share my bath. What is wrong with you?"

I look up to catch her staring wide eyed at my groin. My

pubic hair visible and most likely the base of my cock. I remain that way, neither pulling up my joggers nor removing them further. The partial visibility has Emma considering letting me join her. Even though she's said no, her eyes and labored breaths say yes.

A long, silent moment passes before her eyes dart up to mine and her face grows even redder. Emma spins in the tub, facing away, giving me her back.

"Can you please leave, so I can get out? Then you can use the tub."

I pull up my joggers and settle the elastic band back at my waist.

"Sure thing, Love." I turn to leave but pause before exiting, looking over my shoulder at Emma, who is still turned toward the window. "It really was an accident. I didn't know you were in here. If I had, I wouldn't have come in."

I leave without another word from Emma.

14 - Emma

What happened to the cynic from Dublin?

I pack up my suitcase while Conor is in the shower, both of which don't take long. He's in and out much faster than I was. Before he interrupted my bubble bath, I'd been in there a good thirty minutes. My body ached from all the extra walking and strain of travel, and I had to take advantage while I could.

We check out of the hotel and make our way to his car parked in a lot down behind the building. Rolling my one small suitcase at my side and carrying my messenger bag I'm packed almost as light as he is with only one leather duffle slung over his shoulder. Conor side eyes me, and my suitcase.

"Is that all you packed?" he asks.

"Yup. I like to pack light."

"That seems lighter than most would pack for an international trip for multiple weeks."

I can understand why he would be confused by my lack of over packing. Although I brought enough pairs of underwear for every day of my trip, I had planned on washing my clothes while here. It's safer to wash them than to have to check a suitcase. And if all else fails, I can always buy a new shirt if needed.

"It is, but it's more efficient. Besides, there are these things called washing machines. I don't feel the need to travel with ten pairs of shoes and two dozen outfit choices when less will suffice just as well."

Conor steers me around a corner and down an alley into a small lot behind the hotel where a dozen or more cars are parked. I follow him toward a grouping of them. I don't know which is his.

"Fair enough," he chuckles, "Just never seen a woman pack so light before. It's impressive."

"Thank you."

Conor drives a newer model black SUV. I'm not a car person, so I have no idea what make or model it is. Now if he told me the make and model, I could probably tell him all the safety statistics and ratio of accident to decapitation numbers. But looking at it, I haven't the foggiest.

The driver's seat is on the opposite side from American cars, which is weird. Sitting on the left without driving is confusing my brain, as is driving on the right side of the road. Riding in the bus was different because it was so large, but in a regular size car, it's more noticeable.

It's comfortable though, large enough for him to fit without being cramped and has leather heated seats. Which I am taking full advantage of at this very moment. My butt is warm, which continues up my body and into my chest, making me very comfortable.

Although the continued silence isn't as comfortable

anymore.

I've barely spoken to Conor since we left the hotel. I'm sure I'm still blushing. The bubbles of my bath covered most of my naked body, but the way he looked at me so suggestively and lust filled had me thinking he could see more. Not to mention his own shameless arousal and partial nudity. That man is carved out of pure diamonds. His chest and abs like chiseled marble.

He said he was a professional fighter. I understand on a logical level that that means he is in peak physical condition. But I didn't connect the dots between fighter and abs that could double as a brail encyclopedia. I was two seconds away from allowing him to join me in the tub when he started pulling down his pants.

That tempting peek of manscaped groin. *Holy shit.* I definitely saw at least an inch of cock shaft. From what was easily visible through the pants material the hand to cock ratio is indeed accurate in his case.

Stop daydreaming about Conor's dick, Emma. He's sitting right next to you. He's going to see it written all over your face.

Shifting my eyes ever so slightly to watch Conor in the driver's seat next to me. He has *his* eyes on the road. One hand loosely draped over the steering wheel and the other on the gear shifter between us.

Everyone in Europe apparently drives manual transmission cars. I barely ever risk driving and automatic. I can only imagine the outcome if I attempted to drive a manual.

I'm getting bored listening to the sound of the tires rolling on the pavement and watching the fifth herd of sheep in a field pass by. Without asking I reach over and turn on the radio. I don't know what kind of stations Ireland has, but there has to be something better to listen to.

Scrolling through the stations, I find a classical channel and stop. It's playing what sounds like Chopin. Perfect.

"What the bloody hell is that?" Conor reaches over and clicks a preset radio button, switching it from peaceful and relaxing Chopin to some sort of death metal that feels like someone is stabbing my ears with a nail file. "Much better."

"What? This is not better," I yell over the horrendous music.

I immediately turn it back to the classical channel, saving my poor ears and head from the inevitable headache.

"It's my car. I control the radio. If you want to listen to music, you listen to what I pick. And we are not listening to that droll boring classical shite. It'll put me right to sleep, and I'll drive off a cliff."

Considering we're on an island known for its massive cliff sides that's a high possibility. I consider that for a moment, looking out the windows. We are nowhere near cliffs.

"I'll take that risk."

He only scoffs and clicks the preset on the radio, once again returning to the metal rock station. I cover my ears with my hands growling in frustration at him. He smirks.

"I can't listen to this. It's going to make my ears bleed. You're already walking on thin ice. Do you really want to push me over the edge? You want your precious good luck back, don't you?"

Reaching down, I lift the glass ball pendant and dangle it mockingly at him. He frowns and watches me from the corner of his eye, always keeping the other firmly fixed on the road ahead. At least he's a responsible driver.

I reset the dial to the classical station once again. Conor

continues to flash glares at me. I think I've won the music argument when he doesn't respond for a good minute. That is until he reaches over and pushes the preset button again.

"Nope, can't do. You'll just have to deal."

"No, I won't."

I reach out around his large paw and change the station. He tries swatting my hand away, but I'm too fast. As soon as I get the classical channel back, he changes it to the rock station. Our hands collide and tangle as we go back and forth, the music in the car changing drastically from soothing piano tones to blaring guitar riffs and drums and back again, mixing with whatever music bleeds through in between.

"Oh, come on, no one hates classical music."

"I do," he growls.

Our hands continue to battle with one another and the radio when glass shattering Opera music blares from the speakers.

"For fuck's sake. Turn it off," Conor yells over the soprano notes, removing his hand from the controls to allow me to change it.

The radio station doesn't change. It stays stuck on the Opera channel.

"It won't change."

"What do you mean it won't change?"

"I mean what I said. It's stuck."

I continue fiddling with the knobs and buttons, poking and twisting on the verge of punching it, but it doesn't budge. Not even when I try his stupid preset rock station. I think it actually gets louder.

"Just turn it off."

"What?" I can barely hear Conor over the ridiculously

loud music.

"TURN IT OFF," he says again louder this time.

I hit the power button, which—thank baby Jesus—works, and the cab of the SUV falls blissfully silent again.

"How did you manage to break my radio? This car is only a year old."

Conor looks irritated but not angry, thankfully.

"I didn't break it. You did."

"Did not."

"Did too."

"It's because of your shite luck it broke."

I laugh. For once it wasn't because of my stupid curse. "Nah ah. I don't have bad luck anymore. That's all you now big guy."

I poke at his ridiculously large black cloth covered and muscular arm, which doesn't budge a centimeter.

Conor gapes at me until he groans and rubs a hand over his face, pulling at his stubbled jaw.

"Look we have a couple hour drive to the cliffs, so why don't we just . . . try not to agitate the curse. Okay?"

I let out delirious sounding giggle. "Ooooh so now you believe it's a curse. What happened to the cynic from Dublin?"

"It has proven me wrong."

"Mmmm. Pissed ya off, didn't it? Turned a normal walk down the street into an all-out battle for survival. Welcome to my world," I say with all the cynicism I possess. It's rather nice for someone else to finally understand what it feels like to be me.

Conor's fingers tighten around the steering wheel and the leather creaks and groans under the pressure. Wow. He is much stronger than I thought.

"I've never lost a fight, at least not professionally. I think the last time I lost I was twelve and wrestling my older sister," he grumbles, scowling deeply at the road ahead as if it were the thing offending him.

Many times, the curse did such a thing to me. I've never won a raffle, a coin toss, a carnival game, or a race of any kind. For someone whose entire profession is winning, having my bad luck curse might be a hinderance. I understand his desire to get rid of it. He just doesn't understand my desire to *remain* rid of it. I've lived with it for multiple decades. It's someone else's turn to deal with it.

Without the radio to fill the space our drive is rather quiet until I see signs for the Cliffs of Moher. This is the one stop on the trip I dread the most. It has the highest possibility of death.

The Cliffs of Moher have vertical cliff edges that drops down over seven hundred feet to the Atlantic Ocean below and stretches nearly eight miles along the coast. Visitors crawl on their bellies to the edge to look over, a few brave—or stupid—souls walk directly up to it. I will be doing no such thing. Perhaps if Conor and the curse stay a good distance away, I might attempt it. The crawling, not the walking to the edge. I'm not that brave, or stupid.

We arrive at the visitor's center and park. Learning we can pay a fee to have access to all the amenities, or we can walk the cliffs for free. Considering we've been driving for hours, and I'm starving and really need to pee, we pay the small fee and make our way toward the restrooms. Once relieved, I regroup with Conor.

"Can we get something to eat first? I'm starving." I point toward the small food court, and he agrees.

We pick up a few sandwiches, chips, and a drink each.

There's not much seating inside, but it's so beautiful outside I don't want to stay inside anyway.

Conor picks up a cozy looking plaid picnic blanket from a lending counter, and we make our way outside.

Rays of sunshine break through the clouds overhead, streaming shafts of light down on the green expanse of landscape. The blue of the Atlantic shimmers with tiny diamonds in the distance. The edge of the cliff is lined with a paved walking path, parts of which have a short stone wall along it to protect from people falling over the edge in the more crowded and populated areas.

We make our way down the path until we find an open, grassy area overlooking the cliffs. There aren't too many people here today. Whether that's due to the time of year, time of day or the weather I'm not sure. Either way, I'm glad for it. It allows me and Conor to sit in relative peace alone on the cliffs.

I stand and watch dutifully while Conor unfolds and lays out the picnic blanket. The gesture is unexpected. A big tattooed tough guy like him sitting down on a blue plaid blanket to have a picnic. He's a bit of a gentle giant. Underneath that muscled exterior is a warm heart. The juxtaposition of his big body in jeans, a black long-sleeved thermal, and black knit hat surrounded by the natural elegance of the cliffs and green grass is contradictory. Although one could argue the hard lines of his muscled body mirror that of the sharp edges of the cliff, but I digress.

He finishes setting out the blanket and like a gentleman reaches out a hand to assist me in sitting.

"Thank you."

"You're welcome."

I sit, then he sits. He takes up far more of the blanket that

I do, but I don't mind. My earlier embarrassment from the bathtub has long disappeared. Now I'm more curious about this man I barely know who is willing to drive a stranger around the country for a clover.

"I never would have pegged you for a picnic kinda guy."

He laughs and unwraps his sub sandwich. "Why's that? Because of the tattoos?"

"Partly, I guess." I take a bite of my sandwich and look closely at him, trying to see if I can figure out what kind of guy he is.

"You know you shouldn't judge someone by their appearance. There are many things about me that might surprise you."

Half of his sandwich is already gone, and he leans back on one hand, stretching his long legs out in front of him. I sit with my legs crossed and turn to face him better. The line of the cliffs stretches out behind him in a snaking pattern. It makes for quite a view, and I am not complaining.

The small cut on his lip from before is healing quickly, with only a small pink line now. But the bruise on his cheek is darker. It'll still be some days before that heals completely. Neither deter from his rugged good looks, with a strong jaw line and slightly plump lips.

"Okay, then. Surprise me," I challenge.

He stops chewing and swallows, the corner of his mouth curling. "Well, one thing you would never guess about me is I know how to crochet."

"Liar."

"I would never. I even made this hat." Reaching up, he pulls the black hat off his head and holds it out to me, gesturing for me to take it. I do and inspect it. The yarns are thick and fuzzy, soft under my touch. There's a pattern across the crown. One that, for some reason, makes me believe it has a deeper meaning than just to be pretty. It looks homemade but only because it's not perfectly finished like a machine made one would be. You can see where the ends of the yarn have been tied and tucked, even if barely visible. The material is well worn and warm.

"My Nan taught me when I was a kid. She tried to teach me to knit, but I couldn't figure out the two-needle thing." He holds up his hands and mimes knitting but in an uncoordinated way. "Wool and yarn is kind of in the family blood."

"How so?"

"My family owns a sheep farm. We make wool and yarn and sell it to shops and companies all over Ireland. My grandparents started it, but now, my mum and older sister Bridget run the company."

"That's so Irish of you."

Conor laughs good heartily, and I cringe inwardly. That was rude and stereotypical of me to say. "I'm sorry. That was rude."

"It's alright. It is very Irish. We are the number five country in wool production. I don't blame you for making that assumption."

I take in a calming breath and let my shoulders relax.

"Did you know the risks of small run wool production is fairly low compared to large industrial scale operations. Less risk of injury in large machinery. However, the risk of inhaling bacteria and hair while scoring and brushing is always present. If you practice proper protection, respiratory issues can be deterred or avoided."

I ramble off the first things that pop into my head about

wool production. I've researched and assessed almost every profession there is. Somehow, the basic information and risks always stick with me. The exact numbers and percentages may be elusive, but I still recall high and low-risk possibilities.

"You know everything about everything don't you?"

I turn to face Conor who's watching me with barely hidden amusement and a hint of fascination.

"No." I sigh, looking down to fiddle with the yarn of his hat, "It's more like I know a little of everything, and a lot of nothing. I can tell you risks involved in any profession, the likelihood of an employee getting injured on the job, production numbers, and investment risks. But I can't tell you how to do any of it. I've never experienced it. I don't know if it's enjoyable or how much physicality it takes. I read about things and calculate numbers. I never do any of it."

I've never admitted so much to anyone other than Jules and even then it was masked under a heavy layer of excuses and diversion tactics. There are so many things I've researched that I wished I could do.

But that's what this trip is all about, isn't it? Finally breaking the pattern and doing rather than watching.

"Well, perhaps we can change that."

"What? Are you going to teach me how to sheer a sheep?" I ask, laughing lightly imagining me trying to wrangle and shave a sheep.

"Maybe. We'll see." Is all he says.

Looking up, I see him watching me again. He does that a lot. Most people never pay that much attention to me, and if they do, it's not for good reasons. I feel the opposite when Conor looks at me.

A strong gust of wind rolls off the cliffs and blows my hair all around my face, blocking my vision. I try to pull the strands down and wrangle them into submission. Only partially successful.

I can hear Conor's warm chuckle at my continued struggle. "Here, let me help you." His hands join mine, trying to gather all my hair, but the wind keeps blowing it loose. "I have an idea."

With one hand he removes his hat from mine and with the other presses his large palm to my forehead and pushes all the hair back in one swipe. Before I know it, his knit—sorry, crocheted hat—is fitted snug on my head, holding my wayward hair in place.

"Much better."

"You don't mind if I wear this? Your head isn't going to get cold?" I joke. His hair is almost as thick as mine. I doubt he'll even notice the cold. Besides, don't guys, like, run hotter than women, anyway?

"Not at all. It looks better on you than me." Conor's hand lingers, fingering strands of my hair and tucking them under the edge of the hat. The pad of his thumb brushes the lobe of my ear, and I shiver from more than just the cold wind.

His dark auburn hair glows amber under a stray streak of light. The wind causing so much mayhem with my hair jostles his, but it's short enough to not bother him. He removes his hand and runs his fingers through his tousled hair, which does nothing to tame it. The strands blowing this way and that the moment he releases them.

I adjust the warm hat, pulling it down over my ears and pushing my hair back. He turns his attention back to his sandwich, picking it up and taking a giant bite. We finish our meal quietly, surrounded by the crashing waves and squawking seagulls.

It's so peaceful and serene I could sit here for hours. Even once we finish our food, we remain sitting and watching.

15 - Conor

Aren't you going to enjoy the scenery?

After our impromptu picnic, we clean up and walk along the paved pathway farther down the cliffs. Emma still wearing my hat. I wasn't lying when I told her I crocheted it myself. I had. One of the few things I've made in recent years. I don't make things like my Nan and sister Bridget. They're the ones who run the wool and yarn business, not me. Not so much Nan anymore, although she started the company years ago, she's just helps out when she can now.

Emma looks cute in it, though. It matches perfectly with her outfit as if it were something she had picked out for herself. I follow her, allowing her to enjoy the sites of the cliff and Burren while I enjoy the site of her arse in those black leggings again. Her denim jacket rests just above the rounded swell.

She stops and leans against the barrier wall, looking out over the ocean. Turning her face to the sun that keeps playing peek-a-boo through the clouds today. It lights up her freckles, and she closes her eyes to soak up its warmth before opening them and returning to staring out.

Leaning against the wall, I gaze at her, captivated by her beauty, rather than the Cliffs' infamous allure. I've seen them. They are magnificent. But the beauty standing next to me is a sight I may never see again. I want to enjoy this time, even if it is just to get back that clover, and my luck. If it weren't for that, I would have thought of another excuse to seek her out. Two chance encounters was not enough.

Emma turns and her eyes catch on mine, watching her.

"Aren't you going to enjoy the scenery?" she asks. The apples of her cheeks turning pale pink from the chill rolling off the ocean.

"I am," I answer not removing my eyes from her. Roaming her face more thoroughly, enjoying the scenery.

Her cheeks darken slightly and Emma fidgets, the ends of her hair twisting in the breeze. It's mostly contained under my hat now, but the ends still shift in the breeze around her neck and jaw. Emma pulls her long hair to one side, exposing her slender neck. My gaze wonders down and under the open collar of her denim jacket. The white V-neck shirt underneath gifting me a limited view of her collar bone and the golden horseshoe necklace resting there.

"Are you going to use your new good luck and risk looking over the edge?" I ask nodding with my head toward the cliff but not removing my gaze from her.

"Uhhh . . ."

Emma crosses her arms over her chest and stares warily out, standing on her tip toes and angling her head up to better see over the edge.

"I'm not sure that's a good idea. I can see just fine from

here."

"Nonsense. You can't come all this way and not look over the edge. You hung over the gaping hole at the Blarney stone. This is far easier."

"Doubt it."

She doesn't move to go to an open area to crawl to the edge and look over, but she eyes the area suspiciously only half a dozen meters down the path from us.

"Come on, Love. You have to try things in life or else what good is living?"

I tug on her elbow to draw her away from the wall, her arms dropping and allowing me to pull her along.

"Usually, when I try things, they don't end so well," she whispers.

I can tell she's still on the fence about trying anything new. Her curse always held her back in the past. Now she can't use that excuse, and I won't let her. She can't hide from the world forever just because of the possibility of failure or loss.

I may not know what it's like to lose, but I've had my fair share of failure. Every time in training when I would be put on my arse by someone bigger and better it only motivated me to be better, work harder and overcome my shortcomings. The rest of life is much the same.

Guiding us to an on open area with no barrier wall we stop three meters from the edge, and I drop her elbow from my grasp. The wind picking up speed and strength momentarily billowing around us.

"Walk halfway there, then crawl on your hands and knees. When you're close to the edge, lay on your stomach and shimmy the rest of the way. You don't need to pull yourself far over the edge, just enough to peek over. Simple. People do it every day.

I think you'll be pleasantly surprised by the outcome."

Emma worries her lip between her teeth and eyes the edge of the cliff. Her fingers twist the strap of her bag nervously.

"Are you sure it's safe?"

"As long as you don't run and jump."

I try to break her tension with humor. It works, a little.

A tight smile pulls at her lips. She wants to laugh but is still too nervous to relax. She stands firm for a minute then her hands untangle from her bag strap, pulling it off over her head and handing it to me.

"Okay. I'm gonna do it. You just stay back here. I don't want the curse to affect me while I'm dangling over the edge of a cliff," she says with firm determination.

I laugh. "Okay, no problem. I'll stay right here."

I take her bag and sling it over my shoulder. Watching as she takes in a few deep breaths and strides forward. Doing just as I instructed, she walks halfway, then crawls on her hands and knees and then her stomach. With each centimeter closer to the edge, she gets her pace slows. Pausing each time the breeze blows over her.

Remaining in my original position, I watch her closely, making sure she doesn't stumble or trip or fall, putting her in actual danger. I may also be admiring the scenery again as her arse takes center stage in her crawling.

Emma isn't what could be considered a small woman, even though she's small to me. She's taller than most, with lean shapely legs and a curvy figure she hides under her jumpers and jackets. What I wouldn't give to discover her shape under all those layers.

~Emma~

Oh my fucking God. I can't believe it. I'm actually laying on my belly looking over the edge of the Cliffs of Moher. This is crazy. For a minute, I didn't think I was going to do it. Conor's steady presence and affirmation made me feel safe enough to try. Also, knowing I have the four-leaf clover hanging around my neck doesn't hurt.

I lie here marveling at the massive sheer drop below me and watch as the water hits the rocks and splashes white against the cliffside. A bird flies by, *below* me. *I'm actually higher than flying birds.*

The nervous anxiety I felt before melts away the longer I lie here. Who would have known laying on the edge of a cliff would be relaxing? It sure as hell isn't something I would have ever considered before.

Conor's hat keeps the cold wind from sinking in and from my hair blowing all over the place. If he hadn't of let me wear it, the panic that would have ensued could have been catastrophic. The last thing I need is my hair blocking my vision while I hang on the precipice of possible death.

A week ago, I would have stayed a good mile away from a place like this. I never would have risked it. Things are changing now. Jules was right. I needed this trip. Even if I hadn't met Conor and stolen his luck, I still would have done it. I've spent enough time not doing things and not enjoying life. Not anymore.

When I can feel the cold filtering in through my jacket, I shimmy backward and retrace my steps I took to get here. Returning to Conor and relieving him of purse holding duty, a giant grin plastered on my face.

"That was amazing. I can't believe I almost didn't do it."

"Told you, you would like it."

"Yes, you did."

We continue on the pathway, heading away from the visitor's center, walking for at least a half hour before turning around and walking back. This time, far more optimistic about the trip ahead.

Conor and I chat about random things to pass the time. How the weather here differs from the heat of Texas. About my ridiculous excuse for a scarf and how I need to buy a new one. We also discuss his tattoos, which he rolls up his sleeve to show me.

Close up, I can see all the intricate knot detailing and elegant designs surrounds a tree and various symbols.

"What does the tree symbolize?" I ask, lightly running the tips of my fingers along its branches and around the swirling trunk.

"It's the tree of life. It represents balance and harmony, connecting heaven, Earth, and the underworld."

His voice is low and deep as he watches my hand trace his tattoo. Goose bumps rise on his skin in the wake of my touch. Our bodies are close, blocking the wind which has died down some. The chills couldn't be caused by the cold, so it must be my touch. A thrill runs through me, knowing I affect him.

I clear my throat. "It's beautiful. So detailed."

"Thank you. I did it myself."

"Did what?"

I stop running my finger along his forearm but keep my hand resting there and look up at him confused.

"I drew and tattooed a good portion of my sleeve," he

admits with a rather proud smirk on his lips.

My head cocks at him even more confused. "You drew them *and* tattooed them?"

He nods.

"I thought you were a professional fighter? Not a tattoo artist."

He rotates his arm, showing me more designs along the other side. "I am. I do it as a hobby. I always liked drawing and tattooing intrigued me. That's why only my left arm is done." He holds up his right hand and wiggles his fingers. "I'm right-handed."

I laugh and feel so at ease around Conor it's as if I've known him for years. While I don't know everything about him, I know he's funny, a bit cocky, sometimes a gentleman, can crochet far better than I ever will, and has an affinity for loud obnoxious music. And now that he's secretly a very talented artist.

Looking at the designs inked on his arm, I know he could have easily done this professionally.

"I always found tattoos interesting but never was brave enough to get one. I don't know what I would want permanently inked on my skin."

"Well, I can draw something up for you, if you'd like." Conor offers.

I drop my hand from his arm and shove both in my jacket pockets. Tilting my head farther back I stare up at Conor. "Well, if I think of something I'll let you know."

"You do that. And if you stay long enough, maybe I'll even tattoo it on you."

A deep smooth timber rolls through his words, sending a heat through my body that coalesces low in my stomach.

"I don't think that'll happen. I may be on an adventure, but that's very permanent."

"You never know. You might change your mind."

We don't talk about tattoos anymore and make our way back to the car. Stopping to use the facilities before climbing into his SUV and venturing off to find a hotel for the night.

16 - Emma

It is not a sexcation

We find a hotel in a small town near the Cliffs and make our way inside. It's similar in style to the one in Blarney, with a pub on the first floor and a small check-in counter to the side.

A girl with dark blonde hair stands behind the counter dressed in jeans and a loose-fitting T-shirt with some logo of a sports team on it. At least that's what I think it is, I know nothing about Irish sports teams.

"Afternoon. What can I help you with today?" she asks, smiling warmly at both Conor and me. I appreciate being included in the conversation. Conor tends to divert attention.

Her eyes widen, and she does a double take on Conor. "Oh my God. You're Conor O'Shea." She points at him her mouth gaping open.

"That I am," he agrees and smiles politely. Apparently, MMA fighters are popular in Ireland. He takes her enthusiasm in stride. Not being overly pompous or cocky.

"Fucking hell. My mates are not gonna believe me when I tell them I met you today. Can I get a picture?"

She pulls her phone from her back pocket and holds it up eagerly.

"Sure."

She squeals happily and rounds the counter, holding her phone out in front of her to take a selfie. Conor crouches to get his head closer to hers in frame and smiles.

"Thank you so much. The lads are gonna freak."

"No problem." He waits for the girl to return behind the counter, then continues. "Could I get a room, please?"

"Of course. Just the one?" She looks up at him adoringly. It's kind of cute. She couldn't be over twenty and practically has tiny hearts in her big blue eyes.

"Yes. Just the one."

Hold the phone. Did he just say one? I thought we cleared this up already.

"What? No. We need two."

He looks at me over his shoulder. "One," he states firmly.

"I thought we discussed this? We are not sharing a room—"

"We're not," he interrupts. "*I* only need one room. *You* will be getting your own. I may be driving you, but I'm not paying for your room too."

"Oh," I say stupidly. He's just getting his room, and I have to ask for my own. I suppose that makes sense.

I step back from him and look down, trying to conceal my blush of embarrassment. Even without my bad luck it seems I can still embarrass myself no problem. Guess that'll always be just my luck.

"So just the one room then?" the girl asks again.

"Yes. Thank you. With a king bed if you have it."

She types on her computer and clicks a few times, frowning at whatever she reads on the screen.

"The only king we have is part of a two-bedroom unit that's linked with a jack and jill washroom. The other room has a queen size bed. The only other room I have available is a single." The girl looks up at Conor, then behind him at me. "If you two are traveling together, perhaps you wouldn't mind sharing a washroom?"

The poor girl looks truly apologetic about not being able to give the hunky MMA celebrity his own private king bedroom and bathroom.

Conor sighs and nods. "That's fine. I'll take a shared washroom over a tiny bed."

Great. More opportunities for him to walk in on my naked. I'll have to double check the locks on the doors work before taking a shower.

They both look over at me, waiting for my approval. "Yeah, that's fine."

The girl books us both in—separately—and gives us each a key. Not the gold skeleton style key, just a standard normal one on a plastic keychain with the hotel name and room number printed on it.

"Second floor, up the stairs to your right." She points to the stairs nearby.

"Cheers." Conor calls to the girl as we head toward the stairs.

The rooms are clean and warm with furniture that has more style than I ever will. And just as promised there's a door in each that leads to a large, shared bathroom. First thing I do is check the locks work. They do.

"I'm going to take a nap before we head down for dinner.

If that's alright?" Conor asks from the door in the bathroom that leads to his room.

He's already removed his shoes, and his arms are braced on either side of the door frame. He looks soft, disheveled from the wind, and a bit sleepy. Most likely due to sleeping on the small chaise last night. Perhaps I should have shared the bed. It was big enough.

"Sure. I could use a rest, too. Oh." I reach up and pull the hat off my head to hand back to him. "Here."

He shakes his head. "Hold on to it for now, you need it more than I do."

"Thanks."

I've only just relaxed on the bed when my phone rings on the nightstand. Danny's name flashes on the screen. Sitting up I lean against the head of the bed and grab my phone. Swiping the screen to answer, I'm met with not only Danny's face but Jules's. Split down the center of the screen in a three-way call. My greeting gets stuck in my throat.

They both look extremely unhappy.

"Hey, guys. What's up?" I ask tentatively.

"Will you please tell her she can't purchase a three-thousand-dollar couch for your apartment to replace the damaged one?" Danny demands.

"Can you please tell him I'm allowed to buy my friend a gift if I want to?" Jules argues back.

"Wait. What is going on? I'm confused."

They both open their mouths to speak, but Jules beats Danny by a nanosecond.

"I told him I wanted to buy you a new couch as a welcome home present for when you get back, and this butthead said I couldn't."

"I never said you couldn't," Danny retorts, "I simply said you should wait because she's considering moving and the couch might not be appropriate for her new place."

He rolls his eyes, and I can see the vein throbbing in his temple from here. I bite down on my lips to keep from laughing. Only these two would argue so much over a couch.

"You did not!" Jules shrieks, "You said, and I quote" I can see her raise one hand to create air quotes next to her head. "You can't buy her everything, some people like to pick out their own couches," she mocks in a deep voice while scrunching up her face on the screen. "If I had known you were considering moving, I wouldn't have pushed."

"Like that would have stopped you. You're always so pushy. Forcing Emma to do this or do that. As a matter of fact, isn't this whole Ireland trip your idea?" Danny stares at the screen, raising an accusing eyebrow.

"Yes. And I would gladly do it again. She needs to get out more, and you, and I both know it."

Danny is silent, his eyes softening, shifting on the screen. I'm assuming to look at me now.

"She does have a point there, Em. You do need to get out more, but I would have suggested to the bar down the street not one across the globe."

The softness that was just present fades as he quickly turns his scowl back on Jules.

"I didn't suggest she go to Ireland for a bar. I was trying to help get rid of her bad luck. Like any best friend would."

"Okay, okay. That's enough you two." I pinch the bridge of my nose and take a steadying breath. Sometimes these two drive me crazy. If they would admit they like each other, then we would all be eternally grateful.

My brother, and my best friend both shift their line of sight to me. Thankfully both stop talking.

"Jules, you know how I feel about extravagant gifts." I begin scolding my best friend firmly but gentle.

Jules bites her lip, looking a little sheepish. "I know, but I just can't help myself. You deserve nice things."

"And I love you for your generous spirit. But Danny is also right. I am considering moving to a new apartment when I get back, so I don't know what kind of couch I might want or need. So just hold off for now. Okay?"

Jules nods in concession but smiles knowingly. "Fine. But only because it's about time you got out of the dodgy complex."

"Agreed." Danny adds.

So nice to know my closest family and friends hate where I live.

"And Danny," I say, firming my tone again and turning my scowl on him.

"Yeah, Em."

"Stop arguing with Jules just for the sake of irritating her," I scold like I'm the older sibling and not him.

"Ugh, fine." He huffs with another eye roll.

"I don't want to deal with another call like this. I'm trying to enjoy my vacation, and you two are stressing me out."

They both apologize in unison.

"Love you both. I'll talk to you later. Separately and not to diffuse an argument."

"Love you too sis. Be safe." Danny smiles and gives me the usual stern concerned big brother look with a smile as he hangs up.

"Bye Hun. Have fun." Jules winks and hangs up as well.

As soon as she does, I immediately redial her. Realizing I hadn't had the chance to tell her about Conor, and our little arrangement. She answers immediately.

"Emma? I thought you were going to go enjoy your vacation?" she asks with a gentle mocking tone but with a smile on her face.

Now that she's not sharing a screen with my brother, I can see more of her. She's sitting on a cushioned lounger in a bikini and an oversized white button-up overshirt. The sun flickers over her tanned skin, and it makes me think I should have chosen somewhere warm and near a beach for my vacation.

Jules is in South Africa now for her shark diving experience. I remember all the risks of the ocean and am glad I'm in Ireland on dry land.

Well, sort of dry. The rain seems to have picked up again outside and the sound of it on the window and roof is hypnotizing. We get plenty of rain in Texas, and I always loved it. Sure, it creates a whole list of risks, but as long as you stay inside, you're unlikely to encounter any of those risks. A rainy day spend inside reading is always a good day.

"I am, but there's been a development."

"A development? Do tell. Is it at least a good one?"

I laugh and relax back into the pillows behind me, propping my hand on one bent knee to keep the phone at eye level.

"Oh, a very good one. You remember Conor the hottie from the pub?"

"Oh, I remember. Still bugs me I couldn't google him," she complains, scrunching her nose.

"Well, now you can. His last name is O'Shea."

"That also sounds extremely Irish. You sure I don't need to add anything else?"

"Nope."

Jules squints at me trying to read my expression through

the screen. When I don't say anymore, I can see her pull her laptop on to her thighs, open it and type. I wait patiently for her reaction when his photo loads.

It comes moments later, when her eyes widen and her mouth drops open. "Oh, my fucking Greek God. Is this him? The MMA fighter?"

"Yup."

"Holy shit."

"Yeah. And get this, I ran into him after I found out the tour company closed and then again, all the way in Blarney, when I was heading to kiss the stone."

"What? Why was he there? Isn't that like in a completely different city?" Jules keeps scrolling through the google results, her face shifting and changing with each new photo she finds. Most including sultry bedroom eyes. I don't blame her.

"Yes, it is. He said he was there to visit his sister, which he was, but that wasn't the only reason."

Jules looks up from her internet browsing and drooling to stare at me.

"What was the other reason?"

"According to him, when he helped me find my four-leaf clover," I hold up the necklace as proof, "he inadvertently gave me his good luck. Since then, he's been having some *unpleasant* experiences. Including losing a fight during training."

"Ha!" Jules barks a laugh, grinning wide and returns to ogling Conor's online photos. "So, he got your bad luck, eh?"

"Apparently. I have been having rather good luck since then. Anyway, he found me to try and convince me to give it back to him. Which, of course, I said no. There's no way in hell I'm giving up any good luck I've found."

"So, this means you did it? You succeeded in finding

good luck. Goal achieved. You go, girl." She holds up a fist in solidarity but doesn't turn her eyes away from the computer screen. Still too captivated with photos of Conor.

"He didn't like that and begged me to give it back to him. I kept saying no, but he insisted. Then he suggested he be my personal driver and take me all around Ireland, so I wouldn't have to take the bus."

Jules stops scrolling and slowly looks at the phone, waiting for me to continue.

"At first, I said no," I begin, my voice getting quieter with each word out of my mouth hoping she won't judge me for agreeing to give up the one thing I came here to find, "But he convinced me to let him be my chauffer and tour guide and in return at the end I'll give him back the clover. I guess he has some big fight coming up, and he doesn't want to lose."

"Hold on." Jules shifts, closing her laptop and focusing her attention back on me. "So, you're telling me, you're going to give up your good luck to travel the Irish countryside with a hunk of hottie man meat as your personal driver?"

"Yes?"

Her scream is high pitched and filled with girlish glee. "Oh my God, girl. You are so gonna get laid."

"I am not oh my God. Could you keep your voice down? He's in the room right next door, and I don't know how thin these walls are."

"Yes, you are. You better. You deserve it. Especially a man like that. I bet he's packing some massive—"

"Okay, that's enough of that. Besides, shouldn't you be like scolding me or something?" I interrupt, before she can start loudly talking about Conor's dick. At the memory of the brief flash of skin and hair and possible shaft my cheeks heat with a blush.

"No way. You getting laid by an Irish hottie counts as good luck in my book." Her eyes widen, as does her smile. "What if to get the luck of the Irish you have to "get lucky" with an Irishman?"

"Oh, jeez, Jules, really?"

Not that I hadn't considered it. Perhaps I literally have to get lucky to . . . well get lucky.

"Anyway. Just wanted to let you just in case something happens, and I go missing you know who to send the cops after."

"Uh-huh. If I don't hear from you for a few days, I'm just going to assume you're getting happily railed by a big dick and leave you the hell alone. No way am I interrupting your sexcation."

"Oh, my goodness Jules. It is not a sexcation."

"Well, it better become one."

We talk for a little longer before I hang up and relax in the bed, pulling the warm, heavy quilt over me and curling up on my side. I also set my phone with an alarm, so I don't oversleep. I'm not missing dinner. It's my favorite meal of the day. Especially here. Whatever I smelled passing through the pub downstairs I plan on eating tonight.

17 – Conor

What are you giggling at, Love?

The two-hour nap I took was the best sleep I've ever had. I could be exaggerating, but after sleeping on that chaise, it felt like heaven to stretch out on a king-sized mattress, naked. It's so much easier to relax when there are no clothes restricting anything.

I woke up from a dream involving Emma with a hard-on, but since we share a washroom, and she was probably awake to hear me, I couldn't jerk off to release the tension. My boner faded after a few moments of deep breathing but the desire it created remains.

Sitting pressed up against Emma's side at the bar downstairs in our hotel isn't helping my unsatisfied dick one bit. She's soft and warm and for once not wearing a giant jumper or jacket. Her V-neck white T-shirt clings to her breasts and flutters loosely around the flare of her hips. The barest hint of nipple teases me through the material.

I avert my attention to the bar, trying to signal the bartender for a drink and some dinner. We had hoped to sit at a table, but no such luck. Place is full despite how empty the cliffs were earlier. The only seats available were two wobbly stools in the middle of the long and packed bar.

I guess this is my luck now.

The bartender finally notices us, well he notices Emma. Who could blame him? I would notice her over me as well. He's older than either of us but has aged gracefully. The kind of aging that could easily garner him a night with a younger lady. The gray speckling the dark brown hair at his temples, is more silver fox than old man, and his blue eyes are bright and focused.

"Hello, sweetheart. What can I get for you this fine evening?"

Sweetheart? Isn't that a little too friendly for a woman he just met? I scowl at him, but he doesn't notice me, even though I'm shoulder to shoulder with Emma right in front of him.

"Hi. Can I get a cider?" she asks sweetly.

"We have a few. What kind do you like?"

Emma scrunches her nose and purses her lips in a way that makes her even more attractive in a sweet, innocent kind of way.

"I don't know. Whatever you think is best."

The bartender smiles devilishly, and I bite my tongue.

"Well, you'll be wantin' a local brew. Best in town." He produces a pint glass from behind the bar and begins to fill it from the tap. Watching Emma the entire time, his smarmy smile still in place.

Emma doesn't seem to notice his illicit staring and obvious ogling. She's completely oblivious to it. She just reads over the menu while she waits, not even noticing him checking her out or me firmly giving him the evil eye.

The bartender sets the pint down on a coaster in front of Emma, diverting her attention back to him. "Can I get you anything else, Love?"

Love? *Love? Did he just call her Love? Why does that annoy me?*

Lots of men call women Love in Ireland. I call her Love. It means nothing, just a friendly term of endearment. Yet it still boils my insides hearing someone else call her that.

"Could I get a shepherd's pie, please?"

"Of course you can."

The bartender doesn't move from his perch on the bar, and I figure now is a good time for me to interject and place my order.

"I would like a—"

I don't get the rest of my order out because the twat turns and walks away, ignoring me. He goes to the computer to enter in Emma's order, and I stare dumbfounded at his back.

That fecker really just did that. He is definitely not getting a tip.

Emma's muffled snicker pulls my attention back to her. She's not watching the bartender she's watching me, with her hand over her mouth smothering her giggles. The light in her eyes has my anger dissipating instantly.

"What are you giggling at, *Love*?" I ask, emphasizing love to make it clear how I feel about him calling her that.

She only giggles more, uncovering her mouth to gift me with her smile. It's wide and lights up her face.

"Oh, nothing. It's just entertaining to not be the unlucky one anymore. I think I might even get my food exactly as I ordered."

"Well, enjoy it because if I can't order my supper, I'm

going to be eating half of yours."

"Ah! You will not. Shepard's pie is my favorite, and I will not be sharing."

She's still smiling when she turns to look for the bartender, who is serving another guest, but somehow notices her instantly. Finishing with the patron and coming straight to her bypassing any waving customers on the way.

"Did you need something, sweetheart?"

Again with the sweetheart?

Emma turns to me, smile growing more restrained as she tries to keep from giggling again. "My friend would like to order something."

"Oh, sure." He finally turns his attention to me, and his smile falters. It's overtaken by shock when he spots me. His eyes quickly scanning the visible half of my body and sobering. "What'll ya have, mate?"

"I'd like a pint of Guinness, and I'll also have the shepherd's pie," I say in a flat and probably aggressive tone.

"Right. Absolutely."

He pours my pint quickly and retreats to the computer to put in my order.

Yeah, you better remember your place mate.

"So, tell me, Emma," Emma turns to face me as best she can in the crammed space. I don't mind it when her thigh presses up against mine, and I get a better view of her. "How in the hell did you manage to put me on my ass back at the cathedral? You're much smaller than me, and I'm a professional."

Emma chuckles lightly and fingers the condensation on her pint glass. "My dad and brothers insisted I knew self-defense. As the only girl and with bad luck to boot they never wanted me to be vulnerable."

"And, so they taught you how to take down a professional MMA fighter? Seems like overkill."

"Yeah, they may have gone a little overboard. They didn't just teach me one or two basic moves. They treated my lessons as if it were a life and death situation. Thankfully, it never has been, but I'm always grateful for the knowledge."

She sighs wistfully, and we both take a drink from our pints. Hers a light golden and mine nearly as dark as the bar top beneath.

I don't know her well enough yet, but it seems like she's close with her family. As someone who is part of a large close family myself, I appreciate that in a woman.

"How many brothers do you have?" I ask. The way she talks about them it sounds like a whole pack.

"Three older brothers and a dad who leads them like a pack of wild dogs."

Her laugh is musical and as she shifts her leg presses firmly against mine. My cock stirs at the friction and the lingering desire from my sex dream resurfaces, forcing more blood to run south. I don't shift or move away, I can't. There's no room. I don't want to, anyway. I never hid my attraction to her. Even before the whole clover luck incident, I desired her. Now my interest has grown from strictly physical to genuinely intrigued to know her more.

She puts a lot of her focus on her curse and managing it but there's more to her than that. No one is only one thing. There's still more to learn about Emma, and I plan on learning it all while she's here.

The realization she will leave and return home to Texas in a hand full of days makes something shift in me. A sharp fleeting feeling of panic and loss. I brush it off before the feeling can take root and go back to focusing on the here and now, and Emma.

"That's a lot of brothers. I don't know what my mum would have done with three of me. I only have two sisters. Aisling, my younger and more annoying little sister who you met, and my older sister Bridget who works with my mum running the farm and wool business."

"I used to wish I had sisters, but I'm glad I have my brothers. They're always so protective, and I love them for it. If I had a sister, we probably wouldn't get along. Girls can be catty."

"Don't I know it," I agree, shaking my head. Dealing with my sisters as the only boy was always an adventure.

"Did your brothers only teach you to fight because of your bad luck? Or would they have done that no matter what?" I ask. Sometimes siblings do things out of love, but other times, it's strictly out of obligation. From the sounds of it her brothers are more than just obligated to help and protect her.

"Probably a bit of both. I think they would have taught me self-defense either way but might not have gotten so aggressive with the training if it weren't for the curse. It's kind of ruled my life since I discovered its existence when I was ten."

"You didn't have it until you were ten?" I ask. What could a ten-year old have possibly done to earn such a curse?

"No, it was there before that. I just didn't know that's what it was until then. That's when I realized it wasn't normal to trip so much, lose so many toys and accidentally break so many plates. It's because of the curse that I got into risk assessment and statistical analysis."

My brow furrows. She got into her fact-finding profession because of her curse?

"How so?"

"When I was a teenager, it became painfully obvious the bad luck wasn't going away, and I had to figure out a way to protect myself and limit the damage it caused. So, I started looking up facts about things and the risks each carried, so I could try and avoid it."

"And that led to making that your career?"

"In a way. I just sorta fell into it. By the time I had to decide a major in college it seemed like the logical thing to do."

Emma grows quiet and turns her eyes away from mine, gingerly sipping at her cider before placing it back on the coaster to continue running her finger around its rim. She doesn't look pleased about being a risk analyst. From all the random facts and knowledge I thought it was something she was passionate about. Like me and fighting. It was the thing that called to her, the thing she was good at and wanted to do.

At the growing frown on her pretty face, I'm rethinking my assumption. I knew she was more than her curse. I just hadn't considered she had let it control so much of her life.

"You don't want to be a risk analyst, do you?"

"What?"

Her frowning face morphs, losing its sadness and turns into confusion with a hint of surprise. Surprise that I saw right through her vaguely shielded half-truth? I wonder if anyone else in her life has ever noticed it.

"Why do you say that?" she asks, trying to cover up her surprise.

"Because it's true. I can tell by the way you talk about your career. It's not something you're passionate about. You do it because it's easy and helps control your bad luck. Not because you enjoy it. Not because it makes you happy."

Her face softens and her lips part of a soft exhale. I'm right, and we both know it. I may get hit in the head for a living, but that doesn't mean I'm stupid. I went to university and got an education in kinesiology. I too am more than just what people see on the surface.

"You're right," she admits. "It's not what I want to do, but it's what is safe for me to do."

"What do you really want to do? And why wouldn't it be safe? Is it professional skydiving instructor? I can see how that would be unsafe."

Emma laughs at my joke, and I see the tension easing in her posture. Mine is easing as well. Pulling me closer to her wanting desperately to know her deepest desires.

"Promise you won't laugh?"

"Why would I laugh?"

"Because my reasoning may sound stupid to you. At least that's what I was told when I admitted it to a friend in the past."

Her cheeks pinken, and she nibbles on the corner of her bottom lip, drawing my attention to her mouth. I watch as the plump pinkness is rolled between her teeth and back again. Growing moist and reddened under her attentions.

"Promise I won't laugh," I admit in a low, gravelly voice. I'm surprised she even hears me over the noise of the packed pub around us. I suppose this close it wouldn't matter how quietly I spoke. She would still hear me.

"Okay." Emma inhales and exhales deeply, her chest rising and falling. Drawing my eyes away from her lips and down farther. "I would really love to be an elementary school teacher, but when I realized my curse could negatively affect those around me too, I didn't want to risk hurting children. What if the curse made me trip with a pair of scissors, and I cut a student? Or I accidentally give a student a cup of glue instead of milk, and they drink it? There were so many possibilities I didn't want to risk."

Three days ago, I would have laughed at her and called her crazy for thinking such a thing. Now, after experiencing the power of her bad luck curse firsthand, I know better. I understand where her reasoning stems from and commiserate with her.

I don't laugh. And when she realizes, she looks up at me.

"You're not laughing."

"No, I'm not. I understand your logic, and I can't laugh at you for wanting to protect others. To protect children. I'm just sad you don't get to do what you love. I hope after you absolve your bad luck with all the good luck of Ireland you get to change that."

Reaching up, I catch the stray strands of hair and push them back from her face, trailing my fingertip over her cheek. She doesn't move while she watches me. Doesn't even breathe, and it's as if the clamor of the patrons around us vanishes. Leaving only me and her in utter silence.

My palm rests against her cheek, and I stroke my thumb along her jaw, brushing the underside of her bottom lip. I want to lean in and kiss her. Apparently, my body got the command before my brain could give it and is already leaning in closer to her.

I'm a mere breath away from pressing her lips to mine when I'm shoved forcefully from behind. I try to brace but am too late and instead of a heated kiss I smack forehead first into Emma. Reeling back quickly to protect her from further harm. It's too late to stop the collision but at least I can try to minimize it.

Emma flinches backward and brings her hand to her forehead, wincing. I feel a tiny flickering pain in my forehead, but the anger growing inside me dulls the feeling.

I push back against whoever ruined the kiss that could have led to more with Emma and stand. Shoving back my stool and turning to face the future dead man.

It's a bunch of rowdy lads who are obviously drunk and laughing at one another. None seemingly realizing they just plowed into someone and caused injury.

"Aye!" I shout over their fumbling noise and laughter.

The four turn in confused unison and look up at me, sobering immediately. I am much taller and broader than them and in this moment am probably spewing smoke from my nostrils like an angry bull.

"You need to watch what you're doing. You just hurt my girl, and you need to apologize. *Now.*" I growl at the lads who rightfully cower and swallow visibly under my ire.

They look behind me at Emma who tries to brush off the incident. Tugging at my elbow to sit back down and ignore it. I most certainly will not ignore it.

"Sorry about that. We really didn't mean to hurt no one," one says.

"Yeah. We really are sorry miss. Please don't let your boyfriend beat the shite out of us," says another.

"Oh, he's not my—"

"As long as it doesn't happen again, I'll let it slide this time."

I've already claimed Emma as mine. Might as well let them think I'm her boyfriend to keep any other interested parties uninterested.

"Right. It won't. We're just gonna go over there." The first one points across the room, far, far away from us. Then they scurry off only looking back once.

I hear one of them as they go say, "Jesus Christ that guy was huge. I thought for sure he was going to beat the shite out of us."

It's their lucky day I didn't. For some reason, it pissed me off most knowing it caused Emma injury.

My face falls, and I turn to her to check on her head. I hope my giant brick of a head didn't hurt her too much.

She's still gently rubbing at her forehead. I step close and remove her hand, inspecting the damage. Holding Emma's chin, I gently rotate her head to the side, so I can better see it in the light. No broken skin and only a small pinkish red spot. Doesn't look like there will be a bump or any bruising, thankfully.

"I think you'll be alright. Doesn't look like I did much damage."

I look down at her, keeping her face cupped in my hand. It's so large compared to her, I can run my fingers through her silky hair and tilt her chin up with my thumb at the same time.

"You didn't have to scare them off like that. They were just drunk and fooling around."

"Don't make excuses for their rude behavior. They were being rough and caused me to hurt you. I won't have that. It's my intention to never cause you pain."

Emma sucks in a shuddering breath, and it's as if the interruption never happened. The heat and desire still present. Only this time I'm standing pressed between her knees, looking down at her and this time without a crowd pushing at my back.

My body picks up right where it left off, leaning into her and angling my mouth toward hers.

I hear the bartender approach and say something but

ignore him. Emma's eyes shift in his direction, and I growl in frustration when she pulls away from me.

"Oh, look, our food's here," she announces in a forced, uneven tone. "Just in time, too, because I'm starving."

Emma slips free of my hold, and I want nothing more than to grab her and take the kiss that I keep getting denied.

Turning, I sit and look down at my plate. It's not shepherd's pie.

"What is that?" Emma asks.

"It's liver and onions," I tell her.

All the heat and desire burning through my veins simmers and dissolves as I stare at the purple red blob of meat on the plate before me.

The bartender doesn't even wait to see if everything is right after he places down the plates. He just turns and walks away without a word. First, he can't shut up and now we don't even get a congenially "I hope you enjoy your meal."

Now I love liver as much as the next guy, but this does not look appetizing.

Next to me, and my scowl of defeat, Emma bursts out laughing hysterically. She's doubling over, holding her stomach, and I can see tears welling in her squinted eyes.

"What's so funny?" I demand. A little of my anger subdued under her humor.

"This is fantastic. My meal is right, and yours is all wrong. This never happens to me." She continues to laugh, wheezing as she tries to control her erratic breathing.

"This isn't funny. I'm hungry too, and I'm not eating this."

I push the plate away and search the bar for the bartender. He's all the way at the opposite end and not looking my way.

"It's okay big guy," Emma consoles me and pats my

shoulder. "We'll send it back and see if they can get it right the second time. You wanna know a secret?"

She leans into me and looks around as if being watched. Her chest pressing flush with the outside of my arm. I want to know anything that keeps her leaning against me like this.

"Sure."

"Whenever a restaurant would get my order wrong, I would steal a piece of silverware to keep as a reminder. I have a whole box filled with them back home." She chuckles and wipes the last remaining laughter tear from her eye. "They got my order wrong a lot."

"Why would you want a reminder that a restaurant made your order wrong?"

"At first, I thought it was funny and was curious how many times it would happen. When it started happening more frequently, it was to keep proof of the curse, I suppose. It's kind of become habit now."

Sliding her spoon from the bar top, she hands it to me with a sad smile on her lips. I take it from her and hold it between us.

"I'll keep it. But not as a reminder that my food was made wrong but as a keepsake of tonight and this trip with you."

While she watches I dip my fork into her shepherd's pie and take a solid bite, chewing the fluffy whipped potatoes and juicy, tender meat.

"Mmm, delicious."

"Hey, that's my dinner!" Emma shields her plate from me as I try to steal another bite.

"I told you if I didn't get my supper, I was going to eat half of yours."

She giggles and tries unsuccessfully to keep my fork out of

her pie. I eat only two more bites before we return my plate of liver and onions. My replacement dinner is a shepherd's pie, but the potatoes are watery, and the meat is cold.

Just my luck. Not only was my attempt to kiss Emma thwarted, but my supper was also ruined.

18 – Conor

Like apples I want to take a bite out of

Sweat trickles down my back and neck as I keep my pace jogging down the street that'll bring me back to the hotel. I woke up early this morning with a massive boner and no outlet for it and decided to go for a run. Not being back home where I can be in the gym all day, I have to do something to keep my muscles from laxing.

Running won't give me the workout I desire, but it's all I can manage right now. The hotel doesn't have a gym, and I don't have any free weights in my car, so this'll have to do. I've run at least five miles, and the clouds overhead look like they could dump a truckload of water on me at any moment. I've managed a semblance of a workout and now need a shower. One inside and warm not out in the cold rain.

I enter the hotel and make my way through the lobby and up the stairs toward my room. As I enter, I pull the damp shirt off over my head, wiping excess sweat from my face with it before tossing it on a chair.

The door to our shared washroom is ajar and from the other side I hear music playing. Not classical music as I would expect to be coming from Emma's room but something far more . . . explicit. The lyrics sound more than suggestive. As I step closer, the volume increases, and I can hear Emma singing along. She knows every dirty word. Interesting.

Peeking through the crack in the door, I try to spot Emma before slipping my hand through the narrow opening and pulling the door farther open. The music grows louder, and I finally catch sight of Emma.

Her back is to me, and she's only wearing a pair of white cotton panties and a matching tank top. She looks absolutely mouthwatering. Every inch of freckled skin exposed and on display. Her soft, rounded arse is visible below the hem of her panties as it sways and rolls as she dances along to the music. Moving in a way meant to entice and seduce. My cock twitches in response and swells the longer I watch her.

Emma bounces and shimmies, shaking her arse and nearly killing me in the process. *Fuck, I want to touch her.* Her skin looks smooth and soft. Those enticing freckles clustered on her shoulders and down her arms spotting her pale skin. And just like the ones on her cheeks and neck I want to taste every single one.

Her body is shapely but not hourglass, with soft natural curves. Her hips flare and then round her heart-shaped arse, with lean long legs strong enough to wrap around any part of me and hold on tight.

Silently I make my way through the bathroom, stopping at the threshold to her room. Leaning against the frame, I settle my arms across my bare chest and continue watching. Waiting for her to notice me. She doesn't at first, and I get a front-row seat to her impromptu concert and dance party.

She moves around without a care in the world. Shifting through the clothing in her suitcase and on the bed. Holding items up for inspection trying to decide what to wear. I'm not paying attention to the items she's looking at. All my attention is strictly locked on her body and every movement she makes.

The music shifts and picks up pace as do her movements. Emma does this hip popping movement that makes me internally groan.

"Tá tú chun mé a mharú Leamhan Beag." *You're going to kill me, Little Moth.*

Emma shrieks and spins to face me at the sound of my voice. She's not wearing a bra, and I can see her tight pink nipples through her top with ease. Her breasts are probably only a palm full, but they are perfect. Like apples I want to take a bite out of. This time, I groan out loud. She really is going to kill me.

"Conor! What the hell are you doing?"

Emma's eyes are big and wide from shock, and she's clutching at her chest with one hand, breathing heavily. Her apple chest rises and falls, keeping my attention firmly glued to it. It's hard to look away from something so tempting. Forbidden fruit indeed. No wonder Adam couldn't resist.

"Just enjoying the show. What music was that? Bach? Chopin? I've never heard that rendition before," I tease.

Her cheeks darken as she reaches over and hits a button on her mobile on the dresser to stop the music. In the silence Emma's posture grows stiff, losing the relaxed fluidity she possessed while dancing.

"It's Nicki Minaj, okay? Sometimes, I like to change things up. Listen to something more upbeat. Especially when I'm happy or in a good mood," she says shyly but firmly.

Wrapping her arms around her middle and chest, she conceals herself from my gaze, drawing my attention to her face. Is this why she didn't want me to see her pajamas? Because they're nothing more than this set of panties and top?

"So, what you're saying is that you're in a good mood?"

My voice is low and suggestive. My mood has vastly improved in the last five minutes for sure.

"I guess so. Maybe."

"Because of your good luck? Or is it something else?"

She doesn't answer immediately. Fidgeting in place only a few meters away from me. Oh, how easily I could close that distance and give her many reasons to be in a good mood.

"There's a lot of reasons, really. It's not just one in particular," she finally answers. A soft flush washing up her neck to her ears.

"Mmmm." I hum thoughtfully. "How much do you weigh?"

"What? What does that have to do with anything?" My question brings her out of her silent stiffness.

"Well, you see I'm a professional fighter. Which means I need to work out regularly to stay in fighting shape. There's nowhere for me to do that while we travel, and all I've been able to do is run." I cock my head and look her up and down as if I haven't already memorized every visible inch of her body.

"That still doesn't explain why you need to know my weight. Besides, didn't you mother ever tell you not to ask a woman's weight or age?"

"My mother always taught us that weight doesn't matter. What matters is happiness. If you're happy, the number on the scale doesn't matter. For instance, I weigh eighteen stone, but I don't care. I'm happy and healthy. *That's* what matters."

"Oh." Emma's mouth forms a small O, and I like that shape on her lips. "I don't know how many pounds eighteen stone is."

I laugh. I forgot American's don't use the same scale we do. "It's around two hundred and fifty, two hundred and fifty-five pounds I believe."

"Wow. That's a lot."

"Yeah, it is," I agree. "So, again, how much do you weigh?"

"You still haven't told me why. When you tell me why I'll tell you how much I weigh." She lifts her chin and stands firm. Still in just her underwear, but she doesn't seem to notice her continued state of undress anymore, and I'm not going to point it out to her.

"You look like I could bench press you. It might give me some semblance of a workout for my upper body."

"Oh well, I weigh about one hundred and sixty pounds or so."

I remain leaning against the washroom doorframe and, without warning, stand tall and stride into her room in three quick steps. She's so stunned by my movement she doesn't have enough time to react beyond dropping her arms to her side and taking a half step back.

"What are you—aaahhh!"

Her squeal is cut off as I bend down and lift her like a log across my shoulders. Wrapping my hand around her thighs and shoulder to hold her in place along the back of my neck and shoulders.

She laughs and wriggles, slapping at my chest with one hand while the other scrambles for purchase to hold herself up. I won't let her fall. She's not that heavy in the least. But it's enough added weight I can get a few good squats in. I can't risk lifting her over head with her moving so much. She could easily slip and fall, and I won't allow that.

"Yeah, this could work. If you would stop wriggling so much."

I hold her firmly and do a few squats while she continues to laugh breathlessly. The soft underside of her breasts rest against my neck and jaw and I want to nuzzle into them, but I control myself. Just barely. I'm trying to be playful, not pervy.

"Put me down. I am not a piece of work out equipment," she squeals between peels of high-pitched laughter. Her breath evening out as she gets control of her breathing and body flailing.

"I could argue otherwise."

"Conor! I . . . Oh my gosh. I'm not even wearing pants. Put me down," she demands, giving me one more slap on the pec. Little does she know putting her hands on me only makes me want to hold on to her longer.

"Keep touching me like that Leamhan Beag, and I'll put you under me instead of over me. Actually, scratch that I rather like the idea of you on top."

Giving her arse a little smack, she flinches and yelps but doesn't argue.

In a breathy, cracked voice I hope I caused, Emma speaks softly near my ear. "Can you please put me down, so I can get dressed?"

"Whatever you wish Leamhan Beag."

Swinging her body up and off my shoulders, I'm far too distracted by the way her soft skin glides down my bare chest, and I hear a bang then crash.

Looking down, I see her long legs knocked a lamp off the

dresser, and it's in broken pieces on the floor.

Shite.

I take large tentative steps away from the debris and place Emma down far away from the pieces that could cut her bare feet.

"Bollocks. You stay here. I'll clean this up. I don't want you cutting your feet."

Emma giggles, and I swivel to face her. Her fingers are pressed to her lips, and she's holding back a smile. Eyes alight with mirth.

"What's so funny now?" She always seems to be laughing at me.

"It's just funny at this point. Everything that can go wrong, does."

"So, would you say this is your fault or mine?"

She looks over the scene of broken ceramic and loose wires then back up to me. "Oh, this is definitely your fault. Your bad luck, not mine."

I grunt. She may be right on this one. It is kind of my fault. "Okay, fine. I'll take responsibility, *this time*."

We leave the hotel after having some breakfast in the thankfully less crowded pub, and paying for the lamp I broke, heading to Galway.

Galway is barely an hour and a half drive from here and Emma has decided that she wants to stop and wonder about for a few hours before continuing on our journey to the Causeway.

Our drive is quick and uneventful, thankfully. When we arrive in the city, I make my way through the streets searching for an area with lots of shops for Emma to wonder through. There's an area called The Latin Quarter filled with bright multicolored buildings and walking only narrow cobblestone streets, with live street music and restaurants. It's perfect for a few hours' visit.

It takes a little longer to find a carpark, but I eventually manage to.

The clouds are still gray in the sky, but that never stops an Irishman. It'll no doubt rain, as it always does but for now the sun squeezes through enough to give the day a hazy appearance. Because of this, the wind is extra chilly, and I pull out my scarf from my back seat that matches the hat I loaned to Emma, which currently rests snug on her head.

I loop it around her neck and tie it in front. "Here, wear this. It's cold out and that poor excuse of a scarf you have won't do you any good."

"Oh, no, I couldn't."

"Yes, you can. You need it and besides it matches the hat." I pull gently on the edge of the hat and a small smile pulls at her lips.

"Thank you. I promise I'll buy my own and return these as soon as possible."

"Don't worry about it. Keep them as long as you need."

She smiles again and nods, pulling her trustworthy bag strap over her head and across her chest. She's wearing both her gray jumper and denim jacket today, so along with my scarf and hat, she should be plenty warm. Even without my hat my wool jumper does more than enough to keep me warm.

Emma strolls down the street at my side, having to take twice as many steps to keep up with my stride. I slow my pace, so she can more easily enjoy wondering the area. I don't doubt she could easily keep up with those strong legs of hers that I have imagine wrapped around my hips more than once since seeing them this morning. I just want her to enjoy her visit to Ireland. She's not here to rush and get to an appointment. She's here to experience the Emerald Isle and discover its many lucky aspects.

Her eyes are bright and in constant motion, looking in every window we pass. There are shops with clothing, books, crafts, art, jewelry and more. One store that grabs her attention is one I'm very familiar with. Wool jumpers, scarves, hats, and more line the shelves and hangs on racks in varying colors and styles.

"Let's go in here. I've been wanting to get a new sweater. And maybe I can even buy my own hat and scarf and return yours."

That makes me frown. I like seeing her wearing my hand made hat and scarf. I don't want her wearing some mass-produced subpar garment. She deserves something better.

Before I can talk her out of it, we're entering the store. Emma oohs and ahs at things she touches and holds up for inspection. They're not bad pieces. This store carries well-made quality Irish made wool. Which can also come with a hefty price tag.

Emma holds up a jumper and checks the tag and cringes, setting it back on the display table.

"Maybe I'll just get a new scarf. I don't think I can afford all three items."

"Why don't you just get the jumper you wanted. You can continue wearing my scarf while you're here. I promise I don't mind. I'd prefer you to. I want to make sure you stay warm while we adventure around the country."

Biting her lip uncertainly she eyes the options on the table and around the shop. The excitement that filled her eyes not minutes before fades away by the second as she contemplates the cost.

"I think I'll look around at other stores. Maybe I can find something a little cheaper."

I want to argue with her and tell her I'll cover the cost, but I'm not sure if she'd allow me to. Instead, I spot something near the till that I think she would let me buy her.

19 - Emma

Let's see how it looks

Not being able to buy the beautiful wool sweater was heartbreaking. As was the price tag. I can't in good conscience pay three hundred euros for one sweater. I'm sure there are stores that sell them for far cheaper. This is Ireland, after all. I'm sure I'll find more options.

Conor is being a good sport, following me around the shops and letting me set the pace we stroll at through the busy pedestrian street in the Latin Quarter. My brothers always hated it when they were forced to take me to the mall to go back to school shopping with me. But it doesn't seem to bother Conor. He looks in the windows and comments on items. I think he's actually having fun.

We exit the wool store and Conor stops me only a few feet down the sidewalk, pulling me to the side by my elbow. Stepping out of the flow of traffic.

I look up at him, confused. "What is it?"

"I bought you something," he says quietly, pulling

something small out of his pocket.

He holds his fist out and unfurls his fingers. Inside the palm of his hand sits a beautiful pink and yellow fat bodied moth enamel pin.

"Now I know traditionally you wouldn't want a moth near your clothes, but I saw this and thought you could use one to remember your trip."

Conor pulls the rubber backing off the pin and tacks it on to my jean jacket right next to my lunar moth pin.

"Conor, it's beautiful. You didn't have to."

"I know. I wanted to. I don't want you to forget about me when you go back to the states."

His smile is small, but when his eyes shift to mine, there's only playful flirtation there. I'll miss him when I go home. Because eventually this trip will end. I'll leave this beautiful country with all its rolling green hills and picturesque scenery. And go back to boring, drab, repetitive, jobless Texas.

Suddenly, looking for a new apartment and new job doesn't sound so appealing.

Conor finishes pinning the new moth to my jacket and looks me over, checking his handy work, and I look down to admire it as well.

"There. Perfect."

When I look up, he's not looking at the pin but at me, and I blush under his stare. It's the same intensely heated look he gave me last night when we were just as close at the pub, when he almost kissed me right before he headbutted me.

The memory makes me blush deeper but also smile. It was quite funny.

"Thank you. I love it," I tell him in a hushed tone.

"You're welcome." His voice is as quiet as mine as we

lean in close, huddled on the side up against a bright yellow building. "Come on. There's more to see."

Wrapping his arm behind my back and resting his hand on my hip, he steers me back into the flow of foot traffic. His hand remains there, guiding me and protecting me while we walk until I spot another store that draws my attention.

I drag Conor into a jewelry store called Claddagh Jewelers. Which is why I ventured in. I've read about the claddagh and traditional Celtic knot work designs and want to see some in person. They looked so beautiful online.

Most guys would freak out being pulled into such a store by a woman they're with. Not big, tattooed Conor O'Shea. Nope, he just smiles and greets the store clerk when we enter and trails closely behind me as I venture to a bank of brightly lit cases.

Inside is a variety of earrings. Studs, hoops, and danglies. Earrings are dangerous for me, so I don't wear them. Maybe, in the future, I'll attempt it, but for now, I'm still playing it safe. So, I move on to another case. This one is filled with necklaces. I have a few necklaces, and they tend to catch on things and break. I'm sure the only reason the long chain I'm currently wearing hasn't broken is because it holds a four-leafed clover. They are beautiful when they catch the light and sparkle back at me, though.

The next case has me pausing and considering. Inside there are dozens of claddagh rings. Rings in silver, gold and some fitted with gemstones at the center of the heart.

"Hi there. Can I help you find something today?"

The female clerk steps up on the other side of the case with a friendly smile on her face and a name tag that reads Deirdre. She has perfectly wavey red auburn hair and again I'm faced with the realization that there are so many redheads in Ireland.

I smile back and tap on the glass. "I was just looking at the claw—clay—claw-dawg." I cringe.

"Claddagh," Deirdre offers in her perfect Irish accent.

Why does an American accent have to sound so crass and clunky compared to something as smooth and lyrical as an Irish accent? Every time Conor speaks, I shiver while listening to his voice. Deirdre's voice doesn't make me shiver, but it is beautiful.

"Right, claddagh," I say slowly to pronounce it correctly. "I read about them online and found them so interesting."

"Do you know the story behind them and how to wear them?" Deirdre asks.

"A little bit, I didn't read the whole history, but I know there's different ways to wear the ring depending on your relationship status, correct?"

Deirdre nods and unlocks the case, pulling out a tray of rings. Some simple and others more extravagant. She picks up a simple silver claddagh ring, pointing at each design element as she explains.

"The claddagh ring actually originated here in Galway. Thought to originally be made by a silversmith named Richard Joyce who was captured and enslaved in Algeria. While there, he fashioned this ring to bring back to his sweetheart here in Ireland.

"The hands holding the heart represent friendship, the heart represents love, and the crown represents loyalty. Many men and women wear them. They may buy them for themselves, receive one as a gift or even inherit one from a relative. May I?"

She holds out her hand to mine gesturing for me to allow

her to put the ring on my finger. I place my right hand in hers, and she slips the ring on my ring finger.

"Wearing the ring like this with the heart pointing out on the right hand signifies the wearer is single and looking for love." She winks at me playfully with a mischievous smile before slipping the ring back off and turning it around.

"Wearing it with the heart pointing inwards signifies that the person is taken, or in a relationship. Showing someone has captured their heart." With this description Deirdre smiles wistfully like a schoolgirl with a crush.

Pulling the ring off my hand, she gestures for me to give her my left hand. She slips the ring on in the same position it was in on my right but now on my left.

"If worn with the heart facing in on the left hand it signifies marriage. Now not all Irish use claddagh rings, but a good number do. It's all up to personal preferences. Are there any you would like to take a closer look at?"

I look down at the silver ring, and against my pale freckled skin, it seems to vanish on my hand. I've always leaned more toward gold because of the way it stands out against my skin and blends well with my hair color.

"I prefer gold over silver," I tell her, slipping the ring off and handing it back to her.

"Lovely. We have plenty of gold options to choose from. Perhaps your boyfriend would like to help pick one out for you?"

I look up at Deirdre from the tray of gold rings she placed in front of me, confused. My brow scrunches, and her line-of-sight veers to my right. I turn to see Conor, who is standing close to me and looking over my shoulder. Which is easy with his height.

"Oh, he's not . . ."

"I kind of like the simple classic design," Conor offers still looking down at the tray on the counter.

Reaching around me, he picks one up and holds it up in front of my face.

"What do you think of this one?"

I'm still staring at him, at a loss for words, and confused as to why he didn't correct the woman's assumption.

"Uh, yeah. Simple, classic," I mutter, trying to pry my attention away from his relaxed posture and demeanor while mine is wound in spirals trying to figure him out.

The ring he's holding between his thumb and forefinger is beautiful. It's a smooth golden band with no jewels or adornments. The style is larger than the others, with a thicker band, less likely to bend or break. The design a little more modern with its smooth lines.

It's perfect.

"Wow. I love that one."

"I knew you would," Conor chuckles against my ear. "Here, let's see how it looks."

Lifting my right hand, he slides the ring on my finger with the heart facing inward. As if I'm taken and in a relationship. Is he doing this for fun because of what the woman said? Either way, the ring fits perfectly and looks amazing.

"I'll take this one."

I don't even care how much it costs, as long as it isn't over three hundred dollars. I'm fine with any number she gives me.

"Wonderful. Would you like to wear it out or would you like me to box it up for you?"

"I'll wear it out."

Deirdre rings me up a few minutes later. The total cost is

only two hundred euro, thankfully. She gives me a polishing rag and a lovely little wooden box to store it when I'm not wearing it.

When we leave, I don't flip the ring around until we get back in his SUV hours later after having a bite to eat at one of the cute little restaurants, where Conor collects his second piece of cutlery. This time a fork to go with his spoon.

20 – Emma

At least I'm no longer cold

We didn't leave Galway as early as we had planned, but it was well worth it to spend the day wandering the shops with Conor. After buying my claddagh ring I didn't spend too much more money. I still need to budget. I am, after all, unemployed now.

I have no idea what the hell I'm going to do for work when I get back to Texas. Since I'm basically blacklisted from all competitive companies, I can't be a risk assessment manager for the next year. What does that leave?

Food service? No, too many probabilities for spills.

Receptionist? Maybe. It has very low risk of anything other than papercuts.

Nanny?

Dog walker?

Huh. None are what I want to do. There's the career I always wanted but never thought I could have that I admitted to Conor, which is an elementary school teacher. Perhaps after all this I could take the proper courses to get my teachers credentials. Find a local school, maybe something near the new apartment I also still have to find.

The issue remains. I need income. I have to pay for living expenses and the courses. I can't do that with the small amount I have in my savings. I know if I asked Jules would gladly give me the money, but I can't do that. No matter how rich she is. I'll figure something out. Work part time somewhere with flexible hours and go to classes on my off days.

Who am I kidding? My luck may be good right now, but after I give the clover to Conor, it'll go right back to the curse it was before. I could never risk the kids. Could never expose them to the curse. I just need to stick to jobs that are low risk and safe.

Here and now, I can enjoy the trip, enjoy the scenery rolling by. The green hills and flowing streams. There's a flock of sheep roaming in a field, grazing and bleating. I can hear their calming song as we pass.

With the radio still stuck on the opera channel neither of us wanted to turn it back on. The cab of the car remains pleasantly quiet between easy conversation. We chat about how Conor got into cage fighting; I tell him all about my apartment getting flooding and losing my job. He tells me all about his family's sheep farm and wool business. We exchange favorites, like favorite movie, food, color, sibling, and music.

"If you want to play some music on your mobile you can," Conor says from the driver's seat.

The rain has started again, and it's getting darker with every mile we drive. It'll be late when we get into Bushmills, the city closest to the Giant's Causeway. I hope there'll be an open hotel with rooms.

"No, that's okay. I kind of like the sound of the rain, and the quiet. Besides, if I play music how will we be able to talk?"

"You sure? I don't mind if you want to play some Nicki Minaj or Beyonce or maybe Snoop Dogg." Conor grins and looks at me from the corner of his eye.

"Ha-ha. Very funny. Although I do have some Beyonce in my iTunes, that music isn't appropriate for right now."

"What do you mean? Why not?"

"Because this is a quiet peaceful drive. Calm. Serene. The sound of the rain is music enough."

Conor watches out the window thoughtfully listening to the rain which has grown heavier again. The pitter patter of the rain on the hood of the car harmonizes with the wipers' rhythmic tempo.

I lean my head back against the seat and listen and watch with Conor. I always loved rainy days. I would curl up in my overstuffed chair and watch as the world went by out my window. Sip on hot mint tea and just listen. Listen to the world, listen to the rain, the sounds of the cars driving by and the splash of feet through puddles. The sound of life going on around me, passing me by.

Now I am part of the sounds. Part of my own life.

"You're right. It is like music," Conor says, interrupting my daydream.

As the rain pours and the sky grows dark, we sit in silence until a new sound joins. A sputtering stuttering accompanied by the slowing of the car.

"What the hell?" Conor mutters looking down at the dash, trying to figure out why the car is slowing. "Feck," he groans.

"What? Is there something wrong with the car?" I ask. He said it was only a year old, so it should run perfectly.

"No, just my brain, and my luck. I . . . forgot to fill up on petrol."

Conor steers the SUV on to the shoulder of the empty road. We had decided a scenic route to the causeway would be more enjoyable. The surrounding landscape is nothing but green rolling hills, low stone walls, and wooden picket fences. I have seen a few buildings and houses spotting the horizon, but there are none currently visible. Even if they were there, I wouldn't be able to see them through the sheet of rain steadily pouring down outside my window. The two-lane road we're on is empty of all other vehicles. People opting to stay at home and not drive in the rain.

The SUV rolls to a stop and Conor puts it in park. Gripping the steering wheel with both hands, he let out an exasperated and defeated sigh.

"Are you saying we're out of gas and stuck on the side of the road?"

"Yeah. That's what I'm saying."

Conor looks so deflated. Groaning and rubbing his large hand over his face and stubbled jaw.

"So, what do we do? Call a tow truck to bring us some gas or." I look out the window hesitant to even suggest we go out in this to walk to a gas station. "Do we walk?"

"I'll call roadside services. They should be able to bring us some petrol. Not sure how long it'll take, considering where we are and the weather."

Pulling out his phone, Conor unlocks it and swipes a few times, then pokes aggressively at the screen, growing visibly more agitated.

"Fucking shite," he growls while tossing his phone on the dash. It clatters and skids to a stop face down. "No service."

"What? Seriously?"

My nose wrinkles in disbelief. There's no way our luck is that bad. I dig my phone out of my bag and check it. No service. Fucking shit is right. Stuck on the side of the road, out of gas, in a rainstorm, and no cell service.

Fuck a duck.

"So, what do we do, then?"

I turn to face Conor. His head is tilted back against the seat, and his eyes are closed.

"We wait."

"Wait? Wait for what?"

"For the rain to let up. Then, we walk."

I eye the rain still coming down steadily outside. It does not look like it's going to let up any time soon.

"And how long do you think that'll be?"

"Don't know. Could be an hour, could be more. Sometimes it'll rain all night," he says, his face still upturned and big shoulders drooping.

"All night?"

We could be stuck in this car all night? It's not the worst place I've spent the night but with the car off and the warmth from my heated seat wanning it's growing cold. The rain here isn't warm and humid like it can get in Texas. It's cold and frigid.

I cross my arms over my chest and rub my biceps. I'm only wearing my undershirt and gray sweatshirt, having removed my jean jacket when we got in the car. All my other clothes are in my suitcase in the trunk. Which I can get to if I climb through the back seat. Maybe if I put on a few layers, I won't get cold. As long as we're only stuck here for a short while, this should be fine. I'll hold off on crawling through Conor's car until it's necessary.

An hour goes by, and it's still raining. It's only gotten colder as we've sat here. Conor reclined his chair with his eyes closed. I wish I could sleep so easily. I'm not tired, but I am cold.

I pull my legs up to my chest and wrap my arms around them, trying to cocoon myself for warmth. Rubbing at my legs with my sleeve covered hands and rocking to create friction I press my nose down between my knees and breathe out to warm my face.

"Are you cold?" Conor asks, stirring me from my attempt to warm myself.

"A little," I admit.

Conor frowns and looks me over before glancing into the back seat, a thoughtful expression on his face. He turns back to watch the rain out the front window.

"I don't think we're going anywhere, anytime soon. We'll just have to get comfortable."

Before I can formulate a response, Conor's big body is in motion, turning in his seat and clumsily crawling into the backseat.

"What are you doing?"

"Getting comfortable."

He grunts and falls on to his ass in the backseat. Moving around the few items we've tossed back there he places them on the floor and situates himself. Stripping off his sweater, he folds it and places it on top of my jean jacket, creating a makeshift pillow. He lies down, shifting and wriggling until he's comfortable. Even though his legs are far too long. One is bent with his foot on the seat while the other stretches out as far as it can on the floor.

I watch him and scan up his long body up to his face. He's

watching me with an expectant expression.

"Well? Take off that jumper and get back here."

Twisting to better face him, I pinch my brow in confusion. Conor just looks at me, still waiting like I'm supposed to know what he means.

"I'm sorry, I don't understand."

Impatiently he waves at me, beckoning me to him. God, I want to crawl back there to him so badly. He looks so relaxed and cozy and warm. But there's no way that's what he means. Is it?

"Take off your jumper and get back here. If we're going to stay warm all night, you're going to have to get a lot closer than that."

Oh. He does mean that. But why do I have to take off my sweater? It's the only thing keeping me warm. I'm only wearing a simple white tank top beneath. I open my mouth to ask him, but he cuts off my words with a glare and a raised eyebrow.

Okay, then. No asking questions.

Tentatively I pull my sweater off over my head and shiver. Fuck, it's cold. Conor holds his hand out, and I stare at it before handing over my sweater. He rubs the material between two fingers and huffs disapprovingly. Apparently not liking the quality of the only thing I had to protect me from the cold.

"Come on, then, Leamhan Beag. You'll freeze if you just sit there."

His eyes are fixed to my exposed neck and arms. Already, goose bumps prickle my skin in the few seconds I've sat here exposed.

I nod absentmindedly and climb through the opening to the backseat far more gracefully than he had. When I get back there, I don't know what to do with myself. It doesn't matter because Conor does. He slips one hand around my waist and pulls me on top of him, forcing me to practically lay on him like a mattress. When he shifts me to slide between his legs, I realize that's exactly what he wants.

He's swapped out his sweater with mine behind his head and holds his much larger, thicker, and warmer looking sweater out.

"Lay down, Emma. I won't bite. Unless you're into that kinda thing." He gives me a wicked grin, eyes half lidded as he looks down to my chest pressed against his.

His body is warm against mine, and my hands grip at the T-shirt stretch taught across his chest. The muscles beneath flex and tighten under my touch. They're strong and firm. His chest rises and falls with a deep inhale.

Never breaking eye contact with him I scoot a little higher and position myself more comfortably on top of him. When I do, I feel the bulge in his pants and Conor bites his lips to stifle a moan that I still feel rumble faintly through his chest.

When I'm positioned where he wants me, he drapes his still warm sweater over top of us both. It covers my torso completely and even part of my butt—it's that big. Tucking the sleeves around my shoulders, Conor engulfs me in his heat and scent. It's an intoxicating mix of leather and smoky sage. I unintentionally take a deep inhale and pull him farther in to me. There are other parts of him I wouldn't mind being inside me. Parts that grow hard against my leg and tease me, causing my core to clench, and my body to involuntarily grind against his.

"There. How's that? Warmer?" Conor asks in a sultry gravel that whispers across my cheek.

I snuggle deeper into him and nod. "Yeah. Better."

"Good."

Warm fingers run up the length of my arm from my elbow to my shoulder and make small circles there. Conor's touch sends a wave of desire through me, settling right between my thighs. I want those fingers to touch me in other places, in every place. He does it again only this time in reverse, and I shiver.

"Still cold?" the words are whispered almost directly against my mouth.

In this position, there's no such thing as personal space. Our faces are inches apart and the rest of us, well there's no space between his hard muscled body, and my soft one.

"No."

We're both silent. Neither willing to break the spell that's come over us. Wrapped around us in this dark car, only the barely there light from the hidden moon and a few flashes of bright white from the lightning break the shadows within.

His other hand not tracing the freckles on my arm, wraps tightly around my back and holds me firmly to him. As if I could go anywhere. I don't plan on moving until he forces me off him. He wanted me here, so here I shall stay until further notice.

His hand on my arm moves again. This time trailing past my shoulder up my neck and along my jaw. I gasp, and my nipples harden. They rub torturously against Conor's chest. Jeez, all he did was touch my neck, and I'm turned on enough to cause wetness to pool in my panties. I'm wet and horny and Conor is hard against my thigh so close to where I want that hard length to be.

It's been so long since I've been with a guy who could make me feel this good. There have been times when I was turned on and ready to be let down by a man who has no idea what to do in bed. There were guys who lasted only seconds, not nearly long enough for me to enjoy myself. Then there were those who could go for longer but were boring, one position, repetitive motion guys. I don't think I've ever been sexually pleased by a man. Gotten close but never been so deep in pleasure that I lost myself.

I could easily lose myself with Conor. I know it. Lose myself in those sage green eyes, in those plump kissable lips, in that voice when he speaks Irish to me. *Damn that voice.* He can speak Irish to me all day long. I don't care if I can't understand him, it's worth it. I have noticed a few words that he's repeated a couple times, as if he's calling me something. I hope it's something good. The way his voice drops when he says it makes me think it is.

As I'm imagining Conor dirty talking to me in Irish, he cups my jaw. His fingers slide through my hair, tucking just under the brim of his wool hat that I'm still wearing.

"Ba mhaith liom na liopaí foirfe seo a phógadh. Ba mhaith liom a fhios ag gach orlach de do chorp. An ligfidh tú dom? Mo Leamhan Beag."

His Irish words are like hot magma poured on top of ice cream. Melting my insides at the first touch of their hot caress.

"There you go again, speaking sexy Irish. You know I have no idea what you're saying, right?"

He smirks and rubs the pad of his thumb across my bottom lip. "Just say yes."

There's no other response than "Yes."

The word is barely out of my mouth and Conor is pressing his soft lips to mine. The hand in my hair holds me tight to him as his mouth meets mine. Part hunger, part longing, and all desire. The kiss starts eagerly, as if he was holding himself back and with my one word of approval, he couldn't wait any longer.

Conor tilts my head to deepen the kiss. His tongue running along the seam of my lips, causing me to open for him. He accepts the invitation eagerly. Sliding his tongue to tangle with mine, pulling a gasping moan from me. He muffles it with one of his own. Groaning into my mouth and grinding his erection against my pelvis.

Fuck. When did I move to straddle his thigh? One of my knees is between his thighs, and I'm unabashedly dry humping his leg while he presses down on my ass with his free hand. Causing my clit to rub against his hard length. The thin material of my leggings allows me to feel every inch of his erection against me.

If he keeps doing that, I might actually come without him ever touching me. No man has ever accomplished that before.

His kiss is unrelenting, and he doesn't back away when I open up further for him. Taking everything I offer and reciprocating three-fold.

"Conor," I whimper against his mouth between kisses.

"Yes, Emma?"

Conor's lips leave my mouth to trail across my jaw and down my neck, stopping at my ear.

"What is it, Emma? Tell me, my sweet Leamhan Beag."

Those words whispered so lust filled against my ear have me quaking. His hand cupping my ass cheek descends further down, his long fingers brushing against the apex of my thighs. So fucking close to my throbbing pussy. It only makes me wetter, makes me moan again, rubbing shamelessly against his cock.

Who the fuck am I, and where did the timid, *never does anything remotely exciting*, safe Emma go? I don't know, and I don't care because I'm seconds away from coming.

"Conor . . . I . . . I'm gonna . . . Oh god, please don't stop."

"As you wish," he whispers in my ear before his mouth descends upon mine again. Claiming me in a kiss that makes me toes curl at the same moment he thrusts up hard and runs his finger right where I want it. Down the crack of my backside and along my hot, wet pussy.

"Fuck."

The word escapes me with a groan as I climax, my pussy aching for his finger to slide inside me. I squeeze my eyes shut and drive my throbbing clit against his cock, wrenching out more pulses of pleasure. My body quivers with each ripple of it shooting through my nerves.

"That's right Emma. Come for me, baby. That is the hottest fucking thing I've ever seen. Jesus Christ you're beautiful when you come. I want to see that in the light next time."

Conor's hands remain firmly in place on my now hot and sweaty body. *At least I'm no longer cold.* His hand in my hair removes the wool hat and tosses it aside, so he can run his fingers through my long red strands. Pressing my head down on his chest, he kisses the top of my head and languidly runs his fingers through the loose strands of hair. It's soothing and in moments I'm breathing normally again.

His hand on my ass hadn't shifted far, still firmly cupping my cheek, but no longer stroking me from behind.

I exhale against his chest and a blush creeps up my cheeks. I can't believe that just happened. "That was . . ."

"Hot as fuck? Yeah, I know. Next time, though, I'm going to have you naked and well-lit, so I can see you. I want to see you come undone around my cock, Leamhan Beag."

I choke on my spit. Did he just say that? He wants there to be . . . a next time?

"Next time?" I ask quietly. I need to confirm he knows what he's saying, and it's not just some lust induced nonsense brought on by his continued hard on. Because it's still there. I may have gotten off, but I don't think he did.

"Yes, next time. Because that is not all I'm going to get. I will have all of you, Emma. I'm going to bury my cock so deep in that pussy you're never going to forget how I feel inside you."

Well shit.

21 – Conor

Someone must have worn you out

I wake up with a raging boner only made worse by Emma's warm, lithe body asleep on top of me. It's a great way to wake up, even when cramped in the backseat of my SUV.

The rain has finally subsided and there's morning light streaming in through the windows. Streaks of sunlight wash across Emma's cheek and hair. Her head rests on my chest and the golden strands of her red hair shine in the dawning light. She's beautiful, and I've wanted her this close since I first met her.

Last night was fuck hot, and I meant every word I said to Emma. There's no way I can't have her completely after that. If I wanted her before, now I crave her. The sounds that came from her lips almost had *me* coming in my pants. She was so pliant and responsive. I know getting her naked and inside her would be the best night of my life.

I keep my breathing shallow so as not to disturb Emma. She looks so peaceful and content on my chest. Our body heat keeping us warm. My wool jumper still firmly wrapped around her back, cocooning us from the morning chill.

Slowly I shift my hand, which lies flat against her back, *under* the jumper. The lightweight tank she still wears has ridden up enough that my fingertips graze bare skin. She's soft and smooth under my rough, beat-up hands. Last night I barely got to feel her marvelous skin. Only her arms were exposed, the rest of her remained clothed. Yet, I still made her come with ease.

My cock twitches thinking about having her naked and writhing. Trapped between our bodies, the twitching only makes my craving worse.

My hand wanders lower down her back side, slipping beneath the waistband of her leggings and continuing south. Her arse is supple and fills my whole hand. I give it a little squeeze and Emma sighs softly under her breath in response but doesn't wake.

That little sound has more than just my cock responding, but something in my chest squeezes at my heart. My hold on her tightens infinitesimally.

I reach up and brush the back of my knuckles across her cheek and brush her hair back, so I can better see her long lashes and slightly parted lips. Her warm breath washes across my chest, and I shiver involuntarily.

"Mmmm." Emma exhales, and her eyes flutter open.

The golden rings of her hazel eyes are brighter first thing in the morning, I realize. She turns her head to look up at me and smiles shyly, partially hiding her face in my shirt.

"Good mornin', Love."

"Morning."

Emma reaches up and rubs one eye, yawning. "Did we

sleep all night?"

"Yeah. Looks like it." I don't move an inch. My hand remains planted on her bare arse cheek, and my other plays with the ends of her tousled hair.

"I don't know how you were able to sleep in this position with me on top of you." Emma's nose wrinkles. "I'm surprised I didn't smack you in the face or something during the night. Normally, I toss and turn and can't stay still."

"You must have been extremely comfortable. Or extremely tired. Something or someone must have worn you out," I tease, giving her arse a soft caress.

Emma's gaze jerks to mine and her eyes narrow on me.

"Is your hand on my ass?"

I give said arse a tighter squeeze. "This hand?"

Emma gapes at me, but I can see the smile she's trying to suppress growing at the corner of her lips. "Yes, *that* hand."

"Nope."

"Oh. Am I imagining the large strong hand down my pants, then?"

"Maybe. You could be dreaming. Because I have no idea what you're talking about."

I grin at her poor attempt to scowl at me, the smile on her face keeping her from appearing anything but amused.

"I think you're right. Perhaps I should sit up and stretch to wake up." She pushes on my chest, preparing to rise. I band my free arm around her back and tighten my hand on her arse, holding her in place.

"No. I don't think that's necessary. How about we keep dreaming?"

I pull her down and press a soft kiss to the underside of her jaw. She softens under my affection and eases back down on top of me. Her mouth angles down, and I steal a kiss before she changes her mind and tries to rise again. Our kiss is languid and unhurried. Meeting with as much passion as the night before but with far less urgency. Now that I know how keen she is on getting naked with me, I'm going to take my time. I will explore and appreciate every part of her she's willing to share with me.

Our kiss ends far too soon for my liking. I groan my disapproval while continuing to press kisses to her jaw and neck, brushing my nose along her freckled skin.

"I think we should get up. Maybe find a gas station," Emma mumbles, distracted by my continued worship of her flesh.

She tastes like sunshine and smells like dandelions in a grassy field.

"Five more minutes?" I ask, but don't wait for an answer. Instead, I press my open mouth to the juncture of her throat and shoulder and suck lightly.

"I don't think what you have in mind will only take five minutes."

"You're right. I'll need all day."

She laughs and squeezes my biceps where she holds on to for support. "Conor."

My name is a whimper on her lips, and although I'm sure it's supposed to be an admonishment, but it only deepens my desire.

"If you say my name like that again, Leamhan Beag, we're never leaving this car."

Emma giggles and reluctantly pulls away out of reach of my eager mouth. Sitting up and straddling my hips since there's nowhere else for her to sit. I appreciate the position and give my hips a little roll, pressing my aching erection into the soft heat between her thighs. She moans and bites her bottom lip, turning a torturous glare on me, smacking me playfully in the chest.

"None of that. We need to find gas and get on the road. We're way behind schedule."

Groaning I sit up and take her with me, keeping her firmly planted on my lap straddling me. I turn and press my back to the seat, stretching my legs out, working out the stiffness from sleeping in such a position. Big guys like me were not meant to sleep cramped in a backseat. But it was well worth it to break through the barrier with Emma, to get us to this point together.

I was more than willing to not get sexually involved with Emma if that's what she wants. But I'm also extremely willing to get sexually involved with Emma if she'll allow it. I'll take last night as the green light to keep moving forward with her until she tells me no.

Emma settles on my lap, resting her hands on my shoulders. Although I see desire and want in her eyes, I also see reluctance. Is it because of who I am? Because she's just a tourist? Or is it something else?

Goose bumps appear on Emma's arms and my jumper, which we used as a blanket slipped off her shoulders and pools around her hips. Picking it up, I hold it above her head, signaling for her to put it on. She pauses for only a moment before reaching her hands up and sliding them into the far too large sleeves. It practically swallows her whole, and most likely will reach her knees when she stands. She still looks perfect in it. Nan would be proud of me giving my jumper so such a woman to keep her warm.

"Thank you," Emma whispers once the dark wool is settled on her shoulders.

"You're welcome. I wouldn't want you freezing now that you don't have my body heat to keep you warm."

"No, we wouldn't want that now, would we?"

For a moment, I bask in her disheveled hair and pink cheeks. Wrapping her in the circle of my arms and memorizing every freckle on her face. She too remains quiet in contemplative silence. Her hands, which are mostly covered by the sleeves of my jumper, fiddle with the collar of my shirt.

"What's going on in that pretty little head of yours, Love?"

She shrugs one shoulder, keeping her eyes trained on my chest and her fingers. "Nothing."

"I may not know everything about women, but I do know when they say 'nothing' it's not actually nothing."

Emma grins and looks up at me from under her lashes. "Your sisters taught you well, huh?"

"Aye, they did."

"I'm thinking a lot of things, but the most important is . . . I really need to pee."

I laugh and pull her closer into me and press a soft kiss to her lips. "Your wish is my command. Let us venture out to find you a toilet."

We crawl out of the backseat of the SUV, and I stretch and everything cracks from the stiffness.

I am never sleeping in my car ever again.

I grab a fresh long sleeve shirt and Emma grabs her bag before we venture out on foot in seek of a petrol station or farmhouse. Anything really where we can use the toilet and call roadside services.

We walk over one small sloping hill and instantly come upon a petrol station. Isn't that just my luck? If we'd have gone a mere hundred meters farther, we would have gotten petrol and continued on to the causeway. I think I rather like how my night turned out despite being stranded on the side of the road.

By the time we arrive in Buchmills, it's nearly lunch time. I'm hungry and desperately need a shower, no matter how much I don't want to wash off the scent of Emma from my skin.

I find us a hotel much nicer than the ones we've stayed at. It's large and looks to be a refurbished castle. Emma's eyes are wide and bright when we enter the castle hotel. Looks like I chose well.

Approaching the front desk, we have to wait in line behind three people to wait for a room. When it's finally our turn we step up to the counter and I smile at the lad working the check in and nod in greeting.

"We need two rooms please. Preferably near one another if possible."

Emma stands at my side, a little closer than she had before. Her arm gently brushes against mine. I use my free hand to pull my wallet out of my pocket.

"I'm sorry Sir we are at capacity tonight. I only have one room available," says the lad who just became my new best friend.

Sharing a room and bed with Emma is completely fine by me.

"Of course, there's only one room left. And let me guess; only one bed?" Emma asks the man sarcastically, cocking her head at him slightly in mock frustration. Her words convey irritancy but her tone and body language lean more towards playful. As if she were expecting this to happen.

He looks up from his computer and smiles flatly while trying to retain his professionalism. "Yes miss. One king bed."

"Of course, because apparently my life is a RomCom novel."

"I'm sorry?" the clerk asks confused.

I'm a bit confused as well. "What does that mean? What does one room being available have anything to do with your life being a RomCom novel?"

"Because in every romance book or movie ever the main couple always arrives at a Hotel or Inn and there's only ever *one* room with *one* bed available. Forcing them to spend the night together even though they're not 'together'. Which inevitably leads to—" She pauses in her breathless explanation, eyeing the clerk before continuing. "Other things."

"Other things, eh? I think we've already ventured into *other things*, Love. Don't you? Sharing a room for one night isn't anything more than we've already done." I keep my voice low speaking close to her ear. Her blush is instantaneous, and I love that shade of pink on her.

"Well, that's awfully presumptuous of you."

"But am I wrong?"

Emma's cheeks darken further and the color spreads down her neck as her lips part on a soft inhale.

"Am I wrong Emma?" I ask again. If she doesn't want to stay with me, I'm not going to force her to, but I will have her tell me one way or the other. I need to know what she wants, and if it includes me.

"No," she admits on a whisper, her tongue slipping out to lick at her bottom lip.

I reach up and notch her chin upward with my knuckle. "Good."

I place a soft kiss on her nose, and she smiles. No matter what's good luck or bad luck and who has which, all I know is meeting Emma was meant to be. There's something about her, about us, that feels like we're right where we're supposed to be. Even if it is only for a short while.

Turning back to the patient clerk I smile broadly and pay for the one room with the one bed. Threading my fingers through Emma's, I lead us towards the lifts, room key in hand and ready to let our forced room sharing lead to these "other things" she spoke of. Since I already desired such an outcome my day just got a little better.

"Come on, Love. We both need a shower and a change of clothes. Then we'll go get some lunch and see the historic Giants Causeway. Okay?"

Her shy smile grows wide, and she nods at me, her body easing against mine. I pull her under my arm at my side and we make our way to the lift to go find *our* room.

22 - Emma

I'm not the little mermaid

The Giant's Causeway is just that, giant. It's huge and beautiful and magnificent. Running along the edge of yet another coastline, the numerous hexagonal columns vary in height. Some towering over head others short enough to walk over. Creating Lego-style building blocks in the remnants of a long past history.

Like many ancient sites, no one really knows where the stones came from and why they are all shaped exactly the same stacked one on top of the other. Legends say it was a giant who wanted to create a bridge to cross the sea to get to his enemy. If you believe in such creatures, I suppose it might make sense. But then why shape them as they are? To a giant, each stone would be equivalent of a Lego, and that just doesn't seem affective.

Either way, what remains is a sight to behold. The stacks look as if with one swift brush of a hand they would all come toppling down. Since each probably weighs as much as I do, that's highly unlikely.

Conor and I climb up and down the steps careful not to slip on the water that has pooled in the small divot worn in the top of the stones filled from the ocean gently crashing at its base. Thank goodness I had the forethought to buy waterproof tennis shoes. Me and puddles are not friends, and I've arrived at work with far too many soaking wet socks for my liking.

The causeway doesn't exactly have any history of instilling good luck on a person, but it's still a place everyone should go when visiting Ireland.

"So, is it as amazing as you imagined it would be?" Conor asks.

Stepping behind me, he wraps his arms around my waist and pulls me close to his chest, resting his chin against my temple. The position is personal and familiar, soothing to my chaotic thoughts. His embrace warms not only my body, but my soul.

"Yeah. It is."

"Good. I'm glad you like it."

His hold on me tightens, and I blissfully melt into his touch. Accepting the affection openly. I probably shouldn't. I'm only here for a short time, but I can't reject it. It's too nice, too perfect. All I want is more.

I've had boyfriends in the past who held me, kissed me and showed me affection, but none were Conor. None felt like he does. It's concerning what I'm feeling toward the large man holding me after only a few days' time.

In the past, when something appeared to be too good to be true, it always was. Nothing ever is good or true for me. There is only disappointment. Why would this time be any different? Why is Conor different? Perhaps he's not. Normally, I would turn around and run away. Escape from the inevitability of heartbreak and rejection. Yet I can't force my legs to step away, I can't force my body to disengage from his. I don't want to, no matter how much my logical brain is telling me to.

Just once, I want to be the impulsive daredevil that Jules always is. Leaping in blindly, letting fate guide me and hoping I land safely. I'm always running away from everything so concerned with what might happen or go wrong instead of enjoying what is going right. What is right in front of me. Being in the moment has never been my strong suit. I've always been so concerned with the future to enjoy the present.

Not anymore.

Conor's strong hands rub my arms, drawing my focus away from my spiraling thoughts and back to the beautiful scene in front of me. Back to the present and serenity of the ocean water and crisp sea breeze and comforting presence behind me.

After our *separate* showers earlier, I asked Conor if I could continue wearing his sweater for today. It smells of him and is the warmest coziest thing I've worn ever. I don't know if it's because of the wool yarn, that it's handmade or because it's his that makes it such. I let the thoughts of unhappiness and impending doom drift away on the wind and snuggle deeper into his sweater and arms. Embracing what life has put right in front of me.

There's nothing that says I can't enjoy myself a little while on my vacation. Actually, there's a rather loud voice in my head that sounds suspiciously like my best friend Jules telling me to do the exact opposite. I decide to listen to it for once.

"Come on, Love. There's more to see."

We roam the causeway climbing up and down. I slip a

few times and Conor catches me. We laugh and enjoy the afternoon together. There isn't much to do at the causeway and after an hour of wondering we leave to explore a castle on the sea nearby.

The castle is ancient and made of stone with pieces broken from it exposing the overgrown interior. And when he said a castle on the sea he wasn't joking. The stone structure looms ahead perched on a rock the size of a city block jutting out of the ocean. Connected to the mainland by only a reinforced rope bridge that sways over the water below.

The bridge looks sturdy enough but the sight of it concerns me.

"You want me to cross that?"

Conor chuckles. "What? Are you afraid?"

"Afraid? Absolutely. The odds for a normal person may be slim to none of falling off a rope bridge but for me? They quadruple."

Although I promised to focus on the present and not stress about the future, my pervasive fear of death makes it challenging. I back away, no longer liking the idea of visiting a castle on the sea. I'm not the little mermaid, places like this are not meant for me.

"Oh, no you don't. Get your pretty little arse back here. You can't run away from everything just because of the possibility something might go wrong. You never know. Maybe everything will go right. But you have to actually try things to find out."

Holding my hand tightly he pulls me toward the slightly swaying bridge I know will bring my doom, smiling the entire time. We reach the edge of the imposing cliff and look down over the edge.

White water churns below crashing harshly against jagged rocks, and I swallow hard. That does not look like a pleasant way to die.

Conor haughtily walks onto the bridge backward, grinning like the Cheshire cat as he takes one slow step after another. Putting more distance between him and the safety of solid ground. As well as from me. He holds on to each side of the rope banisters and stops midway to watch me.

"Come on Emma. There's nothing to fear. Just put one foot in front of the other. I promise I'll catch you if you fall."

"Are you going to magically sprouted wings or perhaps gills? Because that's the only way you'll be able to catch me when I fall because I'll be plummeting straight down to my death."

His grin doesn't falter a millimeter. Extending one hand out he curls his index finger, beckoning me to him. If he weren't standing on a questionable structure, I'd be over there in a heartbeat. As it is, I only manage to step one foot on the bridge before freezing in place.

Conor briskly and effortlessly crosses back to me not caring one bit when the bridge sways under his abrupt movement and the wind. Placing two hands on my hips he gently pulls me out onto the bridge, and I hold on to the rope sides like a barnacle on a boat's ass.

"That's it, Love. One foot then the other. Good. See? Perfectly safe."

I can't speak and keep my eyes glued to Conor's. If I look down, I know I'll freeze and then promptly freak out. Conor guides me by the hips the entire way, barely make it to the other side without incident. We finally make it across, and I blow out a heavy breath finally able to breathe again.

"See," Conor beams down at me, "you made it in one piece. The bridge didn't disintegrate, we didn't fall to our deaths. The world continues spinning."

I chuckle and press my face into his chest absorbing his rugged sea salt infused scent. Instantly my overwhelming panic and anxiety calm.

"Thanks," I whisper into his chest.

"You're welcome."

He kisses the top of my head and presses a steady hand to my low back. And here in his arms by a castle on the sea I feel like I've finally found myself. Found the thing that has been missing, the piece that kept falling out of place and never quite fitting, finally clicking. A piece of my heart I never knew was missing until I found it. And the thought that, in a few short days, I could leave it all behind to return to the life I never wanted but settled for scares me.

I love my family and love all the time we get to spend together. But in this moment, I don't want to leave. I don't want to go home to Texas. Is that even an option? I shouldn't be jumping to conclusions just yet.

Conor and I have only made out once. Okay it was a little more than making out, but we remained clothed. We've only known each other for like four days. Am I really willing to give up everything back home to stay here? With him?

There isn't enough time in the world to answer that question. If the time comes when I have to decide I'll just have to let my gut, and my heart decide. Until then I'm not going to calculate the risks. I'm not going to stew over the many things that could go wrong and the many outcomes that could end in disaster.

Leaning my head back I look up at Conor and stand on

tippy toe to reach his lips with mine. The kiss is chased, and I don't linger, if I did things would get out of hand. Conor's surprised look turns heated, and I take that as my cue to back away before he does anything about it.

"Come on big guy. Let's explore."

The castle on the sea proves more entertaining when a stray sheep wanders its way through the overgrown ruins. Eating its way through the foliage and ignoring all attempts of people to pet and befriend it.

We stay till the sun begins to dip below the crest of the world and make the treacherous journey back across the rope bridge to leave. I tried to convince Conor we could live on the island in the castle ruins forever, but he promptly pointed out the lack of plumbing. Which I must admit is a deal breaker.

The entire drive back to our hotel, Conor keeps his hand on my thigh, squeezing occasionally and rubbing his thumb across my leggings. The tips of his fingers rest under the hem of his sweater that fits me more like a dress that a top. The quiet serenity of the drive and the sunset washing colors across the horizon soothes the tangle of nerves that always seem to be at odds inside me.

23 – Conor

Her kisses are my kryptonite

Today was not anything that I expected when I suggested my chauffer services to Emma. I figured we would chat, maybe flirt, I would follow her around as she did typical boring tourist shite and then she would give me back my good luck clover, and I would go on with my life. If I were lucky, I might have a little more fun with the alluring American but nothing more.

Today was more. So much more. I could feel myself slowly shifting. From simple amusement to true interest. My purpose for this deviation in training becoming more than a good luck retrieval. Hell, I haven't even thought about that stupid clover in at least twenty-four hours.

When Emma is near I can't stop myself from touching her. Brushes of my arm against hers, my hand resting on her thigh as I drive. I remain close to her as we walk through the hotel lobby and down the street to a small restaurant for supper. Even when we sit across from one another I stretch out my legs to press against hers under the table. Unable to break this newfound closeness we've developed since last night.

We've eaten our food and, in true Irish fashion, have a pint to end our night when my mobile rings. Thankfully it's been silent all day, but I'm curious who would ring me at this time of night.

Pulling it out of my pocket I see my mum's photo on the screen.

"I have to take this, I'll be right back," I tell Emma apologetically as I set down my pint and stand to walk to a quieter area to speak with my mum.

We talk pretty regularly, so it's not completely unheard of for her to ring me for no reason.

"Hey, Mum."

"Hello, honey. How's everything?"

"Grand. Just having some supper."

"Lovely."

I can hear her smile and like a horrid son, want to end the call without suspicion to be with Emma. She's finally loosening up, and I do not want to miss out on relaxed fun Emma.

"What's going on?" I ask, hoping to get her to admit the reason for her call, so we can hang up sooner.

"Oh not too much. Nan is stirring up her usual amount of mayhem and your dad is still having those back pains."

Shite. This feels like a 'let's catch up and chat for a bit' kind of call. It won't be easy to end it without suspicion. She knows I stay in most nights so saying I'm out she'll ask who I'm with, what I'm doing. Considering the time it would take to explain the whole situation with Emma I don't want to get into it right now.

"Sorry to hear that. How's the farm doing?"

"Splendid. We're hard at work getting all the sheep sheered for Woolapalooza next week, but I'm not sure we'll be able to get it all done in time. We're a little shorthanded with Ian out on Holiday."

And there's the reason for her call tonight. Like most mums, mine loves to guilt trip me into helping out on the farm whenever she can. Starting with "everything's grand" before effortlessly slipping it in that they have lots of work to do and not enough people to get it done in time.

"Uh-huh, I see," I say noncommittally. I've been through this song and dance with her plenty of times. She wants me to offer to come and help and that's not going to happen. Especially not now when I have Emma.

I look over to our table to check on Emma. She's happily watching the musician in the corner playing his guitar and singing in Irish. He too is looking in her direction, a grin growing on hip lips. He probably thinks she's here alone and is planning his pickup line that he won't get to use on her. I need to finish this conversation before his set ends.

"Your father just isn't the spry young lad he used to be and can't do as much as he once could."

"Yeah, getting old is a shame. Gets the best of us," I quip. I hear Mum scoff on the other end of the line but there's a light chuckle at the end.

"If you're not too busy we could really use some young muscle around the farm to get all the sheering done, so we can process all the wool in time."

And there it is.

"I don't know, Mum. I'm really busy with training for my next fight, and I don't know that I'll be able to get away to help right now."

It's not often I tell my mother no, any smart Irish lad wouldn't dare. But this is poor timing.

She sighs and pauses for effect before speaking. "Fine then. I understand. Your poor dad will just have to push through the pain."

"Look, Mum, I would come if I could, but I just can't. I'm really sorry. If anything changes, I'll let you know. Okay?"

I try to assuage her before she starts laying it on thick. Plus, I see the smarmy musician wrapping up his set.

"Okay."

"Great. I really gotta go, I'll talk to you later, Mum. Love you."

I hang up before I can hear her response, making my way quickly across the dining hall to Emma at our table. This time taking the seat right next to her and draping my arm over the back of her chair. Marking my territory like a goddamn dog. Leaning in I whisper in Emma's ear, I give the long-haired musician a glare over her head that communicates everything he needs to know.

Emma is mine.

"You look like you could use another drink," I whisper to Emma. I had nothing to say to her before leaning in. I just wanted to get close to get my point across to the lad eyeing her and trying to see beneath my jumper Emma still wears.

Emma giggles and looks down at her half empty pint glass. She's stuck with cider, not the thick Guinness like myself. She is much smaller than me so that's probably best.

"Well, maybe just one more. But that's all. I'm not much of a drinker and tend to be a light weight."

She looks up at me with bright golden eyes made glassy from the one and a half pints she's already drank. She's still clear though, still focused. I raise my hand to wave down the server and order two more pints for us. Sticking with the pear cider Emma seems to enjoy most.

"So, tell me, Love. Are you feeling any luckier?"

"Oh, loads more lucky than I ever did. I've had multiple meals in a row delivered just as I ordered them and haven't once stubbed a toe on anything. Not to mention I haven't broken anything, lost anything or spilled anything in days. This is fantastic!"

Emma is animated and smiling broadly with every energetic word. Since she's in a such good mood I figure I could ask her a little more about her bad luck.

"Have you ever wondered why all the bad luck?"

She taps her chin and pinches her lips to one side thinking. "I've had theories but none of them made any sense. Eventually I just figured the stars all aligned improperly when I was born causing this fluctuation in the cosmos that ended with me getting the short end of the stick."

"Why would your birth be the cause?"

"I was born on Friday the thirteenth, at one thirteen pm. Or in military time, thirteen hundred and thirteen hours. So you see? Doomed from the start."

Emma smiles and takes a sip of her fresh cider the server sits down in front of her. I play with the ends of her long red hair that hang down her back, relishing in the soft strands wrapped around my fingers.

She doesn't seem too upset about the supposed jinxing of her birth. I'm not sure if she believes it or not. Perhaps after so many years it's just fact to her.

"You know the number thirteen is considered lucky in some cultures. You could actually be the luckiest person and just not realize it. Have you ever considered that? That maybe all the things you think are bad luck are actually just a precursor to the good?"

She stops drinking and sets down her pint glass, making sure it's on the little paper coaster before turning her attention to me. There's curiosity in her eyes and a far-off pondering. I don't think she's ever looked at her luck as anything but purely bad and just taken it at face value.

"What do you mean? That me losing my luggage on every flight was a blessing? That breaking every high heel I've ever worn was positive? Or that being swindled by an out of business tour company was good luck?"

Her initial reaction was hopeful, but as she lists things that, yes, seem like bad luck, she grows more and more disbelieving. I think about it for a minute, considering each of her points. Nan always said everything happens for a reason, that there's always a silver lining if you're willing to look for it.

"Okay, so losing your luggage sucks, but it did teach you to be more efficient with packing. It also keeps you from checking a large suitcase and paying that ridiculous fee the airlines all charge now."

Emma's pinched brow shifts and softens a little considering my argument. She says nothing, but I can see her mindset shifting, so I continue.

"Breaking a high heel forces you to always wear flats. Keeping you stable on your feet and from falling over or rolling your ankles. And as for the tour company being out of business, well . . . If it weren't for them, we wouldn't be sitting here right now enjoying a pint together. We wouldn't have been forced together. We would have missed out on all this." I gesture with my hand to the table and restaurant around us.

The crease between her brows and the pinch in her lips vanish as she looks around and rubs the condensation on her glass. I pick up my pint that I haven't touched since the server sat it down and take a hearty gulp. Giving her a minute to digest my altered perception of her bad luck.

"So, every bad thing that happened wasn't actually bad?"

I shake my head with a little shrug. "I can't say for sure everything had a silver lining. Sometimes life is just shite. But there's a chance most things led to something good."

"And I'm actually lucky?"

"Maybe. Sometimes all it takes is a different perspective to see everything in a new light. Manifest destiny, and all that."

Emma nods quietly. "I'd never really thought of it like that. You could be right."

"I usually am," I give her a wide smile and playful wink.

She bumps me with her shoulder and laughs. It's just as heart melting as before but this time feels lighter, more optimistic. I did that, I made her feel that way. The thought swells in my gut and churns in a way I've never felt before.

"Come on, then, Love, finish your pint before the restaurant closes because you took forever sipping it."

We sit for a little longer finishing our drinks and listening to a new musician that replaced the flirty one from before. Leaving to walk down the street back to our hotel both with a little buzz going that causes us to sway and laugh at everything.

I keep Emma wrapped in one arm the entire way back to our room.

When I got the room earlier, we were sober and in the light of day. Now in the darkness of night after a couple drinks the one bed shines like a beacon in the dim room. Making it very clear that we both agreed to share a room and a bed and now the time has come to do just that.

Emma doesn't seem to come to the same realization as I do, if she does, she doesn't mention it. She just slips off her shoes and sets her purse on the dresser against the wall. I remove my own shoes lining them up next to her much smaller ones. I kind of like how they look next to each other.

Watching her I remain still as she pulls my jumper off over her head and lets it fall to the floor. She's only wearing a thin tank top beneath, this one black. All of her curves are visible now. The slight flaring of her hips, the full roundness of her arse and soft curve of her breasts. Those freckles I like so much bared and tempting. Calling me to discover them all.

Hanging on the wall above the dresser is a large mirror allowing me a view of both her front and back, from my place behind her. Emma's eyes are half lidded as she runs her fingers through her hair making small little mewling sounds of pleasure as she works out the tangles in her long tresses. Pulling her hair to one side she exposes her neck and shoulder.

Stepping closer to her I bring our bodies nearly flush and wrap one hand around her hip and slip the other into her hair close to her scalp, holding her still. Her half lidded eyes find mine in the mirror, and we don't need to speak to know what the other wants. She can see it in my heated gaze and feel it in my growing erection pressed to her backside.

Her head tilts a tiny bit more to the side. Asking, pleading for me to take her. Slowly I lean down and press a soft open-mouthed kiss to her tender throat. She sucks in a sharp breath and arches into my touch, pressing her arse harder against my cock. I moan into her skin, gripping her harder.

I bring my lips to her ear and nip at it playfully, relishing in her response.

"Ar mhaith leat dom fuck tú, Leamhan Beag?" I ask as Emma gives a little whimper and shiver against me. Fuck I like that. "An maith leat é nuair a labhraím Gaeilge leat?"

"What did you say? You're always speaking Irish to me, and I have no idea what you're saying, but it sounds amazing."

I chuckle against her skin peppering it with soft kisses. "I asked if you like me speaking Irish to you. And if you want me to fuck you."

Her plump arse presses harder against my cock with another gasp followed by a soft groan. I love the way her body responds to mine. Releasing her hair my hand runs down her side finding the hem of her shirt and slides underneath. Feeling the hot press of her stomach against my palm makes me groan. There's so much of her body I have yet to see but have fantasized about.

Where are all her freckles? Does she have them on her inner thigh? Between her breasts? What noises will she make when I lick every single one?

There are so many things I want to do to this woman, with this woman it surprises me.

"Yes," she responds in an uneven breath.

"Yes what?"

"Yes, I like it when you talk Irish to me. Even though I have no idea what you're saying. I kind of like guessing what you're saying."

Emma rolls her head back, reaching a hand up to loosely wrap around my neck, holding me close to her. Pressing my mouth close to her ear I nibble on her lobe which causes a shiver across Emma's skin.

"And what else, Leamhan Beag? Tell me."

"I want you to . . ."

"Yes?"

"Fuck me." The words are a whisper on a breath, but that doesn't matter. She still said them.

I growl, growing harder. My hand finds its way up her top and cups her breast. Her bra little more than a thin piece of fabric allows me to feel her beneath easily, with no elaborate lace or padding. When I grip her all I feel is her, and her taut nipple hardening under my fingertips. I roll it between forefinger and thumb before pinching it gently, and she lets out a moan that has my other hand traveling south, cupping her pussy and grinding my cock against her.

"Are you sure, Leamhan Beag? Don't tease me, I can't take it right now."

"Yes, I'm sure. I've wanted you to touch me and do all the naughty things to me I've dreamt about but never been bold enough to tell a man I wanted."

Her nails dig into the soft skin of my neck, and I groan again, sucking on the soft flesh of her shoulder, trying to devour her.

"I'll do anything you want me to, Love. Just say the word Emma, and I'm yours."

I run my finger down her hot pussy through her leggings. Her head lulls back on to my shoulder, giving me a perfect view down her shirt. With my other hand, I knead her breast and those perfect nipples. I want to suck on them, play with them and drive her wild with my touch.

Emma's head turns toward me, allowing me the perfect angle to kiss her, sealing our lips together in a devastatingly demanding kiss. Our tongues tangle in a battle for dominance. She's needy and insistent, seeking as much as I give. Her free hand slips down to cover mine pressed between her thighs. Pressing my fingers harder against her heated core.

"I want you Conor. More than I've ever wanted any man."

Her words send me spiraling. She's going to be mine, and I feel at the same time I'm going to be hers.

Removing my hands from her body I spin her by the hips to face me and reconnect our mouths as soon as she's facing me. I can't stop kissing her. Her kisses are my kryptonite. They make me weak, and I would do anything she told me to if she were to just keep kissing me.

Her hands reach for my jeans undoing my button and zipper pushing at my waistband. We make quick work of the clothing between us. She slides my jeans to the floor, and I kick them away, ripping her tank top over her head. I peel her leggings off her long, toned legs. Before the night is over I will have them wrapped around me. Around my shoulder, or my hips, if I'm lucky both. And I will discover and memorize every freckle on her body.

I groan loudly when she grips my shaft through my boxer briefs. I'm so painfully hard now. She still wears her bra and panties and I want to pull them off with my teeth. As a matter of fact that sounds like the perfect plan.

With one arm under her arse, I move Emma to the bed, spreading her out preparing to indulge and feast upon her. Crawling between her spread legs I place lingering kisses on her skin, trying to find as many freckles as I can, until I catch her panties in my teeth. She makes sweet little whimpering noises under me that only make me need her more.

With her cute little black cotton panties between my teeth, I remove them from her body and bask in her beauty. Her bare pussy glistens with her arousal. I don't hesitate to lean down and swipe my tongue from her opening up to her pretty pink clit.

24 - Emma

I always wanted to be a headboard knocker

My mind goes blank when Conor licks up the center of my pussy sucking on my clit and circling it with his tongue. Guys have tried oral on me before, but they weren't very good at it. I had to either step in and help out or fake it, so they would move on.

There is no faking it with Conor. His talented tongue is not only good at seducing me in Irish but in knowing exactly how to make me squirm. My toes curl, and my back bows as he continues to feast on me like a god damn deity. He already has me climbing that peak to my first orgasm. *Fuck. Is he going to make me come more than once?* That would be a first.

Conor introduces his fingers pressing two easily inside me while continuing to do devilish deeds with his tongue. Pushing my pleasure higher and higher as his fingers slide in deeper and deeper.

I grip his thick dark hair that looks more brown than red in the dim light of the hotel room. His customary copper strands dulled without the gleam of the sun to brighten them. Squirming and pulsing from his focused attention on my needy pussy. I've never been so needy before. But I crave Conor, crave his touch, his kiss, and his naughty Irish words.

Two more strokes, and he's pushing me over that edge effortlessly. My legs clamp around his ears, and my pussy pulses with my orgasm which he elongates with his continued licks and sucks while his fingers remain buried inside me.

"That's it, Love. Come for me."

His hot breath brushes over my sensitive sex, and I shiver as he places soft kisses against my inner thigh and even softer ones on my clit and pussy knowing how sensitive he's made me.

Fuck.

This man might be perfect.

Unlocking my legs from around his neck, he explores my pliant body, his tongue lingering from my belly button to my covered breasts. Reaching behind me he removes the thin bra effortlessly throwing it to the abyss of the hotel room floor already scattered with the rest of our clothes. Immediately he sucks one hard nipple into his mouth. The sensation ripples through my body and makes me shake.

"You taste like heaven, Leamhan Beag," Conor whispers against my skin his short beard tickling as he shifts from one nipple to the other. Hardening it further with little flicks of the tip of his tongue before sucking it into his mouth.

"What does that mean?"

"Hmm?" Conor hums distractedly.

I try to focus on getting an answer out of him rather than the wicked things his tongue is doing to me.

"That name Lame hon bee og."

"Leamhan Beag."

"Yeah that. What's that mean? You've called me that a number of times now."

He hums again and removes his mouth from my nipple to bring his face level with mine. Laying on top of me he holds his weight up on one side. Using one powerful arm to steady himself while his free hand brushes against my cheek.

"It means Little Moth. Because like the moths you love so much you are beautiful and entrancing. Only here for a short while before you're gone. And when you do leave, my life will have a little less beauty in it."

His words are spoken in truth with no mockery or pretense. He means every single syllable, and I melt a little inside. That's what he's been calling me this entire time? Thinking of me in such a way? And here I was calling him big guy and ogling his muscles and tattoos.

Tattoos which shift and ripple with every flex of his muscles beneath.

"Oh." Is all I can manage through the haze of lust and post orgasm brain. "Who knew beneath all the muscles was a poet."

I internally smack myself in the head. *Real smooth Emma.*

Conor just chuckles and presses and long, languid kiss against my lips that has me softening into his touch. When he pulls away, I've forgotten what we were talking about.

"Don't worry, Love, the only thing poetic about me are my words."

Conor rolls over to reach down to the floor where he plucks something from the pocket of his jeans. His wallet, from which he produces a condom.

"Did you expect to get laid on this trip?" I ask partially

annoyed if he thought he would be hooking up with girls while we were traveling together.

He rolls back over on to his side facing me, a lust filled grin on his lips.

"Calm down, Leamhan Beag. The only person I was hoping to get naked in bed with is you," he says grinning at the frown on my face, which lessens as I watch him tear open the packet.

He hasn't removed his boxer briefs yet, and he shoves them down and kicks them away releasing his erect cock. It's thick, long and pink at the tip that leaks with a drip of precum. I unconsciously lick my lips while watching him roll the condom over his massive erection. He has a well manscaped groin, the dark hair trimmed and framing his proud cock.

To clarify the hand to dick size ratio is one hundred percent accurate in Conor's case. Just in case you were wondering.

He gives himself a quick squeeze and strokes down his shaft to cup his balls giving them a little tug to ease his aching. It only makes me wetter watching him touch himself. I always liked watching a man stroke himself.

Conor notices my interest and groans while giving himself another long stroke. A little whimper slips past my lips, and I wriggle rubbing my thighs together, the need building between them again.

"Easy, Love, or you'll make me come too soon," he chides in a playful and tortured tone.

"We wouldn't want that now, would we? I haven't even gotten to play with you yet."

Conor rolls over caging me with his body, pressing his hips between my legs, forcing them apart to make room for his massive body and cock.

He's so wide. His shoulders flex and block the little bit of light coming from the table lamp across the room. His tattoos are dark inky lines patterning his skin that make him appear even more devilish in the low light. My own personal devil willing to do all the naughty things of my dirtiest sex dream.

My hands roam his chest tracing the lines and sharp edges of his muscles. Then across the swirling intricate design of the Celtic knot work tattoo sprawling across his shoulder and pec. Venturing further I scrape his abs, which contract on a sharp inhalation as I keep moving south. I feel his Adonis belt and the light trail of hair leading me to his hard cock.

I reach it and grab hold giving it a tight squeeze. Conor's eyes practically roll back into his head. The bruising around his eye socket and cheek now a light yellow and the split on his lip is nearly healed. The small injuries adding to his devilish appeal.

Conor instinctually pulls back lifting his hips to bring his cock back to line up with my pussy. I'm already wet and ready for him, I've been dreaming of this for days ever since I first saw him shirtless.

He lines himself up and slides in, slowly stretching me to accommodate his size. The pressure he creates feels incredible. Past experiences don't hold a candle to Conor and his cock. Not only is he generously proportioned, but he moves in smooth thrusts with a purposeful roll of his hips that sends him deeper with each movement.

"Fucking Christ," Conor curses, pressing his face into the crook of my neck burying his face in my messy hair. Growling he rolls his hips and presses himself inside me.

I moan and meet his hips with mine, pressing up to bring him deeper. My pussy clamps around him, and we both groan in unison.

"You feel fucking perfect, Emma."

Conor's strong arm slides beneath my back and tightens. Locking us together chest to chest, lifting me partially off the bed. I lock my legs around his hips and grip him even tighter.

His mouth trails down my chest until he can pull one tight nipple into his mouth. He nips it with his teeth and a shudder runs through my entire body at the prick of pain and pleasure. His pelvis moves, shifting his cock inside me but not pulling out one inch. It feels maddening. I want him to fuck me, pound into me like a mad man and ravage my body. I'm desperate for it, for him. Never in my life has anything felt so good, so right.

"Conor, please move. I need you to move, to fuck me."

His teeth nip at my nipple again, but he does as I ask. Pulling out and pounding back inside in a long hard stroke. Then he does it again, and again, and again.

"Yes, just like that. Shit you feel so fucking amazing."

"That's it Emma. Take from me what you want. I'll give you everything and more," he rasps against my breast, now pumping faster and harder, rocking the bed with his motion, knocking the headboard against the wall.

That's fucking hot. I always wanted to be a headboard knocker. To have a man to be so ravenous for me he couldn't hold himself back. Taking me and fucking me until we were both partially dead.

Placing my hands on either side of Conor's face I pull him up to mine, brushing a soft kiss against his stubbled jaw. Rubbing against him like a cat wanting to rub its scent on its property.

"Don't hold back Conor. I want all of you. I want the animal lurking beneath the surface," I breath into his lips.

Conor growls and pumps into me fast and hard a few times before wrapping both arms around me lifting me off the bed completely. Sitting back on his heels Conor holds me easily wrapped around his torso with his cock still buried deep inside me. My arms wrap around his neck, and he doesn't stop his motion. Gripping my ass with both hands he lifts me off his cock and swiftly thrusts up while pulling me back down.

Conor fucks me sitting up and moving for the both of us, lifting me like I weigh nothing. He thrusts upward when he pulls me back down. All that can be heard are heavy breaths, skin smacking with every hard thrust, and the bed thumping against the wall.

I don't know if there's anyone in the room next to us, but they're probably not happy right now.

My body is wound so tight, and I'm so close to coming again I can't stand it.

"Are you going to come for me again, Leamhan Beag?"

"Mmhmm," I wine, biting my lip. "I'm so close. Please make me come again, it feels so fucking good when you do."

Conor's movements become slightly erratic his own release imminent. He presses me down on his cock rubbing my clit against his hard muscles and that's enough to send me over the edge. I scream and bite into the muscles of his shoulder to muffle the sound. My pussy throbs and pulses against his thick shaft. My body quaking with the unbelievable orgasm shooting through my body.

"Fuck, Emma. God damn it, you're gonna make me come."

I roll my hips and another bolt of pleasure shoots through me as Conor growls out his own release. Stilling inside me as his cock twitches and pulses as he comes. Conor groaning loudly against my shoulder, his face buried in my wild hair.

Our bodies are slick with sweat and other bodily fluids, but we remain sitting in the same position. Locked together and breathing heavily.

I lean back enough to lift Conor's head from where it dropped against my shoulder. Cupping his face, I press a kiss to his lips that seems to relax him even further.

"Let's get washed up, then we both need some rest," he says.

Stepping off the bed on to the floor Conor walks us to the bathroom without disengaging from me and goes right to the shower. Never once breaking our lazy kisses.

25 – Conor

Can I keep you?

Falling asleep with Emma wrapped around me is heaven. Waking up to her kicking me in the shin, not so much. In her sleep she's sprawled out next to me, face down and limbs spread wide. One leg is hitched up and the other stretched out. The sheets and blankets a tangled mess at the foot of the bed.

Emma shivers in her sleep, and I reach down to pull the blanket back up over us. Even covered I fear she may be too cold. I remedy that by sharing my excessive body heat with her once again, just as I had in the backseat of my SUV last night.

Reaching out I thread my arm between her thighs and grab on to one perfect ass cheek. She put on a simple pair of panties after our shower, stealing my T-shirt that lay haphazardly on the floor. She looked so sexy in it I couldn't deny her. Especially when she looked up at me through her lashes with giant doe eyes.

What is it about women with big golden hazel eyes that

just melts away all my control? Perhaps it's not all women, just Emma.

Once my hold is secure on her I effortlessly pull her smaller frame close. Slipping her leg over top of mine and cradling her hips against my stomach, I twine our bodies together. Wrapping one arm around her back and pressing my face close to her chest. She smells like a mix of us and sex. The scent is intoxicating. Even in my half-asleep state, my body stirs at the memory of her body tensing and softening against mine when she came.

Emma makes sleepy sounds of disapproval which turn to quiet moans of contentment as she settles against me. Her own arms circling my shoulders and neck.

My entire being alters when she sighs and relaxes back into sleep against me. Her trust in me even in sleep does something to the soft spot inside me underneath all the hard muscles and MMA fighter exterior.

Perhaps it's because I grew up around so many women, but to have earned the right to hold her and protect her after sharing ourselves with one another so intimately feels like a gift of the highest worth. More valuable than diamonds or jewelry or gold. More precious and desirable than even winning the most important fight of my career. I would lose every match if the alternative was to hold Emma every night like this.

Perhaps I am a poet after all considering the things I want to say to her, to do for her.

Curled and entwined with Emma I fall back asleep to wishful thinking of a future with someone like her. No not someone like her, but *her*. With Emma. If only there were a way to convince her to stay.

When I wake again, she's still in my arms. Now laying

more on top of me, her leg hooked around my thigh and her head nestled in the crook of my shoulder.

She wakes slowly, blinking away the sleep and rubbing the glassiness from her eyes. Her crooked smile stretches as she yawns.

"Good morning," she says, waking a little more fully.

"Mornin' Love. Sleep well?" I ask with a knowing smirk on my lips. I doubt she'll remember me pulling her to me during the night. She was out like a light.

"Mmhmm," she murmurs while snuggling back down against my chest.

I wrap my arms tighter around her and let her settle in, not wanting her to go anywhere anymore than she seems to want to. We're both content lying here in the hazy morning light.

I run my fingers through her tangled hair trying to smooth it down while pressing a soft kiss to the top of her head. Her sigh is deep and warm across my chest. There have seldom been times that I've enjoyed cuddling with a woman like this. I've stayed the night with women and even held them in bed, but none felt like this. None drew me in so deeply that I never wanted to move again.

I want to stay here forever, in our castle room locked away from all our responsibilities outside these four walls. Because I know eventually after leaving this room the realities of the world beyond this unplanned holiday will sink in.

I haven't even thought about my upcoming match in days. Emma taking over every moment of my consciousness. It's probably the first time in the last decade I haven't been thinking about training or matches constantly. I can already hear Rory telling me *I told you so.*

No matter how much I don't want to get up we have

to eventually, rising slowly to get ready for another day of adventures. One of the few I have left with Emma. And I plan on making the most of our time together. Maybe even enacting a few of the plans I concocted last night while falling asleep to convince her to stay.

I touch and kiss Emma every opportunity I get. Trying my best to distract her while she dresses and pull her back into bed. I manage a short make out session and almost get her naked again, but she stops it before we can go any further sadly.

Reluctantly I dress, and we pack up our bags, checking out of the hotel and making our way back on to the road. Emma doesn't have any specific places to visit on the way back to Dublin, so I decide for us where we'll be going next.

There's a place my sister once told me about, it's nothing like the cliffs or the causeway, but I think Emma will like it. All I want now is to make her smile, to show her a part of Ireland she would miss were she to leave.

Our drive is filled with easy conversation, and when I'm not shifting gears my hand rests firmly on her thigh. My thumb stroking soothingly. Most of the time her hand rest atop mine stroking the skin between my knuckles. It doesn't seem to be a conscious action, just a natural reaction to my hand being there.

Maybe there is a chance for more beyond the next few days.

The thought has me smiling and trying to hide the giddiness a grown man shouldn't possess. It's hard not to when the possibility of having more time with Emma is a real option. I would give her anything she asked of me to keep her with me. If she wanted to fly to Texas every week to visit her family I would agree. I'd probably even agree to moving to America if she wanted it.

For years I've been looking for a partner, a love to call mine. I thought it would be a local Irish girl. I thought it would be easy and obvious. We would meet and go out and the rest would be history. I never thought an American cursed with bad luck with a time limit would be the one to make me fall. To make me desire that forever with her. Fate works in mysterious ways.

"Are you ever going to tell me where you're taking me?" Emma asks while watching out the window trying to decipher our destination.

"No. You'll just have to wait and see."

"That's no fair."

"Yes it is. We've been doing everything you want to do and now you're just going to have to trust me."

I turn and give her a teasing grin. She tries to smother her smile by biting her lips between her teeth, but there's no hiding it. She's wearing her denim jacket again and fiddles mindlessly with the yellow and pink moth pin I gave her. The gesture is endearing.

I give her leg a squeeze, and she tucks her chin to her chest returning her gaze back out the window.

When we turn on to a gravel road Emma begins to appear worried. Looking around for some structure or sign, but she won't find one. Where I'm taking her isn't in any tourism book or listed on any blog site. It isn't a historic landmark or well-known place. Which is exactly why I'm taking her there.

There won't be a visitors center or swathes of people lingering about taking photos. It'll be only us.

It only takes a few minutes to get to our destination. The trees around us opening up to expose a wide field filled with a plethora of wildflowers. Dandelions mix with daisies and a few patches of purplish bluebells.

Emma plasters her face to the window and is jumping out of the car as soon I park. Her eyes alight with wonder as she surveys the flower field. On the far side resides a small loch with a stone structure across the water that appears to be a castle or home. Castles are prominent in Ireland, and many have been renovated into manors and homes.

There aren't any cars or people I can see around it, so we appear to be alone. Except for the butterflies and bumble bees that land on the flowers collecting the pollen within.

"Oh my god. It's beautiful," Emma gasps and walks farther into the patches of flowers. Most don't reach higher than her shin making it easy to walk through the field.

Still, she walks gingerly trying not to trample a single bud. Even being careful as she is tiny white puffs flutter free from the dandelions as they tend to do at the gentlest touch.

She stops and turns in a circle, absorbing the entire site around her. Smiling wide and instilling even more hope in my heart.

"Do you like it?" I ask sheepishly coming to stand beside her.

Emma turns her sparkling eyes on me and laughs. "Do I like it? Of course I like it. Who wouldn't? It's beautiful Conor."

"Good. I wanted to bring you somewhere we could be alone. To show you some of the everyday beauty of Ireland." *To convince you this could be a place you can stay and live with me. To show you that you can be happy here.*

I keep that last part to myself, still not ready to ask her to stay. If I ask too soon before I've convinced her she can choose to stay she might say no and retreat to her fear of all the things probable but highly unlikely.

"Come on there's more."

"More?" She raises a brow at me, and I can't wait to show her not only what I have planned for today but for the rest of the foreseeable future.

~Emma~

The sight before me is indescribable. Conor has brought me to a fairy wonderland. Only the gentle lapping of water and distant sounds of bees and birds can be heard, no cars or city noise. There's even butterflies. Not as amazing as moth's but still beautiful. This is a place I would have killed for back in Texas. Somewhere quiet and serene with no one around. There are so many places I'm finding in Ireland that make me feel like I've died and gone to heaven. Not to mention the god like man standing next to me. It's because of him that I get to experience this place. He looked nervous when we first arrived unsure how I would react. How anyone could react other than in utter awe is inconceivable.

This places ethereal beauty transcends reality.

Conor said he had more to show me than the field of dreams. He doesn't elaborate, but he does walk back to the SUV and pull out a few paper shopping bags. Where they came from, I have no idea. He must have secretly gotten whatever is in them when we stopped at the gas station, and I went to use the bathroom.

He returns, standing in the middle of the flowers waiting patiently, and very curious.

"Come on," he gestures with an elbow, and I slip my hand around his bicep and let him lead me to wherever the hell he wants.

We don't go far, finding a clear space where soft mossy clover like grass grows surrounding a centuries old tree stump. I half expect to find a fairy circle in its center. Thankfully it's clear of mushroom and flower circles, so I don't have to worry about upsetting the fairy folk.

Conor sets down the bags and from one of them produces a woven wool blanket in the most beautiful shade of crimson. Unfolding it and shaking it out to cover a section of the soft grassy ground next to the tree stump.

"A picnic?"

"Well, there isn't much to do in a field of flowers, now is there?" Conor raises one sardonic eyebrow at me, and I smirk back at him.

"I could think of a few things."

His expression shifts to a wicked knowing gleam. "As can I, Leamhan Beag. Perhaps we can eat what I brought first, then partake in more . . ." His eyes roam over my body hungrily before he continues. "Entertaining activities," he finishes.

"Maybe," I say playfully shrugging one shoulder, trying to hide my blush and grin but fail miserably.

"First things first. I brought lunch and dessert."

He opens another bag and pulls out one food container after the other setting them on the blanket. I move to sit on the blanket and help him arrange the containers, opening each to inspect its contents.

Conor has chosen simple items for our lunch consisting of a mixed fruit salad, a container of meats and cheeses as well as a bag of bread rolls and a sealed cylinder of hot soup. For dessert he's bought far too many items to eat in one sitting. There's chocolate cake, a sugared ball that could be a truffle, a yellow substance resembling peanut brittle, clover-shaped sugar cookies, a green frosted cupcake, and....

"Gummy bears?" I give Conor a bemused grin. With all the specialty desserts I hadn't expected something so simple.

"I didn't know what you liked, so I grabbed a bit of everything, figured if you weren't a fan of the baked goods, you might like something simple, recognizable," he says with a self-conscious laugh.

He's so cute when he's nervous. It's hard not to smile at the big, tattooed guy who worries about what dessert I'll like. He eases when he sees my approval.

"No worries. Normally I wouldn't eat anything I don't know but things are changing now."

"Yes they are," he says low. His intense green eyes never wavering from mine.

I feel as if we both mean more than we're saying. A girl can hope. When a man like Conor stares at you like he's staring at me know it's impossible not to. With his heated stare watching me expectantly hopeful with so much restrained emotion I want to curl up in his arms and never leave.

Conor sits next to me on the blanket and leans back against the tree stump, allowing me to choose what I want to eat first.

We share a delicious creamy potato soup. Conor chuckles when he tries to take a bite, and I pull the large cup out of his reach. I doubt he couldn't reach it if he wanted to, but he allows me to finish the potato-y goodness before I taste every piece of dessert he picked. My favorite is the chocolate cake which he informs me is made with Guinness and an Irish buttercream frosting. Saving the gummy bears for later, they'll be a nice snack on the drive.

We finish our meal and put the containers back in the bag and off to the side. Allowing us to spread out on the blanket and get comfortable.

Conor pulls me in-between his legs and leans my back to his front. Caging me between his powerful thighs and loosely draping his arms around my middle. I rest my head back against his solid chest and revel in the picturesque site before me.

For a long while we remain like this, silent and content. It's the most comfortable I've ever felt. And the most relaxed. I'm not thinking about the possibility of a rainstorm which is highly probable in Ireland, or ants getting into the bags of sweets, or wondering where I might go if I need to pee and worrying about getting stung in the bare ass by a tenacious bee. I'm not thinking about any of that. The only thing in my mind is . . . nothing.

For once I sit and don't think of anything, I just watch the flowers sway in the breeze and listen to the quiet sounds of nature around us. The heat from Conor's body keeping away the slight chill in the spring air.

Conor's shifting arms pulls my focus away from the crystal-clear blue lake and to the man running an exploratory finger along the underside of my breast outside my shirt.

I chose not to wear either of our sweaters today instead choosing a black V-neck shirt, my jean jacket, and worn in "boyfriend" jeans.

Conor's touch isn't sexual yet. More like he's mindlessly moving his fingers in a soothing manner. He doesn't move them higher or lower or shift behind me. Yet.

"Do you know that dandelions grant wishes?"

His question comes out of the blue considering the comfortable silence we've been sitting in. I look around at the surrounding puffy white balls.

"I know as a kid we would always blow on them to spread their fuzzy white seeds in the air and watch them float on the breeze," I answer absentmindedly, picking a dandelion from a nearby patch I can reach without leaving the circle of Conor's embrace.

I bring the white fuzz to my cheek and rub it against my skin feeling the barely there tickle of it.

Conor reaches up and holds the stem of the flower, and my hand within his larger one, bringing the dandelion in front of my mouth.

"You make a wish before blowing on the seeds and that wish floats into the world to become a reality."

Inspecting the dandelion closer I watch as he twists it in our hold. Most dandelions back home are considered weeds, unwanted by any gardener. Yet here they seem larger, fluffier, more than a weed. The white of the fuzzy ball is bright and pure and full looking like a soft gold ball on the tip of the stem.

"Go ahead, Emma. Make a wish."

Make a wish? But what would I wish for?

A week ago I would have wished for my bad luck curse to be broken. As I have had little bad luck lately I consider other things I might wish for; a new job, for Danny and Jules to finally get along, to find a great new apartment . . . love. The last lingers in my mind.

Love.

To wish for true love is always what little girls wish for. To find their prince charming and live happily ever after. I had long ago given up on finding true love. But perhaps now . . . ?

Forming the wish in my mind I inhale a large breath through my nose and blow strong but slow through my mouth at the dandelion. The tiny white seeds separate and drift in the air, lingering and swirling around for a moment before being swept away into the sky. All are gone except for two left on the stem.

"They also say the amount of seeds left after a girl blows on a dandelion is the number of children she'll have," Conor tells me in a matter of fact tone.

I turn my head around to face Conor and look up at him questioningly.

"I always wanted two kids. One boy and one girl."

He looks down at me one corner of his mouth curling just slightly in a smirk. His unspoken meaning left to hang in the air for me to interpret as I wish. I dare not consider it for what I hope it to be. That would be too dangerous.

The dandelion is released from our hands falling to the red blanket beneath us as Conor reaches up to slide his hand around my nape. Leaning in ever so slowly he places a soft kiss to my lips. A kiss so devastatingly loving my body instantly responds, turning into a soft pile of mush beneath him.

He doesn't stop at one mind melting kiss, he continues with one after another until my breath is stuttering against his lips when he pulls away. If my mind weren't blank before it is now.

Soft lips trail down my neck and behind my ear. I turn my head again back to facing the most beautiful scenery I've ever beheld, so he can have better access, his hand sliding from my nape and holding gently against my throat. His thumb pressing under my chin to tilt my head where he wants it.

My fingers dig into his denim clad thighs as he licks in just the right spot to send goose bumps along my spine. A tingling settles in my tailbone that reverberates directly at the apex of my thighs, causing wetness to pool there, readying me for him.

His lips press a soft kiss to the shell of my ear before he

speaks low and soft.

"Can I keep you, Leamhan Beag?"

I want to answer. To tell him that yes, he can keep me forever. But the words don't form, they don't come no matter how hard I try to make them. Whether from fear or pleasure I don't know. Whatever sound I make he takes as confirmation to continue his slow seduction and reign over my body and soul.

"You're mine now Emma," his grip tightens infinitesimally against my throat at the rough declaration. His words aren't angry or hard but conclusory. A declaration of what is. And I have no argument.

I am his.

No matter the future or what is to come, here and now in this moment in this field of flowers I am his.

Behind me I feel his cock hardening against my ass, and I give in. Give in to desire, to feeling, to the present and to him.

26 - Conor

You look so pretty covered in my cum

Emma softens against me, and I know she's given over to the same sensations I have. The desire that's plagued me since the moment she threw salt on me in that pub.

Her body is pliant as I cup her pussy in a possessive hold that leaves no space for argument. She is mine, and I am hers. I don't say it, but she has to know it. Know that she holds as much of me in the palm of her hand as I hold her in mine now.

Emma swivels her hips grinding her pussy into my hand and whimpers at the friction we create.

Here in a place of such natural beauty with no other human around to interfere, I plan on having her once again. Coming undone around me, under me, on top of me.

Her small breathless pants and moans has my cock throbbing behind my zipper. I press my hand against her core shifting her pretty little arse back against my cock. The pressure feels incredible. I suck on her neck as her head falls back against my shoulder and her eyes shut under the onslaught of sensations.

"I want you right now Emma," I growl into her ear. She only nods in agreement. My beautiful little moth, not at all shy, even out in the open like this.

"Take off your jacket, Love."

Emma leans forward and quickly slips her arms free from her jacket and tosses it to the side. Returning to me as soon as it's gone. I press a kiss to her neck as a reward.

"Good girl, now the trousers," I demand in a soft but firm tone.

Emma doesn't even hesitate, reaching down to unbutton and unzip her jeans. In an impressive move she shimmies them down her legs without standing and kicks off her shoes.

I follow her actions, doing the same with my own trousers. Undoing the closures and getting them and my boxer briefs down to my knees before stopping due to Emma's sweet naked arse blocking further progress. I'm not complaining.

My horny girl did more than I commanded, removing her jeans, shoes *and* underwear leaving her bare from the waist down. My cock twitches with approval.

Fucking perfect.

I lift her by the waist and bring her back to me, this time to sit on my lap, my erect cock slipping between her thighs. Emma leans back against my chest as she had before, my shirt riding up enough to feel her against my lower stomach.

Her wetness slicks my cock and abs beneath her. Fuck, she's so wet and ready for me. Glad to know I'm not the only one going out of my fucking mind with desire.

She settles against me, her legs on either side of my own, spreading her wide, baring her sweet pussy to the open air. My cock nestles against her hot wet core, slipping between her folds and rubbing her clit with the tip.

We both moan at the contact and her body jerks, her back bowing and pussy rubbing harder against my shaft. One free arm bands around her middle, holding her tight to me and the other grips her inner thigh. Her skin soft and supple under my fingers. I hold her open, so I can peer over her shoulder and get a glimpse of her perfect pussy.

Her pussy has a light dusting of red hair trimmed and neat, which allows me a view of her glistening sex rubbing against my hard cock. The sight makes my cock pulse, and I roll my hips, guiding my shaft through her wetness, teasing her clit with each slow stroke.

Emma moans loudly against my ear, and I want to record that sound to hear whenever I please. Her hands grapple for purchase, trying to hold on to my forearm and wrapping up and behind my neck. Her fingers grip the hair at my nape as she wriggles on top of me.

"You're fucking perfect like this. You know that, Emma? Opening for me and rubbing against my cock with your pretty little pussy. Do you want me inside you, Love? Do you want me to make you scream?"

I murmur the words into her ear. There's no one around to hear or see, but the words are for her and only her. I want her to feel them in her toes.

My hand gripped around her waist shoves upwards, pushing her shirt and bra over her breast revealing her perfect apple tits and tight pink nipples. I cover one with my hand and squeeze enough to make her let out a small yelp of pleasure.

"Yes, Conor. I'm yours," she purrs. "Just know after you make me yours, I'm going to make you mine."

My heart stammers a staccato rhythm. She's claiming me as I have claimed her.

"Yes, my sweet Leamhan Beag. I am yours."

Emma turns her head to face me and her lips find mind in a possessive kiss, our tongues seeking each other out. She sucks on my bottom lip, and I'm so distracted I don't realize she's lifted her hips and is already sliding my cock inside her tight pussy.

"Emma, Love," I growl, pressing my forehead to hers as she sinks on my cock, sheathing me in her tight channel. "Fuck, I didn't put a condom on yet."

"I know," she says softly against my lips, "I want to feel you. Is that okay? I'm clean. I get tested regularly."

Of course she would. I doubt she's ever let a man inside her without seeing his test results first. She let me inside her without a second's hesitation. She trusts me, and I will not break that trust.

"Me too. Can I come inside you?"

Even the thought of coming inside her has my cock stiffening in anticipation. Flexing inside her and rubbing deliciously against her inner walls. To feel her contracting around me as I spill inside her would be more satisfying than any sex I've ever had, by far.

"No, I'm not on birth control. Just pull out and come on my stomach."

Holy fucking mother of Jesus. This woman is my dream girl.

"Fucking hell Emma. You keep saying shite like that, and I'll have to pull out now. You'll have me coming before I want to."

She giggles, and I can feel the contracting of her stomach along my shaft. Before I can chastise her for laughing at me, she rolls her hips and begins moving. My hold on her spasms as the most sensational feelings jolt through my body.

Leaning back against the tree stump, using it as a back rest, I bring Emma with me. Lounging us both back, creating a new and agreeable angle that allows me to press my feet to the ground. Giving me the ability to thrust up into her.

"Conor, oh shit. Yes, that feels . . ." Emma rocks her hips, fucking my cock in the way she pleases, and I tilt my hips against her movements, causing my balls to tighten.

"That's it, Love. Fuck me just how you like."

Pinching her nipple, I suck on her neck as her movements quicken. Our bodies rocking together in a fluidity and cadence all our own. A tempo that you wouldn't think would work but does.

Feeling her body begin to shake, I shift the hand from her thigh to where we are joined. Placing my palm flat against her, I can feel my cock sliding in and out of her pussy, and I groan. My balls pull tighter as I thrust up harder into her. Moving my hand up to her clit I circle the sensitive bud gently at first. Running my finger down to the bottom of her swollen clit, where my cock continues a punishing pace. Pumping into her pussy I flick the underside before circling it again.

Her cries of pleasure block out all other sounds. Their continuous increase in volume telling me she's getting close to coming.

"Harder. Fuck yes, I'm gonna come. Oh god, yes," Emma rambles as her legs quake and her pussy tightens around my cock. Her orgasm only a few more thrusts away.

I pound harder up into her when her movements stutter, and she shatters, screaming into the emptiness of the field as she comes. Her pussy strangling my cock still inside her as her walls contract and pulse out her orgasm.

The pride I feel when her entire body shudders and twitches as she comes down from her peak, has my own orgasm growing. I push in deep and fuck her in shallow fast thrusts, enjoying the sounds our bodies make together. Her pussy grips me, and the sensation of her bare against my cock is something I will never forget as my release grows at the base of my spine and shoots up my shaft.

"Fuck, Emma, I'm coming," I warn her because I'm going to need a little assistance sliding out of her because if she doesn't lift up, I may not be able pull out.

Thankfully, she has more control at the moment than I do, lifting her hips to slip me out of her just in time. She sits on my abs and holds my cock against her hot pussy. Stroking and rubbing my shaft sending me into oblivion.

I come on a hoarse growl, burying my face in Emma's soft red hair. My cock pulses out streams of hot white cum that coats Emma's stomach and even the one breast not covered by my hand. I slide my free hand to her breast, a small splatter of my cum dripping from her taut nipple, rubbing it into her skin. I love the way she whimpers when I do.

"You look so pretty covered in my cum. You know that, Leamhan Beag?"

Her head nods against my shoulder where it rests, her hand still firmly holding my flagging cock against her sex. It's as if she doesn't want to separate from me just yet. I feel the same. I have no desire to move away or clean my mess off her yet.

Emma holds true to her word. After resting, we clean my mess off her with napkins and she claims me as hers, this time using a condom. Even though I have been hers for a while now. We had sex with her riding me and then with Emma splayed out like a fairy goddess on the blanket slow and sweet. Our bodies meeting in long languid movements coming together with our lips locked together.

I don't care if it's not considered manly to make love slow and sweet on a blanket it the middle of a field of wildflowers. I fucking loved every minute of it.

Since the meadow is empty of all life except us, we don't dress or rise immediately after. Lying naked on my side, I face Emma, who lies just as naked on her back next to me. Her body relaxed and a peaceful content smile on her lips. The light afternoon sun lights up her skin and hair like a golden red beacon.

Lazily I run my fingers across every inch of her I can reach. Trailing nimbly over her hip and soft stomach, around her impeccable breasts moving the pendant with the clover that sits between them out of the way, and up along her elegant neck then back down again, taking an alternate path. Seeking out every piece of her, wanting to imbed her in my memory forever.

Her arms are raised over her head and her eyes remain closed, though I know she's not asleep. Resting my head on my hand propped up on my elbow I gaze down at her and relish in the moment. In the unencumbered freeness in her posture. She's beautiful, and I can't look away.

My body is exhausted in the best way possible, and I want this time with her to continue. If the past two hours have been any indication, so does she. But how to bring it up?

"What are you staring at?"

I shake the concerning thoughts from my mind and focus back on her. Her eyes are now open, and she's shielding them from the sun, looking up at me.

"What?"

"You were staring off into space. What were you thinking about?" she asks with a sweet smile curling the edges of her kiss-swollen lips.

Shite. Should I tell her now? It's the perfect opening. But I don't want her to think I'm asking her now because of the great sex. I need her to know I want her to stay for more than that.

I want her to stay, so I can continue to go on adventures with her and help her crush her fear of the unknown. I want to turn that Claddagh ring on her finger in the opposite direction and maybe someday even place it on her other hand.

When she stripped out of her clothes, she failed to remove her jewelry. The long necklace with the clover inside rests on the side of her pink-tipped breasts and the gold claddagh ring still on her right ring finger, heart facing out.

I internally scowl at the offending jewelry, outwardly I grin at her not letting her see the displeasure I have at seeing it publicly announcing she's not yet fully mine. I fiddle with the ring nonetheless twisting it and wondering if she would notice were I to remove it and replace it the other way around.

"You, Love. I'm always thinking about you."

"What about me?" she asks a playful light in her golden eyes.

"Well, for starters, I was wondering if you always have sex in public places. Is this a thing you do often?"

Emma laughs out loud, the corners of her eyes crinkling

with mirth as she relaxes her head back down on the back of her forearm using it as a pillow. Her other hand still resting on her stomach where I play with her fingers and ring.

"No, this is most definitely not something I've done before. But I have to say I think I rather like it. It's freeing to be outside and naked."

"Agreed."

She chuckles again and rounds her eyes on me, pinching her mouth to one side while still smiling. "I think you would agree to anything that consists of me naked."

"Absolutely. If I could have you naked at all times but keep other people from seeing you, I would."

"You're such a man," she says this lightheartedly and snuggles closer to my own naked body. Rubbing her smooth leg against mine and pressing her hip against my dick, which responds even after all that we have done. Even if just a little. I can't help it. She does things to me I can't control.

"I love it here," she sighs wistfully, ignoring my slowly hardening cock against her thigh and looking out among the flowers and light fluffy clouds rolling across the darkening sky.

We've been here for nearly the whole afternoon now, having driven a couple hours to get here from the causeway. The day is now creeping from afternoon slowly toward evening. We'll have to leave soon, but I'll stay here as long as she wants. Even if that means sleeping under the stars on this blanket.

"I wish I could stay. Everywhere we go is better than the place before. Nowhere in Texas feels like it does here."

"I know what you mean."

This is the perfect moment. Tell her now. Tell her she can stay and enjoy all of this whenever she wants. She can stay with you.

As I open my mouth to do just that, Emma speaks again,

silencing my words.

"I only have a few more days before my flight home. Is there somewhere you would suggest we go? Somewhere like this?"

Emma looks up at me from the corner of her eye. She's subtly reminding me that she isn't here long term, that she's not staying. Or is she trying to see if I'll correct her? Offer her a reason to stay?

I don't know which. Women are so hard to read sometimes. And I'm not a subtle guy. Reading innuendos isn't my best quality. So, not willing to risk she's asking but not asking if she can stay. I go with a safe answer to her question.

"Yeah, I know a place. I have to warn you though, when we get there, you might be a little . . . overwhelmed. My family can be a bit much."

"Your family?"

Sitting up, Emma turns to face me and places her breasts right at eye level and mouth level. I lick my lips, focusing on her nipples instead of her face.

"Yeah. My parent's farm isn't far from here. It's picturesque there, you'll love it. But my family will ask a lot of questions. I haven't told anyone other than Aisling about you. Which probably means they all know about you by now anyway, if I know my sister at all."

"Oh, well . . ."

I don't listen to her response because I can't be face to face with her perfect tits and not take a taste. Leaning forward, I suck one soft nipple into my mouth and tease it with my tongue sucking and nipping at it till it's hard.

Emma's hands thread through my hair, and I can hear her sounds of pleasure at my attentions.

"You're not getting out of answering my questions that easy. You can't just distract me by sucking on my nipple every time."

"Sure, I can, watch me," I get out while switching to her other breast, giving it the same attention.

"Uhh. Conor."

My name is a curse and a command on her lips.

"Yes, my Love?"

Her breath hitches, and my cock somehow is almost hard again. Round three, here we come.

My plans to be balls deep inside Emma for a third time is cut short when small drops of rain begin to fall and land on my cheek and hot skin. I pull back to see droplets of water splash on Emma's creamy freckled skin and run down in rivulets between her breasts. It has the opposite effect it should. Instead of cooling me off and forcing me to leave the open field, it intensifies my returning craving for her.

Instead of answering me she just laughs and stands grabbing her clothes and the food while I reluctantly follow, picking up my own clothes and the blanket. Chasing her naked to the car to sounds of her gleeful laughter. Emma makes it to the vehicle first, lifting the back hatch to toss everything inside shielding herself from the now quickly falling rain.

Crashing into her, I drop everything in the back and lift her, wrapping her legs around my waist and seal my mouth over hers. She eagerly and happily returns the kiss. Latching her arms around my neck and shoulders smiling into my mouth as I slide my tongue inside and taste her sweetness. The sugary flavor of the desserts I bought her lingers on her tongue. If I could remain standing here naked in the rain holding Emma and kissing her for an eternity, I would be the happiest man in existence.

27 - Emma

I think she may be my favorite

Conor tells me about his family that I can expect to meet at his parent's farm as we drive in the rain. Most guys dread introducing the girl they're sleeping with to their family, but Conor doesn't bat a lash. He's fine taking me to his family farm and introducing me to not only his parents but his grandmother. Which if I'm reading him right is an important person in his life to him.

We're not even technically dating. We're not technically anything. Sure, we've had amazing sex, and I want to kiss Conor every opportunity that arises, but what are we to each other? Chauffer and tourist? Friends with benefits? A vacation fling? Or something else?

God, I wish it were something else. With every hour I spend not only with Conor but in Ireland I want to stay more and more. I feel so free and at ease here. Back home I always felt smothered, weighed down. Not here. Here I feel like I could be happy if I allowed myself.

Is it stupid of me to want to stay because of a man? It sounds so cliché and lame. But it feels somehow right. How do I know the right decision to make? Maybe I should ask Jules?

Grabbing my phone from my bag I pull up my messages and open the thread with Jules. It's been a few days since we spoke, so she doesn't know everything that's happened. It's too much to put in a text. Instead, I decide to be vague.

Emma: *How do you know what the right decision to make is?*
Jules: *Decision about what?*
Emma: *Nothing specific just in general. How do you know what's the right choice?*
Jules: *Well I usually go with my gut. It knows best.*
Emma: *Even if your gut leads you somewhere scary?*
Jules: *Sometimes the scary places are the most fun.*
Emma: *But is it worth it?*
Jules: *In my experience, yes. But I'm also careful and make sure I'm safe. Which is why I have you to tell me if anything is going to kill me. If it isn't then it's worth it.*
Jules: *Why? Whatcha thinkin about doin? *winky face**
Emma: *Nothing, yet. I'll let you know if I do.*
Jules: *If it involves hunky Irish boy I say go for it.*

Smiling to myself, I put my phone away and steal a glance at Conor, who's tapping out a beat on the steering wheel. I watch those hands, watch how they effortlessly move. Remembering how they played my body as easily as he taps out the beat in his head.

Am I safe with Conor? I believe I am. I don't think he would ever intentionally hurt me. But that doesn't mean my heart is safe. It can never truly be protected from all harm. I just have to decide: is it worth it?

In the hour it takes us to reach his family farm he lists off who we may encounter there; his parents, sisters, grandmother, or Nan, as well as his cousin who is also his manager who might show up. I doubt I'll remember all their names, but at least I'll be somewhat prepared when we arrive.

Apparently, they're all preparing for a big wool event called Woolapalooza, where they sell their raw untreated wool, undyed and dyed yarn, and other wool products. They've been trying to get everything ready but have been shorthanded with a worker out. Originally Conor told them he couldn't help since he was busy with me, but with our turn of events and me wanting to see more of the countryside, he relented.

Conor called ahead to inform his mom that we were on our way and would be there before dinner. Informing her that he would be able to make it home after all and is bringing a helper. Which she wasn't at all surprised to hear as Aisling had indeed told them all about the American woman he was ushering around. So, when we pull up the drive there's already a welcome party waiting for us under the cover of the front door entry. Half a dozen people are smooshed together, watching us pull up and park. All eager to meet the American that's drawn the attention of their son and brother.

Multiple smiling jovial faces, all ranging in similarity to Conor's, smile back at us warmly. Waving eagerly as we approach.

They are really excited about us being here. It only makes my stomach flip uneasily knowing all their cheerful anticipation is wasted on me. I'll be leaving in a few days. My flight is scheduled for two days from now. Leaving me only forty-eight hours to spend with Conor. To . . . to do what?

Confess I feel more than lust for a man I just met? To uproot my life and start a new one in a new country? To ask Conor if I should stay? If he wants me to stay. Seems like a lot for only forty-eight hours.

His parent's house is two stories tall and runs wide from side to side with a scattering of windows across the front. The exterior is painted stark white while the main door is fire engine red. It looks old but well maintained and loved. The house isn't the only structure on the property there are a few other large buildings that I'm guessing house sheep, and all the equipment for sheering and processing the wool, but it's hard to see any of it through the sheets of rain now pouring down.

As soon as we pull to a stop a large older gentleman breaks through the gaggle of people with an umbrella in hand and strides quickly to the back of the SUV. I don't get out of the car immediately but wait for Conor to come to my side and open the door. He's holding an umbrella overhead, so I can exit without getting drenched.

We make it to the open front door in half a dozen hurried steps. The people there, mostly women, descend on us. Taking the umbrella, and our coats, all kissing cheeks and chatting animatedly to Conor. Hugging and greeting one another in that way only family can. It makes me smile to know he has such a relationship with his family, even through the slight heartache.

"Oh my goodness. And you must be Emma. Come in dear and get warm. How was the drive?" a woman I can only assume is his mother says. Speaking openly and quickly while guiding me into a sitting room and planting me on a rather comfortable couch. A steaming pot of tea already set and waiting on the low wooden table in front of me. A colorful knitted cozy is wrapped around the ceramic tea pot.

I look around, trying to find Conor, who I've lost in the few short steps I've taken into the house. He spots me from through the arch way and forces his way to me. No doubt trying to qualm the panicked expression on my face. I'm a friendly person, but the circumstances around my presence here are rather odd, and I have no idea how to act.

Conor's mother pours two cups of tea for me and Conor as he sits on the couch next to me.

"Mum, you barely gave her a chance to say hello," he scolds his mother, who bats away his comment with a wave of her hand.

"Nonsense. After all that time cooped up in the car, there's no need for her to be crammed in the entryway with everyone crowding her. They can come in and introduce themselves like civilized people."

Conor gives me an apologetic look and says quietly into my ear, "I'm really sorry about all this."

I smile back at him hopefully reassuring him that I'm capable of handling his family. At least now that we have space to speak civilly, as his mother put it.

The rest of his family joins us in the sitting room. Each coming over one at a time and shaking my hand introducing themselves. First his father Brian, then his sister Bridget, and of course, his mother Cara. Each giving me a warm smile, not at all disturbed by the fact that I'm a stranger their son ushered around the country on a whim.

Aisling, whom I've already met, gives me a quick hug and a conspiratorial smile. Not sure what we're conspiring about, but I'm all for it. Aisling is a hoot. Lastly, and according to her most importantly, I meet his grandmother, Moira, who insists

I call her Nan. I think she may be my favorite. She looks like even more fun than Aisling, and I realize that's probably where she got it from.

All of his family look similar enough in appearance to know they're related. His mother has the same dark auburn hair, his father the obvious source of his height and build, and his Nan sharing his soft jade eyes.

"So, we hear you've been going all around Ireland seein' the sites," Cara says. Her eyes alight with intrigue at the presence of her son here with a woman.

As a matter of fact they're all staring at me like I'm the first girl he's ever brought home.

Oh crap.

Am *I the first girl he's brought home?*

Shit, that's not good.

Or is it? I'm not entirely sure. Either way, this has to be sending a message, and I don't know what it's saying. That we're an item, that we're dating, that there's more here than meets the eye? Whatever it's saying his family seems to approve. Since they're all grinning and eyeing me.

"Yes. Conor was kind enough to offer to drive me when I discovered the tour company I booked my trip through, was out of business." I leave out anything about the clover and the bad luck curse. That's a different story for another time.

"And how is it you two met again? Aisling didn't tell us," Nan asks.

She's at least in her seventies maybe even eighties, her hair gone pure white but still thick and resting in soft waves around her shoulders. She's aged beautifully, her wrinkles showing her years of joy like a badge of honor. She wears a knitted shawl similar in style to the sweaters Conor's worn except hers is a vibrant amethyst with tassels on the ends.

"Oh, I accidentally threw salt on him in a pub."

"Did you now?" Nan asks, smirking at her grandson next to me. "Was he doin' something he shouldn't?"

I laugh, the initial tension of meeting Conor's family dissipating under their kind welcome. "No, not at all. I was trying to counteract some bad luck and well because of it I think I had the best luck meeting Conor."

His Nan and mother both tilt their heads in *aww how cute* gesture as their faces transform into something soft and almost heart eyed. Aisling rolls her eyes good naturedly at their swooning.

"I suppose it was good luck for my brother. You're the only person who's been able to convince him to take a day off in years. We should be thanking you," Bridget says from her spot in an armchair across from us next to her mother.

She's older than Conor by a few years and has chestnut brown hair that's pulled back into a loose braid. She, too, wears what appears to be a wool knit sweater. I suppose it makes sense they would all wear wool items since they run a sheep farm that produces wool. It's like being a walking advertisement for your business. An easy way to show possible clients or customers your product without being overly obvious.

"Oh? Is he a workaholic?" I ask, quirking a brow in Conor's direction.

We hadn't talked extensively about work since it's a bit of a sore subject for me. From all his rankings online, I knew he was good at what he did, and that he has a big match coming up soon, but that's about it.

"He has a very strong work ethic," Cara offers in her loving motherly voice.

"It's not a strong work ethic it's obsession. He never takes a Holiday and getting him to take a weekend off to visit is like pulling teeth from a bear," Bridget corrects. "We see him more on the telly during his matches than we do in person."

I turn a playful scowl on Conor, now joining his mom, Nan and two sisters in glaring at him for not spending more time with them.

"Don't you start. I already get it enough from them. I don't need it from you, too," he grumbles, holding his hands up in exasperation.

We all begin laughing at him in unison. Except for his father who stands behind his wife trying to hide his chuckle behind a cough and his hand.

"How long are you able to stay, son?" Brian asks, trying to divert the conversation.

"Only until tomorrow night. We have to get back to Dublin for Emma's flight home."

Conor's amusement fades from his eyes and a flat smile turns down his lips enough to see it's forced. Maybe he doesn't want me to go either.

"Oh, what a shame. We were hopin' you would be able to attend Woolapalooza with us this year. It's been so long since you went." Cara says with a disappointed furrow on her brow.

"Sorry, Mum. Maybe next year."

"Are you sure you can't stay longer?" Nan asks with a sad smile and twinkling eyes, that I'm sure could convince a priest to rob a bank. "I would really love to spend more time with you."

"Sorry Nan. Emma's flight is in two days, and I have my match. I could probably come back next week though, after . . ."

After I leave.

Why does the thought sting my ribs? I just met these people. I shouldn't be fraught with guilt and sadness I won't be here to spend more time with them and Conor. Yet the woeful feeling doesn't subside right away. Lingering in my chest and clogging my throat.

A heavy silence fills the room, and I try to fill it by picking up my floral teacup and sipping the hot tea. I barely taste the hot liquid. The quiet remaining even after I set my cup down. Thankfully Aisling breaks it unable to stand it any longer.

"Okay, so you two must be tired from your drive. How about Conor shows you to your room, and you rest for a bit before supper?"

I give Aisling an appreciative smile and exhale, relaxing my shoulders.

"Good idea, Ash."

Conor reaches out a hand to guide me to stand, and I take it eagerly wanting something to cling to. I don't let go once I'm standing next to him and keep holding on until we make our way upstairs.

They've set us up in one room, not even pretending we're sleeping apart. I don't know how they figured that out since we weren't "together" when I met Aisling. They must have either read between the lines or have been hopeful Conor was bringing home more than a new friend. Or the less desirable option: I'm not the only girl he's ever brought home. I could be the hundredth and this is just par for the course.

Conor enters ahead of me and turns on the bed side lamp, illuminating the spacious room. The walls are a dusty blue with white trim and the windows look out to green fields beyond still being washed with the rain.

"You bring girls home often?" I ask dryly as I enter the room that looks to have at one time been more than just a guest room, with its worn area rug and lived-in feel. Not like how empty unused guest rooms normally feel. It feels, cozy and familiar.

"Why do you ask that?" Conor turns to face me with a confused expression.

Raising my hand, I gesture to the room around us. "They already assume we're sharing a room. I just thought maybe this was a normal thing."

"No," he states firmly, dropping his bag on the floor forgotten to cross the distance to me.

Reaching out, he removes my suitcase from my hand and discards it too. Holding my face between his two large hands and gently forcing me to look him in the eye.

"I haven't brought a girl home since secondary school when I brought my very first girlfriend home to meet my parents. And we most definitely did not share a room. No one assumed anything about us, Emma. I told Aisling when I called earlier that we would be sharing a room. I think that's why they were all a little extra enthusiastic about meeting you."

The weird jealous tightness that had begun to irrationally overwhelm me fades under his words. At least now I know why the eager welcome downstairs.

"You hear me, Leamhan Beag?" Conor rubs a thumb against my lips, easing my tension even further, melting me like hot butter under his hands. "You are not just another girl I brought home for a quick romp. You're special to me. I wouldn't have brought you here otherwise."

I nod because really there's nothing more I can do. I can't speak or form words in response. No one's ever said such a thing to me before, and my brain can't comprehend it. It seems too good to be true, and historically with my luck, too good to be true never ends well. Even with my changing luck and proof that good things can happen there's still the long lingering fear engrained in me to revolt at such things.

"Why don't I show you around the house a bit, eh? Supper should be ready soon."

"Okay."

Leaning down, Conor presses a gentle, prolonged kiss to my lips. Melting my insecurities and diminishing my doubts that he is less than the decent man I know him to be.

28 – Conor

I'm addicted to her taste

Aisling finds Emma and I to tell us supper is ready when we're still mid tour of the house. I still haven't shown her some of the rooms in the main house or the sheering building, and all the sheep. That'll just have to wait till tomorrow after the rain stops. Not like the sheep are going anywhere.

I brought Emma here to show her my home and more of Ireland like she wanted. Perhaps in hopes she falls in love with it enough to consider staying. It would be too much to believe she would fall in love with me in such a short time. A lad can still hope.

Either way, I'm sure Mum and Dad will expect us to help out with the sheering while we're here. Sheering is fairly simple, and I'm sure Emma will enjoy learning. She did, after all, ask me to teach her how. She might even help with the processing of the wool. Nan can even show her how we make the yarn, if there's time.

We only have until after dinner tomorrow to spend here. Emma wants to return to Dublin the night before her flight to ensure she doesn't miss it. Her bad luck habits still direct her life. Sure, she's spent the last week with me with little planning while working to counteract her bad luck with the luck of the Irish.

Which I plan on taking away from her by forcing her to give me her well-deserved four-leaf clover.

I don't even give a shite about the fucking clover anymore. It was ridiculous of me to believe something like that controlled my ability to fight and win matches. I can't say I regret making that deal. It brought me Emma. It gave us this time together.

Like I told her before, even bad luck can lead to something good. Everything happens for a reason and there's always a silver lining. Sometimes it's not as bright as others and takes a keen eye to see, but it's there. With Emma, I don't have to look hard to see it. It shines every time I look at her. Every time I kiss her.

She is my silver lining.

She is the reason I lost my match. So, I could spend this time with her to learn that she's the one meant for me. I've waited years to find the woman who sees through the celebrity, money, and prestige to the man beneath. To me. To my family. That woman is Emma, and I will do everything I can to keep her.

I lead Emma by her hand through the sitting room, family room, and my mum's office that's messier than usual. Ending in the dining room, where the large table is being set by Bridget, who is lying down Mum's good china plates.

They are really pulling out the big guns now. Emma's already made an impression, and she's only just met them.

"I see Mum is using the good plates," I dead pan to my sister with a raised brow. She returns the look with one of her own before it morphs into a gleeful grin in Emma's direction.

"Yes, well, we have a guest. She thought it best."

"I'm sure she did."

Why do mums always insert themselves in their kids love lives? Not that I'm complaining. I'm glad my family is so open and accepting of Emma. Maybe seeing how accepting they are of her will sway her to stay.

"Here, let me help."

Emma extricates her hand from mine firmly holding on to her and moves to help my sister set the table. I release her begrudgingly, allowing her to assist my sister. Bridget hands her the stack of plates and goes to the side table to retrieve . . . yep, the good silver. Way to be subtle mum.

Leaning in closer to Emma so my sister doesn't overhear I say, "Don't steal any of my Mum's silver cutlery, eh? I promise the food will turn out perfect. If you want a fork to remember this by, I can grab you one of the mismatched pieces we normally use."

Emma snickers and smiles up at me with humorous eyes.

"No promises. This cutlery is probably the finest I've ever used. It would make a great addition to my collection."

Well maybe just one. But perhaps the dessert spoon no one ever uses." I wink at her conspiratorially.

She laughs but doesn't take any of the silverware for her collection. Later I'll pick out an old spoon for her instead. I know for a fact the food will be delicious, this spoon will be a reminder of an perfect meal instead of a tragic one.

Watching Emma side by side with my sister setting our family table for a meal with all my siblings and parents causes me pause. The sight engraving into my memory and a permanent brand on my heart. No one I've ever been with has come home to meet my family. None have ever been worthy. Emma is worthy of it and more. She's worthy of everything.

In an attempt to be helpful, I look around the table and count the place settings spotting three extra seats.

"Are Liam and the lads coming?"

"Yeah. They should be here any minute. Boys had school and Liam went to pick them up before you arrived."

Emma finishes placing the cloth napkins on the plates and gives me a questioning glance across the table.

"Liam is Bridget's husband. They have two boys Finn and Riley."

She makes an oh face nodding in understanding.

"How old are your boys?" she asks Bridget, genuinely interested in learning more about them.

Most of my exes would vaguely inquire about my family, but none were genuinely interested in learning more. Simply asking out of formality to appear proper. Emma however is bright eyed and smiling at my sister as she tells her all about my two nephews. Finn the younger at five years old and Riley the oldest at nine. Bridget and Liam have been married for just over ten years, and although adding two grandsons appeased our mum, it only slightly lessened her inquiries as to when I'll be giving her more.

Giving my mum and dad grandkids has always been my plan. Marrying and building a family all my own is something I've always wanted. Growing up with my parents and sisters showed me the joy that comes from building a life with a partner and children. The love and companionship that my parents have always resonated within me, driving me to find it for myself. Until now, I've been unsuccessful.

I knew I would eventually one day find it. I never thought I wouldn't. Finding it in a pub after being showered with a handful of salt wasn't what I expected but how I found her doesn't matter, only that I did.

Liam and the boys arrive shortly after we finish setting the table, in a frenzy of muddy boots and raincoats paired with sounds of happy screams and laughter. Mum finds them immediately for granny hugs and kisses. Followed directly by Nan for more of the same. It makes me hopeful that soon I'll be able to add my own little minions to the parade of laughter and love.

For supper mum made her famous Irish stew and soda bread paired with a locally made whisky for the adults, the boys get juice. I also grab a glass of juice for Emma, knowing she's not much of a drinker. She gives me a grateful smile as I sit down next to her at the bustling table.

Our dining table is made of sturdy handcrafted wood with a well-worn smooth top from generations of O'Shea's eating at it. A handmade white wool runner stretches down its center, decorative bowls holding the food placed along it. This table has been in the family since my great grandfather made it in the nineteen-twenties and can seat up to ten people. Which tonight puts it at capacity with four generations pressed up to its edges.

Mum, Dad, and Nan are religious Irish Catholic and always pray before super. We were all raised this way, and all know what to expect even if we aren't actively as religious, and dutifully bow our heads in a silent prayer. Emma follows suit folding her hands in her lap and waiting respectfully.

As soon as he finishes, we all begin talking and serving

food. Relaxing into a familiar rhythm we all know so well.

"This looks and smells amazing Mrs. O'Shea."

"Please call me Cara, Emma. No need to be so formal."

Says the woman who busted out the good China and real silverware.

Emma accepts a soda bread roll while I ladle steaming spoonfuls of stew into her bowl. Filled with hearty chunks of beef, potatoes, carrots, and other vegetables.

We're halfway through our food when Mum starts asking her questions. The ones I knew she was dying to ask Emma from the start. Preemptively I reach around and rest my arm on the back of Emma's chair, rubbing my fingertips lightly across her arm. Hopefully the movement is comforting. When Emma looks at me from the corner of her eye and her features soften, I know it is.

"So, Emma, where are you from? Where is it you call home?"

Swallowing the mouthful of stew, she was chewing Emma wipes her mouth with her napkin before answering. "I'm from Dallas Texas. But right now, I don't really call any place home."

My mum frowns at Emma from across the table looking rightfully concerned. It sounds as if Emma is homeless, which I know she's not since she told me about her apartment flooding. Which coincidentally lead her to be here today.

"You see, I have an apartment, but it flooded before I came to Ireland. So right now, all my belongings are in storage while it gets repaired. However, I'm on a month-to-month lease and lately I've been considering moving."

"Oh?" mum says, perking up. I know exactly what she's thinking because I'm thinking the same. "Where exactly were you thinking of moving?"

I've stopped eating, stopped blinking, and probably stopped

breathing while waiting for Emma's answer. I, too, would like to know where she was thinking of moving. She hasn't mentioned it before and knowing she's open to a move has my heart stuttering behind my ribs.

"I'm not really sure yet. I just thought maybe it was time for a change. I'm in-between jobs at the moment as well, so it seemed a fitting time."

A lightness fills my chest. She's thinking of starting something new, making a change. Perhaps I could be that change for her? Perhaps Ireland could? I've never been so hopeful for something in my entire life. Not even winning a match.

"Have you considered Ireland? It's definitely a change from Texas."

"Mum," I quietly scold her not wanting to force Emma to discuss such a thing in front of so many prying eyes. No matter how much I want to hear her response.

"What? I was just saying. No harm in considering."

Mum turns back to Emma, who doesn't look as apprehensive as I would have thought. She actually looks thoughtful, as if this isn't the first time the idea has crossed her mind.

"No, I suppose it doesn't hurt to consider anywhere right now. My options are pretty open, I guess. There's no rule that says I have to stay in Texas. But moving so far from my family would kind of suck."

"You have a big family too?" Aisling asks from the other side of Emma.

"Oh yeah. I have three older brothers. One is married with a little boy of his own, the other two are still single though. We actually have relatives here in Ireland somewhere."

Emma relaxes as she talks about her family, the subject an

easy one. Allowing her to return to her stew to finish the last few bites. She's polished off the entire bowl and two soda bread rolls.

I keep my arm around her chair. Not only because it seems to comfort her, but I rather like having it there. The need to constantly be touching Emma one I'm not entirely familiar with, but one I don't at all mind.

"Really? Are you visiting them while here as well?" Aisling asks.

"I have no idea who they are. All I know is that my great great grandfather immigrated to the US, but the rest of his family remained in Ireland. So, there's cousins and aunts and uncles we've never met. I'm sure if I asked my dad, we'd be able to look up the family tree. Maybe try one of those family heritage sites."

"Wouldn't that be lovely? To find some Irish relatives to assist with relocating?" I give my Nan a stern frown, which I know she sees. "If that's something you're considering, that is," she adds to appease me and appear nonchalant. Although the glint in her eye gives her away.

My family is seriously pushing it right now.

I love my Nan, but I think I underestimated her ability to appear innocent while subtly suggesting Emma move to Ireland to become part of our family and give them more grandbabies.

"Maybe," Emma replies a little awkwardly.

"Just ignore them. They're all acting like eejit's because I brought you home with me. They think that means they have the right to assume things they shouldn't."

I try to ease her tension, but the deflation in her posture and expression isn't the sort I was hoping for. She seems less assuaged and more despondent. That's not what I had intended.

Brilliant, Conor. You're not helping the situation.

I try to quickly recover not wanting her to think I don't want her here. "Unless moving to Ireland is something you might be considering. In that case I would be more than happy to help in any way you need."

Big, round golden hazel eyes peer up at me more hopeful than before, and I can't deny the matching optimism in my own. A shadow of a grin crosses her lips. It's shy and small, barely even visible. But I still see it.

She likes the idea.

Supper thankfully goes on with no further discomforts. Discussing easier subjects like the weather, and Woolapalooza, and all the yarns they plan on taking. Emma tells everyone about her brother Danny and best friend Jules, who has had some love-hate relationship ever since they met. And the endlessly entertaining arguments they have over Emma. She tells them about her old job and how that, too, may be an area where she makes changes.

She doesn't tell them her secret hope of wanting to be a schoolteacher. But I can see the light ignite in her when she mentions finding a new profession.

We don't bring up her impending flight back to America in less than two days. Maybe not speaking about it will make it less real.

After dinner I continue my tour of the house as we hadn't finished before. The rain has finally let up, becoming nothing more than a misty drizzle, making it easier for me to show Emma the place I'm most excited to share with her. Not because it's anything special but because of what's inside it.

Exiting the side door of the house, we walk down the damp gravel driveway to a small shed workshop behind the house. It's set up as a craft room of sorts with plenty of storage and space to work. Over the years, it's been filled with more yarn than anything else, but there's still a section with paints, markers, and paper for the boys. As well as a place for me to store my tattooing machines and tools when not in use.

It's always been a hobby, never a career, so I don't have much need for them on a regular basis. The craft shed is kept clean, and I'm thankful for it. If Emma agrees to my request, I'll want a clean space to work on her in.

It may have been a year since I put needle to skin, but I'll never forget how. And this tattoo may be the most important of my life.

Before we reach the small workshop, I reach into my back pocket and pull out an old soup spoon. One of the larger ones that no longer matches any of the other cutlery in the drawer. I figured none would miss it.

"Here. I snagged this for your collection."

Emma takes the spoon and looks down at it for a moment then up at me. A questioning look on her face.

"But the meal was amazing. Nothing was 'wrong' and I'm pretty sure I ate more than you did," she smirks.

"You're probably right, but I thought maybe you could start a new collection. Saving a piece of a positive meal instead of a negative one. Something you want to remember rather than forget."

We stop walking and stand outside the workshop not yet entering. I look down at Emma, waiting to find out if I've crossed a line with my spoon gift.

"Thank you, Conor. I love it. And you might be right. I

shouldn't save things connected with bad memories. I should save them to remind me of the good and happy times. Of things that make me smile that I never want to forget."

She rubs the head of the spoon like a worry stone before slipping it into her pocket.

"You're welcome, Love. I hope your new collection is far larger than you last."

"I hope it will be too."

I give her a reassuring smile before opening the door and gesturing Emma inside. We step into the small building, and I flip on the lights. Emma looking around the space. It's not much. Storage shelves and cabinets line one wall with a spacious drafting table settled under a picture window. The interior is painted a bright, cheerful lavender with a few splatters of paint from the boys, being a tad over excited during craft time.

"Wow. This looks like a fun shed. So many crafts to play with. Do you call it the fun shed?" she jokes.

"No. But I will from now on."

I give her a sultry grin that suggests the kind of fun we could have in this shed all alone out of earshot of my family. She smacks me playfully on the arm, her laugh light and easy.

Letting her peruse a colorful basket of yarns, I pull a large black case from a shelf and set it on the table under the window. Emma steps up close at my side, watching me unlatch the case that holds all my machines and needles and small collection of inks.

"What's that?" she asks, unable to wait until I open it to see.

"Be patient, and you'll see."

She makes a face up at me filled with mirth and playfulness, scrunching her nose adorably. I slow my movements to prolong her anticipation, and my enjoyment at her huff of displeasure at me for making her wait. Chuckling I lift the lid to show her its contents.

My machines, needles, inks, soaps, and tracing papers are all still neatly tucked in their proper places among the foam cut outs holding everything in place. They're still as clean and pristine as when I left them. Having not been used frequently I'm glad to see my parents kept them properly stored.

"Are those?"

"Yup. My tattooing equipment. How do you feel about testing your luck?"

Coppery crimson locks whip back and forth as Emma vehemently shakes her head no. An automated response from the looks of it, because the look in her eyes does not match the movement.

"Are you sure about that? You look like you might be interested."

"I'm definitely interested, but . . ."

"But you're concerned something might go wrong?"

She nods, biting on her lip as she continues to stare at the equipment. Fiddling with the bottles of ink, she pulls out a brilliant emerald green. A color that I had considered in using for her tattoo. It would look beautiful against her skin tone and red hair. Hair that is currently hiding her face from me in a curtain.

Reaching out, I brush it back behind her shoulder and tuck it behind her ear. Revealing her freckled cheeks and thoughtful expression.

"How about I show you the sketch I made for you and then you can decide?"

The lip between her teeth is pulled even farther into her

mouth as she chews on it, contemplating her response. A glimmer appears in her eyes as she turns the ink bottle over, watching the green liquid shift in the light.

"I guess it wouldn't hurt to take a look. I mean I have always wanted a tattoo."

"And looking won't hurt. I promise."

That tortured bottom lip of hers still being assaulted by her teeth. On impulse, I cup the opposite side of her face, turning it to face me, so I can lean down and gently coax her lip from her teeth with a kiss. Sucking gently and pressing feather light kisses to her quickly yielding mouth.

Her posture eases as her body slackens against mine. Pressing closer seeking more. More that I am willing to oblige. After I ink my design into her body.

Easing back from the kiss I look down at Emma, a pink flush splotching her cheeks. She looks gorgeous.

Pulling out the folded paper from my back pocket, I unfold it tentatively. I had sketched out the drawing one morning when she was in the shower. The idea came to me, and I had to get it down on paper just in case. A few elements I filled in before tearing the sheet from my sketchbook tonight.

"It's nothing fancy, but I thought you would like it."

I hand her the paper, and she turns it over to see what I've drawn for her. It's a fine line drawing of a fuzzy bodied moth, wings extended out at its sides with long delicate tails. I took liberties with the pattern design in the wings. Incorporating a few Celtic knots, a clover, a horseshoe, a spoon, and fork, a heart and crown from the claddagh, and a fluffy dandelion. Some elements are more obvious than others that blend in with the pattern until you look closely to find them.

Emma's eyes go wide and her mouth drops open a fraction.

A good sign, I hope.

"Do you like it?"

"It's beautiful, Conor. Where would you put it?"

That's not a no.

"Well, I believe it would look perfect right," I gently grasper her wrist and twist her arm, exposing her inner forearm. "Here. With the head of the moth just below your inner elbow and the tails dangling down toward your wrist."

She stares down at her arm, and my fingers trailing a path in the spot I had imagined tattooing her.

"That seems large. Would it fill my whole arm?"

"No. We can make it smaller. It doesn't have to fill the whole space or reach all the way to your wrist. It could end about halfway. Say here?"

I point mid-way down her forearm. That seems to appease her concerns about getting an overly large tattoo.

"It would be fine line work only." I take the green ink from her hand, holding it up between us. "Maybe in this green, if you like."

"No black?"

"No black."

"Would that look okay?"

"On your fair skin, it would look lovely."

Emma looks down at her arm, then to the ink, and then to the drawing still held in her opposite hand.

"It is quite lovely, and I do really like that green."

She nibbles on her lip again before turning her expectant eyes on me. I want to suck that lip right out of her mouth and soothe it with my tongue again.

"Will it hurt?"

"So, that's a yes?"

She hesitates for only a moment before answering, firm but soft.

"Yes."

"I won't lie, Love, it will hurt. But not for very long. I'll be as gentle as possible."

I pull over a rolling chair and stool, sitting Emma in the chair before extricating all the items I'll need from my case. Setting them all up one by one with deliberate precision. Wiping down the table and covering it with plastic wrap, sanitizing everything. I make a copy of the design onto the transfer paper using my mum's all in one printer, scanner, copier in the corner. Making sure Emma approves of the size first.

When everything is set up and ready, I pull Emma close and wrap the arm of the chair for her to rest her arm on while I tattoo.

"Are you comfortable?"

She nods and smiles big and wide up at me. "Yes."

"Are you ready?"

"Absolutely. I've always wanted to get a tattoo or a piercing but was too afraid of the possible negative consequences. Statistically less than six percent of people who get tattoos get infected, but it would be just my luck that I would fall into that six percent."

Though her words are pessimistic, her smile is not. It's infectious, and I can't stop the small grin from crossing my own lips.

"I promise my needles are clean, and you won't get infected from them. And with proper care, the healing process should be fairly easy as well. I use a product called second skin. It's a full adhesive strip that covers the tattoo, allowing it to heal properly. You can leave it on for days and even shower with it without it peeling off."

"I trust you, Conor."

With her simple declaration of trust, I have all that I need to give her the best tattoo she'll ever get.

It only takes me two hours to ink the design into Emma's arm. The emerald green contrasting beautifully against her pale skin. A few pale red brown freckles add to the beauty of it. The moth looks vibrant enough to fly off her arm.

For all that she worried about the pain she managed it well, only cringing and wincing a few times. I was as gentle as I could be while also trying to take the least amount of time. I'm happy to report my tattooing skills are still as brilliant as they were last time I tattooed.

Now that it's done, her smile spreads her entire face, lighting up every inch of it.

"Do you like it?"

"Like it? I absolutely love it Conor. It's so beautiful. Thank you."

Flinging herself at me, Emma wraps her non tattooed arm around my neck and squeezes tight. I respond in kind, hugging her close with both arms around her waist.

"You're very welcome, Love."

I pull back far enough to press a kiss to her head, not allowing myself more until after I've cared for her new tattoo.

Cleaning it and covering it with the second skin ensuring an easy healing process.

"There. You're good to go. Nothing is getting in there to infect it."

"I wasn't worried about it."

"Is that so?"

"For once, yeah. I know the risks, but I wasn't afraid of them. I knew with you here they wouldn't be an issue."

Emma looks at me with such openness, and warmth churns in my gut.

"I would never let anything hurt you, Leamhan Beag. Especially nothing guided by my hand. It's getting late. We should head inside and get some sleep."

Standing I replace all the items back in my case after cleaning them and dispose of the needles and plastic wrap in the bin. Returning everything to where it originated.

We return to the main house, again her hand securely held in mine, where everyone else has retired for the night. Leaving it quiet and dimly lit. Making our way upstairs and into the now guest room that was once my room. Little remains of that time, with it having been so any years past since I've lived here.

There's a few sports trophies and photos, a few pieces of memorabilia, but nothing more. The rug covering the original hardwood flooring is still worn where the legs of my bed and desk used to sit. The sight a nostalgic reminder of my teen years.

The bed that's in here now is not my old one, but a newer one than thankfully doesn't creek with every little movement. The mattress is also a hundred times better. No more metal coiled springs poking through the surface to cut into my thigh in the middle of the night.

Emma strips down to her panties and under shirt for bed, while I remove every stitch of clothing. Sliding into bed naked and half hard from watching Emma undress. She turns off the light and crawls in next to me. Tucking herself close to my side while keeping her newly tattooed arm resting on my chest. Her nipples graze my side through her thin shirt, causing my half hard cock to upgrade to fully hard.

Tucking my knuckle under her chin, I tilt her head up to line her mouth up with mine. It doesn't take long before I'm stripping her panties down her legs and settling my shoulders between them.

With the first swipe of my tongue, I have her writhing and whimpering under me. I'm addicted to her taste. Her little whimpers of pleasure increasing my own, making me rock my hips into the mattress as I press my tongue inside her.

To keep from shouting, Emma bites down on the soft flesh of her hand just below her thumb. I watch her the entire time. Staring up between her parted thighs and over her small pert breasts. Those pink tipped nipples calling out to me.

I'll get to you, don't you worry. Once I finish devouring Emma's pussy, I'll give you the attention you deserve.

Emma comes, shaking around my tongue and gifting me the taste of her pleasure. And just as I had internally promised I trail kisses up her body and lavish her breasts with my tongue and teeth. Causing a wave of tingles to settle in my balls.

Lining up the broad head of my cock with her core, I slip inside her wet heat, her accepting pussy taking every hard inch. Grinding slow and in long leisurely strokes. Stoking the fire of her desire once again until she's writhing beneath me. Meeting every roll of my hips with one of her own.

Her hands claw at my back and her heels press hard into

my arse. Forcing me deeper inside her. My pace increases as the pulsing in my shaft matches the clenching of her channel.

I love feeling her around me, nothing between us. I'm also thankful for the sturdy, *silent* bed frame. Concealing the sounds of my increasing thrusts as I reach up with one hand and grip the wooden frame of the headboard to steady myself. Curving my other hand under her flexing butt cheek, cupping her soft flesh and helping to lift her. Adding to the intensity of my thrusts.

Our breaths mingle, and our tongues tangle in a frantic need for each other.

"Tá tú liom anois, Leamhan Beag. Agus níl mé ag ligean duit dul riamh," I whisper into her ear between panting breaths.

"I love it when you speak Irish. Please tell me you're saying dirty things."

I chuckle. They may not be dirty words, but they are a vow. That she is mine, and I will never let her go. Of course, I don't tell her that, instead I tell her what I know will force her second orgasm from her and milk mine from me.

"I said I want to feel your sweet pussy come on my cock before I pull out and cover you in my cum . . . again."

Her moan barely makes it past her lips before I swallow it in a punishing kiss, and she comes around my cock. And I do to her exactly as I promised. Pounding deep and fast into her sweet release pulsing around me until my balls throb, and my own orgasm rips through me.

Pulling out, I trap my twitching cock between our bodies, coming hard on her stomach. Coating us both with my cum. It's sticky and warm and I couldn't give a shite.

I remain pressed tight to Emma, coaxing tiny shivers from

her body as I continue kissing her until we're both sated and relaxed.

Thankfully my room has an attached toilet with a bath and shower. Cleaning up is quick as I retrieve a warm damp cloth, first gently wiping Emma clean and then myself. Rinsing and hanging the rag when done. I learned the hard way you do not put a cloth in the hamper still covered in cum. Because when your mum does your laundry and find the hard material, she knows exactly what you were doing and brings it up over dinner the following day. Just to embarrass you.

Crawling back into bed, Emma settles herself across my chest without hesitation. Her arm with the fresh tattoo draped atop me. I tighten my hold around her and trace the outside of the tattoo, not touching it and wondering at my art on her body.

Regardless of what happens in two days, if she returns home, if she stays, or if I follow her to America, she will always have it. She will always think of me and this time we spent together whenever she sees it.

Again, my attention catches on the glinting gold band around her right ring finger. The claddagh ring still with the heart pointing out. Now more determined than ever to keep her, I twist the gold band. Slowly easing it off her finger. She doesn't protest. I hold it up, turning it over in my fingers before sliding it back on hers. This time, heart pointing in.

Emma is nearly half asleep and doesn't seem to care that I'm playing with her ring. Nor does she look at it to notice its new position. She will eventually. But by then I hope to have convinced her I'm worth the risk. That *we're* worth the risk. And I will do anything she asks of me to make her happy.

29 - Emma

I'm sweaty, dirty, and ready for a shower

Morning comes sooner than I want it to. Wrapped in the warm heat of Conor's body I don't want to get out of bed. Perhaps staying under the covers will pause time, relieving me from the unforeseen but now unavoidable choice.

Conor's still asleep next to me. The steady rise and fall of his chest under my head lulling me back to sleep. That is until I hear the door creak open slowly.

Lifting my head to look across the room at the door, I see it ajar, but no one there. Weird. Maybe one of Bridget's boys opened it and ran off when they saw us still asleep? Either way, I am still completely naked under the quilted blanket and am not risking flashing Conor's dad first thing in the morning.

Ignoring the partially open door I rest my head back on Conor's strong chest snuggling up closer to his neck and reach up to curl my fingers through his thick hair. He lightly growls in his sleep, pressing into my touch. His eyes remain closed, and I don't want to wake him just yet. He's so cute when he's asleep.

"Baaaaaaaaahhhhh"

Shrieking, I jolt into an upright position so fast I smack Conor in the face, trying to pull the quilt up to cover my naked chest.

"Fuck's sake. What the hell?" Conor grumbles half asleep and rubbing his nose.

"Baaaahhh."

The noise comes again from closer to the bed this time.

"What is that?" I ask in a high-pitched shrill voice that doesn't sound like my own.

Conor groans rubbing his face and muffles a throaty laugh beneath his hand. Not exactly what I was expecting in response to my obvious distress.

"What are you laughing at?"

"That's just George," he says casually through a yawn.

"George? *Who* is George?"

"My sisters pet sheep."

I'm sorry, his sister's what now? He didn't just say *pet sheep.* Did he? I shouldn't be surprised to find a sheep on a sheep farm, but I did not expect them inside the house. Inside our bedroom.

"Baaaahhh."

Comes George's insistent bleating again.

From the floor, a small black-and-white sheep with big vacant yellowish-green eyes gazes up at me, its neck adorned with a green bow tie. His wool is clean and trimmed, looking well cared for. White around his fluffy body and black at his tiny hooved feet and face. His black ears flopping downward only increasing his cuteness.

"Aww. He's so small and cute. Look at his adorable little

face," I coo down at the most adorable creature I've ever seen.

"Yeah, but he's a sneaky little gobshite. He'll steal your socks and eat your underwear if you let him. So, keep a keen eye on him unless you want to go commando."

"Really? But just look at him. He looks like a sweet little gentleman with his bow tie."

Leaning farther over the edge, I reach down to pet George. He lets me, nuzzling his little black nose against my hand. He has a mop of curly wool fur on his head, and his ears and face are covered in short soft black fur.

"Why do you call him George?"

"Aisling named him because after Curious George. It's why he's a pet and not just another sheep out in the barn. He was curious about everything and always getting into stuff, so Aisling decided she wanted to keep him and named him George."

Conor lets out a deep breath, rising to a seated position to join me in looking over the edge. Even giving George a little scratch behind his ear.

"Ever since she's pampered him and even house trained him. Said he was Gentleman George and gave him that ridiculous bow tie."

He chuckles light heartedly at his sisters' antics. I haven't known Aisling for long, but it sounds like something she would do.

"Well, I think he's precious."

"Yeah, just wait till you can't find your panties. You'll change your tune."

Conor shoo's George out of the room, flashing me his naked ass on the way to the door. Returning to bed as soon as the door is shut.

He prowls over me and begins pulling the quilt down to uncover my naked body, kissing every new exposed part. Obvious in what he's seeking, if his stiffening cock is any indication. Even after last night, my body responds to him, growing wet under his touch.

That is until a swift, loud knock on the door pauses Conor's journey to the apex of my thighs. His body stilling halfway down with his lips brushing my hardened nipples.

"Yes?" he asks impatiently.

"Get up, lazy bones. Breakfast is ready and if you're not downstairs in five minutes mum said she's going to send the boys in there," Aisling calls from the other side of the closed door.

Conor groans into my boobs and rests his forehead between them. I stifle a giggle at his reaction. Biting my lip to keep quiet.

"I can only hold them off for so long. You might as well come down," she calls before I hear her footsteps moving down the hall then down the stairs.

"Well, there's a boner killer if there ever was one."

We both laugh but get up and dressed to go downstairs for breakfast.

At the same table we ate dinner at there is now a marvelous spread of delicious looking breakfast food both familiar and not. Sausage links, slices of grilled tomatoes, beans, toast, thick slices of bacon and some pancake-looking thing. It's shaped like a pancake but lumpier.

Conor's father Brian circles the table, serving fried eggs to everyone as they all fill their plates.

"Would you like some coffee or tea Emma?" Nan asks from the side table along the wall under the large, picturesque window I didn't realize had such a beautiful view outside last night, since the rain was so thick and dark.

"Yes, tea would be lovely. Thank you."

Nan fills a cup with tea from the same ceramic tea pot from last night, setting it on a matching saucer.

"Sugar or honey?"

"Honey, please."

She sets my honeyed tea in front of me and sits in the seat at the head of the table.

"What would you like for breakfast?" Conor asks in my ear from my side, sliding a hand over my thigh and squeezing softly.

I threw on leggings and my lightweight oversized gray sweater, since the sun was shining brighter than it had in days. Warming everything a few degrees higher. A heavy sweater or jacket is not needed today. But it's not exactly a southern summer here. A cool breeze still made its way in through the open window of our bedroom, forcing me to put on something more than just a thin T-shirt.

Conor's large hand circles my thigh his fingers wrapping almost halfway around they're so large. The tips brushing dangerously close to my center. Suppressing a grin and ignoring his blatant attempt to rile me up, I observe the bounty on the table.

"Everything. But what are those?" I ask, pointing to the lumpy pancakes.

"Those are potato pancakes. Trust me, you'll love them."

After the tastiest breakfast I may have ever eaten Conor, Aisling, Liam and Brian lead me out to the large barn to show me the sheep and sheering process.

I'm instructed very carefully by Conor and Aisling on sheering. They do it with such practiced ease that makes it looks as easy as brushing your own hair. But when I try it, I realize how much strength and technique it takes to maneuver the sheep and giant wool pelt properly.

I fumble constantly and the sheep nearly escapes me three times. In the end Conor and I work together to hold the sheep and sheer it. I think Aisling sheered three in the time I finished one.

We spend hours in the sheering barn helping to get as much done as possible. By midday I'm sweaty, dirty, and ready for a shower.

Conor insists on showing me the rest of the property before we head back to the house since the sun is shining warmly overhead, giving us a rare sunny spring day.

I don't argue. The land here is beautiful. Everything is green. The grass, the trees, the leaves of the wildflowers. The sky is a crisp, clear blue the white fluffy clouds mimic the sheep grazing in the fields.

For a moment I stop and stand still in the middle of it all, listening to the wind roll over the hills and sway the tall grass. You never realize how loud and noisy life is until you stand still and listen to the silence.

Looking down from my perusal of the sky, I realize Conor has gotten far ahead of me. I have to jog to catch up with him.

"Where are we going now?" I ask as we cross through a green pasture with wandering freshly sheered sheep nibbling at the grass.

"It's a surprise. You're going to love it."

"You really like surprises, don't you?"

"I just like seeing the look on your face."

"And what look is that?"

Conor stops and turns toward me, holding my gaze with

his. "That look when your eyes go wide and bright and your mouth just barely drops open on a soft gasp. I love seeing the joy you experience."

"You're kind of weird. Ya know that?"

"But in a good way, right?"

He moves closer one slow step at a time, prowling similar to how he did this morning. Smug satisfaction on his handsome face. The fading bruises and cuts now gone. Leaving striking moss green eyes, a formidable jaw line and day-old stubble, I want to run my nails over.

"We'll see."

One dark brow quirks up at me quizzically. "Is that so?"

"That's so."

Conor steps close in front of me and without warning smacks my ass abruptly. A challenging look in his eyes.

"Come on, Leamhan Beag, before I change my mind."

His grin is wicked, but I know he's teasing. I follow Conor and his wide set shoulders through the pasture and around a crop of trees. The sound of lapping water growing steadily louder.

"Where are we . . ." I begin the ask again, but the words fade from existence at the appearance of a scenic pond straight out of a fairy tale.

A small trickling waterfall burbles on one side of the blue green water. The other side thinning into a small stream that snakes its way down a hill and farther into their property. Daisies line the edge of the water, and one solitary duck floats on the surface of the water, bobbing and diving for fish and bugs.

Conor watches me a satisfied grin on his face. "There's the look."

"You keep showing me magical places. It feels like you're trying to persuade me to stay. Because who could possibly want to live anywhere but in a place so beautiful?"

"Maybe I am."

Untucking his dirty green T-shirt from his jeans, Conor pulls the fabric over his head, disposing of it somewhere. I don't pay attention to his shirt because his sweaty chest glistening in the sunlight draws my every attention. The light emphasizing his black intricate tattoos. Reminding me of the one now on my forearm.

Jules will freak when I tell her about it. She'll also be extremely proud that I went with my gut just as she said to. It seems to be leading me somewhere. Somewhere good.

I stand, speechless, watching Conor strip out of his jeans and boxer briefs. He just smirks at me and walks backward toward the pond.

"Come on Emma. You said you wanted to wash up. What better way than in a freshwater pond?"

His feet reach the water, and he wades in slowly, only reaching his knees before he stops.

"Take off your clothes, Emma, and join me."

Looking down at my dirty hands and leggings, I take a subtle sniff and wrinkle my nose at the smell of myself. I suppose bathing in the pond isn't much different from the shower inside. Except the whole being out in the open in public where anyone in his family could see us.

"What about your family?"

"Don't worry about them. They'll leave us be."

I give him my best disbelieving *are you serious* face. He just smiles wider and rolls his bottom lip between his teeth, running inviting hands down his abs and hips, avoiding his groin and growing hardness.

"Fine," I agree haughtily and breathily.

Conor makes his way completely into the pond as I undress and set my clothes on a nearby log. The water is cool but not frigid as I expected and feels like heaven against my heated skin. Washing away the sticky sweat and dirt.

The water reaches mid chest on Conor when he stops, which means even on my toes it still reaches up to my chin. I don't have to worry about it for long. Conor pulls me close to him, wrapping my legs around his waist and holding me high enough the water doesn't risk drowning me. Not that I was too worried about it.

His hair is damp from dunking under the surface of the water, tiny droplets drip from the ends of his disheveled strands. It makes him look like a water god, come to the surface to steal the hearts of young maidens.

Although I can feel the hard ridge of his cock nestling under my ass, he doesn't attempt to slide it inside me. Completely ignoring it. His hands are gently strong, one circling my waist the other cupping one butt cheek. Holding me and nothing more.

My bare breasts press against his firm chest, and our faces are only inches apart. In the warm golden sunshine subtle freckles, I hadn't noticed before, appear high on his cheek bones and nose. Beautiful in their simplicity and elusiveness.

No matter how much bare skin presses together his intentions are purely nonsexual in this moment. A noticeable fondness in his expression.

"What did you mean before?" I ask. My thoughts still caught on his comment earlier.

"Before when?"

"When you said maybe you are."

"Oh, you mean me trying to persuade you to move to Ireland because of its magical beauty?" he says, without even a hint of sarcasm. His face serious.

"Yeah, that."

"Would you be opposed to living in Ireland?"

Looking between his sparkling green eyes, I look for the humor, the moment when he'll laugh and says he's kidding. But it's not there. He doesn't laugh, just waits patiently for me to answer.

"No. I wouldn't be opposed to living in Ireland."

"So maybe you could stay? At least a while longer. Maybe take a closer look. See all that it has to offer?"

Conor's words are low and gravely, tentative in their delivery. Shifting eyes watch to see any reaction from me. A cautious hopefulness swimming in their emerald depths.

"Like what?" I ask on a whisper, needing to know more.

I need to know why I should stay. What Ireland or he has to offer. A move that great would need a strong reason.

"Well," he begins. Rubbing his hand under the water against my waist soothingly. "We have an abundance of fairy tale ponds, lochs, and castles. Not to mention all the four-leaf clovers you could ever want to keep your good luck."

He looks down pointedly to the chain with the clover still around my neck, bobbing on the surface of the water. I'd completely forgotten about it.

"There's also all the cider you could ever want in all of our many pubs," he continues. "Then there's me."

My hands circled around his neck tighten, and I hold him closer. Hope blossoming in my chest, the seeds of it spreading through my veins like the seeds of a dandelion drifting in the wind.

"What about you?"

The corner of his lips twitch, but the smile doesn't fully form yet.

"I want you to stay, Emma. To stay with me. I want to fall asleep next to you every night and wake up with you draped across me every morning. I want to have more chaotic family dinners with you and watch you dance around in your underwear to Nicki Minaj when you're happy, which I hope will be often.

"I want to show you that you don't have bad luck. Because, without the bad luck you hate so much, I never would have met you. I never would have fallen in love with you. I would still be waiting for you. I want to help you become the schoolteacher you dream of being and take you to see a moth sanctuary and listen to my family tell you embarrassing stories about me.

"I want to meet your brother and parents. And this friend Jules you keep talking about and thank her for forcing you to come to Ireland."

I'm breathless under his confessions. It's more than I ever expected him to say. I hoped he would ask me to stay at least to get to know me better, spend time together and possibly date.

But this?

A confession of love? How do I respond to that? Do I tell him I feel the same? That I've never felt so drawn to a person in my life?

"Conor . . . I . . . I . . ." I choke on my words, emotion clogging them in my throat.

"It's okay, Love. You don't have to say anything. Just think about it. It's a big decision. I don't want you to jump in without considering everything first. I just want you to know, if you want to stay there's a place for you here."

Pressing his forehead to mine I close my eyes and inhale his scent of leather and woods tinted with his salty sweat and the crisp water surrounding us. Inhaling deep I relax through my exhale. Calming my racing heart.

His lips are gentle against mine in a kiss so devastatingly loving I'm glad Conor's holding me because I would have sank below the surface and drowned otherwise.

Breaking the kiss, his lips remain hovering over mine but not touching. "Just think about it, Leamhan Beag. You let me know when you decide. Until you decide to get on that plane and leave, you're still mine."

I nod in agreement. All that I can do since I've lost my ability to speak. Conor's hand releases my ass and slides up to cup my cheek a possessive hold on my chin.

We stand in the center of the pond. The only sound our thudding hearts pounding a heavy rhythm against each other and the gentle trickle of the small waterfall. That is until a now familiar sounds breaks the silence.

George the curious sheep bleats loudly from the edge of the pond. Conor and I both turn to look at him and his demanding tone. He's standing near the log where I draped my clothes. Nosing eagerly at the fabrics, until he finds my underwear.

Fuck a duck.

"Don't you dare George," I scold. He doesn't listen but pulling insistently at the white cotton, trying to free them from my leggings. "George! Drop them. No, no, no, no."

I wiggle free of Conor's hold trying to make it to the shore before the little fluffy devil can steal them. I am unsuccessful as I scramble butt naked onto the mossy grass, trying to snatch my cotton panties from George, but he runs off with them clamped between his teeth, bleating happily as he bounces away white cotton panties dangling from his mouth.

Conor's laugh is deep and hearty as he joins me on the shore, dripping wet and brushing dampness from his hair.

"I told you to watch your panties," he chides.

The heavy seriousness from our conversation dissipates in the fading bleats and laughter.

"I suppose I didn't need underwear today."

"I know I prefer when you don't wear them."

With a light smack on my ass and a kiss to my temple Conor retrieves his own clothes, which were thrown over a higher branch where curious panty hungry sheep can't reach them.

Back in the house I head straight for the bathroom to shower. We may have rinsed off in the pond, but there's still wool, hay, and dirt in my hair.

Warm water streams down my back and through my hair, and I've barely squirted the shampoo into my hand when the shower curtain is flung open by a very naked Conor.

"Ah! You almost gave me a heart attack," I screech, smacking him on the chest and clutching my other hand to my heart dramatically.

Chuckling, he pulls me against him as he steps into the tub. No longer disinterested in our combined nudity. He is very much paying attention to it now. Pressing his erection into my stomach and claiming my mouth with his.

His tongue desperately seeking out mine. Tongues tangling and teeth clacking in a frenzy for more. My hands slide down his wet torso, smearing the unused shampoo on his hard abs. Feeling every ridge until I find his eager cock. Gripping it in both hands, I squeeze and stroke him, pulling moans of approval and desire from his lips that are still attached to mine. Wetness not from the shower pools between my thighs and slicks my pussy, wanting him there.

But first I want to taste him. Something I haven't had the pleasure of experiencing yet. Breaking our kiss, I pepper kisses along the underside of his jaw, down his neck and chest. Nipping and biting as I go creating a trail of goose bumps in my wake. Conor's hand slides into my hair and grips gently as I go lower and lower. Finally settling on my knees his beautiful erect cock at eye level.

Licking the tip like frosting on a cupcake his entire body shudders, and his dick bobs against my lips. I press a wet open-mouthed kiss to the leaking tip and suck up his precum. His skin tastes salty and sweet.

I open my lips and suck the swollen head into my mouth, licking the underside with my tongue as I do so. Conor's breath stutters above me, and he mutters something in Irish so low I can't hear. Not that I would understand it anyway.

Taking his increasing heavy breaths and tangled fingers in my hair as a good sign, I continue. Relishing in his unhinged convulsing under my touch. His cock is thick and hard in my mouth as I press it deeper into my throat. Taking as much as possible, which is about seventy-five percent of him before he hits the back of my throat. Using my hand to wrap around the remaining length of him. Stroking with the movement of my mouth moving up and down his cock.

He groans, and I hear a hand slap against the tiled wall.

"Emma, Love . . . fuck your mouth feels fantastic."

I hum around his cock, and he groans again. He starts to say something more but is interrupted by a male voice loudly calling his name from outside the bathroom.

"Conor? Where the feck are ya, you eejit? I know yer here. Your mum told me so."

"Fucking shite," Conor curses.

I pull my mouth free of his dick to look up at him mouthing, *who is it?*

My cousin, he silently mouths back at me.

"Conor!" a pounding knocks on the door loudly. "I know you're in there. Open up."

"Go away, Rory. I'll be out in a few," Conor yells back frustrated with the interruption. He's not the only one.

"Not a chance in hell, mate."

The door opens since neither of us thought to lock it, and I hear heavy footsteps enter the small bathroom. Then I hear a loud growl from Conor above me.

"Look I know you said you needed to take a holiday and get yourself straight before the match, but you really need to come back to the gym to train before the fight," Rory begins rambling and chastising Conor. He must be the one who is his manager.

Ignoring the ranting on the other side of the dark curtain, which thankfully cannot be seen through, I return to my previous position. With Conor's dick deep in my mouth. Above me, Conor bites his fist to contain the moan at my sudden sucking.

Smiling at Conor's wide pleading eyes, looking down at me, I double my efforts. Sucking and stroking not caring about the irate Rory just feet away. The look on Conor's face, one of pure pleasure, disbelief and utter hatred for his cousin in this moment, is worth it.

Gripping the back of my head Conor rocks his hips against my mouth, sliding his cock in and out. His eyes burning bright as he watches his length slip between my lips.

Rory continues talking and Conor seems too close to coming to accept his unwanted presence any longer.

"I swear to God, Rory, if you do not leave right now, I will fire your arse, then beat you senseless."

Conor's demand is punctuated with heavy breaths as he tries to control his arousal but doesn't fully succeed. His shaft pulsing between my lips. I can tell he's close to coming, and I don't care as much that Rory is here to witness it as Conor seems to be.

"I don't give a shite if you beat me, but later. Your match is TOMORROW. You need to get back to training now in order to be ready."

"For fuck's sake, Rory, get the fuck out of here!" Conor roars in agitation, so close to coming in my mouth.

Cupping his balls in my hand, I give them a good squeeze and hold them there as I continue my ministrations. Circling the head of his cock with my tongue, then my fingers.

"You're not in there alone, are you?" Rory asks hesitantly.

"No," Conor answers hoarsely, the light rocking of his hips growing more desperate as his release nears.

"She's in there with you, isn't she?"

"Yup."

"Right, then. Okay . . . I'll just . . . wait downstairs."

"You do that."

The door shuts and as soon as it does Conor moans,

focusing on me kneeling between his legs.

"You are in big trouble, Love."

Not wanting to remove his cock from my mouth I shrug one shoulder in response.

His body tenses, and he bends slightly at the waist, angling himself further down my throat. I gag a little at the invasion but quickly pull back enough to continue sucking and fucking him with my mouth.

I don't want him to stop. I want to see him fall apart and taste his desire. Massaging his balls, I let him move but continue my own rhythm matching his perfectly.

"Jesus fuck, Emma. I'm gonna come, and you're going to keep my cock in your mouth until you swallow every last fucking drop as punishment for your little stunt."

Personally, that doesn't sound like a punishment to me. Neither does my body as my pussy throbs and grows wetter the harder he thrusts and longer he talks.

The ache is too great, and I release his testicles to slide my fingers down into my needy pussy. Slipping one finger along my slit then circling my clit.

"That's it, Love, play with yourself. Make yourself come while making me come."

And I do. Slipping my fingers into myself and grinding my palm against my clit as Conor throbs and pulses out his release into my mouth, holding my head tight against his cock. The ecstasy of my own orgasm thrums through my veins and pulses out around my fingers as his cock continues to spasm between my lips.

After the shockwaves from both of our climaxes settle, Conor helps me into a standing position and brushes a tender kiss across my lips.

"You continue to surprise me, Leamhan Beag."

"As do you. Your fight is tomorrow?"

Conor nods without a hint of concern, altering his expression. He's either extremely cocky or very confident. Possibly both.

"Why didn't you tell me?"

"I didn't want to concern you with it. You had so many other things going on. My fight shouldn't affect your decisions."

I look up at him, brushing away a strand of wet hair that clings to my face. He means that. I can understand how, initially, his life might not have concerned me. But now? Now with his declarations and offers, his life is very much important.

"However, if you stay, I would love for you to be there. Having you near makes me feel like I'm the luckiest lad in the world. Like I could do anything."

"Because I still possess your good luck clover," I say flatly with a forced smile.

He scoffs and a chuckle rumbles low in his chest. "I don't give a shite about the fucking clover Emma. Keep it, toss it in the bin, burn it. I don't care. All I want is you, Love."

My heart hammers in my chest nearly as fast as it had a few minutes ago. "Nothing more?"

"Nothing more, nothing less than all of you."

30 – Conor

I'll give her anything she asks of me

Rory's a lucky man right now. I was fully intending on beating that gobshite into pulp if he continued to run his mouth while my cock was shoved inside Emma's. If he hadn't had left when he did, he would be on his way to hospital right now. Bleeding from multiple wounds. He's my cousin, and I love him, but he would have deserved it. Would have done the same, too, had I walked in on him and Erin and didn't leave.

Instead of weeping tears of blood he's sitting on the couch in the living room with Aisling and Nan when I come downstairs, a dopey grin on my face. The grin only wavering for a moment as I spare a glare at Rory before dismissing his error earlier. You can't hold on to negative feelings, or they'll taint all the good.

"Sorry about earlier, mate. I didn't mean to interrupt anything," Rory mutters.

He understands what he did wrong. There's no need to

berate him more for it.

"What did he interrupt?" Aisling asks like the nosey little sister she is. If the giant shit-eating grin on her face is any indication, she absolutely knows what he interrupted.

"None of your business."

Aisling smothers a laugh and sticks her tongue out at me like the mature adult she is. Nan giving me a knowing smirk from her spot in her chair where she's working on yet another jumper, scarf, hat, socks, or something else to gift to one of us grandkids. This time in a burnt orange. I hope it's not for me. Orange isn't my color.

"Where is Emma? Will she be joining us for an afternoon drink?" Nan nods toward the low table where there is not only tea, but whiskey set out.

My family has a proclivity for the old Irish tradition of mixing their tea and whiskey. The two pair nicely and makes teatime a tad more bearable when company is lacking.

"She'll be down soon."

"I like her, Conor."

"You'd like anyone I brought home."

Nan shakes her head. "No. I've seen the girls you've been with before."

"How?" I ask, shocked that Nan is someone mysteriously following my love life.

I turn a much narrower glare on Rory, expecting him to be the culprit spilling my dating habits with my family. Holding up his hands in surrender, he shakes his head back and forth adamantly.

"Not me, mate. I didn't say nothin."

I turn my glare on Aisling, the family gossip. She too stares back at me wide eyed and innocent.

"Not me," she admits, sipping from her teacup. The picture of perfect innocence I know she isn't.

"Don't blame them. I read the gossip tabloids. I see the photos of you going out with those women. They all looked . . . fake. Like they were putting on a show, more interested in smiling for the camera than you."

Well, she's not wrong. That pretty much sums up the entirety of my recent years of dating.

"Nan," Aisling gasps in mock surprise. "I never knew. We could have been having far more interesting conversations all this time?"

Nan laughs but continues her knitting, pretending to be a boring grandma who doesn't know which Kardashian is in the headlines this week. She turns her focused grass green eyes back on me, her hands never faltering in their movements.

"This one is different. She's . . . good for you."

"Good for me?"

"Yes. You needed someone real, someone who is with you because of you. Not because of your money or status."

My smile falters, and I plop down on the couch next to Aisling, my body slouching against the familiar cushions. Nan gives me a curious look, not expecting a negative response to her declaration. She believes with the right motivation Emma will turn from tourists to resident. Aisling, on the other hand, knows the whole story how Emma and I met and gives me a pathetic, pitiful look. Like she feels sorry for me.

Don't feel sorry for me yet. Emma might choose to stay.

The thought has my mood improving, and I perk up a bit. Because Nan's optimism might not be misplaced. I asked Emma to stay. Offered her the choice, and she didn't immediately say no.

"I think you're right Nan."

Nan just nods in agreement. Aisling furrows her brow at me, and Rory is completely lost. He knows nothing about Emma. At least I didn't think he did. I never told him anything. But when he interrupted us in the shower, he said, "She's in there with you." Which means he somehow knew about her.

I turn to face my cousin and manager—and if I were being honest, my best friend—and give him a quizzical look.

"How did you know about Emma?"

"Aisling told me. So did your mum and Bridget and even your dad. As soon as I arrived demanding to see you they very excitedly told me about this woman who you brought home. I don't really know the whole story though. I gather there's a lot more to it that I'm missing."

I huff out a laugh and rub a hand around the back of my neck. "You have no idea mate."

Rory raises an eyebrow at me, waiting for me to elaborate. I just shake my head at him. I'll fill him in later. Now Emma's sock clad feet appear on the stairs, and I don't want her to think we were talking about her. Even though we were.

Emma enters the room with a tentative smile on her lips. She has nothing to be embarrassed about, and I won't let her. Standing I cross the room to where she's stopped at the threshold, obviously unsure if she should join. Of course she should fucking join. I want her to stick around and join in every family gathering possible.

Wrapping an arm around her waist, I press a kiss to her temple and feel her posture relax under my touch. Guiding her to the couch, I gesture for her to sit between me and Aisling. Knowing her being near my sister will put her even more at ease.

The thought warms my chest. Emma and Aisling already seem to be becoming fast friends, and I couldn't be happier about the development. Some might not like their girlfriends getting to know their siblings and befriending them in such a way, but I only want more of it.

"Emma, this is Rory. My impatient and sometimes deaf cousin and manager."

Emma waves at Rory, her cheeks pinkening slightly. "Hello. It's nice to meet you, properly."

"Nice to meet you as well," he says but thankfully says nothing more about the shower. I thank him silently for not bringing it up in front of others.

"Oh my," Nan interrupts the introductions. "Is that Conor's jumper?" she asks, eyeing Emma who is, once again, wearing the black jumper I loaned her when we were stranded on the side of the road.

The material swallows her, and she's rolled the cuffs up multiple times so the tips of her fingers poke out the bottom. It nearly reaches her knees. I still like seeing her in it.

Emma blushes again and tucks her chin down to look down at herself. "Uh, yeah. He let me borrow it because it's warmer than mine and the ones in the store were too expensive."

"That was nice of him. But I think I have one that might fit better. I have plenty of jumpers I've made in my room if you're interested. Although if you prefer his I can understand, but I'd still like to give you one. As a gift."

Emma thinks it over, her eyes watching Nan expectantly. Waiting for what? A punch line? A just kidding? When nothing comes, she exhales and nods.

"Okay, sure. I wanted one of my own anyway. I'm sure Conor wouldn't mind getting his back."

"You can keep it for as long as you want," I state, not wanting her to give it back.

"Even so, let's go find you one of your own."

Nan smiles and stands, placing her current project on her empty seat. She reaches out a hand and takes Emma's. She follows willingly, and the two head out of the room toward Nan's room on the lower floor. Stairs don't agree with her hips anymore.

Emma looks back over her shoulder, and I give her a reassuring smile before they disappear down the hall. Nan gabbing the whole time about colors and styles.

"I think Nan likes her," Aisling loud whispers next to me, leaning over to elbow me in the ribs.

"That much she's said," I agree, still watching down the hall, even though I can't see either of the woman anymore.

Supper is served earlier than it was last night since we still have to drive back to Dublin after. It's just as loud the second time around. My family just as welcoming to Emma. This time with the addition of one more, my cousin Rory. Who is shoved at the edge of the table next to my nephews across from me.

He doesn't seem to notice the boisterous boys next to him trying to instigate a food fight. His curious eyes keep shifting between me and Emma, who is now wearing a new jumper curtesy of Nan. The fit still large but far more fitted to her size than my giant one in a color I called pink and was immediately corrected on. The pink is specifically "dusty rose."

Emma hasn't given me back my black jumper yet, so she's accepted I want her to have it.

Again, Nan tries to sneak in suggestions about moving to Ireland, and all the positive attributes of living here might have for Emma. One of which is her ability to show her how to properly turn raw wool into the yarn she uses to knit all our Christmas gifts. And then teaching her how to knit said jumpers.

The way my Nan instantly invites Emma to be part of the family is endearing, and extremely helpful when trying to convince her we're worth the risk.

Me finding a woman to settle down with is not only something I want but the rest of my family as well. Especially Mum and Rory. Anything that gets me out of the gym twenty-four-seven is something he supports.

After supper everyone says their goodbyes. Hugging both me and Emma with encouraging words of either a safe return home or invitations to come back whenever she pleases. With or without me. I'm fine with that. Because that means she'd be in Ireland.

Rory heads out before us since his goodbyes take far less time. Our luggage is loaded in the boot of my SUV, and we finally begin the short but long journey back to Dublin. The drive itself should only be an hour, but it'll be the longest hour of my life. Knowing when we arrive, she may want to go her separate way. Turn down my offer and leave, which she has every right to.

If she doesn't, I'll give her anything she asks of me.

The sky remains blissfully clear, not a rain cloud in sight. Fitting that, now, the rain would let up. No more getting caught in the rain for us. Nothing to stop her from returning home or extending her trip even a day or two more.

For the entire drive, I keep my hand firmly on Emma. Her thigh, her shoulder, her hand. Keeping contact reminding her I'm here. I'll always be here until she doesn't want me.

Without the sounds of the rain hitting the car, the lack of radio is far more obvious. Emma doesn't seem to mind. Her eyes drifting between the road ahead and out her window, then back to me. She seems far too deep in thought to interrupt, but I have to know.

"Will you stay with me tonight? At my place? Or did you want to go to a hotel?"

Her hand grips mine resting on her thigh, her thumb rubbing in restless circles.

"I'll stay with you."

"Good." I give her hand a grateful squeeze, and my nerves settle.

The day fades into night and the sky is clear enough to see the light twinkling of stars as we drive. Which are replaced with the streetlights of the city as we get closer and closer to my flat. Arriving all too soon.

I park in the underground lot and guide Emma to my floor, flicking on the lights as we enter my front door.

My flat consists of two bedrooms with plenty of windows looking out over the streets below. The area I live in is more residential than commercial and has far less noise in the evening. With the absence of heavy tourist crowds and pub patrons, it makes it a highly desirable area for locals.

Emma inspects every room leisurely. The living room with the large leather sofa and flatscreen, years of MMA memorabilia hanging on the exposed brick walls. a well-stocked kitchen I use regularly, have to keep in good health in my profession or, so my well-paid nutritionist says. The washroom with large walk-in glass shower and deep soaking tub for those nights my fights get more aggressive than others. The second bedroom, which, not surprisingly, is set up as a small home gym, with a bench press, free weights, and a treadmill for those days I don't get to the real gym or ring to train.

Finally, my bedroom with the large king size bed centered on the back wall, draped in a messily folded quilt Nan made for me when I moved into my flat years ago, in shades of fading blues and grays. The floor is covered with a lush navy rug, my shoes and gear strew about the floor, a few shirts overflowing from the hamper. I didn't have time to do laundry before running after Emma to get back my luck. The dresser is sparsely covered with photo frames, a watch my mates gifted me after my first main card win, loose coins, receipts, and random things that ended up in my pockets then on the dresser never to move again.

I try to keep my home organized and clean but sometimes life happens, and it has a lived-in feel I prefer over stark cleanliness.

The suitcases are tucked inside my walk-in closet filled with unfolded clothing and fitness gear of unknown cleanliness. I don't bother unpacking just yet. There are more important things and people to focus on tonight.

Rory wants me in the gym first thing in the morning to train before the fight tomorrow night. After nearly a week out, I'm adamant to get back in the ring. But doing so without knowing Emma will be there to cheer me on has my ever-present desire to train dwindling. Shifting to a nervous anxiety that I may never see her again after tonight.

Who am I kidding? Even if she returns to Texas, my lovesick arse will probably book a seat on the same flight to follow her like a damn puppy dog.

I follow Emma back to the main living space where she leans against the island counter that divides the kitchen from the living room. She looks like she belongs here.

"Are you thirsty? I have a few options."

Walking around the island, I make my way to the fridge and open it, listing off what's left inside.

"Milk, orange juice, water. I can make coffee or tea."

I close the fridge door and gesture to the small array of liquor bottles on the counter in the corner. "I also have something stronger, if you're interested."

"Orange juice is fine," she offers with a wary smile, her eyes downcast on the countertop at her clasped hands.

After getting her a glass of juice and watching her swallow it in two massive gulps, I steer us to the sofa wanting to ease into its familiarity with Emma curled up on my lap. If this is the last night I have with her, I don't want to spend it standing at my kitchen island making idle chitchat.

She comes willingly falling easily into place across my thighs, stretching her legs out across the leather. Her shoes falling to the floor as she kicks them off, getting more comfortable.

When she nuzzles her face into the crook of my neck, something inside me liquifies, my entire being sinking into a complete state of serenity.

I spread my legs farther apart, Emma's backside slipping between cradled in my thighs. Everything is quiet and still, and I fear if I breathe too hard everything might shatter.

"So, when is your fight tomorrow?" Emma's soft voice breaks the silence but not enough to shatter the feeling steadily growing inside me.

"It starts at five in the evening. I'd love it if you came to watch me."

"My flight is at five."

"Oh."

We sit in a new type of silence, one that rests heavy on my heart, waiting for her to push me away. She doesn't. But having the knowledge out there ringing in my ears like a siren has my hold on Emma tightening.

"If I were to stay," she begins a quiet yearning in her voice. "What . . . what would happen then?"

"For starters, you'll stay here with me for as long as you desire. Then, I don't know. We could see about finding you a job. One as a teacher. You'd have to get a work visa. I have no idea what kind of certificates are required for teaching, but I'm sure we could figure it out."

Emma is quiet in my arms, keeping her face pressed close to my chest. Her hand fiddling with the collar of my shirt, soft fingertips grazing across my skin with every other stroke.

"What if . . . what if I'm not sure I want to stay? What if something happens? Between us."

It's obvious she's concerned. Who wouldn't be? It's a big change, and she'd be leaving behind a lot. I won't let her think I'm forcing her to stay or that I won't fly her entire family out here to live with us if she wants it.

"How about we don't plan anything permanent yet? You can stay with me, and we can see where things go for a short time. And if you change your mind, I'll buy you a first-class ticket back to America. I promise I won't force you to stay, but I want you to know I very much would like you to.

"And if you're concerned about seeing your family, I will

gladly pay for them to visit. Or we could visit them for a time. Spend half our time in America the other half here in Ireland. I have to travel for my matches anyway. I don't care where we are, Leamhan Beag, as long as we're together.

"I've never met anyone like you. I've never felt so strongly, so completely for someone before, like I do for you. I always planned to get married and have children but never found the right girl to do it with. They were all lacking. Lacking in humor, heart, love."

Her hand slides from my collar to circle around my neck, her lips pressing softly to my throat causing me to swallow hard and a shiver to run down my spine.

"I want you, Emma. Physically, emotionally, eternally. I won't hurt you, at least not intentionally. And I have enough money to ensure your comfort and fulfill your every need. Just say you'll let me. Say you'll let me try."

My strangled heartfelt confession ends on a pathetic pleading lament. All the strength training and fighting ability in the world couldn't make me strong enough not to beg this woman to stay.

"I'll have to sleep on it. I'm still not sure," she answers honestly. Her voice as small and as cautious as mine.

I kiss the top of her head and sink further into the sofa settling in. I plan on sitting here until she falls asleep, then carrying her to my bed and holding her close all night, hoping my shockingly tangible feelings for her absorb into her skin.

"I have to go to the gym in the morning to prepare. I wish I could stay with you but . . . I'll have a car here for you at two o'clock to take you, well wherever you want to go. If you decide to stay, the driver will bring you to the arena where I'll be fighting. If not, it'll take you to the airport. It's your choice."

I can feel her nod against my shoulder, but she doesn't speak. Neither of us does. I don't turn on the telly or move to do anything. Remaining firmly in place, running my fingers through Emma's silky ruby hair. Watching the strands flow like water over them. Memorizing its shade and the sound of her breathing and the rhythm of her heart beating steadily against mine.

"Is tusa an grá a cheap mé nach bhfaighfinn choíche agus an grá nach scaoilfidh mé as." *You are the love I thought I would never find and the love I will never let go of.*

I whisper the words, knowing Emma can hear them, but she doesn't ask me to translate this time. I don't think I could. Saying them in Irish made it easier. But to say them in English, would break me.

31 – Emma

Fuck eloquence

The morning comes in annoyingly bright rays of sunshine through the large window in Conor's bedroom. Its warmth sinking into the exposed side of my face. The rest of me is engulfed in Conor's arms. Our bodies so close I'm surprised I hadn't woken in the night.

I remember falling asleep in his lap on the couch and nothing else. One moment I'm dreading falling asleep and losing time with him the next I'm waking hours later in his bed. My internal clock waking me as soon as the sun crested the horizon.

The clock on the nightstand reads seven-o-five. I wonder when Conor was planning on leaving to train. I wish he didn't have to. But it's probably better. I'll be able to call Jules and get her sound honest advice. It'll probably come as a shock considering the last time we spoke nothing had happened between Conor and I yet. Now so much has.

They say good things come to those who wait but great

things come all at once.

Should I consider this a great thing? If I turn away now and leave, will I regret it for the rest of my life?

I have a feeling I would.

However, leaving Texas, and all my family behind, no more family dinners and quick trips to Danny's for drinks or to Sean's to play with my nephew, would be immensely difficult.

Although it's not as if I would never see them again, considering Conor said he would pay to bring them here. We could travel to America, and I could show him my old life, introduce him to my family. Watch my brothers sizing him up and calculating their ability to take him down if needed. They could try and possibly succeed, but my money would be on Conor. High school wrestling and a few jujitsu classes does not a professional fighter make.

Conor shifts under me and yawns. His body elongating in a stretch before his hands find any part of my body he can reach. One settling under my butt, cupping the cheek and kneading it.

His massive body repositioning and pulling me on top to straddle his thighs. Conor's mouth finds the crook of my neck and sucks softly.

"Good morning, Love."

His voice is pure sin dipped in gravel and coated in lust. The large hard length of his cock settling comfortably against my pussy, forcing a breathy gasp from me.

"Good morning," I pant.

"Are you going to tell me your decision before I have my way with you? Or are you going to make me work for it?"

The playfulness in his words has my anxiety easing and the stress of deciding washing away. Focusing on the man below me kissing a path up my neck and jaw before finding my lips. Pulling my bottom lip between his teeth, he sucks on it gently before releasing it to press a punishing kiss against them.

I don't deny him all that he wants because I want it too.

The kiss shifts from desperate to tender and worshipping. An exploratory and adoring kiss. The frantic energy of our previous lovemaking becoming something softer, smoother.

Undemanding hands explore by body, which I realize is mostly bare with only my panties remaining. He must have removed all the other clothes when putting us to bed last night. They brush and grip and hold every part of me.

Reaching for the only clothing on my body, Conor twists each side of my panties around his fists and pulls. The sharp tearing sound breaking our dazed kiss.

"Did you just tear off my underwear?"

"Yes, I did. You have a problem with that?" Conor retorts flatly, ignoring my feigned disapproval and continuing to kiss any part of me he can reach. Which is mostly my neck and collarbone.

"Not particularly. But I seem to be running low on panties since your sheep ate a pair, and you just destroyed another."

"Not my sheep, not my fault," he grumbles against my breast sliding me up, so he can better reach my nipple to suck it into his mouth.

All other protests or sassy remarks are cut short when he does. He doesn't want to talk anymore and neither do I.

Our movements become a practiced dance we somehow learned without even trying. Mouths knowing exactly where to suck and kiss, hands knowing where to hold and stroke, hips rolling in unison. Coming together in a now recognizable movement.

My knees pressing to either side of his hips lift me enough for him to position himself at my entrance. His hard arousal meeting my wetness. He presses up into me slowly, languishing in every inch he advances. Unhurried and controlled.

His arms wrap around my waist, keeping my chest pressed close to his as if he wants no space between us. Mine wrap around his shoulders and neck, allowing him to take control of the speed and movement of our bodies. Slow, long thrusts in and out as his hips roll and undulate.

My orgasm builds slowly, so slowly I don't even realize I'm coming. The tightening in my core, a wave rolling through my body, baring down on Conor's cock, still thrusting faster now but still far slower than before.

His body tenses, and he groans, pressing his hips flush with mine, and I can feel him coming inside me. His hot release coating and spraying. His cock twitching and pulsing out his release. It feels like pure bliss, and I convulse around him at the sensation. My orgasm rolling back and forth settling tight in my core.

"Conor." His name comes out a breathless whisper against his lips.

"Shite," he groans. "Fuck . . . I'm sorry, Love. I didn't think . . . I forgot . . ." He trails off trying to speak but is still wrapped in the pleasure of his release.

He doesn't instantly pull out. What's the point? It would change nothing. I should freak out and run over the numbers on how likely I am to get pregnant. Right now, I couldn't care less.

"It's okay, Love."

Conor's eyes shoot to mine. He's only ever been the one to call me, Love. Hearing me call him that has him looking mystified. A glimmering approval in his glowing jade eyes.

"It is?"

"Yeah. I'm sure it'll be fine. I have less than a twenty percent chance of getting pregnant. Even less if I'm not ovulating."

"That still seems like a large percentage."

I shrug. At this point I might as well live my life on the edge. I no longer believe I'll always fall into the small percentages out of bad luck.

"It's actually harder to conceive than you think," I say, noticing his look of apprehension doesn't seem fearful or angry that it could happen. More like concern for me and how I feel about it.

It makes me smile down at him and peck a kiss to his nose, washing away the look completely.

"If you say so, Love," he concedes, half-lidded with a smile.

We get up slowly making our way to the bathroom to shower and dress. We don't have sex again, but that doesn't mean we don't touch and kiss and fondle.

By the time we get out of the shower Rory has called three times and Conor hurries to dress and eat a quick breakfast consisting of two protein bars and an apple. We linger at the door to his apartment, starting another make-out session neither of us wants to end.

"If you decide to leave, please just let me know. Let me know you make it back safe and if anything comes of this morning."

He means the unprotected sex that could possibly end in pregnancy. I give him a small nod, toying with the cuffs of my new sweater. A gift from Conor's Nan. It's soft and warm and my new security blanket.

"I will. I promise."

"Good. I really hope I do see you later, though."

I can't answer him. I still haven't decided, and I only have a handful of hours left to do so.

"Just in case, and not to try to sway you or anything, but you should know, and I want to tell you." He pauses and cups my face between his hands, lining my face up with his. "I love you, Emma Johnson. Know that."

He presses a kiss to my forehead, and his hold tightens before releasing me completely. Without a goodbye he turns and leaves. Looking at me one last time over his shoulder as the door closes behind him.

Not caring what time it is, I dig my phone out of my purse on the entry way table and dial Jules's number. It takes a few rings, but she answers.

"Somebody better be dead or dying to be calling at this hour," my best friend growls out as soon as she answers the phone.

"Not dead but possibly dying inside."

"Emma? Is that you? Are you okay? Do I need to send a fixer?"

"What the hell is a fixer?"

"Someone who fixes things, duh. They just usually include bullet wounds or stalkers."

My mouth falls open at the weirdest exchange of words I've ever had with Jules. That's saying something when we've discussed the likelihood of our entire world being an alien's science experiment.

"When have you ever had a bullet wound?" I ask flabbergasted.

"Not me. Other people. Whatever it doesn't matter. What's going on Em?"

Shaking my head clear of the fixer and bullet wound comment, I try to focus on why I called.

"Well, you're not going to believe this," I begin.

"Probably will but go on."

I chuckle and delve into the story of me and Conor and all that's happened in the past days. Jules listens intently, making small noises throughout to confirm she is listening and following along but letting me get it all out before saying anything. I pace frantically back and forth from one end of the apartment to the other, nibbling on my fingernail nervously.

"So now I'm in his apartment trying to figure out what to do. Get on the plane back home or go to his fight and stay and see what happens."

"Stay," she says firmly no longer groggy in the least.

"What? Just like that? No thinking about it or anything?"

"What's there to think about, Em? You love the guy, right?" she asks haughtily.

I do love him. But I shouldn't, right? Not so soon. It couldn't be love, it's just lust clouding my brain with endorphins and orgasms.

That's not right. It's not lust. I've felt plenty of lust. It wanes and fades after the initial satisfaction. It doesn't leave my heart melting on to the floor pining over the man.

"Well . . . maybe. I don't know."

"So, that's a yes. You've never loved a guy before, Emma. Why would you decide to run away from the one you finally fall for? And a fuck hot rich one at that."

"Eloquent as always Jules."

"Fuck eloquence," she scoffs, laughing lightly.

My best friend and life advisor everyone.

"But what about my brothers and parents?" I argue, trying

to convince myself, only because I already know the answer I want to give but can't seem to accept.

"What about them? They'll be happy for you, hun. Don't worry about them. It's not like you'd be moving to the moon it's only Ireland. There are these amazing inventions called *airplanes*," she says sarcastically. "We can fly to you; you can fly to us. It'll be great. Maybe I'll even get a place over there. I've been meaning for a change of scenery. New York is getting boring."

"Only you would think New York is boring, Jules."

"Well, it is," she pouts. "And what about your bad luck curse? Do you think it's gone?"

I haven't even thought about the curse in days. My luck didn't matter when I was busy getting naked with Conor. If anything, I've had great luck since I met him.

"Maybe. I haven't really thought about it."

"*You* haven't thought about your bad luck? Conor really has been keeping you busy, hasn't he?"

"Ha-ha Jules, you're so funny. I guess I've just had other things on my mind lately. It's kind of like as soon as I stopped thinking about it all the time it went away. Conor thinks I don't have bad luck at all."

"Really?" Jules asks obvious disbelief in her tone, laced with a tinge of hope. We would all love for it to be true. Past experiences argue the contrary, but when looked at in a different light, I can see what Conor means.

"He says that everything happens for a reason. You just have to look for it. Sometimes it may not be as obvious as others, but there's always something."

"I think I like Conor even more now. So?"

"So what?"

"Are you going to stay?"

Am I going to stay? A large part of me wants to, but a small part still argues that things could go terribly wrong if I do.

"Well, you know my opinion. Jump in feet first and hope you stick the landing."

"A life motto we should all live by," I deadpan.

"In all seriousness, Emma," her voice lowers, and all humor fades. With Jules, that rarely happens, so I know she's trying to focus. "Conor sounds amazing. A life with him would be a hundred times more than anything you have waiting for you back in Texas. There's nothing there for you anymore. Not a job, not an apartment, not a caring, loving man willing to give you the world on a silver platter. Take the opportunity. Fate opened the door for you. Now all you have to do is walk through it."

"That's all? Just walk through the door and say yes? Leave the rest to fate and not worry about the what ifs?" I ask weakly, feeling my stubborn resolve to fight waning.

"Yes."

Yes?

32 - Conor

Now is not the time to be popping a boner

Walking away from Emma and leaving her in my flat pierces my soul and bleeds tar. But I have to do it. I have to let her choose. If she doesn't want this, want us, I'll accept it, no matter how much it hurts.

I've been punched, kicked, twisted, broken bones and bled in the ring. None of that hurts as much as this. None would compare to the pain I would feel if she were to leave.

Throughout my entire workout and warm up, I keep silent unable to hold any conversation. My mind solely focused on one thing only. The clock on the wall ticking down to my fate, my possible future.

Perhaps there's already a future growing inside Emma. The thought has my heart rate picking up speed and causing me to stumble.

"You okay, mate?" Rory asks, watching me carefully.

I told him about Emma as soon as I arrived. Made him reserve her a seat and ticket at the arena in case she shows.

Ring side, right by him and the rest of my team. The team that ensures my career continues. I should give them a bonus or something. I don't give them enough credit for what they do. Especially Niall who always tends to take the brunt of it, literally.

"Yeah. Fine," I answer, returning to the speed bag swinging rapidly from the low mounted frame.

My fists come back up and resume fast hard movements against the small teardrop shaped bag, re accelerating its speed. The black bag becomes and blur and I blindly swing at it, allowing my muscle memory to take over. My body moving of its own accord while my mind drifts from here back to my apartment this morning.

The way she straddled me and let me set our rhythm, how I came inside her. My dick in my shorts perks up at the memory, and I have to push it away.

Now is not the time to be popping a boner.

"Are you ready for this fight?" Rory inquires from behind me, concern lacing his words.

"Yeah mate, I'm grand don't worry."

"You sure don't look it. You've barely spoken since you got here and told me you confessed your love for a girl you just met."

My fists fall from the bag. I swivel on my heel to come face to face with Rory, my fury a palpable taste in my mouth.

"You will speak of her respectfully, or I will ensure you can't speak again."

My threat is met with disbelief and a tinge of fear. He's not sure I'll follow through. I will. I don't give a shite who he is and what he's done for me. He can either speak of Emma respectfully or not at all. It's his choice.

Rory slowly raises his hands, palms out defensively. "No worries, mate. Didn't mean to offend, just meant you've been a bit distracted. Just want to make sure you're focused enough for the fight. It's my job to make sure you come out of it unbroken."

"Something always breaks when I fight."

"You know what I mean, Conor."

I know what he means. He has good intentions, but my nerves are like live wires and if anything comes near them, I snap.

"Sorry, Rory. I am a little distracted but don't worry. When I'm in the ring, all that matters is my opponent and winning. You don't have anything to worry about."

"If you say so. Should I call Erin to be there to console you if she doesn't show?"

I huff out a large breath and roll my eyes at him. "No. I don't need your fiancé to treat me like a weeping eejit. I'll be fine."

"Good. Then, get back to it, mate. We don't got all day," he commands, forcefully turning me around to the now still speed bag.

Hours later, we're at the arena. The clock on the wall reads four exactly. I still haven't heard from Emma. I have no idea if she chose to go or stay. The car showed up at my place at two. I know this; I checked. Just to make sure there were no issues. I didn't ask where she told the driver to take her. I'd rather hope until the last possible moment instead of hearing she'd already left. It would crush me, and I don't know how well I would perform, knowing I had no heart in the fight. Because it had just gotten on a plane and flown to America without me.

I've weighed in, dressed, wrapped my hands, and warmed up so much I'm sure my internal temperature has risen five degrees. Anxious energy courses through every nerve ending in my body.

Normally, before a fight, I'm calm, lighthearted, and excited to get out there. My heart doesn't stutter in my chest every time the door opens and closes and it's not Emma. Like right now. The door opens, and I stand from the bench, my worn-out heart accelerating, just to drop when Rory walks in.

He sees my crestfallen expression and sighs. No longer mad I keep asking after Emma and if she's shown up, but sad for me. Knowing he once again is going to tell me that she's not here.

He shakes his head, confirming it, before crossing to meet me.

"Sorry lad. She's still not here."

"You'll tell me the moment she is? Won't you?"

"Of course, mate."

He claps me on my shoulder, and we go over the plan for my walkout. It's the same as it always is. Long walk down the tunnel surrounded by my team and security, ignore the camera, and look straight ahead, focused on the ring and the fight. Smile, wave, slap a few hands if I feel so inclined. Sometimes I even do a little jig.

Despite the brutality of MMA, I am a fighter who always maintains a positive and friendly demeanor with the fans.

Tonight, they won't get the smiling friendly lad but me in my dire mood. No smile, no joy. Not without Emma here. I fear for my opponent's safety. I feel like I could kill a man tonight.

An hour passes and still no Emma. My hope is all but gone. She would either be here by now or be on the plane home. I know which she's chosen.

My walk-out song pick for tonight? "Paint it, Black" by Ciara.

I can hear the buildup of the song as I walk through the tunnel, my face flat and movements sharp. Eating up the distance between me and the ring in long, swift strides. Forcing my entourage to match my pace.

We exit the tunnel and into the throng of screaming bodies and waving arms. People are packed into the large stadium, filling it to the brim. I don't notice a single one. I ignore the outstretched arms. The cries for my attention fade into the chaos. None of the sounds register as I keep my eyes locked straight ahead.

The ominous sway and beat of the music keeps my feet moving forward. My arms remaining at my sides, and my mouth in a hard flat line. The tape around my hands pinches at my skin as I ball my hands into fists.

Nothing matters anymore, not winning, not losing, not defending myself against injury. I won't feel a thing, but my opponent will. He'll feel the pain killing every nerve ending and washing a numbness over me, and it will leave him bleeding and broken. Just like my heart.

By the time we reach the ring I can't even feel the bite of the tape on my hand anymore. Numb from the neck down. It's obvious to all the mood I'm in and a palpable knowing drifts across the crowd only making them more eager for the fight.

People surround me and unzip my hoodie, pulling it down my arms and removing it. I don't look at them even when they call my name. When they talk to me. Tell me things I already know. Things I don't give a shite about. My focus is on the man across the caged ring and what I'm going to do to him.

Until a quieter voice says my name, a cool hand pressing against my chest. A touch that sends a shiver across my skin, and I look down. Down to see my Leamhan Beag, my little moth, staring up at me.

"Conor? Are you in there?" she asks a teasing smirk on her beautiful pink lips.

She's here.

"Can you hear me or has the crowds shouting caused you to go deaf? Because I think it might make me deaf."

"Emma?" my hoarse throat craoks out.

Her expression turns apologetic, and she pinches her lips to one side. "I'm sorry I'm so late. Traffic was horrendous trying to get here. I just barely made it in."

"Emma," I say again around a smile that takes over my entire being.

I don't care that I'm minutes away from a huge fight and that there's thousands of people watching us right now. I wrap both arms around her and clutch her to my chest, lifting her feet of the ground, and she wraps herself around me. Clinging to me with as much desperation as I feel.

Burying my face in her crimson hair I inhale her fresh scent and the numbness that possessed me evaporates under her touch. Instead, my body comes to life feeling every tickle of her hair against my nose and scratch of her nails and heals against my skin.

"You're here."

"I'm here."

"You didn't leave."

"I didn't leave."

Emma leans back, and I tighten my arms around her, not ready to let her go yet. But she doesn't wiggle out of my hold. She only pulls back enough to bring her lips to mine in a possessive kiss, tongue and all. A claiming kiss that makes it clear to me, and everyone watching through the camera that is no doubt streaming this to the large screens overhead, that she is mine, and I am hers.

My hand finds her arse and grips her possessively. Again, my cock responds to her, thickening in my shorts.

Again, not the right time to pop a boner.

Emma breaks the kiss and giggles against my lips. The sound pure balm to my soul.

"Does this mean you're staying?"

"Well, when I looked down at my hand and saw my claddagh ring already turned with the heart facing inward I figured I had no choice."

"You always have a choice, Leamhan Beag. You're the boss here, not me."

Her smile widens and then she does wiggle free of my hold, sliding down to place her feet on the floor but not backing away yet.

"Good. Now as your boss I'm ordering you to get in that ring and win this fight. Am I understood?" she says in a mock stern voice, pointing first at the caged ring and then poking the same finger into my chest.

Leaning down, I steal another kiss, still smiling against her mouth.

"Whatever you say, Love."

As I've done to her on several occasions, she reaches around and slaps my arse in a *go get 'em* gesture.

I get in the ring and do just as she ordered. Winning my match to the sounds of my Little Moth cheering me on from the sidelines.

Her voice carrying louder than all the others.

Her smiling face, the only one I see when the ref lifts my hand to claim me the winner.

Her hand the only thing I feel as I hold on to her for the rest of the evening, through all the interviews and celebration.

Her ear the one I whisper confessions of love into at night when I take her home and call her mine.

Because wouldn't you know it, it's just my luck I fell in love with the woman who threw salt on me in a pub one random night.

Epilogue – Emma

Two and a half years later

The dress doesn't fit.

Fuck a duck.

Of course it doesn't. I bought it four months ago before we knew. Before I started gaining weight. Before I was eating for two, not to mention stress eating during finals.

Yesterday was my last final toward gaining my PME, Professional Masters in Education, making me a certified teacher in Ireland. As long as I didn't fail the test, which is highly unlikely. Conor stayed up for hours studying with me, and I knew every answer to the questions on the test. I feel confident in my final grade. These days I look on the brighter side, the positive side, instead of focusing on the negative and what could go wrong.

Conor taught me that. Over the years he's taught me many things. He's shown me how to be optimistic and not let small diversions hinder my happiness.

Today I am immensely happy. It's my graduation party.

Everyone is here, from both sides of our family, for the party and then my graduation ceremony next week. My family flew in a couple days ago, including all my brothers, sister-in-law, nephew, parents, and of course, my BFF Jules.

Even though we live even farther apart now than we did when I lived in Texas, I've seen her more than I ever have. She says I'm far more fun now and Ireland is far more interesting to visit than Texas. I completely agree with her.

Unsuccessfully I fight with the dress zipper again, hoping this time it'll work. I picked the dress out with the intention of wearing it today and for the graduation ceremony. It was fitted when I purchased it, and prior to my initial trip to Ireland I would never have chosen something like it. But I loved the way it hugged my body, and the shade of green reminded me of Conor's eyes.

However, now the stubborn zipper won't go past my waist.

"Damn it."

"Having a bit of trouble, Love?"

Conor saunters out of the bathroom and into our bedroom buttoning up his silver-gray dress shirt looking all kinds of sexy. My hormones have been in overdrive since finding out about the pregnancy, making me ravenous for his cock all day every day. Although we already had a very healthy sex life, it doubled in the past few months. We've fucked in nearly every part of our house. A two-story townhouse Conor bought for us last year, when we decided it was time to leave his bachelor pad.

We both had discussed future plans and knew children would always be in the picture. We almost had an unplanned pregnancy that first time on the day of Conor's fight and the day I decided to stay in Ireland. Although we both would have loved that child, we weren't ready for one then and it seemed the universe agreed. I got my period and life went on.

The baby currently growing in my belly wasn't planned, either, but that doesn't matter to us. We haven't told our families yet and planned to do so today. But first I need to put something on that actually zips.

"I can't get my dress zipped," I whine, giving him an overly dramatic pout in the mirror's reflection. My arms flopping to my sides in defeat.

Conor steps up behind me and slips his arms around my waist, settling his hands on my stomach and our unborn child. His lips press soft, loving kisses to my neck and a chill runs down my spine, igniting my now ever-present horniness.

"That's because baby O'Shea needs more room to grow."

Conor's breath brushes my sensitive skin, and I shiver, pressing my ass back against his groin. He responds in kind, pressing his bulge against my ass and chuckles in my ear.

"Naughty Leamhan Beag. We have guests waiting for us downstairs. That will have to wait."

I pout even more, stomping my foot like a child. It only makes him laugh harder. Stepping back far enough I can no longer feel the warmth from his body pressing against my back, Conor turns me to face him and places a kiss on my nose. He's so freaking sweet. He will be a great dad.

"What am I supposed to wear?"

"What about that cute dress you bought when you went shopping with Aisling?"

Shopping trips with Aisling have become a regular occurrence for me, at least when she's in town. She's graduated from university and is now deep in the thralls of her new business, which seems to be getting off to a great start.

A few weeks ago, we went out, and I went on a bit of a

shopping spree. I really wanted to go into the baby stores but withheld since Aisling didn't know about the pregnancy. So instead, I subtly looked for clothing that was stretchy or flowy that would accommodate a growing baby bump.

"Which one?" I ask still sulking, in mourning for my perfect green dress that I'll now have to wait at least seven months to wear.

"The one with all the dandelions on it. I like it because it reminds me of when I took you to the dandelion field by the loch. When I first realized I wanted more than just a few days with you, I wanted forever."

Swoon.

"Well, how can I say no to that?"

"Then hurry it up."

With a pat on my ass, he urges me toward our closet. I change, and the dandelion dress is far more comfortable around my belly. Flowing from an elasticized empire waistline with small hat sleeves and thankfully no zipper. The dress hits just above my knee, and I match it with a pair of sparkly white ballet flats.

Staring at myself in the mirror once more before venturing downstairs, I take in my appearance. I'm wearing clothing I never would have considered because of their pattern or color. There's a small growing swell to my stomach where our future child grows, the gold claddagh ring now on my left-hand ring finger.

So much has changed in the past couple of years. And all because I lost my job, and my apartment flooded.

Our wedding was a spur-of-the-moment decision also. So, unlike how I used to be. But when we realized that without a visa I would have to go home to Texas after ninety days

Conor immediately proposed. We threw on some nice clothes, kidnapped Rory to be our witness and went on down to the registrar's office, said our I do's and that was it.

I had my claddagh ring that Conor happily shifted to my opposite hand, but we had to buy his later. He, too, wears a traditional claddagh in gold to match mine. He later purchased me a green, emerald stone wedding band. Claiming he had to purchase one of my wedding rings since I had purchased the claddagh for myself.

Smiling, I take in a deep breath and let it out, then turn to join him waiting for me at the door with an open extended hand and head downstairs.

Most of the family is congregating out on the porch and in the kitchen where our moms are drinking flutes of champagne, and no doubt discussing their next big scheme to get more grandchildren. Little do they know they will have one more before the night is over.

Jules greets me as soon as we enter. Circling me in a massive hug.

"Oh my goodness, honey. You look beautiful, practically glowing."

Jules winks at me with a huge smile on her beautiful face. She's the only one who knows about the pregnancy because she was the one I called when I wasn't sure and needed her support to take the test. I had to make sure before telling Conor, I didn't want to get his hopes up if I weren't. He was a little bummed when the first possibly pregnancy didn't happen. I didn't want to see that sadness in his eyes again.

"I love this dress. So flowy and *stretchy*."

Okay, I get it, Jules. I'm pregnant and going to need an adjustable waistband.

"Hey, sis."

Thankfully Danny appears to end this conversation before Jules ruins our surprise. Placing a kiss on my cheek, then positioning himself at Jules's side, placing a possessive arm around her waist and a kiss to her cheek. Jules looks up at him in the way that I look at Conor. Another big change that came from my trip to Ireland.

True to her word Jules came out to Ireland for a few months after helping me pack up or sell off my belongings back in Texas and moving into Conor's apartment, sorry flat—I'm still getting used to the Irish lingo—in Dublin.

Soon after her arrival, my brother Danny decided he needed to come out and delegate so Jules wouldn't buy us a house or something. During their joined time in Ireland, they finally moved past the hate part of their love-hate relationship and dove headfirst into the love part. They are now engaged, but Jules hasn't allowed him to set a date yet. Her free-spirited nature still clinging on to the last bit of her single life. Even though they live together and do everything together.

Danny usually takes a few weeks' vacation during the year, and they both come to Ireland to visit. Mom and Dad came out once. This is only their second time in Ireland. We've made trips to Texas with Conor's parents as well. Our parents get along swimmingly.

Speaking of our parents, here comes my mom.

"Emma, sweetheart, you look lovely," she says donning the Irish terminology. I think she wishes it were her that moved here. After I tell her I'm pregnant, it wouldn't surprise me if she convinces my dad to sell their house in Texas and move here. Not that I would mind. But with my brother and his family still living in Texas I'm sure my parents would want to still spend a good amount of time there too.

"Thank you, Mom."

"Here, have a drink."

She hands me a flute of champagne. Well, no time like the present I suppose.

"No, thank you. I'm not drinking."

Mom freezes. The realization of why I wouldn't be drinking a celebratory glass of champagne at my own graduation party slowly transforms her face. Her eyes widening and glimmering with hope.

"Not drinking? Cara!" she calls over to Conor's mom loud enough to draw everyone in the room's attention. "Cara! Emma isn't drinking!"

"She isn't drinkin'? Why wouldn't she be—"

Our mothers share a weirdly telepathic look and Cara turns her big eyes on me. She nearly sprints over to our small group, others in the room turning to watch, curious what's going on.

"You're not drinkin'?" she asks, obviously seeking clarity. I clear my throat before answering, knowing this will become a full announcement.

"No, I am not drinking."

"Please don't tell me it's because you've just decided you don't like the taste of alcohol anymore," my mother begs.

"No. It's not that." Steadying myself with a deep breath, Conor plants himself at my side, placing a supportive hand on my back. "I'm not drinking because . . . I'm pregnant."

The entire room breaks out into happy cheers, the loudest of which is my mother. Hugging me and Conor, in turn, talking nonstop about baby names, cradles, and strollers, ending, of course, on spending more time in Ireland to be here when the baby is born.

"I knew it," Nan proclaims. "I sensed it the last time you came over."

I hadn't been over to their house in a month. How could she have possibly known, then?

Reaching into her oversized purse, she pulls out a familiar-looking item made of their customary undyed wool yarn. She holds it up and reveals the baby size onesie with little footies and all. A black and white sheep with a green bow embroidered on the front.

Holy shit, she was really sure about it wasn't she?

"Doesn't surprise me. Nan knew when both my nephews were going to be born." Conor accepts the first baby gift we've received and kisses Nan on the cheek. "Thank you, Nan. It's perfect."

With all the love and affection going on around us, my fluctuating hormones kick in. Tears well in my eyes and blur my vision. I try to stop them, but there's no stopping a pregnant woman from crying. Conor immediately notices and wraps me in his arms. Holding me close to his chest he coo's reassurances and calming sounds against my hair. Pressing kisses to my head and face in between words of love, which, of course, only makes me cry harder.

"What can I do? What do you need? Tell me, and I'll get it, I'll do whatever you tell me to."

He tries to assuage my supposed upset, but I'm not upset. I'm extremely incandescently happy.

"There's nothing I need or want that I don't already have. I'm just really happy," I finally say between short gasps.

The tears finally shut off, easing the water works that have my husband on the verge of a breakdown of his own. He hasn't witnessed one of my crying fits yet. He better get used to them because I have a feeling it's going to happen often.

"You sure? I can get you the plushie that always seems to make you happy."

I laugh, knowing he would gladly run and get me my sheep plushie with a hidden pocket for a heating pad I use when on my period and have horrible cramps.

"No thank you, Love. I don't need it."

Conor sighs in relief. His shoulders visibly relaxing.

"You'll let me know when you do need something. Anything. You're growing a human inside you. The least I can do is get you a cup of tea or a pillow when needed."

"When my stomach gets so big I can't tie my shoes, I'll definitely take you up on that. Don't worry, there'll be plenty of opportunities for you to help."

With a gentle large hand, he wipes away my drying tears and places a sweet kiss on my lips.

"Good, because I don't plan on ever leaving your side."

With that we return to the party celebrating more than our guests had expected to today. Congratulations for my pregnancy and the beginning of my new career. When the summer ends, I start work teaching first year primary school kids, and I can't wait.

Realizing that all of my dreams are coming true I start to cry again and catch sight of my large husband practically having a panic attack when he sees my tears again.

THE END

Acknowledgements

Thank you to the talented Nat aka Speckledplum for once again making a beautiful cover to add to the series. You always blow me away, and make the cutest animals.

To Lucia aka LucielArts for continuing to create beautiful character art ;-) You really bring my characters to life for all of us to enjoy.

To my BETA's who always point out my errors and make sure I put out my best work possible. And to my Irish correspondent Aine for answering all my weird questions and double checking my Irish lingo was correct.

For more information on Rebecca's books please visit her website at
www.RebeccaRennickAuthor.com

Books in the Gummy Bear Orgy Series

Pinky Promise
Her Favorite Jack-O-Lantern
Just My Luck

Note from the Author

Throughout my life I've lived by the belief that there is always a reason for everything. The year before I published Pinky Promise the first book in the GBOS and started on this journey, I lost my dream job. I was crushed, devistated, and spent four days crying on the couch after. But I always believed there was a reason for it and I just had to wait to find out what it was. I believe it was so I could have more time to write and begin this new adventure. So if something bad happens just remind yourself that there's a reason and a silver lining. Some day you'll find it. Sometimes it just takes a positive outlook on life to manifest good.The Gummy Bear Orgy is a series of stand alone's that can be read out of order. They will not interconnect in any way. If you don't want to read one of the colors, you don't have to. Please use these stories to have fun, laugh and smile, and maybe even blush.

Milton Keynes UK
Ingram Content Group UK Ltd.
UKHW041001040324
438885UK00006B/399

9 798218 333621